"Ancient Rome boils with sordid power pl[a]
rituals, and eruptions of bloodshed in Eck[e]
An entertaining sword-and-politics saga f
and sharp drama."

—*Kirkus Reviews*

† † † † † *Robert Eckert*

The Year of Five Emperors

"It is the sort of tome that contains multitudes (literally), creates a world (here a thoroughly-researched and believable Rome, where I indeed I read it for the first time), and peoples it with historical figures that seem very far indeed from the schoolbooks of my youth, let alone my Latin lessons... We are plunged into every social and political level of Rome, seeing things as much from the street and domus-level as from the more rarified air breathed in manors and Senate." Don Device, EICAR (International Film and Television School)

"While the political side of the plot in The Year of Five Emperors will interest historical fiction buffs, those more interested in the people of that day will find themselves quite enthralled by the other insights presented in this book... As a result, readers come away from The Year of Five Emperors feeling that people truly haven't changed all that much over the centuries: the men and women of that time faced so many of the same issues we are still dealing with today." Viga Boland, Readers' Favorites

"What this boils down to is a sprawling drama taking the reader from the mighty Urbs of Rome herself to numerous intrigues stretching from the wind blasted wastes of the Antonine Wall to the Channel to the sunny cities of Antioch and Alexandria. Each of these settings is lushly brought to life." Doug Welch, Amazon customer

Copyright ©2023 by Rober Eckert

ISBN: 978-1-77883-107-2 (Paperback)

978-1-77883-110-2 (Hardback)

978-1-77883-111-9 (E-book)

All rights reserved. No part of this publication may be reproduced, distributed, or transmitted in any form or by any means, including photocopying, recording, or other electronic or mechanical methods, without the prior written permission of the publisher, except in the case brief quotations embodied in critical reviews and other noncommercial uses permitted by copyright law.

The views expressed in this book are solely those of the author and do not necessarily reflect the views of the publisher, and the publisher hereby disclaims any responsibility for them.

BOOKSIDE Press

BookSide Press
877-741-8091
www.booksidepress.com
orders@booksidepress.com

TABLE OF CONTENTS

MAPS AND NOTES

The City of Roma

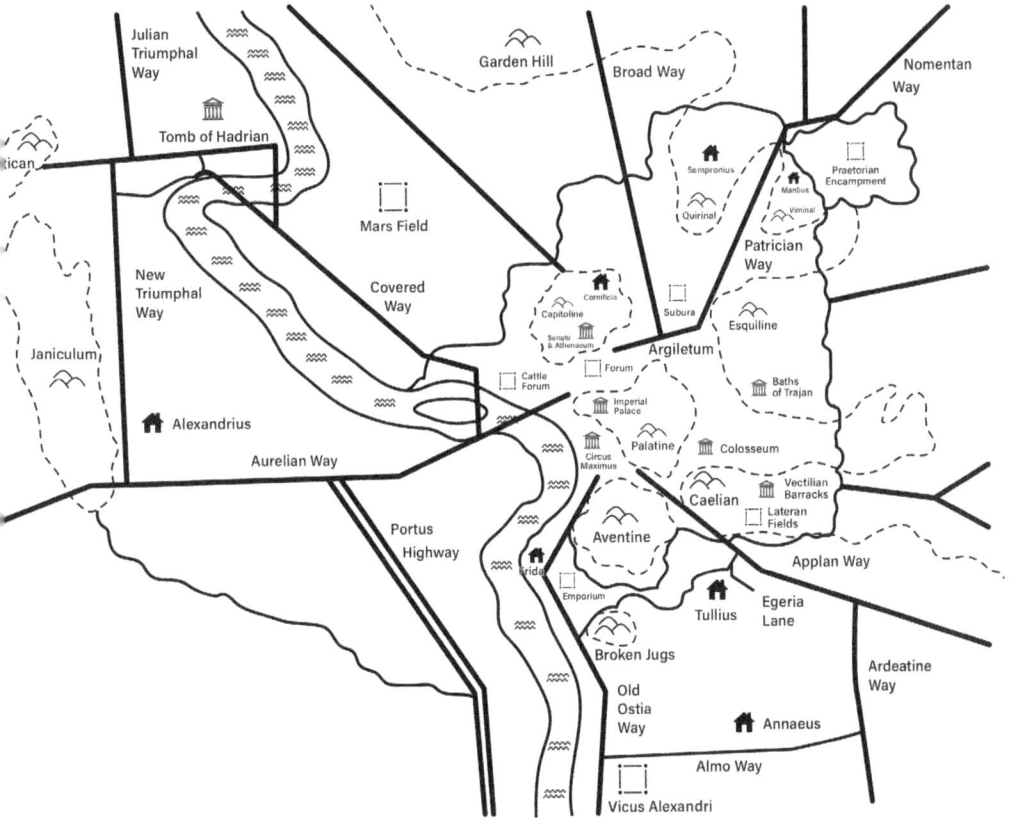

Julian Triumphal Way

Garden Hill

Broad Way

Nomentan Way

Tomb of Hadrian

Vatican

Mars Field

Sempronius

Manlius

Praetorian Encampment

Quirinal

Viminal

Patrician Way

New Triumphal Way

Covered Way

Cornificia

Capitoline

Subura

Esquiline

Janiculum

Senate & Athenaeum

Argiletum

Cattle Forum

Forum

Baths of Trajan

Alexandrius

Imperial Palace

Palatine

Colosseum

Aurelian Way

Circus Maximus

Caelian

Vectilian Barracks

Portus Highway

Aventine

Lateran Fields

Applan Way

Emporium

Tullius

Egeria Lane

Broken Jugs

Ardeatine Way

Old Ostia Way

Annaeus

Almo Way

Vicus Alexandri

1

THE WESTERN EMPIRE

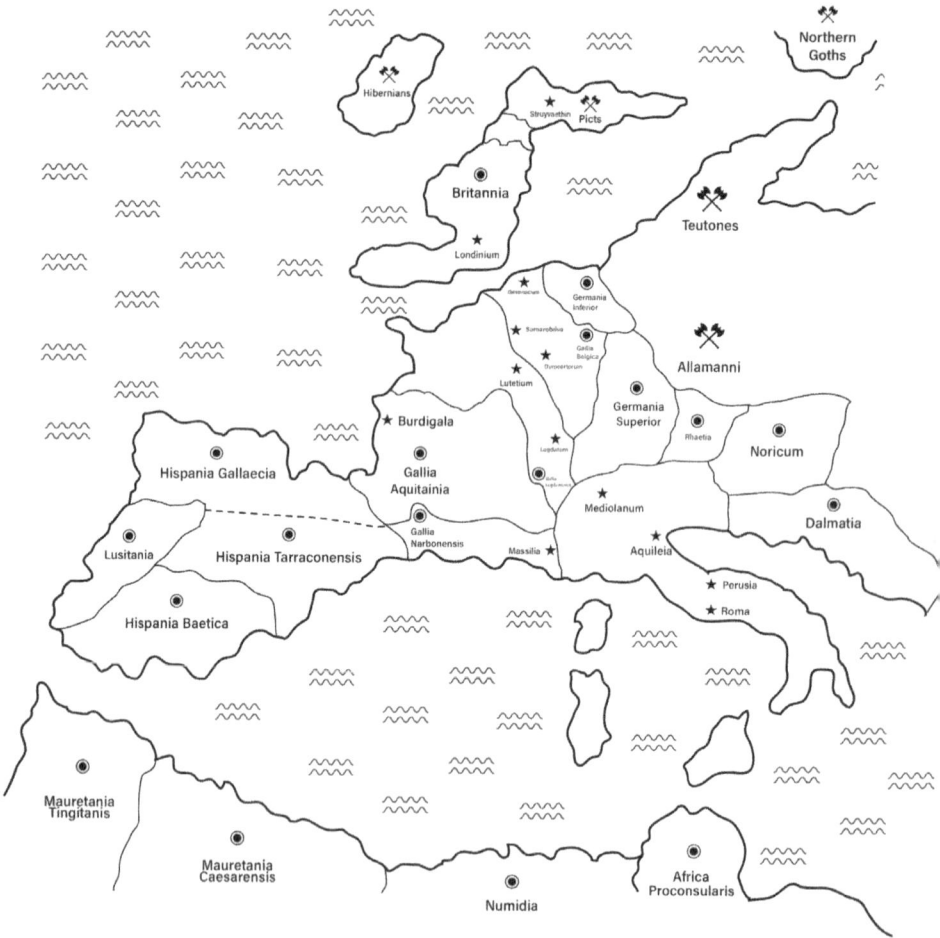

Northern
Goths

Hibernians

Struynaethin
Picts

Britannia

Teutones

Londinium

Germania
Inferior

Gesoriacum

Samarobiva
Gallia
Belgica
Durovertorum

Allamanni

Lutetium

Burdigala

Germania
Superior

Lugdunum

Rhaetia

Noricum

Hispania Gallaecia

Gallia
Aquitainia

Mediolanum

Dalmatia

Gallia
Narbonensis

Lusitania

Hispania Tarraconensis

Massilia

Aquileia

Perusia

Roma

Hispania Baetica

Mauretania
Tingitanis

Mauretania
Caesarensis

Africa
Proconsularis

Numidia

Cities   Barbarians   Province   Other Kingdom

2

THE EASTERN EMPIRE

Rossolyani

Southern Goths

Alano Scyths

Hunnish Horde

Marcomanni

Yazyges Dacia

Cimmerian Bosporus

Media Atropatene

Hyrcania

Carnuntum

Moesia Inferior

Calidа

Greater Armenia

Pannonia Superior

Sarmium

Moesia Superior

Thracia

Trebizond

Lesser Armenia

Media Parthica

Pannonia Inferior

Byzantium

Bithynia Pontus

Parthia Deserta

Macedonia

Nicaea

Cyzicus

Galatia

Cappadocia

Assyria Adiabene

Epirus

Nisibis

Osroene

Arabia Hatrena

Lycia

Cilicia

Seleutia Ctesiphon

Persia

Antioch

Babylonia

Characene

Achaea

Cyprus

Syria

Neapolis

Palestina

Alexandria

Arabia Petraea

Lepcis Magna

Libya Cyrenaica

Aegyptus

Note on the Maps

The familiar ancient walls of Rome, entirely enclosing an expanded "pomerium" (official city limit) well beyond the original Seven Hills, did not yet exist at the time of this story. They were the work of Emperor Aurelian eighty years later. As of the Year of Five Emperors, several areas between the pomerium and the old walls of King Servius Tullius, namely Mars Field, the Emporium, the Public Pool, and the Porta Capena district, were completely unenclosed, and the Trans-Tiber district had only a partial, fragmentary wall, an unfinished project of the late Republic. The Praetorian Encampment was outside the pomerium, but had its own walls. A stretch of the original wall of Romulus, which enclosed little more than Palatine Hill, still stood between the Palace and the Forum.

The maps of the West and of the East are drawn in accord with the Geography of Claudius Ptolemy, and represent the most accurate topographic knowledge of the 2nd century CE.

Note on Currency

The word "gold" is used sloppily here for two different things: a physical gold coin (the *aureus*) weighing a little more than a Victorian sovereign or an American half-eagle; and a unit of account, the "thousand" (*milia*) divided into 250 "pennies" (the *denarius*, the common silver coin), thus in early-modern English terms more like a "guinea" than a "pound sterling". The penny was divided into ten "coppers" (the *aes*) or more commonly into four "farthings" (the *sestertius*, Latin for "halfway to three", that is 2 ½ , *aes* so that the *millia* was 1000 *sestertii*). The copper was originally subdivided, in the West into four "quarters" (the *quadrans*; King James Version renders this "farthing" but that makes more sense for ¼ penny than 1/40), or in the East into eight "bits" (the *lepton*; KJV renders it "mite"), or anciently into twelve "ounces" (the *uncia*). The quarter was a token coin, but marked

4

on the back with three tick-marks because it could be exchanged for three ounces (about 90 grams) of bronze (by no means pure copper). However, before the time of Marcus Aurelius the small change had ceased to be redeemable and then ceased to be minted. By comparison, an American cent is a little over a gram and can no longer be pure copper because that metallic content would be worth more than its face value: the Roman quarter thus was more or less equivalent, in terms of the metal it could purchase, to an American quarter as of the late 20th century, and the "thousand" roughly to $2500. But that is only in terms of metal.

Modern equivalencies are difficult because metals and luxury goods were more valuable relative to foodstuffs and basic goods, which in turn cost more relative to labor, than is the case in more modern times. The New Testament gives a penny per day as a typical wage for unskilled labor (Matt. 20:1-16), and since these were long days we can equate the penny to about a dozen times the minimum wage. But that much money nowadays would buy dozen of loaves of the cheapest bread, and whole ounces of silver. While a penny was certainly expected to buy several loaves of bread (Rev. 6:6 lists "a measure of wheat for a penny" as a sign of dire conditions in the end times, the "measure" being enough for a two-pound loaf), the laboring class did have to work longer for their food. And the metallic content of the penny was an ever-shrinking fraction of an ounce, ultimately only a thin wash of silver over a copper core (a deceit which fooled no-one). Here we have another difficulty with converting Roman currency: the penny was depreciating, and would by no means still buy a day-laborer at the time of our story (at least not in Italy, though out in the boondocks coins were still rare and valued). The traditional "donative" of ten *millia* per soldier paid to the troops by a new Emperor was much more than even officers earned in a year. More extravagant donatives had a fiscal effect comparable to doubling the entire State budget for the year. So naturally, this was a period of currency debasement and price inflation. The *aureus* more or less retained its weight and purity even while *denarius* the fell. Julius

Caesar had fixed the *denarius* as 1/25 *aureus* but an approximate value for the *denarius* of 1/250 *aureus* is probably more like it for the Year of Five Emperors.

Note on Language

The process by which the "classical" Latin of the late Republic evolved into the "vulgar" Latin of the Empire, which broke apart into regional dialects, to become eventually the Romance languages of today, was a long one. The early stages are obscured because the educated upper classes continued to imitate the classical style in their writings. It is not certain to what extent they also imitated, successfully or unsuccessfully, classical Latin in their speech. We are told, for example, that Septimius Severus had an atrocious accent, although he was from a well-to-do family. But then, he was raised in Africa and spent much of his adult life in the frontier provinces rather than in Italy; here it is assumed that in Italy, at least, classical versus vulgar speech was a marker of social class. It may be surmised that as one travelled further and further from Rome, the Latin became less and less "classical" under the influence of native speeches, since for many people in the western Empire, Latin was distinctly their second language and not their first. In the eastern Empire, for most people Latin would not even be a second language: Greek was already established in that role before Rome.

We do get some evidence for the differences between vulgar and classical Latin from grammarians tut-tutting about common errors, less formal writings which exhibit the errors the grammarians complained about and others besides, and reconstructions by Romance linguists of stages which the later languages must have passed through. There was some replacement of vocabulary, but more pervasively a tendency to strip down the pronunciation by simplifying some vowels and eliminating some consonants, especially in the endings. So, here a more vulgar style of speech, often indicative of a lower social status, is indicated by some slangier vocabulary, greater use of contractions, and omitted endings on proper names. Thus, where Tullius Secundus says "Britannia, Gallia, Hispania," Septimius Severus says "Britain, Gaul, Spain." But social and regional dialects should rarely have been so divergent, at this stage of the history, as to cause significant barriers to mutual understanding.

Words which have come down to us through the Latin have sometimes changed their meanings enough that another word is preferred as a translation. To describe the quintessential social relationship between *patronus* and *cliens*, "patron" still conveys the right meaning, but "client" now suggests a mere business relationship, so "protegé" is used instead. Similarly, "spirit" is used for *genius*, since "genius" and "genie" now have quite different implications. The political term *res publica* is usually rendered "the State," reserving "the Republic" to mean the old regime prior to the civil wars of Julius Caesar against Pompey, and Octavian against Mark Antony. As far as the Roman mind was concerned, however, "the Empire" was still the same *res publica* as before, simply with the addition of a novel office with wide powers. The formal title of "the Emperor" was *Augustus*, a word which had to be spoken with reverence and is left as "the August One"; *imperator* could be used to refer to him less formally, but was still the generic word for "commander" and would also be used for various high-ranking military officers. For that usage, *imperator* is translated "General" without regard to what particular title that officer might hold, and similarly "Governor" is used for the presiding officer in any province, without distinguishing whether *proconsul, procurator,* or *praefectus* was his title. This is for simplicity's sake, but Romans were keenly aware of the subtlest distinctions of rank.

DRAMATIS PERSONAE

Romans often had a lot of names. Alphabetization here is by the most used. Asterisks indicate historical figures; footnotes add information where liberties have been taken with historical figures.

*ABGAR: Throne-name recurrently used by kings of Osroene. Abgar IX (Latin name Lucius Aelias Megas) was reigning at this time.

ACHILLES: Deceased son of Smaragda. Father of Narcissus.

*AELIUS CORDUENUS: Eldest of the Senators.

*AGACLYTUS: Majordomo of the palace under Commodus. Succeeded by Eclectus. Husband of Sabina.

AJAX: Slave in the imperial palace. Trained gladiator.

*ALEXANDER (ABONOTEICHITES): Ventriloquist and cult leader. Claimed succession from Apollonius.

ALEXANDRIUS: Son of Pescennius Niger. Roommate of Diodoros, then of Quintilian. Brother of Florentius. Student of Fulminatus.

ANICIA: Lady of noble family, dubiously claiming descent from Augustus and Tiberius. Friend of Titiana. Mother of Julia Aniciana.

(CLAUDIUS CLEMENS) ANNAEUS: Young Senator. Secret Christian. Patron of Clemens.

*ANNIUS: Husband of Biba. Father of Fustus. Grandfather of Pescennius Niger.

*ANNULINUS: Chief of staff for Septimius Severus.

*(TITUS AURELIUS ARRIUS BOIONIUS) ANTONINUS PIUS (HADRIANUS AUGUSTUS): Emperor 138-161. Final adopted son of Hadrian. Father of Faustina. Adopted Marcus Aurelius and Lucius Verus, who jointly succeeded him.

*APOLLONIUS (OF TYANA): Reputed miracle worker and teacher of wisdom, from whom several subsequent cult leaders claimed to trace their authority.

ARDOGENT: Harbor master of Gesoriacum. Cousin of Boudogur.

ARPENTUS: Gaulish merchant. Business associate of Diodoros Tigranos. Former patron of Frida.

*ARTAXERXES (Persian ARDASHIR): Son of Sasan. Grandson of Papak. Later became the first Persian Emperor of the Sassanian line.

*ASELLIUS AEMILIANUS: Governor of Asia. Distantly related to Clodius Albinus.

*(GAIUS JULIUS CAESAR OCTAVIAN) AUGUSTUS: First Emperor until 14. Grand-nephew and adopted son of Julius Caesar. Accumulated power and titles until by 27 BC his supremacy become official. "Augustus" was not a personal name but the most important of the titles which were conferred on all subsequent Emperors. Succeeded by Tiberius.

*AVIDIA PLAUTIA: Wife of Ceionius Commodus. Mother of Lucius Verus.

*(GAIUS) AVIDIUS CASSIUS: Protegé of Marcus Aurelius. Reputed lover of Faustina. Served under Lucius Verus. Briefly claimed the imperial throne in 175. Probably related to Avidia Plautia. Descended from the Seleucids, former royal family of Syria and environs.

BASILIDES TIGRANOS: Deceased father of Diodoros Tigranos.

*BASSIANUS: See CARACALLA.

(SEVERA) BATTANITHA: Libyan freedwoman. Former nursemaid to Septimius and Junius Severus.

BIBA: Nubian freedwoman. Wife of Annius. Mother of Fustus. Grandmother of Pescennius Niger.

BOUDOGUR: Gaulish merchant. Cousin of Ardogent.

BURRANUS: Roman soldier. Captive of Qenmaethin. Husband of Malduve.

*(GAIUS JULIUS CAESAR AUGUSTUS GERMANICUS) CALIGULA: Emperor 37-41. "Caligula" was a nickname from his "little boots"; he was generally called Gaius Caesar during his reign. Great-grandson of Augustus. Grand-nephew and adopted son of Tiberius. Nephew of Claudius, who succeeded him. Assassinated.

CAMILLA: Mother of Sempronius.

*CANDIDUS: Officer serving under Septimius Severus. Husband of Philoxena.

*(LUCIUS SEPTIMIUS BASSIANUS) CARACALLA: Emperor 198-217, at first jointly with his father Septimius Severus and brother Geta.

*CASTOR: Slave of Tullius Secundus.

*(LUCIUS) CEIONIUS COMMODUS (AELIUS CAESAR): Deceased heir of the Emperor Hadrian. Husband of Avidia Plautia. Father of Lucius Verus, two daughters, and perhaps others. Related to Clodius Albinus.

CHEIRONIOS: Prefect of Byzantium. Protegé of Meherdates Tigranos.

*CHOSROES (or OSROES in Latin, from Persian KHOSRAU): Son of Vologases IV, half-brother of Vologases V, rebel against both. King of Media Atropatene, claimed to be rightful Parthian Emperor.

*(LUCIUS FABIUS) CILO: Senator. Protegé of Septimius Severus.

*(APOLLOS) CITHARIUS: Greek musician. Protegé of Titiana.

*CLARA DIDIA: Daughter of Didius Julianus and Scantilla. Wife of Repentinus.

*(ERUCIUS) CLARUS (VIBIANUS): Consul in 193. Colleague of Falco. Cousin of Scantilla.

*(TIBERIUS) CLAUDIUS CAESAR (AUGUSTUS GERMANICUS): Emperor 41-54. Nephew of Tiberius. Uncle of Caligula. Adopted his grand-nephew Nero, who succeeded him.

*CLEANDER: Deceased former Praetorian Prefect.

CLEMENS: Deliveryman to palace. Secret Christian.

*(DECIMUS) CLODIUS ALBINUS: Governor of Britannia. Claimant to the imperial throne 193-197. Husband of Plautilla. Father of Priscus and a younger son. Patron of Servilius, Placidius, Pescennius Niger, Diodoros Tigranos, and Junius Severus.

COCINA: Slave of Tullius Secundus. Granddaughter of Hibernius. Mother of Cocinilla. Second cousin of Narcissus. Daughter of a slave who had also been called Cocina.

COCINILLA: Child slave of Tullius Secundus. Daughter of Cocina and Magnus. Formerly the name of Cocina, when the elder Cocina had still been alive.

*(LUCIUS MARCUS AURELIUS ANTONINUS) COMMODUS (CAESAR AUGUSTUS): Emperor 177-192, at first jointly with his father Marcus Aurelius. Brother of Lucilla, Cornificia, Fadilla, and Sabina. Husband of Crispina. Lover of Marcia. Named for, but not blood-related to, Ceionius Commodus.

*CORNIFICIA: Sister of Commodus, Lucilla, Fadilla, and Sabina. Daughter of Marcus Aurelius and Faustina. Second marriage to Didius Marinus.

*(MARCUS LICINIUS) CRASSUS: Roman politician. Commanded the forces which defeated the revolt of Spartacus. Mediated between Julius Caesar and Pompey to form the First Triumvirate. Died attempting to invade Parthia.

*CRISPINA (BRUTTIA): Wife of Commodus.

*DIDIUS MARINUS: Husband of Cornificia. Protegé of Didius Julianus.

*(MARCUS) DIDIUS JULIANUS: Emperor March-June 193. Husband of Scantilla. Father of Clara Didia.

*DIO CASSIUS (COCCEIANUS): Author. Protegé of Cornificia.

DIODOROS TIGRANOS: Protegé of Clodius Albinus. Patron of Tausius. Father of Meherdates Tigranos. Son of Basilides Tigranos.

DEMETRIOS: Merchant in Antioch. Secret Christian.

DIONYSIUS: Leader of the Greek community in Alexandria.

*(TITUS FLAVIUS CAESAR) DOMITIAN (AUGUSTUS): Emperor 81-96. Son of Vespasian. Brother and probable killer of Titus. Assassinated. Succeeded by Nerva.

*ECLECTUS: Majordomo of the palace under Commodus and Pertinax. Husband of Marcia.

*ELEUTHEROS: Bishop of Rome. Succeeded by Victor.

*FABIA: Daughter of Ceionius Commodus. Sister of Lucius Verus. One-time fiancé of Marcus Aurelius.

FABIOLUS PROLECTUS: Junior magistrate hearing the case of Mercurius.

*FADILLA: Sister of Commodus, Lucilla, Cornificia, and Sabina. Daughter of Marcus Aurelius and Faustina. Daughter-in-law of Fabia.

*(QUINTUS POMPEIUS SOSIUS) FALCO: Consul in 193. Colleague of Clarus. Brief attempt to claim the throne in March 193.

*FAUSTINA: Daughter of Antoninus Pius (her mother was also named Faustina). Wife of Marcus Aurelius. Mother of Commodus, Lucilla, Cornificia, Fadilla, and Sabina.

FAUSTUS PARISIUS: Postmaster of Lutetia. Friend of Quintus Curtius.

FLORENTIUS: Son of Pescennius Niger. Brother of Alexandrius.

FORTUNATUS CURTIUS: Protegé of Sempronius. Brother of Jovialis. Cousin of Quintus.

FRIDA: Wife of Tausius. Formerly mistress of Arpentus.

FULMINATUS RHETOR: Attorney for Commodus, and later for Mercurius. Teacher of Alexandrius.

*FUSTUS: Father of Pescennius Niger. Husband of Lampridia. Son of Annius and Biba.

*(LUCIUS LIVIUS OCELLA SERVIUS SULPICIUS) GALBA (CAESAR AUGUSTUS): Emperor 68-69, imposed by army. Assassinated. Succeeded by Otho.

*(FLAVIUS) GENIALIS: Manager of the Circus Maximus and Colosseum, given the rank of prefect by Didius Julianus.

GERMANUS: See Phaeton.

*(PUBLIUS SEPTIMIUS) GETA: Co-Emperor 209-211. Son of Septimius Severus and Julia Domna. Brother of Caracalla, who killed him. Also the name of a brother of Septimius Severus, lover of Tullius Primus.

*(PUBLIUS AELIUS TRAIANUS) HADRIAN (AUGUSTUS): Emperor 117-138. Grandnephew-in-law, cousin once removed, and putative adoptive son of Trajan. Successively adopted Ursus Servianus, Fuscus Salinator, Ceionius Commodus, and finally Antoninus Pius, who succeeded him.

HERMES: Deceased runaway slave of Jovialis Rhetor. Twin brother of Mercurius.

HIBERNIUS: Deceased slave of Tullian family. Brother of Smaragda. Grandfather of Cocina.

*HYACINTHUS: Eunuch slave in the imperial palace.

JOVIALIS CURTIUS (RHETOR): Attorney of Narcissus. Protegé of Sempronius. Brother of Fortunatus. Cousin of Quintus. Owner of Hermes and Mercurius.

JULIA ANICIANA: Daughter of Anicia. Friend of Tullia Minor.

*JULIA DOMNA: Wife of Septimius Severus. Mother of Caracalla and Geta.

*JULIUS CAESAR: Roman politician. Conqueror of Gaul. Formed First Triumvirate with Pompey and Crassus. Defeated Pompey after the death of Crassus to become dictator. Often considered the first "Emperor" but was never granted the titles and powers of an "Augustus" and in his time "Caesar" was simply his personal name. Assassinated. Great-uncle and adoptive father of Augustus Caesar.

JUNIPERA: Slave in the imperial palace. Wife of Narcissus.

*(CAIUS) JUNIUS SEVERUS (LEPCIUS): Appointed Governor of Britannia but never served. Cousin of Septimius Severus.[1]

*KUGLAS (ARGENTOCOXUS): Son-in-law and heir to Qenmaethin.[2]
*(QUINTUS AEMILIUS) LAETUS: Praetorian Prefect. Fiancé of Popilia.
*LAMPRIDIA: Wife of Fustus. Mother of Pescennius Niger.
LANGORIA: Enslaved under questionable circumstances in the imperial palace. Sister of Tausius.

*LUCILLA: Deceased eldest sister of Commodus, Cornificia, Fadilla, and Sabina. Daughter of Marcus Aurelius and Faustina. Wife of Lucius Verus, then of Pompeianus.

*LUCIUS (CEIONIUS COMMODUS AELIUS AURELIUS) VERUS (CAESAR AUGUSTUS): Co-Emperor with Marcus Aurelius 161-169. Son of Ceionius Commodus and Avidia Plautia. Adopted son of Antoninus Pius. First husband of Lucilla.

MAGNUS: Slave of Tullius Secundus. Trained gladiator. Father of Cocinilla.

---

[1] We have no indication that Junius Severus was really related to Septimius Severus (the name "Severus" could occur in multiple families) but for narrative purposes he is. We only know that he was a drinking companion of Commodus, sent to relieve Clodius Albinus shortly before the death of Commodus. But Clodius retained Britannia, and we don't hear how that happened. If Junius had been killed, we would probably have been told that, so most likely he decided that discretion was the better part of valor. The praenomen and agnomen assigned to him are invented.

[2] Caledonian language is here reconstructed as, though not yet Gaelic (that would come with post-Roman settlers from Ireland), some kind of Q-Celtic distinguishing uvular Q (corresponding to Brythonic P) from velar K (corresponding to C). The energetic chief of the Maethi who later fought Septimius Severus is recorded as Argentocoxus "silver-lame," an odd name: here argento- is taken as translating glas "gray" and -coxus as either imitating the sound of the Celtic name, or as a personal attribute, or both. The Maethi dominated mid-Caledonia from the 2nd through 7th centuries from their stronghold at Struyvaeithin (M-to-V between vowels was a regular shift), now Stirling.

MALDUVE: Caledonian woman. Wife of Burranus.

*(GNAEUS) MANLIUS: Senator. Father of Scantilla.

*(LUCIUS) MANTENNIUS (SABINUS): Prefect of Alexandria, later Governor of Egypt.

*MARCIA: Mistress of Commodus, then wife of Eclectus. Intermediary between Commodus and Victor.

*MARCUS (ANNIUS) AURELIUS (ANTONINUS CAESAR AUGUSTUS): Emperor 161-180, at first jointly with Lucius Verus. Husband of Faustina. Father of Commodus, who succeeded him, and of Lucilla, Cornificia, Fadilla, and Sabina.

MARIA SEMPRONIA: Cousin of Senator Sempronius.

MEHERDATES TIGRANOS: Son of Diodoros Tigranos. Patron of Cheironios.

MERCURIUS: Slave of Jovialis Rhetor. Twin brother of Hermes. Client of Fulminatus Rhetor.

*(LAURENTIUS) MOTILENUS: Deputy to, and sometimes replacement for, Laetus as Praetorian Prefect.

*NARCISSUS: Enslaved under questionable circumstances in the imperial palace. Husband of Junipera. Grandson of Smaragda. Second cousin of Cocina.[3]

---

[3] There was a Narcissus, described as an "athlete" and implicated in the assassination of Commodus. But he is also described as having obtained for Pescennius Niger his first major post, so he was no minor servant. The case of Mercurius, a runaway slave purporting to be from a secret family of Commodus Ceionius and suing for property, was a real one (except that the plaintiff's name is not preserved), but the connection to Narcissus is a narrative invention here.

*NARSAI: Exiled prince of Adiabene in Mesopotamia, later King.[4]

NATHAN: Jewish boy in Alexandria. Grandson of Ptolemy.

*(LUCIUS DOMITIUS AHENOBARBUS) NERO (CLAUDIUS CAESAR AUGUSTUS DRUSUS GERMANICUS): Emperor 54-68. Great-great-grandson of Augustus. Great-grand-nephew of Tiberius. Nephew of Caligula. Grand-nephew, stepson, and adopted son of Claudius. Committed suicide. Succeeded irregularly by Galba.

*(MARCUS COCCEIUS) NERVA (AUGUSTUS): Emperor 96-98. Nephew of one of the last descendants of Augustus. Elected by Senate as a stopgap after assassination of Domitian. Adopted Trajan, who succeeded him.

*NONIUS MURCUS: Senator. Protegé of Pertinax. Patron of Pescennius Niger.

*(RUFUS) NOVIUS: Legionary commander. Protegé of Clodius Albinus.

OCTAVIUS EMESIANUS: Governor of Syria. Distantly related to the imperial family.

*(MARCUS SALVIUS) OTHO (NERO CAESAR AUGUSTUS): Briefly Emperor in 69. Expected to be adopted by Galba but turned on him when he favored another. Committed suicide when Vitellius rebelled.

---

[4] The syncretist religion here ascribed to Narsai is loosely based on his neighbor, Abd-as-Samiyah of Arabia Hatraea. The ruins of Hatra (now sadly vandalized by ISIL) contain temples to deities of multiple nations, identified with each other in various ways. Arabia Hatraea seceded from Media Parthica, changing Abd-as-Samiyah's title from "commander" to "king," during the Year of Five Emperors, in alliance with Narsai and Pescennius Niger. In consequence Septimius Severus made futile efforts to besiege Hatra.

*PAPAK (Persian BABAG): Nominal King of Persia. Father-in law of Sasan. Grandfather of Artaxerxes.

*(PUBLIUS HELVIUS) PERTINAX (CAESAR AUGUSTUS): Emperor January-March 193. Husband of Titiana. Also the name of his son.

*(JUSTUS) PESCENNIUS NIGER: Claimant to the imperial throne 193-195. Son of Fustus and Lampridia. Father of Alexandrius and Florentius. Protegé of Nonius Murcus and Clodius Albinus.[5]

PHAETON (SIGISMUND, GERMANUS): Slave of Tullius Secundus. Purported descendant of Woden.

PHILODEMOS: Greek jeweler in Alexandria.

PHILOXENA: Greek freedwoman. Governess of Tullia Minor. Wife of Candidus.

(VALERIUS) PLACIDIUS: Governor of Gallia Belgica. Protegé of Clodius Albinus.

*PLAUTILLA: Wife of Clodius Albinus. Mother of Priscus and a younger son. Related to Avidia Plautia.

---

[5] It is controversial how "black" Pescennius Niger was. One source (but a late and unreliable one) says that the nickname referred only to a dark birth-mark on his neck. For narrative purposes, he is as black as Barack Obama. Skin color was not the issue it would be in later centuries, but his middle-class-at-best social rank was. He and Pertinax were from the humblest origins of any imperial claimants until the "Barracks Emperors" period. The names and social statuses of his ancestors are genuine, except that the Nubian grandmother is invented. He did have two sons, although their names are not preserved. He was in fact still Governor of Syria when Commodus died: the fictitious transfer to Egypt is for narrative purposes. Sometimes Clio must give way to other Muses.

*(TIBERIUS CLAUDIUS) POMPEIANUS: Second husband of Lucilla. Adopted son of Marcus Aurelius. Turned down the imperial throne three times. Patron of Pertinax.

*(GNAEUS) POMPEIUS MAGNUS: Roman politician. Formed First Triumvirate with Julius Caesar and Crassus. Defeated by Julius Caesar after the death of Crassus. Fled to Egypt where he was murdered.

POPILIA: Fiancée of Laetus. Friend of Tullia Minor.

*(PESCENNIUS) PRISCUS: Son of Clodius Albinus and Plautilla. Named for Pescennius Niger.

PTOLEMY: Jewish merchant in Alexandria. Business partner of Fustus. Grandfather of Nathan.

QENMAETHIN: Chieftain of central Caledonia. Father-in-law of Kuglas.

QUAERIUS ANATINUS: Tax collector.

QUINTILIAN (VITERBIUS RHETOR): Attorney for the State in the case of Mercurius.

QUINTUS CURTIUS: Postmaster of Massilia. Protegé of Sempronius. Cousin of Fortunatus and Jovialis.

*(SEXTUS CORNELIUS) REPENTINUS: Senator. Husband of Clara Didia.

*SABINA: Sister of Commodus. Daughter of Marcus Aurelius and Faustina. Second marriage to Agaclytus.

*SASAN: Grand Magus of the Zoroastrian faith. Son-in-law of Papak. Father of Artaxerxes.

*SCANTILLA (MANLIA): Wife of Didius Julianus. Mother of Clara Didia. Daughter of Manlius. Cousin of Clarus.

(CAIUS TITIUS) SEMPRONIUS: Senator. Patron of Quintus, Fortunatus, and Jovialis Curtius.

*(LUCIUS) SEPTIMIUS SEVERUS (PERTINAX CAESAR AUGUSTUS): Emperor 193-211. Husband of Julia Domna. Father of Caracalla and Geta. Patron of Cilo.

*SERAPION: Patriarch of Antioch 191-211.

SERVILIUS: Faithful retainer to Clodius Albinus.

SICARIUS: Hired assassin.

*SILIUS MESSALA: Senator. Protegé of Sulpicianus. Briefly Consul in 193.

SMARAGDA: Slave of Ceionius Commodus. Sister of Hibernius. Grandmother of Narcissus.

(FLAVIUS) STRASTIVUS: Sarmatian merchant and smuggler.

*(TITUS FLAVIUS CLAUDIUS) SULPICIANUS: Senator. Father of Titiana. Patron of Pertinax. Brief attempt to claim throne in March 193.

*TAUSIUS: Officer of the Watch. Protegé of Diodoros Tigranos. Brother of Langoria.

*TIBERIUS (CLAUDIUS NERO JULIUS CAESAR AUGUSTUS): Emperor 14-37. Stepson and adopted son of Augustus. Adopted Caligula, who succeeded him.

TIGHER INISSEAN: King of the Eqendi/Epidii "horse people" on the Hebrides.

*(FLAVIA) TITIANA: Wife of Pertinax. Daughter of Sulpicianus. Descended through her mother from both Vespasian and his brother.

*TITUS (FLAVIUS CAESAR VESPASIANUS AUGUSTUS): Emperor 79-81. Son of Vespasian (whose name was identical to his). Destroyer of the Temple. Brother of Domitian, who succeeded him (and may have killed him). Uncle by marriage of Trajan.

*(MARCUS ULPIUS) TRAJAN (AUGUSTUS): Emperor 98-117. Nephew-in-law of Titus. Adopted son of Nerva. May or may not have adopted Hadrian, who succeeded him.

TULLIA MINOR: Daughter of Tullius Secundus.

*TULLIUS CRISPINUS: Praetorian, given the rank of prefect by Didius Julianus.

(MARCUS) TULLIUS PRIMUS: Deceased elder brother of Tullius Secundus.

(MARCUS) TULLIUS SECUNDUS: Senator and financier. Father of Tullia Minor. Owner of Castor, Cocina, Cocinilla, Magnus, and Phaeton. Employer of Philoxena.

*(TITUS FLAVIUS CAESAR) VESPASIAN (AUGUSTUS): Emperor 69-79. Commander against the Judean Revolt. Prevailed during the Year

of Four Emperors. Father of Titus, who succeeded him, and of Domitian. Great-great-great-grandfather and great-great-great-uncle of Titiana.

*VICTOR: Bishop of Rome.[6] Preceded by Eleutheros. Succeeded by Zephyrinos.

*(AULUS) VITELLIUS (GERMANICUS AUGUSTUS): Briefly Emperor in 69. Attempted to abdicate peacefully in favor of Vespasian but was assassinated.

*VOLOGASES (Persian BALAGASH): Name of six Parthian emperors. Vologases V, previously King of Persarmenia (the portion of Armenia assigned to the control of the Arsacid line of Parthian emperors), had just succeeded Vologases IV, but the succession was briefly contested by his half-brother Chosroes.

YA'AQOV: Leader of the Jewish community in Alexandria.

*ZEPHYRINOS: Senior assistant to Victor, later his successor.

---

[6] Victor is the first "Pope" from whom we have any substantial record. What we have indicates that the Church operated in his time as, among other things, a kind of mutual insurance society, taking care of widows and orphans of their members. Victor exercised authority over churches not only in Italy, but also in Spain (Gaul still had its own leadership in Arelate, but some Gaulish Christians were also loyal to Rome), his native North Africa (which not all early bishops of Rome received allegiance from), and Greece (which was not to be transferred to Constantinople's jurisdiction until late in the 4th century), but not further east. He received the eastern leader Polycarp of Smyrna, and they agreed to disagree on some issues, such as whether Easter should be clearly separated from the Jewish Passover. Victor was a staunch advocate of the doctrine that Christ was fully divine, excommunicating any who tried to portray Jesus as an exalted human only. There are inconsistencies in the old lists of Popes as to whether Victor succeeded Eleutheros during the last year of Commodus or during the Year of Five Emperors, and differences of interpretation as to whether Marcia dealt with him as a secret Christian or as an extortionist; on both of these issues the narrative plays it both ways.

BOOK ONE

The Dying of the Old Year

<u>Chapter 1</u>

"Father! I am still so nervous. Must I go?" Senator Marcus Tullius Secundus looked at his daughter with an expression which, he hoped, conveyed patience, and did not reveal irritation, or the amusement he also felt. The Senator was devoted to the Stoic philosophy of bearing with equanimity whatever one encountered in life, tempering one's grief in the face of losses with the reflection that indulgent sadness could do nothing helpful, and tempering one's joys with the reflection that nothing is permanent. He had always endeavored to instill in Tullia Minor these virtues of moderation and prudence, but with little effect, he had to confess to himself. Her temperament by nature often swung wildly between extremes, and today Tullia had viewed the prospect of tonight's celebrations sometimes with giddy anticipation, and sometimes, as now, with panicky dread.

"We are almost there," he said, hoping that would suffice. He knew this not because he could see anything, but from long familiarity with every turning on the way from their home on Egeria's Lane, a little off the Appian Way in the Porta Capena district, to the Palace. A direct route from the head of the Appian Way around the side of the Circus Maximus and up the Palatine Hill was proposed by city planners from time to time, but always thwarted by the needs of the priests to conduct certain rituals at a particular spot at the foot of the Palatine, in honor of Consus, that mysterious numen who manifested as a voice in one's head giving unexpected advice. These rituals had protected the city since king Romulus, and perhaps had protected the village which was there before Romulus, and could certainly not be stopped now. So the last portion of the drive involved some circuitous maneuvers.

The twilight was dimming and they were riding in an enclosed carriage, and as it was a bit chilly, only the merest slits were open for some air. The carriage was stuffed with embroidered pillows and woolen wraps to provide some warmth. The costume Tullius had chosen for the evening was not really suitable for the weather, but he would not be outdoors much. He was wearing a chiton in the Greek style, with a wreath of laurel leaves around his forehead and a quill pen stuck behind his right ear. Tullia at least was wearing two layers of robes, blue over white. She also had a headband, a strip of cloth with *EPATO*EPATO*EPATO* written over and over all the way around, to indicate the character she was portraying, and she carried as a prop the lyre Philoxena had crafted for her out of sawdust mixed with paste. She had at first argued for a different costume, then pronounced herself delighted with what Philoxena had fashioned, then declared that she was not going. Once in the carriage, however, she had begun chattering about how wonderful it would be to see the Emperor's residence at last, until she had fallen silent and, it appeared, fallen into low spirits again.

"Castor could drop you off and take me home, and still be back long before you need him."

"My dear, you are of age now." Indeed, that year she had been admitted to the rites of the Good Goddess. "You must begin to circulate in society." One would almost think she had never set foot outside the house before, Tullius thought to himself, but suppressed the urge to say it.

"But could I not begin with something smaller than the imperial palace on New Year's Eve?"

"It is the perfect occasion. Everyone who is of any importance will be there. And many of them will be looking for wives, if not for themselves then for their sons or nephews or protegés. You must not remain faithful to a ghost forever."

"I am afraid of making a fool of myself. What if I try to talk to someone who has no interest in talking to me?"

"That is very easily avoided. Can you remember and obey one simple piece of advice?"

"Certainly, father!"

"Never speak until you are spoken to. It is not your place to be forward. Let them take your measure and decide if they wish to approach you."

"So am I to be stared at and judged, by strangers, all night long? I do not know if I can bear it."

"There will also be people there whom you know. You will see. Now my dear, you must make an effort to enjoy yourself, or at least to give the impression that you are doing so."

The carriage pulled up to the open gate of the palace complex, twice a man's height and decorated in brass plate with embossed images of protective warriors. Castor, the stout slave who was named after a legendary boxer, got down from the driver's seat to open the door and give Tullia a hand down. Tullius got out without assistance. As they walked through the gateway toward the great front door, Tullia begin to fidget. "This lyre will be so awkward! How will I manage it all night?"

"You will be able to set it down."

"That costume as Daphne turning into a tree worked so well at our little Saturnalia party. Why couldn't I have been Daphne again?"

"Because then I would have had to be Apollo, and only one person can be an Olympian god tonight."

Chapter 2

Castor drove the carriage a little way further, and turned through a far less ornate gateway, typically used by deliverymen, into a wide empty lot adjoining the lower wing of the Palace, which contained stables, kitchens, servants' quarters, and the like. Ordinarily, if Tullius went to a gathering at the house in town of one of his wealthy friends, Castor would have to drive back home, then return for his master at some later, vaguely specified time, unless the host undertook to get his guests home. The problem was simple enough. There was hardly any place to park in Roma. Tullius had a large enough lot to hold a barn out back with horse-stalls and room for two carriages, this fancy one and a one-horse chariot. But he could not have accommodated multiple guests arriving by carriage, and most had much less space than he did. Almost everywhere around the seven hills, or in many of the suburban developments outside the walls, or across the Tiber as far out as the Janiculum area, there were public buildings, fancy houses, and dubious tenements jostling each other tightly, begrudging the streets enough room to get through. Small wonder, then, that prominent men mostly preferred to do their entertaining out at their country estates, and while in the city, they would venture from their houses carried in litter chairs, which could be broken down and folded up when not in use. After all, it was hardly as if horses could make better speed than men, not on Roma's streets. But Tullius never used his servants as beasts of burden in this way. He considered the litter chair vaguely Eastern and unmanly.

There were some open spaces at the edges of the city, especially on the flats by the east bank of the Tiber. Northwest of the seven hills was Mars Field, a great field used to train soldiers, or these days more often gladiators, also used for lesser public entertainments than the exhibitions in the Circus Maximus or the Colosseum. And southwest was the Emporium, which had taken over the former role of the Forum, now that the Forum was a rather congested plaza, as a place for vendors to spread out their goods in booths and stalls on market days, with plenty of room for the vendors to unload, and the shoppers to load, their numerous carts and drays and carriages. There were some public gardens like the Lateran fields and the grounds enclosed within the Temple of Claudius. But a large vacant expanse in the center of Roma, like the empty lots around the palace, was quite a rarity, and this one was of fairly recent origin.

One night a few years earlier, some wretched slave was found in the palace, who could give no very good account of what he was doing there. Commodus Caesar doubtless suspected that some member of his household had let him in, but without a particular suspect it would have been impractical to torture his entire staff. Unfortunately, the emperor undertook to conduct the torture of the intruder himself, with more enthusiasm than skill, with the result that the poor fellow died before the interrogation yielded any information. So he decreed that, to make it more difficult for any other rash intruder, all real estate on the Palatine hill which had come into private hands since Vespasian demolished the Golden House of Nero was to be expropriated, and the buildings demolished, including some tenements favored by those working for the City legion or the temples on the Capitoline who could afford the rents. Romans had long memories, and recalled that, whatever else one might say about Nero, when he acquired all the land for his Golden House project, he had paid generous compensation to owners and tenants alike for their troubles. Commodus did not do likewise. And while the stated purpose was to surround the Palace with a maze of hedges, walls, and ditches, only some fencing at the new outer perimeter of the grounds had actually gone up. Like many plans of Commodus, the proposed defensive works around the Palace fell victim to a shortfall in the funding, and to his tendency to forget his last obsession whenever his next fancy struck him.

A hostler directed Castor next to some other expensive conveyances, as grooms came up to take the horses. The drivers and porters would have their own little party in the servants' wing, and would not even need to dress up in costume. Castor had brought his dice, hoping that tonight he would meet some new people, who did not already know how dangerous it was to gamble with him. Castor was, of course, well known to the servants at the Palace, both slave and free, having driven the Senator here many times. He also brought a satchel. He believed the Senator had noticed him placing it beside the driver's seat, but Tullius was not the kind of suspicious master who asks questions about every little thing. However, one of the Praetorian guards milling around the entrance, whose name Castor could not summon up although they had certainly met before, asked him, "And what is that?"

"Something from Cocina," Castor replied vaguely. The cook in the Tullian household had some reputation for her skills both in the kitchen and as an herbalist, and she had relatives in the Palace.

"Might I have a taste?" The Praetorian stood blocking Castor's way in.

"It is a preparation for female troubles. Do you need some?"

Someone smaller than Castor might not have gotten away with that, but the Praetorian laughed and let him pass.

Chapter 3

The atrium in the Palace was naturally on a grander scale than atria in the homes of even the richest Senators. Even the vestibule leading from the twenty-foot-high door to the atrium was no stubby little hallway, with pegs for cloaks and mats to rub off muddy boots, but a lengthy corridor, lined with frescoes of past Emperors and their triumphant deeds, curving around a fair portion of the oblong rounded atrium before finally entering. This was for a practical reason. Praetorians were stationed where the vestibule joined the atrium, as well as at the door, so that any would-be invaders would be trapped for a while in a place where they could not see what defenders they had to contend with. The size of the atrium itself, with its impossibly high vaulted ceiling, was beyond any practicality, however, intended solely to make the visitor feel small. The ceiling was decorated to represent the dome of heaven, with the constellations of the Zodiac going around in proper order, but other constellations arranged more for artistic display than astronomical accuracy. Gold leaf, semiprecious stones, and paints containing the rarest purple and azure tints, were not spared in the pictures of the animals and heroes. Orion's dog had a stud on his collar, representing the star Sirius, which was a real diamond of startling size. But the splendid ceiling was a nuisance to clean. In winter, the pool was drained to become a central hearth, and quite a bonfire was required to keep this room warm. Far from all of the smoke escaped out the skylight. Slaves had spent days perched precariously on scaffolding, to scrub out all the black smears in preparation for the New Year's Eve gala.

There were rooms of somewhat more human scale in the Palace, where it would be common to hold a banquet. In warmer months, in the day, the open colonnade around a large outdoor pool would be used. But tonight, tables were set here and there about the atrium, laden with food and drink, and surrounded by comfortable benches, whose paddings were covered with the most expensive silk brocades and cloth of gold. There were breads and cheeses and figs and raisins, of course, but most of the foodstuffs were more exotic. The flamingo-tongue pies were exquisite.

The crocodile meat pickled in brine was not actually very tasty, but had been imported from Egypt to show that no expense was being spared. There was plenty of tetrapharmacum, a specialty of the house, invented by a member of the imperial family a couple of generations back. Though named for a medicine with four ingredients, this dish contained nothing very healthy, but rather, sweet pastry enfolding pheasant meat and two kinds of pork, namely a gamy ham made from wild boar, and a fatty sausage made from the udders of sows. The wine on offer was good, at this hour of the evening. Experienced guests knew to grab this wine while they could, before the rotgut that would take its place as the night progressed.

Eclectus, the majordomo of the household, was guarding a particular jug of wine, on a brass tray with a jeweled goblet. This jug was no ordinary amphora, but was sheathed in silver with delicate traceries. That alone should suffice to warn the party guests that its contents were not for just anyone, but Eclectus stood right by it to make sure. He was wearing a livery scarcely distinguishing him from the lesser servants, but did not mind. He was rather relieved not to have to devise some costume as a legendary figure, as the guests scattered around the room in conversational knots had all been obliged to do, with varying degrees of success. Eclectus was watching the entryway, waiting for a particular person to come in, but turned when the corner of his eye noticed someone approaching, then smiled to see who it was.

"Why, Marcia, my dear, you look positively hideous this evening!" Marcia was usually the very mirror of the latest style. But now she had an improvised headdress festooned with seashells balanced doubtfully on her hair, blue streaks smeared on her face, fake clamshells over her breasts, and a wide sash around her robe painted hastily with blue zigzags intended to be waves. All of this was supposed to show that she was a Nereid, a nymph of the ocean. Anyone else would have found something nice to say to the Emperor's mistress about her costume, or avoided the subject altogether. But Eclectus and Marcia shared a deep affection, and Eclectus did not need to be told who was really responsible for this crime against fashion. It was even worse than the Amazon costume he had inflicted on her last time.

"I'm afraid this is his revenge on me, for the cutting remarks I made about that gladiator get-up he intends to wear when he addresses the public tomorrow."

"Is there nothing we can do to prevent that?"

"He is one of the Consuls again for the coming year. Of course he has to appear."

"But I mean, can't we stop him from making himself look ridiculous? Or at least talk him out of killing some poor souls who are not allowed to fight back?"

"He is impossible today. I think he has been at the opium again, or something worse. When I bathed him, he vomited in the tub. It was disgusting. And while I was trying to get fresh hot water and clean him up, he kept accusing me of poisoning him. I almost told him straight out that no-one needs to poison a man who poisons himself. No, I didn't say anything, but he knew what I was thinking. He said there would be big changes in the year to come. Maybe he means to get rid of me."

"Or me, or both of us. You were missed this morning. He was shouting that you were out with me, and that we must be sleeping together, although he worded it more bluntly. Finally, someone pointed out to him that I was still here, and that Hyacinthus had been the one to drive you. He can hardly accuse you of an affair with Hyacinthus." Hyacinthus was a eunuch. "Where did you go?"

"To the catacombs, to visit my father's grave and seek his blessing for the New Year." Marcia raised her voice a little as she said this, as if to make sure any eavesdropper heard this part clearly.

Eclectus replied in a very low whisper. "Don't tell me you went to meet the Christians again? You know they have no more money for you."

Marcia shrugged. "They always get together on the day of the Sun. Their meetings soothe me somehow. It is hard to explain. I ask nothing from them, and they ask nothing from me."

Eclectus said, "Be careful. Someone is coming." He could hear Laurentius Motilenus, the shifty-eyed second-in-command of the Praetorian Guard, coming in from the vestibule with some people.

Motilenus was saying, "Let me guess. You are a poet, and she is your Muse? The Muse Erato, if my Greek does not fail me?" He was educated enough to know that the P in *EPATO* was a Rho, and that Erato was the name of the Muse for lyric poetry.

"Precisely," Senator Tullius replied. "I am Pindar the odist."

The Praetorians at the entry to the atrium parted to let them pass. Motilenus announced in a loud voice, "Senator Marcus Tullius Secundus, in the guise of the poet Pindar! And his daughter Tullia Minor, in the guise of the Muse Erato!"

Tullia started to curtsey to Motilenus, then noticed that her father was not bowing.

Chapter 4

Tullius and Tullia surveyed the room. Tullius knew Eclectus and Marcia, of course, but Eclectus had the air of one who was on duty, and not really free for idle conversation. And it was not always wise to initiate contact with Marcia, even if she were not precisely the last kind of person he would wish to introduce to Tullia. Uncertain whom to approach, Tullius was surprised to be rescued by his daughter. "Look! There is Popilia!" she exclaimed. "I have not seen her since the festival of Flora. Could I go over and speak to her?"

Popilia was standing next to Quintus Aemilius Laetus, the beefy commander of the Praetorian Guard. Laetus was not in uniform, but rather wore a leather skirt, and a long cape draped from his shoulders, leaving his well-toned bare chest exposed, completing the outfit with a crested helmet and a sword belted to his side. Popilia was in a drab gray robe, presumably borrowed from a servant, and wore a makeshift manacle on her left wrist, made out of the same kind of sawdust-and-paste mix as Tullia's lyre. Clearly he was a Greek hero and she was his slave. Laetus was drinking a cup of wine. Popilia had a cup also, but was not drinking. She was staring up at him adoringly and whispering some endearments as Tullius led Tullia over to them.

"Senator!" Laetus snapped to attention and bowed.

"Laetus, my good fellow!" Tullius nodded in return. "I see you are not on duty this evening?"

"Motilenus was happy to be named head of security for tonight, even though it means he cannot drink." Laetus lowered his voice to add, "I think he might be after my job."

Laetus said that as if it were amusing, but Tullius had to wonder if perhaps his political support was being solicited. He hastened to change the subject. "And who are you, this evening?"

"I am Achilles, and Popilia here is my Briseis. For she has sworn to be mine, all mine!"

"Are you married then?" Tullia gushed. Tullius gave her a stern look, to remind her of her pledge not to speak until spoken to, but if she even saw it, she paid no mind. "I should so love to have been there!"

"Oh don't worry! You haven't missed it!" Popilia answered. "The wedding won't be until the spring. I wouldn't dream of getting married without inviting you, and all our old friends. We will have the biggest wedding ever, won't we dear?"

"Yes, dear." Laetus took another slug of wine.

"And who is... he, this evening?" Tullius asked.

"Hercules again." Laetus rolled his eyes a little.

"And here I sat down to memorize all of Pindar's Odes to Zeus. I shall have to see what I can recall of Pindar's words about Hercules."

Motilenus came into the atrium again to announce, "Senator Publius Helvius Pertinax, in the guise of an Egyptian slave! His wife the Lady Flavia Titiana, in the guise of Queen Cleopatra! And Senator Marcus Didius Julianus, in the guise of Mark Antony!"

Pertinax was currently Prefect of the City. He liked to think of himself as a self-made man who had risen through sheer merit, from his beginnings as the son of a freedman to his current status as a Senator with one of the most impressive resumés of past titles, including the Consulate and important Governorships, of Africa Proconsularis, Syria, and Britannia. Of course his advancement had also been due to his assiduous cultivation of connections, but his great patrons would not have taken him on as a protegé if he had not shown genuine talent even as a junior officer. His marriage to Titiana was a symbolic affirmation of his acceptance into the nobility. She was the great-great-granddaughter both of the Emperor Vespasian and, because of a cousin-marriage, of Vespasian's brother as well. She was indulged when she made occasional remarks comparing the present imperial family unfavorably to her own. Her loyalty to her husband left as much to be desired as her loyalty to the Emperor. She had always regarded herself as a beauty, although few others did, and at her present age took to painting her face quite thickly. She wore Cleopatra's crown as if it were her due, and the asp on the front of the crown looked ready to strike at anyone who would cross her. She glared at Motilenus, who retreated back into the vestibular hall, going out to watch the door for the next batch of guests. Naturally it was Titiana who led the trio across the room.

Or at least, she led Julianus. Pertinax tried to follow, but Eclectus intercepted him. "Prefect Pertinax!" he called out, giving only the most perfunctory of bows.

"What is it, Eclectus?" Pertinax, annoyed, did not even nod to him.

"The August One wishes to honor you with a drink from his own supply of wine." Eclectus handed Pertinax the goblet, and while Pertinax held it, Eclectus filled it most generously, very nearly to the brim.

Pertinax took a sip. "Mmmm! Very curiously spiced!"

"Please! Drink it all," Eclectus urged, in a tone indicating plainly that this was not a request.

Pertinax raised his eyes heavenward for a moment of prayer, and drained the goblet.

Chapter 5

Narcissus greeted Castor warmly, throwing arms around his neck and kissing him on the cheek. "So excellent to see you! We will have all evening to catch up on things, since the August One," at the mention of whom Narcissus bowed slightly without even thinking about it, "isn't trusting me up among the toffs tonight. Someone has to see that the drivers and porters are fed and entertained, and I'm one of the ones charged with that. Hyacinthus promises to sing a little later, and I bet I can prod some of the girls into dancing for us, once the pace in the kitchen slacks off a bit."

Narcissus led Castor in the direction of the kitchens, where many servants who usually had other duties, freedmen as well as slaves, had been drafted to help. And those maids who would be useless helping the cooks, having no purpose in the Palace save to look pretty, and dance sometimes, and bed the August One when he was in the mood, did much of the work of shuttling dainties from the kitchen to the atrium or fetching wine from the cellar, along with the better-looking of the eunuchs. All were under orders to be obliging if any of the guests wanted them for something else. The Palace had many discreet rooms for such purposes. None of the staff, free or otherwise, would dare to sneak even a bite of the dainties, though there were bound to be leftovers later. But there was ample food prepared for the servants of the guests. It would not do, after all, for a porter carrying a Senator home in a litter to feel faint with hunger. And if the wine, too, was off-limits, for this special occasion everyone could drink beer rather than water. The beer and the food were both of good quality, too. New Year's Eve promised to be an enjoyable holiday for everyone, or nearly everyone.

"Will any of the toffs join us, do you think?" Castor asked. It was more common than one might think for someone who seemed very well-bred to tire of the mannerly conversations at these events, and slip off for rowdier entertainments, and not all of them were interested only in sex. Castor's right hand went to the pouch hanging from his belt, and through the leather he began unconsciously fingering the dice which nestled there among the coins. They said that rubbing dice brought luck, and no-one who had diced with Castor could dispute that it worked, at least for him.

"Some of the regulars are bound to get bored, I imagine. Maybe we can fight later." Narcissus and Castor were well-known as an evenly matched pair of sparring partners. When money was around, they would stage a bout for those who enjoyed that sort of thing. Either could throw the fight to the other, whichever way would be more profitable, depending on how bets had been laid down, without anyone being the wiser.

"I was wondering if you knew whether Junius Severus is coming? He lost very badly last time, and I accepted his promise to pay up next time he saw me, but I haven't seen him since."

Narcissus burst out laughing. "He's been posted to Britain. The next time he sees you is not likely to be for years."

"That lying weasel! I trusted him. His word was always good before."

"It was not his fault. Apparently he had to go with very little warning." Narcissus shrugged. "I think he must have charmed some Senator's wife just a little too much."

For a moment, no-one was passing them in the hall. Still, Castor looked up and down warily, and lowered his voice before saying, "Your cousin sends what your friend needs."

Narcissus looked at the satchel in Castor's left hand, which both had pointedly refrained from mentioning. He turned off into a hallway that Castor had never been down before, and had seldom seen unguarded. Castor hesitated, but Narcissus beckoned him to follow. It led to the cramped room, conveniently close to the kitchens, where all of the maidservants slept, nearly on top of each other, at night. Now, with everyone busy elsewhere, it was dark and appeared empty. It still made Castor nervous to be there. Castor thought maybe Marcia herself had a room further down the hall, although he was quite mistaken, for she lived in the opposite wing. He had heard tales of slaves being castrated for intruding into the female quarters in the homes of rich men. Of course, he heard many tales that were not true, but it did not pay to take chances. He wanted to hurry up, leave his delivery, and get out. He found an empty and clean chamber-pot, into which he dumped the herbs from the satchel, since he could not afford to give up a good leather bag. He nearly jumped out of his skin when Langoria suddenly stirred on the bed.

The light from the hall was dim, since the nearest sconce for a torch was not at all near, but even so, Castor could see that she was still in her first bloom of youth, however sadly tear-streaked her cheeks. She moaned a little and stared vacantly. "She has been this way for a couple days now," Narcissus whispered. "The other girls are covering for her, saying that it is one of those ills which only afflict women." That had the merit of being true, even if incomplete. "Did Cocina give instructions?"

Langoria sat up and said, "I am not dead. And I am not deaf. Tell me what to do with these."

Castor repeated what he had been told to say. "Divide this into twenty doses, to be taken three times a day, for a week. Infuse the herbs in a cup of water that has boiled. You must drink it all, though it is very bitter. Sweeten with honey if you must. Do this once after sunrise with a prayer to Kore the maiden, once before sunset with a prayer to Diana the queen, and once in the middle of the night with a prayer to Hecate the crone. Then stand on a bed or a table and jump down hard, saying Begone! But under your breath, for that is not meant for anyone to hear except... what is in your belly."

"Will the little ghost haunt me?" she asked. Neither man could answer that. Castor began to slink out of the room. Narcissus turned to follow, and Langoria said to their backs, "Thank you both. And please send word to my brother that it is done."

Narcissus looked back, and nodded his acknowledgement.

Chapter 6

"My dearest Lady Titiana! You look positively ravishing this evening!" Tullius took her hand and kissed her rather gaudy ring. "And Senator!" he added, with a nod to Julianus.

"Senator!" Julianus nodded back to him.

"Tullius, you flatterer you!" Titiana warbled. "And my! How your daughter has grown!" Tullia Minor curtseyed to her, somewhat star-struck. It had been years since she had seen the great lady.

"Senator!" Laetus bowed to Julianus. "My Lady!" He bowed to Titiana.

"Laetus, I hope this evening finds you well," Julianus said with a nod.

Titiana walked right past him, to go greet another guest across the room. "My dear Lady Anicia! How delightful to see you..."

Julianus turned to Tullia. "And how are you, dear? It has been so long."

Tullia curtseyed and said, "I am well. But is Lady Scantilla not coming?"

Julianus raised his voice to say, "My wife Scantilla is unwell!" But quietly he said, "She is fine. She just hates this kind of gathering." Then in a normal tone he said, "I would have stayed home with her, but Cleopatra needed to have an Antony."

Laetus interjected, "Have I offended her somehow?" Pertinax now came up to join them, and Laetus bowed to him. "Prefect, I would never wish to insult your wife in any way."

Pertinax smiled. "Don't worry about it, Laetus. My guess is that she thinks you ought to have greeted her first. If it eases your mind any, she bristled a bit at Motilenus too, for announcing me ahead of her." He shrugged. "She can be that way."

"Prefect!" Tullius nodded to him. "How is it that you are not her Antony?"

Pertinax nodded back. "Senator, I am but her slave, as ever." He raised the mock manacle on his left wrist, which was similar to the one Popilia wore, though neither Senator had deigned to take any notice of Popilia's presence. "I was afraid that..." He paused and lowered his voice. "A certain person might make remarks that I am not noble enough to portray Antony. But he cannot dispute my right to play a slave." He wobbled a little on his feet. "She argued that if she were Cleopatra, then I must be Antony. I resisted, and finally enlisted the aid of my colleague and successor."

Julianus said, "I am always happy to help." He had not gone to very much trouble about his costume, the same toga any Roman of Senatorial rank might wear on any occasion.

Pertinax turned to Tullia. "And is this Tullia Minor, all grown up? I don't know if you will remember me."

Tullia curtseyed. "Of course I remember you, Senator! You visited the home of Julianus more than once, when I was there to visit Lady Scantilla and..." She broke off, thinking it unlucky to name the dead. From her father she had at least learned the knack of changing the subject. "The two of you are close friends, are you not?"

Pertinax replied, "We have often worked together. He was my colleague the year I was Consul, and he was my successor as Governor of Africa."

"And do the two of you work together now?"

This was a minor *faux pas*, but Julianus smoothed it over. "I am enjoying a year away from public duties."

A silence fell. Laetus broke it. "I am forgetting my manners! Are any of you thirsty? I am going to refill my cup, and would be glad to pour for any of you."

"None for me, thanks," said Pertinax. "The cup which Eclectus gave me is going to my head. I am not feeling very well." He was not looking well, either. He moved urgently over to a bench to recline on, but stumbled before he reached it, and fell heavily against it.

"Husband!" Titiana rushed over to him. "How can you be so undignified?"

A loud laugh broke out. It was the voice of Commodus Caesar! How could they not have noticed him slipping into the room behind them? Tullius and Julianus spun around to give deep bows, while Tullia and Popilia curtseyed nearly to the floor.

He was dressed in a robe made of a lion's pelt. The lion's head rested on top of his hair, with fake glass eyes that stared disconcertingly. A club was tied to one sleeve so that he need not be bothered with carrying it, but Hercules after all had to be depicted with a club. The robe was pinned together in front with brooches, but most of them had come loose. He was walking rather unsteadily, and some wine sloshed onto the tiled floor out of the goblet he was holding, a close match to the goblet Eclectus had served Pertinax from. He stepped on the bottom of his robe, and another brooch came unpinned, revealing that he was naked underneath. "Julianus! I didn't know if you would dare to come! And here you are, coupled with Titiana! Are you so thick with Pertinax nowadays that you're even swapping wives? But wait, where is Scantilla? Don't tell me you took Titiana from him, and you didn't even give him Scantilla? Is he having to service you too?"

Pertinax and Julianus stared down at the floor, afraid to speak. Titiana, however, glared daggers at Commodus. Tullius cleared his throat. "How gladly I sing odes on the theme of Hercules, recalling ancient tales of the highest grandeur! How the son of Zeus sprang, from his mother's womb to brightest light, escaping the birth pangs along with his twin! He was not to escape the notice of golden-throned Hera..."

Commodus interrupted, "That's enough of your shit, Tullius, and Pertinax, why don't you have some more of my wine?"

Chapter 7

That evening, Governor Decimus Clodius Albinus of Britannia was perched most uncomfortably above the wall of Antoninus Pius, at the very northernmost boundary of his province. The Antonine wall was not nearly as solid as Hadrian's wall. Mostly it was a double wooden fence with packed earth in between, the parapet on top scarcely sturdy enough or wide enough to walk on, certainly not usable for patrolling and keeping an eye on the north. It had been intended to face the wall with stone on both sides, as had been done for most of the length of Hadrian's wall. But a shortage of good nearby quarries meant that little of this had been accomplished by the time Marcus Aurelius pulled back to Hadrian's line. And when the Romans returned, they found that the natives had carted away a lot of the stones that had been placed. Timber was not always so easy to obtain this far north, either, so in many stretches the turf was just piled up in a heap, not hemmed in by any kind of fencing, and badly eroded by the weather. This was one of the stretches which had eroded worst while the Romans were away, which was why a gateway was grudgingly allowed to cut through here. Loads of wood had been brought up to construct at least a single wooden fence just north of the turf-heap barrier, and the ditch north of that had been improved with wooden spikes. But there was a gap in the ditch here, to allow a path to the gateway, for traders to pass through if they could afford the customs dues. Watchtowers on either side of the gate were manned day and night.

And now, a high platform had been built in haste, so that the Governor could sit on an imposing chair and look down over anyone on the north side. His trusted aide Servilius sat on a much less imposing stool beside him, at a little desk with pen and ink and birch-paper if any note-taking were required, though the light was very poor, from torches valiantly struggling against a chill wind blowing from Caledonia, or all the way from Ultima Thule as far as Clodius could tell. Despite his famously pasty-white skin, Clodius had actually been born and spent his early childhood in Africa, and had never much cared for the far north. He clutched his cloak tighter, and envied the soldiers in the open field north of the gateway, where numerous fires and torches were lit around a large tent. Meat was roasting, so at least the wind brought with it some pleasant aromas. On the platform, besides Clodius and Servilius, an interpreter stood by with a megaphone, and a half-dozen archers crouched in front, waiting.

Then, abruptly springing from behind an escarpment which the Caledonians had perhaps improved as their answer to the Roman barrier, dozens of barbarian warriors appeared, with two leaders. The half-moon was sinking low, but still the sentries ought to have seen and given warning of their approach. The leaders were easy to distinguish, in their multi-colored and gaily bangled coats. For the others were all naked, in war paint that was mostly blue, except for red and black streaks on some faces and chests. They carried long spears and whooped as they came. The archers cocked their bows, in case the Caledonians had any hostile ideas.

"Well, I have seen better costumes for midwinter revelries," Clodius observed. "Was it really necessary to schedule this parlay for New Year's Eve?"

"The soothsayer said that if this matter is not concluded by the end of the year, it never will be," Servilius replied.

"But need it have been after sundown? This wind is so miserable."

"Sharing an evening meal is how they solemnize an alliance. They believe that the gods will curse any man who shares bread and salt with another, and then breaks faith." Servilius shrugged. "That is not to say that this has always stopped them from warring against a sworn ally."

The Caledonian warriors were in a line, rhythmically shouting as they held their spears vertical and tossed them to each other, half throwing to the left and half to the right, a little faster each time, none failing to catch his neighbor's throw. Then they split into two lines, and began throwing their spears over their counterparts in the other line, jumping straight up to catch the spears overhead, and backing up as they turned the spears around for the next throw so that each jump was a little more difficult than the previous. They began varying their moves into a more intricate war-dance.

"At least we shall not be as chilly as those barbarians. How can they stand it?"

"They believe that nudity confers invulnerability in battle. And it is true that a blade thrust through cloth can cause a badly infected wound, so that a soldier who has no proper armor is better off doing without," Servilius explained. "And I have heard that if you keep moving, it is not uncomfortable to be naked in the cold."

"You have only... heard? You are not speaking from experience?"

Servilius laughed. "No, I have not tried it."

"A pity. For a moment there, I was picturing you fleeing an angry husband some snowy night." He watched for a while. "I hope these fellows have left their clothing somewhere near to hand."

"Remember that we have gifts for them of suits of leather armor, which they should appreciate. Perhaps we should distribute those first, even before the baubles for the chiefs. They are going to some trouble to put on a show for us. In real combat the Caledonians use heavy swords, and when they use javelins, they launch them from throwers. Bare-handed spears like this? Purely for display." He thought a little more. "They are also sending a message that they are not attempting to smuggle any weapons into the banquet tent, but will be hard to bring down if we are the side with treacherous intent."

The Caledonians finished their dance with a loud hurrah and struck a threatening pose. Clodius rose to address them. "Warriors of the... Maeaetae! We honor your fortitude and your valor!" Servilius had coached him on the tribal name, but he still stumbled over it. No matter, for the interpreter repeating the words in Caledonian could pronounce "Maethi" well enough, even if the Caledonians could tell that his mother-tongue was Brythonic. "We have gifts for you, of hardened leather armor with real iron rivets," Clodius added, with a gesture to the Roman soldiers below that they should fetch out the leather suits from the banquet tent and begin distributing them. When the interpreter had repeated this, Clodius concluded, "For we hope that you shall be our friends! Never should we wish to face such fierce enemies!"

The Caledonians shouted a kind of huzzah, which could be taken as either a cheer or a threat.

Chapter 8

In Alexandria, Governor Justus Pescennius Niger had a simpler evening planned. Two guests were invited, and he asked them to arrive late, when few would note their coming. A plate with some bread and a few sausages was on the table for one of his guests to nibble on, along with jugs of wine and water. One of the two tall candles on the tables was lit, the other unlit, and only a few dim oil lamps added to the subdued light in the room. Pescennius quietly admired his new clepsydra. This was a water clock, the pot tapered precisely so that the level would go down at a steady pace, whether the water was high and therefore dripping out the small hole in the bottom under greater pressure, or low and dripping out more slowly. As the float sank, it drove intricate gearwork. The clock was set to ring a chime at midnight. It was from a workshop tracing its lineage to the great engineer Ctesias. Pescennius recalled how the salesman had boasted of the precision of their clocks. Knowing how poorly clocks agreed, Pescennius had laid a trap for him, asking that two of their clocks be set to ring in an hour precisely. He toured the works, which also made hydraulically powered pipe-organs and dancing dolls. He returned near the appointed time, and was astonished when the clocks rang their chimes together. So he bought one for his office. Technology was so marvelous, these days.

A servant showed in his guests and left them alone. One was Dionysius, the ethnarch of the Greek community in the city. Dionysius bowed and said, "My lord governor, I am honored. I could wish for no better company on this occasion."

"You are always welcome here, Dionysius. Come sit by me and help yourself to some refreshments." Pescennius waved him to a place at his right hand. "And Ya'aqov, I am most gratified that you have come." Ya'aqov, the ethnarch of the Jewish community, sat down on another bench on the far side of the table without any kind of bowing gesture. In his dialect the *'ayin* sound in his name was guttural and not silent, and Pescennius was careful to pronounce his name accurately, not slur it into "Iacobos" as most Greek-speakers would do. Most Jews in Alexandria had alternate Greek names, or indeed had only a Greek name, but not this one, and he was reputed to be touchy. "I hope that it is no breach of your religion to mark the occasion of the Roman New Year."

"This is not when our people mark the turning of the year, nor is midnight even the time when we break one day from another," Ya'aqov observed. "But if there is no rite dedicating this occasion to any of your supposed gods, then there can be no harm in it. One time is as good as another."

"Rightly said," Pescennius replied. "For a long time, Romans were accustomed to begin their years in the spring, with the month of March. I confess I know no reason why winter was thought a better beginning."

"In the days of our lawgiver Moshe, our people also began their years in the spring. And I must also confess that I know no reason why fall was thought to be better."

"The Egyptians once started their years whenever the Nile flooded. At least that time was singled out by nature. But for ages now, their New Year comes every 365 days, even though that is not quite right. It is not exactly in the same season as when I was young."

"Any day is a good day for friends to get together," said Dionysius, mixing some water and wine together into a cup, and wrapping a sausage into some bread.

"Ya'aqov, I know that your religion forbids you from sharing with us," Pescennius said. "But know that you would be welcome to share, if you could. There is no pork in this meat."

"I know you for a good man. I know that your hospitality is offered in kindness. But our God, holy be His Name, is strict with us about what meats and drinks we may consume. Even those who wish to respect our ways might make errors in this regard. In this way we avoid accidental impurities. No offense has ever been intended to anyone."

Pescennius may have been content with that answer, but Dionysius was not. "Doesn't your insistence, that your ways are so much purer than any other people's ways, give offense whether intended or not?"

"Please, let's not quarrel," Pescennius said, before Ya'aqov could reply. "In fact, that is precisely why I wished to see both of you, together, and away from other ears. At this time, especially, all quarrels must be settled. I hear disturbing rumors that the Greeks and the Jews are spoiling for a fight again. We can't have another round of inter-ethnic riots in Alexandria, not now."

"It is not the Jews who have looked for any fight. But we will fight back if they try again to beat an innocent boy like Nathan bar-Moshe bar-Ptolemy, whose only crime was cutting through the Greek quarter on his way home."

Dionysius exploded. "He broke into the shop of Philodemos the jeweler!"

Ya'aqov shook his head. "He did no such thing. Nothing at all was found on him, as you know. Yet you beat him half to death!"

"Philodemos was not such a fool as to leave valuables in the shop overnight to be stolen. But locks were broken, and tools were damaged that will be difficult to repair or replace."

"And this has what to do with Nathan?"

"When the friends of Philodemos who live nearby heard the noise, they found no-one else suspicious in the neighborhood."

"Then they missed the real thief. Nathan would never be involved in such a thing. He is of very respectable family. Governor, I mentioned that his father's father was Ptolemy. That is the very same Ptolemy who used to work for your father!" Ya'aqov seemed to think that this was a very telling point.

"I remember meeting him..." Pescennius mused, pouring himself some more wine, mixing it with water, and slipping into a reverie.

Chapter 9

Pescennius thought back to the first time he had visited Egypt. His parents had both been born there, but often spoke disparagingly of it. His father Fustus was the son of a Roman officer named Annius and a Nubian freedwoman, whom Pescennius knew as Biba though that was surely not her name. His mother Lampridia was almost all Egyptian, despite her Greek name. His grandfather's marriage was purely for love, and blighted his chances of promotion. It would have been perfectly acceptable for him to beget a son on a slave woman from the dark lands beyond the Empire, but to grant her freedom? And to acknowledge her as a wife? That was not done. But Annius did not care. His father's marriage, by contrast, was purely mercenary. Lampridia brought money from her mercantile family. Fustus brought Roman citizenship, and the social rank of an equestrian. Lampridia thought that they would go to Roma and rise in the world. She did not understand that the rank of equestrian was not so lofty in Italy as it appeared in Egypt, particularly when coupled with a failed military career. The best post that Annius could obtain, when he retired from the army and returned to Italy, was town supervisor of Aquinum, an old but not very prominent commune in Latium. And Fustus never amounted to even that much, as Lampridia never tired of reminding him. Biba was the only one who ever expressed any desire to go back to Egypt, but she got her way at last, when Annius died and there was nothing for Fustus to do but to take a job in Alexandria, working for Lampridia's brother.

Pescennius had been away from home for a long time by then. He served with distinction on the upper Danube. He wrote to tell his parents that he had been made a military tribune in his legion, charged with disciplining the soldiers and sometimes conducting courts martial. Fustus was pleased, but Lampridia sniffed that an administrative job was nothing to be very proud of. Then his patrons Nonius Murcus and Clodius Albinus sent him to Roma, with a purse full of coin which, they told him, he was never even to think about repaying, and glowing letters of recommendation. Someone at the Palace was duly impressed. Pescennius was enrolled for the fall with a teacher of law, so that he could serve the next year as a magistrate with the rank of *quaestor*, skipping steps in the usual progression. The title of "quaestor" was a high one, responsible for capital cases such as murder or treason, and for complex cases of financial embezzlement. Serving in that office gave him Senatorial rank. He had months free before his schooling began, so he travelled to Egypt to share news of his good fortune with his family face to face.

He found the languid heat of the late spring in Egypt pleasant, though some thought it oppressive. He found the country beautiful, and wondered why his parents had such a poor opinion of the place. But he soon found that he was totally lost. He asked a passerby to make sense of the directions he had been given to his parents' home. The man said, "That cannot be right. Only Romans live out that way." Pescennius could not convince the man that his father was a Roman and so was he. He realized that the relative darkness of his skin was the problem. This stranger seemed genuinely concerned that he might be suffering from some kind of madness, and might be in real danger if he went where he did not belong.

Pescennius had never encountered this before. His darkness was certainly noticed, and the identifying nickname Niger was his for life. But he had met soldiers from Mauretania who were darker than he was, without feeling that this gave him and them much in common. The army bureaucracy delighted in posting soldiers from Syria to Britain, or soldiers from Spain to Dacia. No-one cared what ethnicity a comrade-in-arms came from. Prejudice was rather based on social class. Clodius Albinus had taken him aside to talk about this, when Pescennius said he was happy with what he was doing in the army, and had no real wish to leave it and go to Roma. "Look, you are the most excellent tribune I have ever seen. Your handling of the chicken case was brilliant." Ten soldiers had shared a chicken dinner, and a farmer complained that a fat chicken of his was missing. None of the soldiers would admit to taking it, no matter how much Pescennius blustered that he would execute them all if they did not tell, for all the world as if he meant it. So he ordered that each one of them pay the full price of the chicken, and gave a stern lecture about how the army did not requisition supplies without compensation.

"But," Clodius continued, "this is as high as you will ever go, as a clever man of equestrian class. Do you think that I move from command to command because I am a clever man? It is because I am of the *gens Clodia* family, and my mother from the *gens Ceionia,* as in Ceionius Commodus, the man Commodus Caesar is named for. It has been taken for granted that I would be of Senatorial rank since before I could gurgle 'mama' and 'papa' at my noble parents. You, on the other hand, need a push. I will make Roma give you one of the posts in the Course of Honor, and if you perform it as well as I know you can, they will consider you Senatorial material. After that you can return to the army, if this is where you want to be, with the kind of rank that you deserve."

Fustus understood perfectly what it meant for Pescennius to be named a quaestor. He was bursting with pride and had to show off his son to everyone who passed through the offices of his brother-in-law's export business. Lampridia had her own view of what it meant. "Then it is time for you to be married," she said. "No-one will take seriously a judge who cannot even manage a household. We will see the match-maker at once. I will insist on a woman of impeccable Roman blood." Pescennius had hardly even thought about it. The army strongly discouraged courting the local women, and most of the soldiers were unmarried. It had even been against the law for a long time for legionaries to marry, but that was from the days when enlistments were short-term. Still, even career-military men were often single, and satisfied all their urges with whores, something that Pescennius had never developed any interest in. His own marriage would prove to be one of indifference. They seldom saw each other anymore. She bore him two sons, and that was all that he needed from her. He bought her a villa in Tuscany, and that was all that she needed from him.

It was at the export firm that Pescennius met Ptolemy, a shrewd appraiser of true values, when pushy salesmen thought some goods or other would fetch a high price in Italy. Fustus seemed to regard him as a close friend, yet never invited him to the house. Fustus did invite home business acquaintances who were far less genial. But they were Roman, or Greek, and Ptolemy was a Jew, however Greek his name. Pescennius also met his son, several years younger than himself, who was called Moshe by his father, but Marcus by everyone else. Why did he try to pass himself off with a Roman name, when he was not Roman, and barriers would be put in his way because he was not? Ptolemy sensed that Pescennius did not care about the barriers between nations as much as some did, and asked if he was interested in coming to the synagogue. It was one of their lesser festivals, the Feast of Weeks, for it seems that they not only counted days in sevens, but also counted the sevens in sevens and were celebrating this bit of arithmetic, or something. Ptolemy assured Pescennius that non-Jews would be welcome to attend.

This proved true, more or less, but there was a special roped-off section for the Theophiloi, or God-lovers, as those non-Jews were called who enjoyed hearing the Jewish teachings, but had no intention of undergoing the painful ritual of conversion. Pescennius had been to shrines where women were separated from the men, but never to one which separated by ethnicity. He had been to the Temple of Isis, where he learned that the rites of Isis which Biba had taught him bore no resemblance to what the Egyptians did. But no-one there had asked him how much Egyptian blood he had in him.

The reading in the synagogue proved to be on this very theme. Ruth, an ancestress of the Jews' former royal house, was of the Moabite nation originally. The Moabites, the rabbi assured his audience, were a nation of surpassing wickedness. But Ruth was a good woman, and so she left Moab to join the Jews, out of devotion to the One True God.

Anyone with such devotion was welcome to join the Jews, regardless of what wicked nation he, or she, was born into. Well, it was easier for a "she" than a "he" to join, Pescennius knew. He was not about to let a knife come anywhere near his penis. And he was not persuaded that any god was truer than any other. He wondered about the Moabites. It sounded as if they were all gone now, but in their time they had lived next to the Jews, and no doubt looked very much the same as the Jews, dressed very much the same, and probably behaved neither better nor worse, no matter what the rabbi said. But in the East, all that it took for one ethnicity to despise another was for the two groups to live nearby.

He thought about what Biba said, when she took him to see Sobek the great crocodile. This monster had been brought up from the Fayyum to be venerated by the local Egyptians as the very embodiment of Ra. Egypt had always had many such sacred animals, and the crocodile had once been of only local importance. But now that the Apis bull had been largely expropriated by the Greeks, the Egyptian community wanted a deity peculiarly their own, and what could be more Egyptian than the crocodile? A best-selling book described the miraculous attributes of Sobek. But Biba told Pescennius, "He is big and dreadful, but only here. You find no crocodiles in the sea, because they cannot live there. You, my little Piscis," she said while reaching up to pat him on the head, using a nickname she had called him since he was a little child, arising from a simple misunderstanding of what the name "Pescennius" meant, "should be like a fish who can swim anywhere, from the smallest stream to the encircling Ocean."

He was so glad to have taken the opportunity to see Biba once more before she died.

<u>Chapter 10</u>

Qenmaethin had pledged his daughter, now that she was of age, to Kuglas. That is to say, Kuglas was designated to be the next Qenmaethin. It was more accurate to call the Qenmaethin a war-chief, rather than a king, since succession was matrilineal in Caledonia. Qenmaethin held his position because he was married to the high priestess, whose daughter would be high priestess after her. Their son was irrelevant. That is not to say that the Maethi were ruled by their women, as some from other nations mockingly said of them. Qenmaethin's daughter appeared to be pleased enough by the choice of Kuglas, and Qenmaethin hoped that his wife had always been pleased enough to have him, but neither had had much say in the matter. The Maethi considered this system superior to what they heard about other nations, where an able king might leave his power to a worthless son. Their chiefs were chosen for merit. Or at least, Qenmaethin generally thought that Kuglas was a meritorious choice for successor. On some occasions he thought, rather, that Kuglas showed how much he had to learn. His reaction to the interpreter calling out that Romans would never wish to face such fierce enemies was one of those occasions. "You hear that?" Kuglas exclaimed with a beaming grin. "They are afraid of us."

"No. They are laughing at us inside. But they are choosing to be polite. We must be likewise." Qenmaethin cupped his hands in front of his mouth and shouted up at the wall in Latin. "Great Clodius Albinus of the Romans! We are honored that you praise us, far beyond what we deserve! All the world knows the might of Roma! It is our fondest wish that you might count us among your friends!"

Servilius said quietly to Clodius, "It is surprising that he chooses to speak in Latin, and that his Latin is so passable. His manners also are better than I expected."

Clodius called out, "I greet you, great king of the Maeaetae, in the name of the Senate and People of Roma! For you also we have gifts!"

A Roman soldier brought out a chest from the banquet tent and bowed before the Caledonian chiefs, setting the chest at their feet and withdrawing. The chest proved to contain a gold circlet crown set with semi-precious stones, some gold and silver armlets, and necklaces of various styles. Qenmaethin placed the crown on his head, and a necklace around Kuglas.

Kuglas said, "This is not much. We were hoping for so much more."

"This is only what they start with. They were not about to bring much of value over to our side of the wall before we have reached agreement. Let us make it worth their while to be more open-handed." Again he cupped his hands and shouted. "Truly Roma is munificent! If it is known that Roma is generous to us, the Gwotadin of the north and the Eqendi will acknowledge the Maethi as overlords! The Eqendi will bring friends from over the water! Together we shall crush the unruly Picts beneath our heels! Then all Caledon will be federates of Roma!" He was showing off his Latin vocabulary.

Clodius had to sit down and consider. "What all was he saying there?"

Servilius explained, "These Maeaetae hold the center of Caledonia, and the Votadini the east coast. The southern Votadini are subject to us, if not very loyal. He is promises to bring the northern Votadini, also called the Taixali, into allegiance, and the Epidii of the western isles, with their allies in Hibernia. No Roman governor has ever succeeded in making any allies in Hibernia."

"Is that fellow standing with him a representative of... one or the other of those other tribes you mentioned?"

"No. That is the man Priscus and I negotiated with, to set up this meeting. He has little Latin and a hostile attitude. We know not what his relationship is to the king, but he appears to be more than a mere minister."

"Why was he insulting Picts, calling them unruly and promising to crush them? Aren't these people Picts?"

"Some use that name to mean any of the painted peoples, but strictly it means the more savage tribes of the farthest north. He is not pledging to make friends of those. If he said that, we would know he was lying. He is promising to wage war on them, with all the allies he can buy if we fund him. He must know that our ultimate aim is to finish taking all of this island, and never have to worry about a northern frontier again. He is saying that he will do that for us."

"Is he capable of accomplishing all of what he says he can?"

"He appears to be intelligent and ambitious. We can certainly trust that he wants to conquer Caledonia for his own sake. And if he buys allies with money from us, then he will have to remain our man to keep them. I do not think he would have said in front of all his men that he can bring over the Votadini and Epidii if he cannot do so. Few of them are likely to know much Latin, but some are sure to have picked up the gist of what he said."

"But this is so much more than we were bargaining for. We were only looking to offer some iron for a few years of truce. For something like this, do we offer him gold?"

"We must. The soothsayer was right. This is an excellent opportunity. If he does the work for us, it will cost us little or no blood from our own troops. I say that we offer him all the iron, and a thousand pieces of gold besides. I am sure that is more money than he has ever dreamed of."

"Well, I have less faith in soothsayers than you do, but I do have faith in your judgment."

Chapter 11

Dionysius sought to bring the attention of Pescennius Niger back to the case. "You know that Philodemos is highly reputable as well. He supplies the best men in the city, and their wives!"

Of course, thought Pescennius. It is the same thinking, always, in the East. First the parties should be prejudged by their ethnicities, and then by their social rank and connections. In the West, the connections would have been raised first. The facts of the matter hardly entered into this. Even if Pescennius wanted to know what the facts were, they would be impossible to ascertain. "I gather that the youth is not dead, and I hope that he is in no danger?"

"The doctor says that his bone has set well," Ya'aqov replied, "all praise be to God for His infinite mercies. But he may walk with a limp. The family's just demands for compensation have been rudely refused."

"And the jeweler lost no gemstone or pearl of great price?"

"No," admitted Dionysius. "But he suffered losses. He is the one who ought to be compensated, and if he is not... well, break-ins can happen at Jewish shops as well."

"Do not even think to suggest criminal actions in my presence," Pescennius warned in his sternest tone.

Dionysius lowered his head. "My deepest apologies, Governor."

"But if he is made whole for his costs, he would be content?"

"He would."

"And if the bar-Ptolemy family is paid, they would be content?"

Ya'aqov agreed, "Yes, they would. But, which is it to be?"

"Both of you, submit to Mantennius the amounts required, and I shall pay them myself. And then I will hold the two of you responsible for telling the hotheads in your communities that, if anybody has an accusation against a member of the other community, it should be brought to the proper magistrates. I must have peace in Alexandria at this time."

Dionysius raised his head. "You are very generous."

Ya'aqov pointed out, "If you make a habit of this, some might contrive more incidents, to wring money from you."

Pescennius had thought of that. "It will not be a habit. Let everyone know that if there is a next time, I shall instead levy fines on both of your communities."

Ya'aqov then pointed out, "The Egyptians will resent that we and the Greeks are getting money, and they are not, when they had no part in causing this trouble."

Pescennius had not thought of that. "Good point. They have recently brought up a new crocodile to replace the old Sobek. I should contribute to keeping the poor dumb beast fed."

Ya'aqov stood and gave Pescennius a bow. "You are as wise as our king Solomon, of blessed memory."

"You are not offended that I assist the worship of a false god?"

"You know that the animal is no god, and the fools will do what they do in any case. Seeking peace is a holy endeavor."

"Even my personal quarrels, I have decided that I must set aside at this time. When Octavius Emesianus relieved me as Governor of Syria, I brought the personal guards with me here to my new post. He has demanded their return ever since. This evening I wrote to him, letting him have his way. I said that I would come with the men, to visit him and discuss any other issues. Do either of you have any complaints against the Syrians that you would like me to address?" He knew perfectly well that both of them did, and they spoke up simultaneously.

"The chief rabbi of Antioch writes that the Governor fined his community most unfairly," Ya'aqov said, while Dionysius chimed in with, "Some of our merchants were hit with unexpected fees in Berytus harbor."

"Then write up detailed reports for me, and leave the reports with Mantennius when you see him about the money. I will bring these matters to the Governor's personal attention."

They sat in silence for a while. Pescennius kept his eyes on the clepsydra as its pointer indicated the approaching end of the day, and of the year. A hitherto-silent part of the machinery came alive. The chime sounded.

"Midnight!" exclaimed Pescennius. He lit a long thin strip of wood from the burning candle, held this match aloft while he blew out the candle, then lit the other candle with it. "Hah! I usually fail at that."

"Mazel tov!" Ya'aqov said with a smile.

"Happy New Year!" added Dionysius.

"They say that lighting fresh fire will make the new year better, but we shall have to see."

<u>Chapter 12</u>

The atrium of the Palace was rather the worse for wear. Much of the food had been consumed, of course, but many half-eaten bits were lying around here and there, on tables or benches or often enough the floor. Some of the amphorae of wine had also been knocked over, leaving sticky spots on the floor, or sad stains on the fancily brocaded bench cushions, stains that would never come clean. An owl had flown in through the skylight and was very difficult to shoo away. It would have been impolitic to mention that an owl was considered a bird of ill omen. Senator Tullius attempted to utter some verses about the owl of Minerva, but the bird hooted at him until he had to give it up.

Some guests whose costumes involved props of one kind or another had shed them. Laetus, for example, had shed his helmet, which was not his real helmet with the fashionable crest of red feathers that the Praetorians favored. He had not wanted to involve any part of his uniform, and this improvised pot on his head had gotten stuffy and uncomfortable. Tullia had carefully leaned her lyre against a table, but when she wanted to show it to Senator Sempronius, who was being so friendly, she found that it had been knocked over, stepped on, and broken. The bench it was next to was even lying on its side.

That happened after Hyacinthus performed a bawdy poem, filled with *double entendre*, in which he sang both male and female parts. Tullius reflected that it was a little cruel to make him sing about a topic he could know only in the most theoretical sense, except for that parody of love which Commodus Caesar inflicted upon him. But such a sentiment would not even have occurred to most of the attendees. Fulminatus Rhetor found the performance downright arousing. He was a lawyer, whom many of the other guests thought was above his place to be at this party, regardless of how much money he had, or how many services he had performed for Commodus. He reached over a bench to grope the breasts of Junipera, a slave who was re-stocking a table with more food.

This was intended to be a prelude to an invitation to join him in a side-room. Or perhaps he intended to take her right then and there. Open orgies were considered very low-class, but had not been unknown in the Palace under Commodus, though not when high society was invited. Whether Fulminatus understood the distinction was not clear. Junipera was under orders to co-operate with whatever a guest required of her. Nonetheless, she could not help but make a noise and flinch away from the unexpected touch. This startled Fulminatus, who was a bit too drunk to keep his balance. He fell over the bench, knocking it over, banging his shins on the corner of the bench and his head on the edge of the table.

The cut on his cheek added a much-needed touch of realism to his otherwise unlikely costume as a gladiator with a protruding paunch. His fury turned to embarrassment as he heard laughter from multiple voices, and saw a withering evil-eye directed at him by Lady Titiana. He wished that he could simply go home. Many other tired guests felt the same, but no-one would be allowed to leave for some time yet. And the atrium had no corners in which he could hide. In his desperation to find someplace where he could disappear from view for a while, he stumbled into a side-room where he found Commodus with Ajax, a real gladiator, one of many whom Commodus had purchased. Commodus did not use Ajax as he used Hyacinthus. Rather, the bloody nose and black eye which Ajax sported indicated that Commodus wanted to fight with someone. Of course, Ajax was required to make a show of fighting, without really fighting back. That was something Narcissus was not as good at. "Do you wish to join us?" Commodus asked. Fulminatus fled before he could even finish stuttering out his apology.

Servants continued to bring up more wood for the fire, more food for the tables, and more wine. Marcia spotted Langoria setting down two amphorae of the worst wine in the Palace. "Are you feeling better?" she asked solicitously.

"Yes, my lady," Langoria replied with downcast eyes. Then she decided that Marcia's concern might be genuine. "A wise woman sent me medicine.

I'm told I need boiling water for the herbs. Might I ask, my lady, if you could arrange for me to be assigned to the kitchen for this coming week?"

"You are getting rid of a child." This was spoken as a statement, not a question. Langoria could not answer except to lower her eyes again. "Is it his?"

"You mustn't blame me, my lady. All the gods know, I never wished his attentions." She had made the mistake of protesting when Commodus ordered the apartment building where she lived torn down. She had been held in the Palace ever since.

"How could I ever blame you? Look at me." Marcia put her hand on Langoria's shoulder, and Langoria looked her in the eye. "Have you considered this carefully? It might be an advantage for you to have his child."

"Or it could be only a danger. Narcissus has told me about his family."

Marcia nodded, for all the world as if she knew what Langoria was talking about.

Chapter 13

Kuglas could scarcely contain his glee when he heard what Clodius Albinus had to say now. He could not make out the Latin very well, but the interpreter's Caledonian was clear enough. "Indeed Roma shall be pleased to show generosity to so bold-hearted a king, who makes such wise plans for the benefit both of his own people and of ours! Wagons are coming, which shall soon bring twenty thousand bars of iron for your smiths, and a thousand gold coins for all your needs! Only swear by your gods and ours that you shall be friends to Roma, and accept the hospitality of the feast we are preparing!"

"We are rich!" Kuglas exulted. "Swear to them by our mothers, or by my ballocks, or whatever they ask! We will build walls for Struyvaethin of iron, and drink from cups of gold!"

"Watch, and I will show you how this is done," Qenmaethin replied. He shouted up, "Dearly do we wish to be your friends forever! But we do not wish to deceive you about the cost of this campaign. It would be ill-done to leave the work half-finished, and enemies still unsubdued, thirsting for revenge. We fear it shall require no less than thirty thousand bars of iron, and two thousand gold coins."

Servilius could scarcely contain his annoyance. He said to Clodius in incredulity, "Does this savage want to haggle with us now?"

A messenger in the uniform of the Cursus, the imperial postal service, came riding up at a furious gallop. He dismounted with a leap, grabbed a scroll from the saddle-bag, and began dashing up the stairs to the platform without even looking to see if anyone was taking the reins of his horse. Some of the soldiers below were shouting at him to stop, but he paid no mind. The stairs were just a rickety ladder. They could not be seen from the Caledonian side, after all, so there had been no need to waste any effort on them to make them look impressive, when this whole structure would be torn down tomorrow. The messenger tripped, and fell to his knees on the next-to-last step. The archers had spun around in response to the noise, and already had their bows pointed at him, prepared to shoot him if he made one single more move toward the Governor.

He pounded his chest with his right fist, extended his arm out in salute, and held up the scroll in his left hand. "Very urgent message for Governor Clodius Albinus!" he panted.

Clodius looked at him as if he were mad. "Not now! Can't you see that I am occupied? My son Pescennius Priscus is somewhere down below. Take it to him." Clodius had given his eldest son Priscus the first name "Pescennius" in honor of his protegé Pescennius Niger, but full names were rarely used except on formal occasions or for initial introductions. Clodius used both names to emphasize that this messenger did not know his son, and was acting above his place, as if he were someone important.

"The wild cat is a god's gift! I was ordered to say that, if I were blocked from reaching you, and to put this into no hands but yours, and to do so as quickly as possible."

Servilius pursed his lips. "Then this is from..."

Clodius nodded. "Diodoros Tigranos, yes it must be." Clodius took the scroll, tore open its seals roughly, and began to read. He let out an involuntary gasp, and shouted, "Out of my way!" He stepped past the messenger to go down the stairs in a rush.

Servilius asked, "What is it?" He started to follow.

Clodius turned around and said, "You must stay and handle the barbarian. Give him whatever he wants! You and Priscus will have to handle the banquet. In fact, Priscus may have to handle the whole province for a while. When you are done here, follow me to Londinium, as fast as you can!"

Clodius took the messenger's horse, wheeling it around and galloping off to the south. Servilius returned to the platform, composing his face and calculating what he should say to the Caledonians.

On the north side of the wall, they could not see everything, but what they did see was all very amusing. "I had not thought," said Kuglas, "that such a pale man could grow any paler. He had the look of one who received very ill news indeed."

"But it is a rare piece of news which is not good news for someone," Qenmaethin added.

Chapter 14

Quintus Curtius, the postmaster of Massilia, scrutinized very carefully the document which Junius Severus handed to him. Called a "diploma", it authorized the bearer to use the services of the Cursus, which was not for private business, except by official permission with payment of substantial fees, no matter what some Senators might think. Many Senators and other wealthy Italians had estates in Gaul, and expected the Cursus to send messages, or loads of goods even, back and forth between their estates and Italy for free. A lot of these illegal requests came through Massilia. Quintus had probably said No to more high-ranking toffs, and stood his ground in the face of more verbal abuse, than any other man in the Empire.

It was far from unknown for someone to attempt to forge a diploma. And at first, even if it bore all the correct seals, this one looked highly suspicious. Most diplomas were fairly short and precise. A fellow postman, for example, had come through earlier that month, with a diploma authorizing him to take the fastest horse at any post station in Italy, Gaul, or Britain, for a two-month period December and January, and to draw a certain amount of rations, and at the Channel ports the Cursus was directed to pay for his crossing in either direction. Quintus still wondered what the great hurry had been in that case. Urgent dispatches, with a diploma for fast horse relay, came through from time to time, but usually the messenger had at least some gossip to share about what the message consisted of.

By contrast, this diploma commanded all post stations, anywhere apparently, to give every assistance to Junius Severus, forever as far as it appeared, and specified a long list of the kinds of assistance he was to receive. The post stations were to provide lodging for Junius Severus and all men accompanying him, without any stated limitation on the number. He and his infinite number of men were all to be issued rations, and could take horses, and the Cursus was to pay to hire boats, either on rivers or on the seas, as they might require. Postmasters were to give Junius Severus warnings about any known dangers on the roads ahead, and to advise on possible alternative routes. Quintus was about to dismiss this as the most ludicrous forgery he had ever encountered, when he discovered some coded phrases, which told him that this diploma was issued at the personal request of the Emperor.

"Everything appears to be in order," he said stiffly. "What are your needs tonight?"

"I apologize that we come to you at such a late hour. I hope that it is not too severe an inconvenience."

That was different. None of those who gave Quintus extra trouble had ever before acknowledged to him that they were being troublesome. He decided to unbend. "I am sorry that I have few staff to serve you at present. I allowed most to go into town and celebrate the holiday. We were not expecting latecomers."

"I have marched my men hard for two weeks from Roma." On foot, this was an impressive distance to cover in that time. "Most nights we have camped out, as I have wanted to make as much ground as possible every day without regard to where we might stop. We have drawn rations at the mutation stations, and at a mansion with a bathhouse we changed clothes." The mutations, so-called because a rider might get a change of horses there, and the mansions, reasonably-sized inns, were the smaller outposts of the Cursus system. Neither could accommodate a sizable body of men. "But I told them that if we pressed on into the evening, we could reach a major post station tonight and hope to sleep indoors. It turned out to be a bit further than I thought it would be."

"Well, I am ordered to house and feed your men, however many they might be. But if you are bringing a legion, that is beyond my power. Are those men outside your vanguard, or is that it?"

"I have only the one centurion, and he has only nine tentfuls. The head-count is seventy-four." Roman soldiers typically slept eight to a tent, even though a tent-leader was sometimes called a *decan* as if he commanded ten. A centurion was so named as if he commanded ten tents of ten each, but his unit was always somewhat smaller than a hundred.

The centurion would sleep in a command tent with other officers. Curtius presumed that the centurion in this case shared a tent with this Junius fellow, although Junius did not have the air of a military officer at all. He wasn't even armed. And his precise, archaically classical enunciations put Curtius more in mind of an academy than of a bivouac.

"Oh I see. That we can easily manage, if they are not all expecting feather-beds." This was a joke, as Junius perfectly understood. The men would sleep on hard pallets. "And I am sorry, but I have nowhere near seventy horses to speed you on your way."

"Few of them know how to ride anyway. We shall continue to march."

"But I can provide a good horse for yourself, and another for your centurion."

"If they must be on foot, so will I be. I do not wish them to think of me as merely one of the Emperor's pet dogs."

He might have the makings of an officer yet, Quintus thought. He decided to probe a little. "I am ordered to advise you about hazards on your way. Surely you know that the Channel is a very unpleasant body of water to cross in January?"

"Who said we were going to Britannia?"

"My apologies. There was some message traffic through here for Britain, and I thought there might be a connection."

"Just between you and me, yes we are going across the Channel. They should be immune to seasickness by the time we get there. A few weeks on hard-tack should give anyone a stomach of iron." Junius knew that he should not be divulging anything whatsoever about his mission. But he also knew that postmasters loved to be well-informed, and might do special favors for a bit of news.

"There is nobody here who can prepare hot food at this hour, not in such quantity."

"None of the men would expect that. A warm place to sleep, now that they will appreciate."

"I have very little budget for wine here. But I laid in some beer for the holiday. I didn't realize how many of my own men would prefer to go into town. There should be plenty for each of your men to drink to the New Year."

"You are most kind. I think some of them would kill for a beer now."

"Fortunately, that will not be necessary."

Chapter 15

Dionysius had a question for Governor Pescennius. Their business seemed to be concluded, and yet Pescennius was in no hurry to dismiss them. "You have said repeatedly that you want all quarrels resolved at this time especially. What is so special about this time? Have you heard of some omen, or had some dream from the gods? Does this turning of the year call for more efforts at peacemaking than we should exert at any time?"

"I recently read an account of the dread Year of Four Emperors, after Nero died. The great Vespasian knew how much trouble there would be. So he called a meeting of all the leading men of Egypt and Syria, men who had many differences with each other and with himself, and urged them all to settle everything. I took it as a sign of what I should do. Ya'aqov, I know that your people have reason to curse the memory of Vespasian. I hope you will take no offense that I cite him as a good example."

"He was a wise and strong leader for your people, however unfortunate that was for mine."

"He was right then, and I believe I am right now, to want the East united when there is a bad storm brewing in the West."

"But I thought," said Dionysius, "that those rumors a couple months back, about Commodus Caesar dying, turned out to be totally unfounded."

"They were." Pescennius sighed, and drained his cup. "But they reached Britannia, and somehow Governor Clodius Albinus was persuaded that they were true. He wrote a most unfortunate letter to the Senate about it."

"Do you know what it said?" Ya'aqov asked.

"Certainly I do. Clodius is a dear patron of mine, so I was sent a copy. He went rather beyond expressing happiness at the supposed death, to list all the reasons why he was happy. He accused the August One of converting public funds to his private use, disgracing the dignity of the Palace by filling it with sexual slaves of both genders, and expending too much on gladiator fights and suchlike shows. He urged the Senate to reaffirm its rights to control the public purse. He mentioned that his Ceionius grandparents make him kin to the imperial family, without quite putting himself forward as a candidate for the throne."

"Such terrible things to say! How much the worse that they are all true," Ya'aqov said wryly.

"You know I cannot speak a word of agreement. The Governor of Egypt serves at the pleasure of the August One."

"But," noted Dionysius, "I do not hear you speaking a word of denial. So you are worried for your old friend? Perhaps you may need to go to war for him?"

"I cannot speak of such things. But if he is ordered back to Roma, to answer treason charges, I doubt he will go quietly. And he has very many friends. I tell you these things, because I hope that you are my friends."

"You have done much tonight to make us so," Ya'aqov said.

Dionysius had a hopeful thought. "Maybe in Rome as well, someone succeeded in lighting fresh fire for the New Year at midnight, to bring better luck to all the Empire."

Pescennius prided himself on his scientific knowledge. "It is not midnight in Roma yet. Because of the roundness of the world, midnight comes at a later hour to the west. I cannot pretend to understand that completely, but the astrologers assure me that it is so. So there is time yet, Ya'aqov, for you to pray to your lonely God, and for you, Dionysius, to pray to all your gods, and for me to pray in my own way, that midnight will bring a better year to Roma."

"Peace in Rome would be a blessing for my people as well," Ya'aqov reflected. "I shall pray as you request." Ya'aqov lowered his head and began rocking back and forth, chanting in a low voice. Meanwhile Dionysius lifted his hands and his head heavenward, whispering rapidly.

Pescennius folded his hands, leaned back, and closed his eyes in silence.

Chapter 16

"It's midnight!" Commodus Caesar bellowed. "Or close enough. I want to start out the year the right way. And I am so tired of Marcia! And all the rest of you!" He staggered over to the bench where Tullia and Popilia were chatting merrily about wedding preparations, until this eruption. "It was so kind of Tullius to bring me a fresh morsel. Have you even bled yet?" He grabbed Tullia by the shoulders and pulled her upright.

Tullia gasped a little, but quickly regained her composure. "I do not understand what you mean, O August One!" She tried to make a curtsey. Her father took a few steps closer, then hesitated.

"Sure you do." Commodus leered at her. "I ask again. Have you bled?"

"Yes," she replied calmly. "The Good Goddess has visited me."

"She speaks in pieties! Well isn't that sweet?" Commodus pulled up her robes to take a peek, then dropped them in disgust. "Gaaah! Hardly any hair! No, this one is not ripe." He gave Tullia a shove, and she sat back down with a plop. "This one will have to do." He tried to grab Popilia by her fake manacle, but it simply broke in his hand. Enraged, he pulled her up by her hair. She shrieked. The last shreds of conversation among the guests ceased completely.

Then Laetus shouted, "She is mine!"

"And you don't want to share? You ungrateful wretch! I plucked you out of the sewer, and I can toss you back!"

While he spoke, Commodus let go of Popilia's hair. She bolted away. Commodus lunged after her, seizing her robe. Her robe tore nearly in half. Popilia began to sob. Laetus strode across the room grimly. "Leave her alone!"

Commodus laughed. "Would you dare do anything about it? I don't think so." He tore Popilia's robe completely off, knocked her down, and climbed on top of her.

Laetus drew his sword, and spoke very grimly. "Leave... her... alone."

"Make me, big boy!"

73

Laetus stabbed him in the throat, piercing the carotid artery. Commodus Caesar gurgled and died, with a look of astonishment in his eyes. Tullia took off her outer robe and gave it to the quivering, crying, blood-spattered Popilia as Laetus rolled the body off of her. The Praetorians from the entryway and some of the guests edged closer, moving uncertainly, without saying a word.

Lady Titiana broke the tense silence. "Laetus, we all saw the gross provocation. But you have killed the Emperor, and must expect to give an account of what you have done, to a court of law." She turned to the Praetorians and glared, defying them to contradict her. Perhaps Medusa would have been a better costume for her.

"He asked for it!" Laetus retorted. And in a way, that was literally true. Several voices began speaking at once. Tullius stood up on a bench and raised his hands.

"Hear me Romans!" the Senator shouted, and for a wonder, the crowd quieted to listen to him. "This is no ordinary case, and the magistrates can scarcely be expected to know what to do about it, until the Senate gives them guidance." Many of the guests were Senators themselves, and shared this ready assumption that the Senate had ultimate authority. Unfortunately, all those who were armed in the vicinity, not only here in the atrium itself but around all exits from the Palace, were Praetorians who might have other ideas. "I offer to take Laetus into my custody, in the name of the Senate and People of Roma. He knows that I would allow no lawless treachery to befall him, and you all know that I would surrender him to any authority with an established legal right to demand him. What say you?"

The crowd began to buzz again, but Laetus sheathed his sword, bowed to Tullius, and said, "You are a fair man, Senator. I will trust in you."

"What says the City? And what says the Guard?" Tullius was not nearly so unaware of the need for the local armed forces to be agreeable as his pious legalisms might have suggested.

As Prefect, Pertinax commanded the regular troops of the City, who operated not only within the city limits, but also in the surrounding area, and could block all gates in and out. The Praetorian Guards and the City troops naturally insulted each other and boasted of their own superior attributes on every possible occasion. But the City was not a unit which the Guard could ignore, and it was clever of Tullius to mention them first. Pertinax spoke wearily. "I say well done, Tullius. I must go to headquarters and put the Watch on higher alert. There are bound to be troublemakers when this news gets out. And I must speak to the lictors about convening the Senate." He seemed anxious to leave, or at least, to test whether he and the others would be permitted to leave.

Motilenus seized the opportunity to assert himself as commander of the Guard while the position of Laetus was uncertain. He bowed to Pertinax and said, "Honored Prefect, the Guard will want to be as one with the City at this dangerous time. We shall be entirely at your command. You shall be to us as a Caesar. I am sure that I speak for every Praetorian."

The Praetorians in the room exchanged wary glances as he spoke, but made no protest.

BOOK TWO

The Announcement of January

Chapter 1

The City was, and was not, like one more legion of the army. It was not numbered as a legion. That was because it was far older than any of the various units which had ever been called Legion I, of which confusingly there were three active at this time, Legion I and Legion I Additional on the Danube, and Legion I Minerva on the Rhine. It might have been called Legion Zero, except that of course no Roman had ever thought of such a number. It was the institutional continuation of the original town muster under Romulus, and the inaugural oath of the Prefect of the City still contained embarrassing phrases about how he was to act as the king, whenever the king was absent. The king had been absent now for about eight hundred years. One of the few kingly powers which the Prefect still really had was the right to call the Senate into session if both Consuls were for some reason absent, or on the peculiar occasion of the beginning of January, when the terms of the outgoing Consuls had expired and the incoming Consuls had not been inaugurated. Seldom had this quirk of office been as important a part of the Prefect's role as on this particular New Year's Day. It demonstrated the wisdom of the founding fathers, who always provided emergency backups for every office.

For the most part, the Prefect had a peculiarly hybrid role. He was the military commander of the Cohorts, the most numerous branch of the City. These were the same kinds of military units as in any legion, charged with as wide a defensive zone, including the crucial port of Ostia and major towns in Latium quite aside from Roma itself. But he also headed various bureaucratic departments, like the mayor in any large city. The largest stream of money he administered was a welfare system doling out bread to the poor. Some of the circuses were also his responsibility. City cryers told the inhabitants the news, or at least, such news as the regime saw fit for them to hear. The water department was large, charged with patching defects in the aqueducts, tracking down and fining those who tapped into the system beyond their legal allotments, and maintaining the great underground Cloaca which endeavored, with mixed success, to carry all the sewage downstream. And then there was the Watch, the other armed branch of the City. Like the Auxiliary in other legions, it was open to non-citizens. Indeed, much as the army preferred that its soldiers have no local ties, watchmen were commonly hired from as far away from Roma as possible, provided the applicant could demonstrate good enough Latin. But unlike the auxiliaries, who were armed and trained nearly the same as the cohorts of the legion, and expected to fulfil the same kinds of duties, most watchmen only got batons. The rawer recruits among the watchmen probably could not be trusted to know the hilt from the point of a sword, anyway. Their duties were to patrol, look out for burglars and pickpockets, and often enough, act as fire brigades.

Tausias was an officer in the Watch, entitled to wear a sword. His patron was Diodoros Tigranos, now the ranking officer in the Cohorts, whose father Basilides Tigranos made a lot of money importing Armenian rugs to Roma, enough money to buy citizenship. Tausias came by his citizenship the hard way. He had first worked for Basilides in the East, but always wanted to come to Roma, like so many starry-eyed youth. When Diodoros Tigranos rose to high rank in the Cohorts, he obtained a slot in the Watch for Tausias, and allowed Tausias and his sister Langoria to live in his prestigiously-located apartment on the Palatine hill, although their contribution toward the rent was only token. This was how a patron would help out a promising protegé who might become someone of influence. Tausias got his chance to rise when he knocked out, with only his baton, two of the bold, and better than usually armed, robbers who were trying to take down a coach carrying a large amount of coin to the Palace. The coach was manned by Praetorians, who would usually look down their noses at the Watch, but noted in their report that his assistance had been as timely as it was brave. Tausias was granted citizenship for his valor, and transferred to the Cohorts. He then disappointed Tigranos by saying that he did not like it much in the Cohorts, and had no ambition to rise there, and would rather return to the Watch if he could only have better rank and pay. Tigranos did pull some strings to make this so. Then Commodus knocked down their apartment building, and they did not see as much of each other anymore.

Tausias was coming off of a long night shift. New Year's Eve saw the usual public drunkenness, with some brawls, and some thieves taking advantage of the visibly helpless, but no more so than any other year. Indeed the chilly weather seemed to keep more people at home than usual. After midnight, the Watch was ordered to double its patrols. Tausias was one of those who had to roust watchmen out of bed, when he ought to have been seeking his own. No reason for this was given, of course. Tausias wondered how the Watch would maintain staffing when half the men who should have been on the day shift had instead been kept awake at night. He should have gone home, to the place he now shared with a woman named Frida who sold fish, in an unfashionable neighborhood down the Tiber which was conveniently close to the Emporium but inconveniently subject to periodic flooding. But he had gotten his second wind and was no longer feeling sleepy.

He hung out around the Forum, the old downtown in the crease between the Palatine and Capitoline hills. He idly hoped that someone from the Palace might come by on some business or other, so that he could inquire about his sister, who was now enslaved in the Palace. He strolled by the Circus Maximus to peer up at the Palatine, but it appeared that the Palace was under some kind of lockdown, with an unusual number of Praetorians walking around the perimeter and no-one coming out. He returned to the Forum as the sun was coming out, and saw the cryer, a man whose face was as familiar to everyone as his booming baritone voice. But today his face was painted like the mask of Tragedy. The cryer's four attendants were in black robes of mourning, with ashes poured over their faces and hair, and tear-streaks painted down their cheeks. Not many were up and about at this hour, but all those who were stopped to listen, their curiosity aroused by the cryer's strange appearance.

"It is the Kalends of January, the 946th year since the founding of our City, but how unluckily the new year begins!" the cryer announced. The attentive noticed that he did not call the month "Amazonius" using the new month-names, derived from the full name of Commodus Caesar after he had some ridiculous titles granted to himself. Commodus could never make up his mind which of these names should be assigned to the months or in which order. Sometimes he liked "Marcus" and "Antoninus" after his predecessors, but lately he was replacing those. This left everyone confused, exactly as he liked it.

"Woe!" and "Woe!" and "Woe!" and "Woe!" his attendants cried, one after the other, each trying to outdo the last in woefulness.

"I rend my clothes to tell you of this woeful news!" He struggled to tear his toga.

"Woe! Woe! Woe! Woe!" cried his attendants. Then, since the cryer was still fighting with his toga, they cried "Woe! Woe! Woe! Woe!" again. Finally the cryer achieved a small rip.

"Our mighty Emperor, the noble Lucius Aelius Aurelius Commodus Augustus Herculeus Romanus Exsuperatorius Amazonius Invictus Felix Pius, the Father of our Country, the gladiator who fights without fear, has been slain!" The fourfold cries of woe from his attendants competed with gasps and exclamations from the crowd. A couple of goatherds, driving a small flock of fresh victims up to the temple of Capitoline Jove, laughed out loud.

Tausias, light-headed from lack of sleep, felt like heckling. "So is it really true this time?"

"Our honored Prefect, Publius Helvius Pertinax, assures us all that order will be strictly maintained during this period of mourning!"

Tausias overrode the cries of woe by asking a very pointed question. "So is Pertinax the one behind all this?"

"Laurentius Motilenus pledges the unreserved loyalty of the Praetorian Guard to the Prefect!"

"Motilenus? What happened to Laetus?"

"The Senate is called into urgent session. And that is all!"

Tausias had noticed that there was only one lictor patrolling the Forum, when usually there would be several. All of the Forum, not only the Senate House, was in the jurisdiction of the lictors, not the watchmen. Now he understood that the lictors were busy rousting Senators, who ordinarily did not have to be told about a meeting at the last moment. As he walked behind the retreating cryer, saying "Come on, don't leave us hanging like this, tell us who killed him and what's really going on," the lictor came up to confront him.

"You look like you are in the Watch. Isn't there some other place you should be?"

"I am off-duty."

"Today? I doubt that very much. Why don't you find your superiors and see if they have some use for you?" It sounded as if the lictor doubted that Tausias was of any use to anyone, ever. Tausias briefly considered that the lictor's ceremonial double-headed axe was not really a very good weapon, no match for his own sword.

Then better sense prevailed, and he turned around, heading for home.

Chapter 2

Tullius seldom slept in past sunrise, but indulged the needs of his body a little after the late and stressful night he had endured. It would be sheer pridefulness, he reflected, to injure his health merely to avoid any appearance of sloth. But neither should he stay in bed any longer, when duty called. It would not do to force his household to stand around, waiting to give him the morning salutations. He put on the fresh clean Senatorial toga which Cocina had left by his bed, and went out to face the day.

"Good morning, O most loving of fathers!" Tullia Minor said to him, as she did every morning.

"Good morning, sir!" Philoxena said. She was a freedwoman, with a husband in the army whom she seldom saw. She had been hired to tend to Tullia's needs, teach her some Greek and some weaving, and seek out good tutors for other subjects a noble girl ought to know, such as music. Philoxena had been under the impression that since she was free, she would outrank Cocina in the household, but was quickly disabused of that notion. Tullius rewarded Cocina and Castor well for their services, and allowed them to conduct their own little money-making enterprises, so that all in all, either of them made considerably more than Philoxena's fixed wages. It was undoubtedly her right, however, to greet him before any slaves.

Usually it would then be Castor who said "Good morning, O most generous of masters!" with a bow, but instead it was Magnus, a gladiator he had purchased to supplement Castor's pugilistic skills with some knowledge of weapons. One could never be too careful these days, and a second bodyguard might be good to have. Magnus had less reason than Castor did to praise Tullius for generosity, monetarily at least. Then the new German boy grunted something, and made a slouch that might charitably be called a bow. Tullius could not remember why he had bought that one in the first place.

Cocina had an unusual salutation, but one which Tullius had always liked. "Good morning, O wisest of masters!" she said, and little Cocinilla said it in unison with her, in a high lisping voice. Tullius still sometimes by mistake called the mother "Cocinilla", a habit from when she had been the little girl and her mother was "Cocina". The previous Cocina had that name because she was born in the kitchen where she would spend all her life, although she was also called an unpronounceable name by her father Hibernius. Hibernius, whom Tullius had not thought about for years, was so-called because Hibernia was where he and his sister had been captured, and his native name also was difficult. The names of slaves did not matter and would be changed often. The German boy would probably remain Germanus for a while because he called himself Sigismundus or something like that, which would never do. Tullius had not thought of a classical name that seemed appropriate. Since he was not useful for much except feeding, watering, and brushing the horses, and shoveling out the stalls, Tullius considered naming him Philippus, the lover of horses, but his attitude toward the horses did not seem to be love.

"I have browned the sausages the way you like them, and left them in the warmer," Cocina said. This was her gentle way of reproving him for not rising when she expected and eating her sausages just as she finished them. "And Cocinilla has been to the baker for some fresh buns." So the girl was learning to be useful. That would make her the fourth generation to serve the *gens Tullia* family, and the last. Tullius provided in his will that Castor, Cocina, and Cocinilla would be freed, though no others. Some Romans considered mass emancipations a pious act, so laws were enacted limiting the practice. But Tullius believed with the Stoics that freedom was rather illusory, and that one could be happy in any social estate. He allowed his favorites considerable liberties, and all his slaves knew that there were far worse masters in Rome than him. On his country estates, he did free those who acted as stewards, for the practical reason that a freedman would often get more respect in the conduct of business.

But then, his servants in the country had to deal with people who seldom or never met Tullius personally. Around Rome, none of those who dealt with Tullius would ever doubt that Castor and Cocina acted on his behalf. "Cocina, I need you to go into Ostia today," he said, as he tore off a bit of sausage and a bit of bun to throw into the fire, for a morning offering to the Penates, the spirits of the house and family. "Take my seal, and pester the grain and oil factors all day about the current prices. There should be a great panic today, but by late in the day surely cooler heads will prevail, and prices will come back down. I want you to sell all my holdings at the peak price. Philoxena and my daughter will look after your girl."

"Of course, master." It was understood, since she was being told to spend all day trying for the best price, that she would have plenty of time to do other things on her own behalf. "May I make short sales?" It could be dangerous to sell more than Tullius actually held, but it could be profitable.

"Use your discretion. I will put one-tenth of any earnings into your peculiar account." An account was called "peculiar" when it legally belonged to a master, but one of his slaves had the right to draw from it at will. Tullius had not examined Cocina's peculiar account in some time, but if he did, he might be surprised at how it had been grown. Or perhaps he wouldn't be. Castor had a peculiar account as well, but he had simply never had the same head for money that Cocina did. For a market play like this, on a day when Tullius couldn't possibly handle it in person, Castor would not be the right one to put in charge. That reminded him. "Where is Castor this morning?"

"He is still standing by the back room, guarding our... guest." Cocina had no reason to know the commander of the Praetorian Guard by sight, and no-one had explained to her why a blood-spattered half-naked man was lodging with them. She assumed she would be told in good time.

"All night?" He should have known Castor would do that. Cocina led him back to the best guest room, and indeed Castor was still standing at the doorway. Castor was wearing the sword Laetus had used last night, but at least he had cleaned it off. Did he even know whose blood he had wiped up?

"Good morning, O most generous of masters," Castor said, as he said every morning. "He has been no trouble. He surrendered his weapon, as you see. And do you remember he insisted on riding up with me, rather than bloody the cushions in the carriage?"

"I remember he offered to let you manacle him."

"He is sleeping on the floor, rather than on the good bed, I think again to avoid making bloodstains." Laetus was still sprawled out, showing no sign of awakening.

"Should I bathe him before I head to Ostia?" Cocina asked.

"You may, if you are so eager," Tullius twitted her, "but you should know that he is already betrothed."

"O master, he has nothing I have not already seen."

"And find some appropriate clothes for him. Not a Senator's toga, to which he is not entitled." The commander of the Praetorians was called a "prefect" like many other commanders. But the office of Praetorian Prefect, far from being on the Course of Honor, was forbidden to anyone above equestrian rank. If his power rivaled that of the Prefect of the City, his respectability most certainly did not.

"There are some other togas in the house." This would hardly be the first time a guest had needed a change of clothing. Philoxena taught Tullia how to make a toga in every style.

"Castor won't be able to drive you to Ostia, because I order him to go to bed at once. And Magnus will have to guard Laetus. So it must be Germanus driving the chariot, if you think you can make him understand directions."

"I can manage him." Germanus pretended not to know any Latin, but everybody knew that he understood much more than he let on. "But who will drive you, master, if you need to go anywhere?"

"Lictors will be here immediately, in their chariots since they are in a hurry to call on every Senator. One of them can drive me to the Senate House."

A banging on the door revealed that Tullius was an accurate prophet.

Chapter 3

Caius Titius Sempronius was one of the most recent additions to the Senate. He too was awaiting the lictors that morning, with considerable nervousness. He had attended a couple of sessions at which nothing happened, beyond routine endorsement of decisions already made elsewhere. This time would be far from routine. He grew impatient during the morning greetings. Although his house on the Quirinal hill was scarcely larger than the home of Tullius on the opposite side of the city, it had a larger staff, who were in the habit of making lengthy salutations after years of dealing with the prickly dignity of his father. One poor fellow, trying to dig for some new way to flatter the master, said, "Your presence at the Palace last night must surely have added luster to the occasion!"

"What are you accusing me of?" Sempronius snapped. Then he realized that his household did not yet know what a dismal turn last night's party had taken, and were all taken aback by his outburst. It had been absurd of him to think that the remark implied complicity in the assassination. "I apologize," he said, which appalled all his servants even worse. Over a year since his father was executed, and he still did not know how to conduct himself as the paterfamilias of the house, who should never apologize for anything. "The Emperor was murdered last night," he explained. The dismay was now complete. There were still some slaves who had not greeted the master and were now unsure of what to say. Perhaps they ought to wait for him to elaborate. But he did not seem to want to say anything more about the subject. Fortuitously, someone was at the door.

"That must be the lictors calling me to the Senate," Sempronius said, but he was mistaken. It was Fortunatus Curtius, who served with the Cohorts of the City at Nomentum, several miles northeast of Rome. Other men from his unit waited patiently outside. The *gens Sempronia* were long-time patrons of the Curtius family. The Senator's father had obtained a position as postmaster for Quintus Curtius, for example, and promoted the legal career of Jovialis Curtius Rhetor. Fortunatus was the cousin of Quintus and brother of Jovialis.

"I cannot stay long, but I am so glad of an opportunity to greet you this morning, Senator," Fortunatus said with a bow. "Our unit has been ordered to relieve the Watch on the Quirinal and Viminal hills, and more of the regular troops are on their way." It was unlikely to be a coincidence that this section of Rome faced the main encampment of the Praetorian Guard. "We have been told about the event last night." He was careful not to describe it as a sad event, or a happy event, without hearing what the Senator had to say about it.

Sempronius had no desire to say anything at all about it. "Other, more pleasant things took place last night. I had a delightful conversation with a young girl who is in need of a husband." Fortunatus was in need of a wife, as Sempronius knew, and this sounded hopeful. "She is the daughter of Senator Tullius." Or perhaps not.

"That's way too high for me to aim."

"But she knows many girls, of various ranks, from the female festivals. Now that her father allows her to accept social invitations, and I have befriended her, I could ask her to bring girlfriends to a gathering in honor of the Carmentalia, where I would introduce them to respectable young men such as yourself." The Carmentalia in the middle of January honored a minor goddess. Carmenta invented the Latin alphabet, taught the Sybils how to prophecy, and told her son Evander the most auspicious spot to found a village, right at the foot of the Palatine hill where Romulus would later start his city. While the festival honoring her was principally for women, males were not forbidden to celebrate it, so it was perfect for his purpose. Sempronius hoped that his choice of costume the previous night, as a satyr, had not given Tullia the wrong impression of him, but the conversation had gone well enough.

Fortunatus bowed slightly again. "You have always been so good to our family."

"Is there anything else that you need?"

"My slave Mercurius has run off. He is the twin brother of that slave of Jovialis, the one who disappeared a few years ago. If he is trying to vanish in Rome, perhaps someone will hear something."

"I will keep my ears open. But I do know one other thing that you need. You need to stay here at my house while you are in Roma. The Vectilian barracks will be far too crowded if the City is moving blades onto the streets from all the Latin towns. They may keep you all here for some time." Fortunatus was about to protest politely, but Sempronius raised his hand and said, "I must insist on this."

Now the lictors did come, so Sempronius went out together with Fortunatus to attend to their respective duties, Sempronius carried in a litter chair, Fortunatus marching with his fellow soldiers.

Chapter 4

Quintus Curtius was not surprised to learn that Junius Severus had decided to stay a day and give his men a rest. "If I am out of place, just say so, but I am more or less ordered to advise you."

"I would appreciate some advice. The centurion says nothing but 'whatever you please sir.'"

"I can't understand whether you are trying to move quickly, or slowly. If you don't want to reach the Channel until the weather is better, you should not push the men so. Late January or February would be the worst time to get there. But if you're wanting to hurry, then even if your men are not riders, you could at least load them all into carts. We have plenty of those, and mules and oxen, and if you take all we have, we can get more from Arelate." Arelate was an upstart city compared to Massilia, but had grown larger.

"I suppose I am aiming for the appearance of speed, rather than the reality. I continue to hope for news of some change that renders my mission unnecessary. But if anyone asks my men, they will certainly all say that I have pursued it with maximum diligence."

"I would be the last person to inquire about the nature of your mission." This was of course a lie. He was bursting with curiosity. "But whatever it is, your men are more likely to perform it well if they are not exhausted when they arrive."

"The men have no mission but to keep me alive. There are enough of them to ward off any highway robbers. But they hardly suffice to invade Britannia in force. I suppose, though, that they are more likely to keep me alive if I give them fewer reasons for wishing me dead."

"I think they love you well enough. They drank your health enthusiastically last night."

"They are only grateful that I finally allowed them a real rest, the first one since the bath and wine house by Populonia."

"I also think it is because you impose nothing on them that you do not endure yourself."

"I am nearly at my own limits. But if I follow your suggestion about taking carts, we would have to change animals often, and might need to stop to repair a cart. I want to be seen, and to have to present my diploma, at as few places as possible. I know that word travels up and down among the post stations about who is travelling. I would appreciate it greatly if you send no word north of my coming. It would be best if we board a boat as just one more company of troops, transferred to Britannia for whatever reason the army does such things, with nobody even knowing that we come from Italia. You were commended to me by Senator Sempronius as a helpful man." He had saved this name-drop for the most effective time. "What I most need from you is discretion."

"My lips are sealed. I would never wish to do anything that might hurt a friend of the Senator." Or a man in your line of work, he thought to himself. I would never have taken this young man for an assassin. That must be what makes him so good at it. "The straightforward route for you is to take the Via Agrippa all the way to Durocort and then the west fork to Gesoriac on the Channel." Durocortorum was the capital of Gallia Belgica, Gesoriacum the port nearest to Britannia. "But I advise you not to take it. Governor Placidius regards Clodius Albinus as his special patron, and will be curious about anyone passing through on the way to Britain."

"I am most indebted to you for telling me this. But in this season, it will only be practical to cross the Channel at its narrowest point. There is no place I can sail except Gesoriacum. How else can I get there?"

"When you reach the Icauna, a headwater to the Sequana river, take a boat down to Lutetia. The road north from there joins the road from Durocort at Samarobriva, not too far from the Channel. You can hire local boatmen without showing any papers or giving away where you are headed. The postmaster at Lutetia is a dreadful gossip," as Quintus knew from exchanging gossip with him constantly, "but if you are willing to risk being known to him, tell him you are a special friend of mine. He will be the one who knows exactly what you face ahead of you."

"I have not brought much in the way of coin. A secure strongbox would be a burden and a temptation. I spent much of my money on wine at Populonia, to ration out at our camps at night. It helped to keep the men in tolerable spirits, as long as it lasted."

"Hmmm. I cannot advance you the cost, without knowing the boatman's name or what he will charge. The inspectors like to see receipts for everything when they look at the books."

"How about this, then? Suppose I ride in your carts for a while, and as animals tire or carts break down, I sell them to the locals."

"That would work. You will have to sign for them, but the inspectors won't look at those receipts for months."

"Can you afford to have all your carts and draft animals disappear?"

"That always happens. Goods and supplies go upriver by cart and come downriver by boat. The Rhodane is too swift for it to be otherwise. The Cursus is continually selling off surplus animals up north and buying new ones down around here."

"When all of this is done, I shall be certain to tell Senator Sempronius how very good to me you have been." Junius knew that this was the coin in which Quintus expected repayment.

They were walking outside, near the stables. Quintus added, "You must at least take one good horse with you, for someone to ride ahead and scout along the way, and in case you need a quick get-away. Come see what we have." They went into the stables, and Junius took admiring note of a stallion stamping and rearing in his stall. Quintus said, "We call that one Bucephalus, after the skittish horse Alexander the Great rode. He needs an outing every morning, and he knows it is near time."

"May I?" Junius asked with a tone of pleading. He and Bucephalus had a good ride. As they were coming back, Junius saw his centurion, and said, "We are taking this horse, and you will use him to ride ahead and scout, if you can handle him!"

The centurion appeared doubtful, but as usual said only, "Whatever you please, sir."

Chapter 5

Eclectus woke up in Marcia's bed, trying to decide how much of what he thought he remembered of the previous night was only a dream. This would be far from the first time he had dreamt about Marcia. But seeing her stir beside him, with a languid purr, convinced him that that part, at least, had been real. He sat bolt upright in reflexive fear. What if they were discovered? Commodus would kill them! Or no, could it really be true that Commodus was dead?

His movement woke Marcia up. She reached up to hug him. "Please, don't go yet."

"It is so late! I should have been up hours ago."

"For what? There's nothing for you to do today. Do you think you are going to greet the Emperor? This morning, you are my one and only Emperor." She reached down to toy with his penis, which began to respond again.

"I still have my duties," he protested.

"To whom?"

She was right, of course. There was no way of knowing when, or if, there would be a new ruler in the Palace, or whether this hypothetical new ruler would keep Eclectus on. So he attended to the more pleasurable duties Marcia required of him. Then he used the chamber-pot and the washing-bowl, and ambled in the direction of the kitchens. Surprisingly few people seemed to be up and about, and the few he encountered were nervous, neither saying a word to him nor meeting his eye. Motilenus was the first to speak to him, coming up from behind and startling him.

"Did you have a pleasant sleep?" Motilenus asked with what sounded like a sneer. "Where do you think you are going?"

Eclectus turned to face him and saw that his expression was as unpleasant as his tone of voice. "I am just going to get something to eat."

"Good. No-one is to leave the Palace until further instructions. We don't want anyone out there talking, starting unfortunate rumors."

"The whole city is bound to know by now that Caesar is dead."

"But we don't want anyone saying that the Praetorians murdered the August One."

"There are plenty of witnesses to what happened, respectable men that no-one will contradict."

"The Senators will know better than to gossip to their servants. They will say nothing to anyone until they have met. The Senate will decide what the official story is going to be, and that will be that."

"Not all of the guests were Senators. I would not trust someone like Fulminatus Rhetor to keep his mouth shut."

"That's why Fulminatus is not going anywhere either. You think we let every guest leave last night? No, just the Senators. We don't want a fight with the Senate, or with the City, but someone like the Rhetor? If he doesn't like being detained, he can sue me."

"So are the people going to be told that Commodus committed suicide? I don't think people will easily believe that."

"So maybe Marcia poisoned him. Maybe Marcia and Eclectus conspired together, if you won't stop making trouble. Or he died when Narcissus strangled him. Or when Hyacinthus took his revenge. Aren't you the one who told Narcissus and Hyacinthus to do what they did last night?"

"I told Narcissus to bind up the neck wound." As a boxer, Narcissus had plenty of experience stitching up bad cuts. "We might need the body to look somewhat presentable, if it is to lie in state before the cremation."

"Oh, I very much doubt that will happen. What did you say to Hyacinthus?"

"Hyacinthus? I don't remember speaking to him at all." His memory of events was a little blurry after midnight. He finished the dead Emperor's special wine, and then Marcia took him by the hand...

"If you really don't know what happened, you had better take a look."

Motilenus said no more as he led Eclectus back across the Palace to the atrium. Someone had at least wiped up the pools of blood from the floor. The body of Commodus was lying on a table. The genitals had been severed and stuffed into his mouth. The jaws were now clenched around them in rigor mortis. Some kind of rope was tied tightly around the neck. On closer inspection, Eclectus found that it was a baby's umbilical cord.

"Let's hope the Senate doesn't want any kind of funeral at all, that we can just dump this body quietly. I understand perfectly what Hyacinthus did, and can't blame him in the least, though of course I have to chain him up. But I really don't understand what Narcissus did."

"I do," Eclectus said.

But if Motilenus hoped that Eclectus would enlighten him, he was disappointed.

Chapter 6

Cocina did get her curiosity satisfied, in every respect. She scrubbed the bloodstains off of Laetus, dressed him and fed him. He said, "You are very kind. I hope that I'm not bringing danger to this house."

"The house is strong," she said. Some houses outside the ancient walls of Servius Tullius were still built as if a Gaulish or Punic army might rampage around the countryside any day now, and this was one of them. She did not know what kind of enemies he might have, but wanted to reassure him. "We are built of stone and cannot burn. The doors lock and would not easily be forced. We seldom drop the bar, but when we do, it is a bar of iron not wood. The windows are too narrow for any but a small child to crawl through. Anyone trying to climb the roof and go down the skylight would find little purchase. Unless you have done something to bring a whole legion after you, you should be safe enough."

"He killed the Caesar!" Tullia Minor blurted out.

"Stuff and nonsense!" Cocina exclaimed. "Master would not shelter an assassin!"

"It is true," Laetus admitted. "I had my reasons, as she knows. Most of my fellow Praetorians will still be on my side, I think, but some will think I'm a liability to them all now. Before fights broke out about what to do with me, the Senator thought it safest to take me elsewhere."

"Master is wise. But if Praetorians are arguing with Praetorians, it should be the job of their commander to keep them in line." Cocina had a firm belief in proper order.

"I am the commander. At least, I was until last night. I don't know what I am now."

"Oh. Well, it is none of my affair. I have my own matters to attend to." She could now see why master wanted her in Ostia this day. She pantomimed to Germanus that he was to ready the chariot, although she believed that he already knew that and was looking forward to the outing. Laetus returned to the back room and occupied himself with some calisthenics. Magnus stood outside, more or less as a guard. But

95

if Laetus decided to fight Magnus, Cocina would have bet on Laetus, even though Magnus had a sword and Laetus had given up his. She did not really think very highly of Magnus, and was a little worried that he would be left in charge.

Magnus was Cocinilla's father, but that was all due to a mistake. Tullius bought Magnus because, one day when they were watching the fights at the Circus Maximus, Cocina pointed to Magnus and said that it was a pity he would not live long. Tullius thought that meant she was attracted to him, and also thought that it was past time that Cocina was bred. Actually she only meant that Magnus was one of the less-skilled gladiators, which was why his owner proved to be happy to sell him at a very reasonable price. Cocina did, however, comply with even unspoken wishes of her master. If the relationship between her and Magnus was now cool, and had never been very hot, at least she had a daughter out of it. Cocinilla was watching in fascination as Philoxena and Tullia began to work the loom. Cocina mused that the girl would learn to find that boring, soon enough.

As Cocina was going out, Castor met her in the vestibule. Cocina chided him, "Master ordered you to get some rest."

"There is something I must tell you first. I delivered your herbs last night, and the girl asked Narcissus and me to send word to her brother about it. I do not think Narcissus will be able to get out. The guards were very threatening with me, telling me not to say anything to anyone about what had happened, if I knew what was good for me. I think they are keeping all the servants prisoner."

"So you are wanting me to carry word to the brother?"

"Exactly. Narcissus promised that we would."

"What is his name, and where can I find him?"

"His name is Tausias, but he is in the Watch, and they will be working the Watch hard the next few days, I'm sure. It is hard to tell where he might be made to patrol, and he might not get home much, and home for him has shifted from place to place lately. But he has a good friend in Diodoros Tigranos. You could leave a message with him. He lives below the Janiculum with Alexandrius, who studies law under Fulminatus Rhetor. Their place is just up the Triumphal Way next to the school of Fulminatus. Do you know where that is?"

"I do. But first I will see to what the master has told me to do. And you should do likewise. Get some rest. He may need you to be alert in the days to come."

Germanus drove better than Cocina had expected. He understood horses, even if he did not like them, and had chosen the one he got on with best. They turned on to Appian Way, intending to follow it through the wall into Rome proper at the Capena gate and turn left by the Circus Maximus, to leave the walls again by the Brass Plates gate as an easy way to get to the Old Ostia Way running down the east bank of the Tiber. It had not even occurred to Cocina that the gate would not be open. It was annoying to find that it was not. With irritated gestures, she got Germanus to follow some side alleys to get onto Ostia Way. As they came to the walls which ran for miles to enclose both Ostia proper and the Claudian Harbor, traffic stopped. The gate was blocked by soldiers, who were letting only one at a time through, after checking who was entering and for what purpose. Several people who had evidently been refused entry were shouting at the soldiers, to no avail.

Germanus tugged on the reins and turned the horse off of the road. He gave a crack of the whip and charged down the left side of the crowd. The horse reared and shied rather than trample the soldier coming out towards them with his hands raised.

"And just who do you think you are?" the irate soldier asked.

Cocina had dressed in her best. It would not do to conduct business looking like a kitchen maid. She tried to pass herself off as a free, indeed noble, woman with her most correct and haughty accents. "You must pardon the utter ignorance of my slave," she said. "There is no use talking to him, as he has scarcely a word of Latin. I have very urgent business that concerns the vital supply of grain and oil to the city." She dug in her bag and produced sales contracts in blank and the seal of Tullius.

"Let me see that," demanded the soldier, reaching for the seal. He examined it and asked, "Now, you are not Senator Tullius, and neither is this barbarian, so where is Senator Tullius?"

"He is in the Senate House. Where else would he be on such a day as this?" Her tone made it plain that he must be the stupidest fool in all of Italy. "But he sent me to attend to business which will brook no delay." He thought that this must be the Senator's wife or mistress. Fearing to offend such a woman any further, he let them pass.

The dreary work of unloading ships and warehousing the grain and other goods largely took place in the Harbor of Claudius a couple miles up the coast. The offices where all this business was managed were still in the old town, even though Ostia harbor was mostly silted up nowadays. The old town was filled with temples for every deity any sailor from an international crew might conceivably wish to pay homage to, along with pleasant residential districts, and many shops and taverns. Cocina gave three coppers to a livery stable to watch the horse and car, and more coins than she had planned to give to Germanus to amuse himself.

Germanus looked at her as if worried about whether he was in trouble, but her wink assured him that he had done well.

Chapter 7

Many explanations were offered for why the robes of a flamen were red. The color might symbolize the courage of Rome, or the sacred fire into which they tossed burnt offerings. But the best explanation is probably the simplest. The flamens often ended up covered in blood, and any other color for their robes would have made them a nuisance to clean. Four of these high priests were chanting as they struggled to bind the legs of an uncooperative goat. Then they hoisted the victim onto a large altar-stone, whose top surface had a shallow V shape, both sides sloping toward the central gutter, which in turn sloped toward a cistern to hold the blood. The three major flamens, Dialis for Jupiter, Martialis for Mars, and Quirinalis for the deified king Romulus, always participated in the sacrificial rite for the convocation of the Senate. One of the minor flamens would join them depending on the time of year. On New Year's Day, of course it was the Janualis, flamen for Janus the double-headed god of gates, doors, endings, and beginnings.

The Haruspex, who would examine the entrails for omens, and the priest of Victory, who would bring a portion of the offering into the Senate House itself, stood by but did not assist the others with the bleating kid. The Flaminica, wife of the Dialis, had an intricate dance which she had to perform in time to her husband's incantation. The Dialis had to be married, and the marriage contract had to be the strictest one known to Roman law. Not only was it inconceivable for this pair to divorce, but if either died the other would have to give up the office. The dance of the Flaminica assured the fertility of all the women as well as the fields of Rome, but no-one watching it would have considered it erotic, even if she had been younger and shapelier than she was.

The Janualis had the honor of slicing the throat when the prayers of dedication were finished, and would get first pick of the meat as the priests butchered the animal. He was not, however, happy. "What kind of a scrofulous beast is this? I hope that we did not pay the supplier too much for it."

99

The Martialis said, "From what I hear, none of the suppliers have been paid at all in months. Until the State starts meeting its obligations in a more timely manner, this is what we have to expect."

When the goat had bled out, the Janualis passed the knife to the Haruspex. The Haruspex sliced open the belly and groped among the innards. With a grimace, he passed the knife to the priest of Victory, who sliced out some tripe to throw into a bowl half-filled with incense. The Dialis lit a torch for the priest of Victory, who entered the Senate House together with the Haruspex. The Eldest was waiting for them.

The Eldest was a hundred years old, some thought. He was not quite, but he had to be carried in his chair even within the Senate House. If he was no longer very mobile, his senses and his wits were still keen. His name might have been Aelius Corduenus, but he had not been called anything but "Eldest" for a very long time, and the younger Senators like Sempronius had never known him as anything else. He sat in the front of the chamber, to the right hand of the statue of Winged Victory which stood on a pillar by the center of the front wall. At the rear of the chamber stood a row of twelve lictors facing out, their fasces held high to ward off intruders. Senators filed into the chamber, each waiting for a nod of recognition from the lictors in order to pass, and climbed up into the tiered rows of benches, the older members taking the seats in the first rows. In front of the winged image was an ancient brazier, the Altar of Victory. The priest of Victory stood by this Altar with his offering and the torch to light it with. The Haruspex stood by the priest of Victory. A scribe sat by the Eldest at a desk, writing down the names of the Senators as they entered. All had now arrived who were expected, the scribe signaled to the Eldest.

The Eldest raised his hands. "May Victory ever bless the arms of Rome!" The priest of Victory added the incense and the offal to the coals and oil in the brazier, and set the offering alight. "Haruspex, how are the omens this day?"

The Haruspex frowned. "The entrails were gravely diseased. Could we have expected anything else? Ulcerations told of the bloodshed that has been, and threatened more bloodshed to come. The liver was curiously misshapen, and attacked by parasites. In brief, I have never seen worse omens in all my years."

The Eldest said, "Nonetheless, it is my opinion that this meeting must proceed. How can we postpone to a more propitious day, when we may have no lucky days for some time to come? It is precisely because of the ill fortune that we are meeting. Does anyone object?" The Senate had declined to convene in the face of far less unfavorable reports from the Haruspex before, and if a single Senator spoke up against the risk of displeasing the gods by proceeding in the face of such bad omens, the Eldest would have had to concede. But there was not a sound. After a suitable pause, the Eldest resumed. "I have consulted with the Vestal Virgins, and am informed that the late Commodus Caesar left no will and testament of any kind. Either he believed himself immortal, or he cared not a fig for what should happen after his demise. Tiberius Claudius Pompeianus, you were once named his guardian and must be counted his next-of-kin. You shall have to act as paterfamilias for his sisters," a task no-one would envy him, "and it is right that we should hear first from you. What should be done about his estate?"

Pompeianus was nowhere near the Eldest's age, but was going blind, and needed a cane to walk even slowly. He seldom came to the Senate House anymore, but of course he could not be absent on this occasion. "Eldest, I am too far gone to be any kind of a candidate for succession to his titles. I have not the slightest interest in his collection of gladiators, or girls, or boys, or obscene works of art. Neither would I wish to soil myself with any of his money, when who can say how much of it was pilfered from the State? Yes, when Clodius Albinus said it, we had no choice but to condemn him, but now we can speak openly. As to his various bits of land, the houses, the gilded chariots, the gladiators' gear, the silken finery, and all the rest, much of it was purchased with stolen money. So I renounce it, every bit of it, for myself and all who are under my authority."

"Hear, hear!" numerous Senators cried.

The Eldest was a stickler for exact forms. "There is a problem legally. If you renounce your claim on the estate, then it reverts to the nearest relative after you, and so forth until kinship can no longer be traced. The intermarriages and adoptions have been so tangled that it would require a better genealogist than I am to determine who is in line, and in what order."

Pompeianus had the answer. "Then let me cut the Gordian knot this way. I accept the legacy of Commodus Caesar, and immediately make a gift of its entirety to the State, but with the wish that his slaves should be freed, for they have suffered quite enough."

"I move that this House accept the gift of the estate of the late Commodus Caesar, in the name of the People of Rome, with the warmest expressions of gratitude to Claudius Pompeianus for his generosity." The Eldest seldom formally made a motion himself, but this was an unusual occasion. "Does anyone wish to second?" Many Senators shouted that they did. "I recognize that our honored Prefect of the City, Publius Helvius Pertinax, has seconded the motion. Who is in favor?"

"Aye!" shouted all the Senators.

"Is anyone opposed?"

The Eldest allowed the silence to continue for a moment before directing the scribe to record unanimous passage of the motion.

Chapter 8

Slaves were not the only ones in the Palace concerned about their freedom. Marcia was surprised to find Popilia in the laundry, trying to scour out the bloodstains from the robe Tullia had lent her, before they set permanently. Marcia was in one of her finest robes, with fur trimming around the multi-colored stole. The belt cinching her waist was covered by a wide silken sash dyed purple, nicely setting off the amethysts in her golden necklace. The robe she had worn the previous night had an unfortunate stain, probably from when Commodus had thrown up early in the evening. When one of the maids had cleaned it, for Marcia did not do such work herself, she would give it away rather than ever wear such an unfortunate reminder again. Perhaps Langoria would appreciate it. She had a right to be dressed better than a slave.

"What are you doing here?" she asked Popilia.

"Tullia Minor was so kind to lend me this. I must not repay her by letting it be ruined."

"No, I mean, why haven't you gone home?"

Marcia had her suspicions about the reason, and Popilia confirmed them. "The Praetorians won't let me leave. And I am worried about the servants who brought me here, too. They say that people have been trapped in the Palace and can never get out. Please, my lady, if there is anything you can do to help..." She was trying hard not to cry again.

"Don't worry, I will get to the bottom of this," Marcia promised, stomping off angrily to find Motilenus. She found him and Eclectus in the middle of an absurd argument with a wagoner, at the side entrance to the lower wing. The wagon was bringing a load of hay for the stables, and was then to cart off the manure for the use of some farms a few miles out in the country. This was ordinary routine, and Eclectus was attempting to pick some men to help in the loading and unloading, as usual.

Motilenus, however, was angry at the Praetorians who had let the wagon through the gate in the first place, saying it ought to have been turned away. Eclectus and others were pointing out that the horses would not stop eating, or pooping, merely because the humans were having a bad day. Motilenus did not want any slaves helping the driver, lest they whisper some message for the outside. The wagoner was quite insistent that he would not do the work alone, nor simply go away without payment for his troubles. The Praetorians considered the work quite beneath them. Motilenus became particularly incensed when Eclectus suggested that "Narcissus and Ajax are the two strongest, let them handle this."

"Not Narcissus!" Motilenus shouted. "He might try to hide in the wagon and escape."

"Are you suggesting," Marcia put in, "that he would rather bury himself in a load of manure than spend another day in your company?"

Eclectus explained. "He has suggested pointing the finger at Narcissus as the one who killed Caesar. Or pointing the finger at you, or at the two of us together."

Marcia said, "I would have thought it would suit you just fine to have it known that Laetus did it. Doesn't that leave you in command?"

"But not if the honor of the Praetorian Guard is besmirched!" Motilenus insisted.

"That would be quite impossible," Marcia said snidely.

"True. Our honor is beyond question," Motilenus replied. Obviously Marcia's remark had gone completely over his head. She had always had the impression that Motilenus was simply not very bright. Motilenus resumed ranting. "But you are known to be just his whore! Many people heard him say you were poisoning him. You had cause, because he was getting rid of you. People heard him say that too! And we all know why, because you are sleeping with Eclectus! Caesar was retching and behaving oddly all night from the effect of your poison. Yes, Laetus threatened him with a sword, not knowing the cause of his derangement, and that is why he must be demoted. But then Caesar vomited blood and passed out. And Narcissus garroted him to make sure he was dead. That is how it happened!"

Marcia laughed. "Suppose you convince everyone of this story. Don't you think the people of Rome will be grateful, to whoever rid them of the crazed and dangerous man that Commodus turned into? I loved him once. Many had high hopes for him. But everyone hated and feared him by the end. Would you like to make a wager with me? I bet that the Senate is voting for a formal damnation of his memory even as we speak. If I win, let these people go. If I lose, do to me whatever you please."

"Do you really believe that the people would think of you as some kind of heroine?"

"I don't care what they think of me. I don't even care what happens to me anymore. The reason I came looking for you was to talk about Popilia. Why are you holding her? Do you think she has any interest in telling tales against Laetus, or against any of you? Quite the opposite. You really aren't thinking very clearly about this. Can you at least let Popilia go home?"

"If that will make you stop being trouble. All right, you win. Popilia can go, and Narcissus can shovel shit." Motilenus walked off, feeling very unsatisfied. The Praetorians and servants who had been watching the confrontation mostly drifted away. Marcia whispered to Eclectus that he should go and make sure that Popilia and her servants got out before Motilenus had a chance to change his mind. Then she followed Ajax, Narcissus, and the wagoner into the stables as they wrestled a big bale of hay inside. She thought she had seen the wagoner before, and caught his eye. With a shovel she casually scratched an arc into the dirt. He took the shovel from her and drew an answering arc, completing the sign of the fish. Then he scratched a straight line. She made it into the sign of the cross, then scuffed out the marks with her feet.

Someone was hidden under the manure when the wagon left, but it was not Narcissus.

Chapter 9

Cocina found the merchants of Ostia as full of panicked rumors as Tullius had predicted. Rebels had infiltrated the Palace last night and killed the Emperor, and more rebels were trying to infiltrate Ostia to set all the grain warehouses on fire! That was why the City troops were guarding the entrances, but what if they were not in time? No, no, the City was going to seize all the grain in the name of the State and pay nothing for it! No, it must be that the City was afraid that the Praetorians would seize all the grain. And if the City and the Praetorians were going to fight a battle here, weren't the warehouses in danger of being burned? Someone else said that if the government of the Empire had been overthrown, then pirates would be attacking any day now. Never mind that no pirates had been so daring as to raid Ostia in well over a hundred years, and those had not fared very well.

On one thing they were all agreed. It would be a good idea to own some grain and oil and wine which was stored somewhere else. Cocina mentioned that she was authorized by Senator Tullius to sell any or all of the produce from his estates, and from the estates for which he was an agent, and any other stores he had acquired title to during the previous season. She was immediately besieged by shouted offers. She let the babble continue for a little while, then said that she would return when they were ready to be serious. When a couple of them tried to follow as she walked away, she pointed out how rude it was to follow a woman, and that if her German driver saw them he would be unlikely to understand. She did not actually know where Germanus had gotten off to. She hoped he would not get too drunk or into too much trouble.

She went to the shop of Severa Battanitha. She was an old freedwoman. Of course she was not of the Severan family, but had taken their name when they freed her, much as Cocina would become Tullia Cocina someday. She was from Leptis Magna in Libya Cyrenaica, where she was the nanny for Septimius Severus, now the ranking officer on the Danube. When he was grown she was sold to cousins in Perusia so that she could be nanny to Junius Severus. And when he was grown, the family gave her her freedom and enough money to set up shop in Ostia, where she imported this and that from Libya, using all her contacts there. She was never one to stop writing to anyone she knew, and her boys always remembered their nanny. Septimius wrote from time to time, and Junius would come and visit. Cocina knew that she would not be able to get out of Battanitha's shop without hearing all the latest.

"Good morning, dear. I need more asafetida and silphium." Supplying Langoria had run her nearly out of the needed herbs. Cocina could find wild carrot locally, but asafetida came only from the East, and silphium only from Cyrene in particular.

"Have you heard the news?" Battanitha said, as Cocina had expected she would. "My boy is being given command of the Rhine!"

"I thought Septimius was happy where he is on the Danube."

"He is! He has become irreplaceable there. I had such a sweet letter from him just last month. He remembered the games we used to play at Saturnalia time, when he would pretend to be a judge."

"If they cannot replace him on the Danube, then how can he command on the Rhine?"

"No, no, it is Junius who is going to command the Rhine!"

"Isn't he rather young for that? I did not even know he was in the army."

"But everybody knows that he is brilliant! He came to see me, and said he had to go away to the north and might not be back for a very long time. He could not tell me what posting he was being given, but I guessed his secret."

Now it all made sense to Cocina. She had been told no such nonsense as Junius being given the Rhine, but had spun her own fantasy. There was only one possible reply. "That is such wonderful news!" Cocina then began to brag about Tullia Minor, and how she had grown, and how everyone at the Palace had admired her. Cocina knew little about how the night at the Palace had gone, though she knew it had not ended well. But then, Battanitha knew very little of what Junius was really up to. Cocina was pleased to chat idly for a while. Wasting some time was exactly the right thing to do now.

At only one point did the conversation take a dangerous turn. "And of course you will have heard," Battanitha said, "what that horrible Victor has done!" Cocina knew that Victor was also from Leptis Magna, and had moved to Italy around the same time Battanitha had. She knew this only because Battanitha frequently referred to him as a great enemy of all that was right and decent, and blamed every flooding of the Tiber or outbreak of disease on Victor angering the gods. She did not know why Victor was Battanitha's special bogeyman, except that of course Battanitha believed Leptis Magna to be the center of the universe, and everything that happened in Rome to be the result of what people from Leptis Magna did. As far as Cocina knew, Victor was merely the head of one of the odd little cults which proliferated in Rome.

"So what has he done now?" she asked.

"How could you not have heard? He has killed the Emperor!"

"Ah yes, I have heard, but I did not realize that Victor was behind it." Cocina of course could not divulge that she had actually met the assassin, in her master's house no less. She confined herself to agreeing with Battanitha that it was awful. Eventually Battanitha got around to filling Cocina's order and taking her money.

When she returned to the grain and oil merchants, Cocina was offered higher prices than when she had walked away. This was as she hoped. She accepted some offers, and this caused others to bid even higher. She sold everything Tullius actually held, but refrained from selling more, because it might be difficult to get back into Ostia in a day or two to make the purchases she would need to cover any short sale. She made sure that all the buyers came with her to the temple of Castor and Pollux, to burn incense to the Heavenly Twins and have the priests put their seal on the contracts. Notarization by any priest made a contract legally binding, but she wanted it done in this temple in particular, because the Twins were the special protectors of ships at sea. No merchant whose fortune could be ruined by a shipwreck would want to offend the Twins. Then she went in search of Germanus, and found him at a little shrine to the German Hercules.

The German community could not afford a marble building, but had a wooden roof over an image of a warrior with one eye gouged out. Apparently the German Hercules was not as invulnerable in battle as the Greek Hercules. Cocina would not have worshipped such a god, but knew that the Egyptians worshipped Osiris even though he had been captured by his enemy and torn to pieces, and that Victor's god had been executed as a criminal. Germanus had a little keg of beer, and rather than make a small libation offering and drink the rest, as Cocina would have expected, he poured all of it into the ground. She said something she did not expect him to understand about how she approved of piety.

This provoked him into a recitation of what was apparently a genealogy, a list of a dozen Germanic names, separated by the word *fater* which Cocina could figure out was *pater*. He conveyed to her that he was the descendant of this deity, and was royalty back home. Cocina would believe that as soon as she began trusting Battanitha as a source of news, but made some pretense of being impressed. She had him drive back through the warehouse district to the Claudian Harbor, and up Portus Way. This was a divided highway, with the Rome-bound and Harbor-bound lanes separated. Outside the Roman Empire, there were no roads like it. Within the Empire there were few, and this was the first.

Germanus took the chance to make the horse show what it could do.

Chapter 10

The Eldest moved on with his agenda. "We must address the question of the vacant offices and titles. The late Commodus Caesar was to be Consul, along with our Pompeius Falco, whom we esteem so greatly." Falco bowed slightly to acknowledge the compliment. Somehow he had already gotten hold of his scepter of office, which he should not have had until he had taken his oath. But then, the inaugural ceremony in the Circus Maximus, alongside Commodus dressed as a gladiator and pretending to fight, was not going to happen as scheduled. "He was also Caesar, Augustus, Father of the Country, and..." The Eldest could not remember off-hand all of the titles, ranging from the grandiose to the absurd, which Commodus had created for himself and insisted on the Senate officially voting to confer upon him. "And other titles not previously known to our constitution." The Eldest noticed with annoyance that while he paused, Sempronius had begun whispering animatedly to his friend Erucius Clarus Vibianus. "The House will be in order. I recall a time when even the most junior members knew better than to carry on extraneous conversations. Are you discussing anything that you would like to share with the rest of us?"

"I apologize, Eldest. May I address the House?"

The Eldest had not anticipated that Sempronius would take him up on the sarcastic suggestion that he share his thoughts. As far as the Eldest was concerned, someone like the Consul or the Prefect ought to be speaking long before this young whipper-snapper. But he had asked, so protocol had him trapped. "Caius Titius Sempronius has the floor."

"Thank you, Eldest. My question is a simple one. Should we even be thinking about choosing a new Emperor at all?" There were some gasps at the audacity of this. "I know we cannot go back to the legendary days of the Republic. The army insists that there must be one supreme commander, and we must respect that view. But what do we know about whom the army might prefer? For years now, nobody has dared to speak about the succession. It would have been like throwing a knife at a man, to mention his name as a potential Emperor. Should we not wait to hear who is favored by the legions? Clodius Albinus should be on the way from Britannia. He is well connected in Gallia Belgica and could tell us more about what the troops are thinking on the Rhine. We called him here with words of condemnation, but now that the cause for that condemnation has been removed, is he not entitled to be heard? Indeed, does not his kinship give him a right to be considered as successor?"

At this, some called out "Hear, hear!" while others muttered angrily. The Eldest raised his hands, but did not need to speak in order to restore order.

Sempronius resumed. "I know that the Praetorians express support for Pertinax, who has the loyalty of the City as well. But there are many legions in the army, and we do not know their opinions. For that matter, do we even know the opinions of the Senate? Only half of the Senators are here. That is as usual, but this is no usual question. We have an able Consul in Falco to run the administration. We ought to choose a second Consul, certainly. But I see no need to go further than that today. And we have a fine Prefect in Pertinax. He has the City well in hand, and for a rarity, the Praetorians are in no mood to pick a fight with the regulars. This gives us the benefit of relative calm. I say that we should wait, and consult other voices."

The Eldest said, "Who else wishes to speak? I see Didius Julianus has raised his hand, and Consul Falco has raised his rod."

"I yield to the Consul," Julianus conceded.

"Quintus Pompeius Sosius Falco has the floor."

"Thank you Eldest," said Falco with a slight bow. "And I thank Senator Julianus for his courtesy, and Senator Sempronius for his expression of confidence in my ability. I agree with him as to the need to elect a second Consul, perhaps his friend Clarus. But I cannot agree with him at all that this is any time to wait. Wait for what, or for whom? We have summoned Clodius Albinus, but will he come? I hear rumors that he intends to flout our authority. Certainly that should make his friends in this House think again about his supposed worthiness." At this there began to be some muttering. "And he could only speak for Britannia, perhaps indirectly for the Rhine. Should we send to the Danube as well, and to Syria? How many weeks would we have to wait for a response? Or months? Should we also give a vote to Hispania, or Africa, or Graecia, or Egypt? We are Rome, and the Senate and People of Rome rule this Empire." This, at least, drew some expressions of approval.

Falco continued, "I must also correct his claim that no-one has spoken about the succession lately. You have all heard of the horse named Pertinax." The owner of a champion race-horse had served under Pertinax during his term as Governor of Britannia, and had named the horse for him. "At a recent race, I heard Laetus cheering for Pertinax, and when the horse won, he said to all his Praetorian friends that he should like to see Pertinax win the greatest race. He even said he would lay bets on it. There could be little doubt what he meant by that! I hear that the Guard is for Pertinax because Laetus induced them to be so. I hear that this upstart Motilenus has only declared the Guard loyal to Pertinax in order to put himself at the front of the triumphal march, as it were. In short, I hear that the events of last night may not have been nearly so spontaneous as some have wished to paint them!"

Titus Flavius Claudius Sulpicianus, the father of Lady Titiana and father-in-law of Pertinax, shouted "How dare you!" Although his voice was loudest, he was far from the only one shouting. The Eldest raised his hands, to no avail.

"The House will be in order!" The Eldest had to raise his voice. "The House will be in order! Consul, are you quite, quite finished?" Falco nodded. "Publius Helvius Pertinax has a right of reply."

Pertinax glared at Falco and said, "I have nothing to say to him."

"Then Marcus Didius Julianus has the floor."

"And Severus," added Julianus.

"I do not see Severus here," the Eldest said in some puzzlement. "He ought to be on the Danube. Unless you mean the younger Severus, who someone told me is in Britannia, and in any case does not yet have the right to speak here."

112

"I mean my full name is Marcus Didius Severus Julianus. I must not slight my Severan relatives."

"Then," the Eldest said with some annoyance, "Marcus Didius Severus Julianus has the floor."

"Thank you, Eldest. Let those of us who were present at the New Year's masquerade forgive Consul Falco for his speculations, for he was not a witness. Nor should we think his absence a cause for suspicion. I myself was reluctant to attend, after so long when Commodus Caesar..." Here he paused, searching for the right words. "When he requested my absence from the city. Let us not mince words here. These last years have been a nightmare, under our worst Emperor since Domitian. At the very least we should let the people know that it is safe to be honest about the relief they all must feel. Let us revoke the title of Father of the Country we improvidently awarded to Commodus, and all authorizations for statues to stand in his honor, and resolve that his memory be damned."

"That sounds like a motion. Is there a second?"

Gnaeus Manlius, the father of Lady Scantilla and father-in-law of Julianus, rose and said "I second the motion. Pulling down the statutes will give the mob something fun to do." There were some laughs at this. "That would be a better occupation for their hands than some other things they might get up to."

"Very well, Senator Gnaeus Manlius has seconded." He was a little miffed that Manlius had spoken before being recognized. "Who wishes to speak concerning this motion?" No-one spoke. Those who had a better opinion of Commodus than their fellows knew better than to say so now. Those who shared the loathing for Commodus were annoyed that Didius Julianus had pushed himself forward to be the first to condemn. There was no particular glory in speaking second, which might make a Senator look to be a follower of Julianus, who was not particularly popular. Everyone was glad that Manlius, who already was connected to him, had taken on the role of being his second, however irregularly. "You are all anxious to vote, I take it? Who is in favor?"

All the Senators said "Aye!" though with varying degrees of enthusiasm. Quite a few of them did, after all, owe their positions to Commodus.

"Who is opposed?" There was silence, and the scribe noted the unanimous vote. "Senator Julianus, are you finished?"

"No, Eldest. We must have strong leadership for this troubled time, an Emperor we can all be proud of. Everyone here knows of the many services which our honored Prefect, Publius Helvius Pertinax, has performed for the State. Indeed it would be tedious even to attempt to list all the titles he has held, and all of his accomplishments in those various offices."

Nonetheless Julianus proceeded, for the next hour, to attempt just that.

Chapter 11

"Good day, Victor," Marcia said with feigned casualness. It would be difficult to know that it was day, in this dimly-lit chamber deep under the Vaticanus hill. Victor was working on some papers at a desk, a list of names and amounts, assisted only by a feeble oil lamp, rubbing his strained eyes. Startled, he moved to cover the papers, then relaxed, seeing who it was. The peaked crown of white starched linen which Marcia had seen Victor wear the day before was sitting on the desk, and his tall shepherd's crook leaned against the wall. Marcia's rescuer, accompanying her with a torch although she showed herself familiar with every twist and turn of the way, now retreated into the catacombs to leave the two alone. "I am sorry that my clothes are dirty and smelly. I have had no chance to clean them." The pungent brown stains were incongruous on her finery. Marcia did not explain to Victor how they had gotten there in the first place.

"You worry about cleansing the stains on pieces of cloth, which are but dumb things," Victor said. "Do you have no concern about cleansing the stains on your soul?"

"I am sorry that I stole so much money from you. I need your help now, and I will pay you what I can." Marcia took off her valuable necklace and held it out to him. When he showed no inclination to take it, she laid it on his desk.

"You stole nothing from us. You helped us to redeem our captives from Sardinia, and for that we remain grateful." Marcus Aurelius sent many Christians to the silver mines, where some died from the hard labor, but others lived for years. Aurelius did not consider Christianity a form of treason, as Nero and Domitian had, but something much worse in his eyes, a philosophical error which would lead the people into ignorance. Commodus considered the Christians only as a source of money, and was easily persuaded that their ransoms would bring more than their easily-replaced labor. "Whatever the Emperor demanded, we were happy to pay. What is coin compared with life?" And if Marcia made them pay rather more than the Emperor demanded, well, what agent would not take a commission?

"You do not wish to take my dirty money? You are too pure for that?"

"Of course we will take it," Victor said, now picking up the necklace and assessing the gold and the stones. "We see to the needs of many widows and orphans, and ransoming the captives strained our finances to the breaking point. But I wish you were giving out of a charitable heart, rather than with any thought that you can buy us."

"So you will not help me?"

"We help all who are in need, insofar as we are able. No-one is of more value than any other, merely for possessing wealth, nor is anyone of lesser value, no matter what sins he may have committed. Or she."

"I had nothing to do with the killing last night."

"Odd that you should hasten to deny what I did not accuse you of."

"It is convenient for some to lay the blame on me. Do not believe it if you hear such things."

"We know well what it is to be blamed for what we had no part in. Do you know the Jewish story of the scapegoat? In old times, their ancestors would heap curses on a goat and chase it out into the wilderness, so that the goat would bear the punishment for all the sins of the people."

"As you believe that Jesus did."

"Aha, so you have not been wholly inattentive when you hang about at the back of our meetings. Do not look surprised. It would take far more than wearing a drab and baggy robe, and veiling your face, to disguise yourself from me. Clemens wondered yesterday if it was you, but I did not give your secret away."

"Who is Clemens?"

"The man whose life you just put at hazard. And you did not bother to ask his name? Did you even thank him?"

"You are right. I owe gratitude to him for bringing me here, and to you for receiving me. I am being most unmannerly. I have not even expressed condolences for the loss of Eleutheros." When Marcia began negotiating over the captives in Sardinia, it was Eleutheros who wore the Eastern-style peaked white crown, and Victor was merely his deputy. She had not seen Eleutheros in years and suddenly now the crown was Victor's, so she presumed that Eleutheros was deceased.

"He is not dead, but he has had a stroke which left him incapacitated. Would you like to pay your respects to him?" Victor led her to an even deeper chamber, with niches in all the walls holding urns of ashes. A lamp was lit in one niche, containing a decorated box presumably filled with some especially venerated remains. "PETRUS" was written on the box.

Eleutheros sat immobile in a rare solid-backed chair, with a fixed look of blindness in his eyes. A man Victor introduced as Zephyrinos was spooning watery gruel into his mouth. The old man was not swallowing much of it. Marcia was unsure of what was proper. She curtseyed and said, "God's blessings be upon you." That sounded polite enough. There was no hint of acknowledgment, and she fled the chamber. As Victor followed, she asked, "Wouldn't it be more merciful to let him die? Why pour food down the neck of what is little more than a corpse? If he could speak, he would beg to die."

"Certainly not!" Victor replied indignantly. "Life is a gift from God. No man has the right to decide when it should end."

"Do you suppose he even sees or hears anything? I felt a little foolish addressing a man who could not reply."

"The Lord sees and hears. Never think that any act of kindness or word of blessing is in vain."

"Everything that I say sounds foolish or wicked to you, doesn't it? I don't know why I thought that here was where I should take refuge."

"Of course you know why, my child."

"It was only that I was afraid to stay where I was."

"No, you were not only running away from fear. You were running toward God's love."

"Your god could never love someone like me."

"You are profoundly mistaken. God loves all His children, and wants only that you would renounce the darkness of your sins, and walk in His light."

"Well, I shall not be sinning with Commodus Caesar any longer."

"But is there repentance in your heart? Do you understand the uncleanness of consorting with a man who was married to another?"

"You think I was sinning against Crispina?" Marcia laughed. "She was glad to be rid of him. He may never have legally divorced her, but she's been comfortably banished on Capri for years. They are as divorced as any couple could be."

"There is no divorce in the eyes of God. Unless, indeed, she first broke her oaths to him."

"Crispina would never dare cheat on him, don't be absurd. He had to say that, of course, but he's always been a liar. She said she was pregnant, and then she wasn't pregnant." Marcia did not know, or care, whether Crispina was mistaken about being pregnant, or had miscarried, or had asked Narcissus for his cousin's herbs. "So he said she was useless to him, slapped her hard across the face, and sent her away."

"That is as I thought. So she is still his wife, unless the rumors are true that Commodus finally had her killed. Even so, his sins do not excuse yours. She was certainly alive when you took up with him. In fact, she was still in the Palace when you began, or am I mistaken?"

"You are not. But I was careful never to get with child." In her view, that was a good thing.

"Don't tell me that you have been to that witch Battanitha!"

"I have never heard that name. But if you wish me to confess all my sins, as I know is the custom among your people, this morning I slept with Eclectus."

"Is he married to another?"

"No. I think that he has always loved me, and would not settle for another."

To Marcia's astonishment, Victor replied, "In the eyes of God, then, he became your husband this morning. You owe him your love and obedience."

"I do love him, I suppose, but he never tells me what to do."

"Did you ask his permission before running away like this?"

Chapter 12

"And furthermore," Julianus concluded after detailing the record of Pertinax, "his service as Prefect of the City has earned him expressions of loyalty from the Praetorian Guard, who are seldom heard to praise the City. The Guards have even been heard to say that they regard Pertinax as their Caesar, and theirs is a voice which we should hesitate to disregard. Wherefore, I move that we confer on the honored Publius Helvius Pertinax the titles of Caesar and Augustus, with all the tribunician and imperial powers those names convey." Several Senators raced to shout that they seconded the motion, which was out of order since the Eldest had not yet asked.

"It is recognized that Gnaeus Manlius has seconded," the Eldest said. It was safest to recognize the father-in-law again, as the closest associate of Julianus and the seconder of his previous motion. Picking out some other Senator would risk offending the others. "Publius Helvius Pertinax has the right of reply."

Pertinax looked tired and ill. He had gotten very little sleep the previous night. "Thank you, Eldest. And I thank Julianus and Manlius for the honor. But I must assure you all that I have not sought this, and am most reluctant to accept. Pompeianus, you were my first and greatest patron, and your parentage commends you to this post far more than mine does, vigorous servant of the State though my father always was. You said you were too old to be any kind of a candidate, but I am scarcely a youngster myself. Would you reconsider your renunciation, so far as the titles are concerned? You could serve as Nerva served after the death of Domitian, with the understanding that it is only for long enough to consider the succession in an orderly fashion."

The Eldest observed the formalities. "Claudius Pompeianus, you are requested to speak."

Pompeianus leaned heavily on his cane as he turned to face Pertinax, as if intentionally emphasizing his frailty. "Indeed I have watched you grow old, yet somehow I am still older than you. You have not yet

119

reached the age when Father Time begins to wound you with gross infirmities. I can scarcely see where to set down my walking stick, but this much I can see clearly, that the next Emperor shall have much to contend with, and may have a most unhappy time. I am sorry to push the burden onto you, sonny, but truly I cannot take it onto these bent shoulders."

"Prefect Pertinax, do you have more to add?"

"If no-one else will take it, how can I refuse? You all know that I have never refused any burden the State asks me to bear."

"Who else wishes to speak? Consul Falco is recognized."

"Should we not consider alternatives?" Falco asked, and paused. "Pertinax complains of the burden, which would be lighter if others would share. If Pompeianus has a claim from his family connections, surely Flavius Sulpicianus has an even better claim? Perhaps he ought to be co-Augustus?" Sulpicianus shook his head rapidly, recoiling from the very thought. "Or his daughter, the Lady Flavia Titiana, whose favors so many of us have enjoyed?" The *double entendre* did not go unnoticed. There was some jeering, which the Eldest found disturbing. "Should not she, as the consort of our new Augustus, have the title of Augusta? And should not the name of Caesar be conferred also upon his son?" No-one in Rome had even met Pertinax's son, who stayed with relatives in the country. "And if we are granting titles, should our new Augustus not also be called Father of the Country?"

"Are you attempting to formulate a motion?" the Eldest asked.

"I must speak!" Pertinax interjected.

"You have the right of reply," the Eldest acknowledged.

"I interpose my right as paterfamilias. I will not have it said that I owe my position to my wife, and I wish no titles conferred upon my son until it is seen whether he is worthy of them. I forbid this House to grant titles upon members of my own household without my consent. As for the title of Father of the Country, that ought not be granted when I have done nothing yet to earn it. I would rather be known as Princeps of the Senate, as Emperors in former times were called."

"Have both titles then!" Falco shouted.

"Consul Falco, you are out of order," the Eldest said sternly. "I see that Marcus Tullius Secundus wishes to speak."

Tullius maneuvered Falco into a trap. "I second the motion of our esteemed Consul, that the nomination by Julianus be amended, so that the titles of Father of the Country and Princeps of the Senate also be conferred upon Publius Helvius Pertinax."

The Eldest remarked, "Tullius, I hear that you took Laetus into your custody in the name of us all. I am not certain whether to call that high-handed, or quick-witted, or both at once."

Tullius replied, "I was not certain whether this House would wish him arrested for murder, or given a vote of thanks, or both at once." There was some laughter at this. "He should enjoy that home of mine rather than the other Tullian home." The Hole of Tullius on the Capitoline hill was the oldest Roman prison, a rock cell into which prisoners were dropped, and sometimes never taken out again.

The Eldest returned to the matter at hand. "That must be discussed before we adjourn, but at present there are important motions pending. Who else wishes to speak?" There was silence. "I recall a time when orators could hold forth for hours on such a weighty topic. But you are all anxious to vote? Very well. On the motion to amend, shall the nomination be amended to include the titles of Father of the Country and Princeps of the Senate? All those in favor?"

Most Senators shouted "Aye," but some remained silent.

"All opposed?"

Out of those who did not want Pertinax to be Emperor, or did not want any Emperor chosen this day, most did not care overly much about which honorifics he piled up. Only Falco shouted "Nay."

"Consul Falco, technically this is your own motion."

"Then I withdraw the objection."

"It is unanimous then." The Eldest looked to see that the scribe was recording this. "On the motion to nominate, shall the titles of Caesar, Augustus, Father of the Country, and Princeps of the Senate be conferred upon Publius Helvius Pertinax, with all tribunician and imperial powers? All those in favor?"

Again there was a majority "Aye."

"All those opposed?"

This time there were several voices saying "Nay" if not very loudly.

The Eldest considered. "I should hate to trust to my ears on a matter of such weight. Let us have a division of the House. Julianus and Manlius, as the proponents, stand here on the dextrous side of the altar, and let all those in favor join you. Those opposed stand on the sinistrous side. Any who wish to abstain, remain where you are, and I shall join you in neutrality." As most of the Senators joined Julianus, many of those who had said Nay now decided it would be better to join them. Only Falco, Sempronius, and Clarus stood on the sinistrous side, and only Pertinax, standing, and the Eldest, carried in his chair, were by the benches. Then Sempronius, with a glance at Clarus, decided to move over to the dextrous side, and Clarus and Falco followed him. "You have decided to make it unanimous, then? Very well." The Eldest turned around to face the lictors. "You may hail the Emperor."

The lictors knelt, holding their doubled-headed axes in present-arms posture, and chanted the sacramental oath of loyalty. "Ave Pertinace! Ave Caesar! May all the gods preserve you as our Imperator! May our lives be forfeit if we fail to defend you!"

The Eldest turned to the Senators. "Resume your places!" Then he turned to Pertinax. "O August One, it is your right to preside now."

Pertinax answered, "I should prefer that you continue to preside, with your wisdom and experience." At a nod from the Eldest, his attendants carried him back to the front. The Eldest would have preferred to give up the chore, but whatever the August One wanted, he would get. Pertinax continued, "I should like to make a motion." It was far more customary for the Emperor simply to state his wishes and let other Senators go through the formalities of making a motion. Pertinax phrased his motion rather informally. "I hope to work smoothly with Consul Falco, and as he has expressed that our esteemed colleague Erucius Clarus Vibanius would be acceptable to him as the other Consul, allow me to nominate him for the office."

The Eldest recognized Sempronius as the second this time.

Chapter 13

When the Portus Way met the Aurelian Way, Cocina had a little difficulty persuading Germanus that he should turn left. He knew that they were on the wrong side of the Tiber, and would need to go right to get to the bridge. He pointed that way and repeated the word *domum* "home," the first time she had heard him utter a Latin word, and with a correct ending, no less. She told him they were not going home yet, and he understood. At the last possible moment he tugged on the reins to make the horse do a sharp left turn, which did not quite overturn the chariot. The office and school of Fulminatus was less than half a mile, at Triumphal Way. Just a little up Triumphal Way was an apartment building, wealthy enough to have security guards. She asked if Diodoros Tigranos lived there, and was shown to a door on the second floor. The man who answered looked far too young to command the Cohorts.

Somewhat doubtfully, she asked, "Are you Diodoros Tigranos?"

"No, but he lives here. He is on duty today. I am Alexandrius. Can I be of service?"

"Named for Alexander the Great? That is a nice name." She was evading, for the moment, any statement of who she was or what she wanted, until she had the measure of this man.

"I am named for the city of Alexandria, because I was conceived there, although my father spent only a short time there, and never returned again until recently."

"But you are named for that one night of passion? It must have been a memorable one!"

"If it was, it must have been one of very few. My parents do not get on well."

Seeing that his manners were open and candid, Cocina divulged a little. "I have a message to convey to an officer that Tigranos knows, whose sister is in the Palace and needed some assistance. My cousin in the Palace is her friend, and asked me to get word to the brother that it has been done."

"Which officer is Tigranos supposed to get a message to?"

124

"The one whose sister is in the Palace. Tigranos will know."

"And what is the message?"

"What she asked to be done, has been done."

Alexandrius laughed. "I have met other spies who work for Tigranos, but you are the most cryptic. Please believe me that I am on his side, and would betray none of his secrets."

"I am not a spy."

"A pity. You would be an excellent one. So who are you?"

Cocina relented. "I am Cocina. I serve in the household of Senator Marcus Tullius Secundus."

"And who is your cousin in the Palace?"

"His name is Narcissus."

"Narcissus! My family is greatly indebted to him. He forged the Emperor's signature on a letter appointing my father as a magistrate."

"I didn't know Narcissus took such risks!"

"There was little danger. No Emperor can ever pay as much attention to administration as he must pretend to. There are several people in the Palace whose job it is to put the imperial name on documents that Caesar never sees. Narcissus is not usually one, but he acted that time. My father brought a wonderful letter of recommendation, but it was from Clodius Albinus, and Marcus Aurelius was angry at Clodius for something or other at the time, so no-one was sure what to do. Narcissus took it to Tigranos, who is loyal to Clodius ever since Clodius cleared the way for his father to get citizenship. And Tigranos found an open position for a judge quaestor under the City. My father was not really qualified, but Narcissus thought he could handle it. So you see, you need not worry whether I would be willing to help your cousin Narcissus with... whatever this is."

"Narcissus has befriended Langoria, who is treated as a slave in the Palace, even though she is freeborn and her brother Tausias is a citizen, and an officer of the Watch."

"This is the Tausias who lived with Tigranos before he had to move out here?"

"I didn't know that they had lived together, but I was told they were good friends."

"And something has been done for his sister that you are reluctant to talk about?"

"Exactly, and her brother will know what the message is about. Just tell him, it is done."

"I will pass on the word as quickly as I can, but it is hard to say when Tigranos will be home, or how hard it will be for him to find Tausias, with all the madness today. Do you know that the Aemilian Bridge is closed? My teacher Fulminatus Rhetor did not show up today, after going to the Palace last night. When I tried to go into town to inquire about him, I was not allowed across. If you live on the other side of the Tiber, it may be very difficult to get home."

"No! I didn't know that. I suppose I shouldn't be surprised. The City troops were making it difficult to get into Ostia when I went there this morning. But how can they close Rome?"

"They had to. Crowds of people were coming into town for the spectacle that was going to take place in the Circus Maximus, which won't happen now. They don't want a large disappointed mob in the heart of the city. So they closed the gates and the bridges to turn away as many as they could."

"So I will have to take some confusing detour, with a driver who barely understands me."

"The soldiers will let you through if you have some kind of official business. Can you prove to them that you are the servant of Senator Tullius?"

"I have his seal." She pulled it out of her bag.

"Do you now? Well if your cousin can forge for an Emperor, I'm sure you can forge for a Senator. Try telling the soldiers that you are coming to take him home from the Senate meeting."

"He was fetched to the Senate House by the lictors, so he will need a ride back. But all I have is a little chariot with only room for me and the driver. The master can hardly sit on my lap. I suppose I could walk home from the Forum."

"A woman should not be walking alone, especially not on a dangerous day like today. I will lend you my carriage and horses. Just leave your chariot here, until we can swap them back."

"That is excessively kind of you."

"Not at all. Tell Senator Tullius that the son of Pescennius Niger is happy to assist him."

Germanus enjoyed driving a fine carriage, even with Cocina constantly pestering him to be careful with it.

Chapter 14

Tausias had no real business returning to the Forum. After a few hours of sleep he was called back to duty around noon, to help manage the crowds who had managed to get into Rome before all the gates were closed, and were milling about the Circus demanding their show. What did it matter if the Emperor was dead? They came for a show and they ought to have it, as far as they were concerned. Some acrobats and dancers were brought out to keep them mildly amused. The gladiators, and more to the point their owners, were entirely unwilling to risk injury or death under these circumstances. Flavius Genialis, who managed the state-owned gladiators, had no guidance more recent than yesterday's plea from Eclectus to stop this if possible. Promises were made that the new Consuls, Falco and whoever else it would be, were going to make speeches, which did not sound as thrilling as the performance by Commodus that they had been led to expect.

There were at least some lions and tigers in cages to look at. They ought perhaps have been moved to the Colosseum, where they could be let loose, but the plans had been for a crowd of over a hundred thousand, more than would fit in the Colosseum, so everything was in the Circus. Tausias thought wickedly that turning the beasts loose on the crowd might be the best solution. He was probably not the only member of the Watch to have that thought. But things settled down, and the watchmen no longer needed him to tell them what to do, so Tausias strolled up to the Forum in the vague hope of some news. He was in luck, for the cryer came out again. His face-paint had been sloppily changed into a mask of Comedy, and the rip in his toga had been hastily and badly sewn up. His attendants were now dressed as celebrants, in festive garb with floral garlands, and fixed idiotic grins.

"How the gloom of the darkest night gives way to radiant sunshine!" the cryer proclaimed.

"Hurrah!" and "Hurrah!" and "Hurrah!" and "Hurrah!" his attendants added.

Tausias was still in the mood to heckle. "But you were so sad about it this morning!"

"The cowardly despot Commodus is no more!"

Tausias outshouted the fourfold hurrahs. "We get no funeral games for him, I take it?"

"Never again will anyone call that tyrant the Father of the Country. Let us damn his memory!"

"Then can we tear down his ugly statues?"

The cryer for once answered. "The Senate not only permits, but commands that all memorials to the tyrant be destroyed!"

The crowd in the Forum, much larger than the audience had been in the morning, out-cheered the attendants. One said he had plenty of ropes in his shop, and others began planning with him. Some began arguing about which statue of Commodus was the ugliest and should go down first. It was pointed out that Commodus had put his own head on the Colossus, the great statue in front of the Colosseum which Nero had originally erected, but which had borne various other heads since. And that head was gilded. Scraping the metal off of it could be profitable.

"For we shall erect statues to our noble Publius Helvius Pertinax Caesar Augustus!"

"Hurrah! Hurrah! Hurrah! Hurrah!"

"Noble?" Tausias asked scornfully. "That son of a crooked arms dealer?"

The cryer ignored him this time. "He has become Father of the Country and Princeps of the Senate!"

"And how much did he pay for that?"

"The August One will be generous with all soldiers on the occasion of his accession, paying twelve gold per man, regardless of which unit he serves in!"

"Commodus paid twenty!" That was not quite true. Commodus promised twenty, which for the men in many units turned out not to be the same thing at all.

"Six will be paid at once, and six when funds are available! And that is all."

Tausias laughed at that. He doubted any money at all would reach the Watch. There were other soldiers in the Forum however who were angry. "What kind of insult is that?" was one of the milder remarks. The cryer's attendants dropped any pretense of being anything but bodyguards, striking fighting poses. Lictors closed in around them as they retreated. Tausias drifted back toward the Circus. One of the soldiers, in the uniform of the City, followed him. Tausias worried that he had given offense with some of his remarks, perhaps the one about Pertinax and his father. The Prefect did have many sincere admirers after all, and now that he was the Emperor it was perhaps especially unwise to voice disrespect.

However, the soldier just wanted to tell him that Diodoros Tigranos was looking for him.

Chapter 15

Eclectus was worried, and when he was worried he threw himself into work. He organized the construction of a casket to hide the disturbing corpse. It was the plainest of wooden boxes. All he wanted was to nail it shut as quickly as possible. One of the craftsmen in the Palace asked if it ought not be decorated, in some manner or another. Whatever anyone thought of him, he had been the Emperor after all. But Eclectus said that this could wait, until they heard whether there was to be any kind of funeral. There was no point in wasting effort on something that might only be set on fire or thrown into the river. Eclectus thought it might be some time before any decision was made. Perhaps no-one would even remember that there was a body to dispose of, until the new Emperor, whoever that might be, moved into the Palace and was confronted with the problem. At least, the problem should not be left displayed in the atrium. Eclectus had the corpse boxed up, and was trying to decide what less conspicuous place he should order it moved to, when he learned that he was mistaken in thinking that no-one outside the Palace had considered the matter.

Lucius Fabius Cilo was neither one of the most junior Senators, nor one of the highest-ranking. He was a protegé of the Severan family who had commanded a legion, and served as Governor of Gallia Narbonensis, if only for a year. Eclectus could not recall seeing him at the festivities of the previous evening, but he had been at the Palace with Junius Severus for some drinking and gaming only a few weeks ago. He now appeared at the front gate with a half-dozen men. Motilenus went out through the vestibule to inquire as to his purpose in coming, and escort him in.

"We are come to take the body," Cilo explained to Eclectus.

"Your timing is good. We have just finished sealing the coffin shut. What disposition has been decided upon?" Eclectus half expected to hear that the coffin would be opened so that the mob could tear the body to pieces. He would not approve of that, but would understand it.

"There is plenty of room in Hadrian's mausoleum. Hadrian planned for a dynasty to last more generations than it has. The Senate has been treating Claudius Pompeianus as the heir to that family, so he has the right to decide who may be buried there. He says he has no objections to Commodus lying in that tomb, but wants no part of taking the body there."

"How did you get drafted for this luckless task?"

"I volunteered. My home is near, so I could assemble a team of servants quickly. I am hoping that it will be remembered that I did not shirk when unpleasant but necessary work was called for."

Motilenus asked, "What has the Senate decided to tell the people about how he died?"

"Nothing. Nothing at all. We are to erase him from memory. Like King Romulus of old, he vanished into an impenetrable fog, except that in this case we believe spirits from below took him, rather than gods from above. One thing that everyone agrees, however: it did not happen in the Palace. Nobody who was at the Palace last night saw him at all."

That settled one concern, but Motilenus also wanted to be sure he had not backed the wrong horse. "Is Pertinax to be the new Emperor?"

"He is, and should be moving in here within a day or two. And Clarus Vibanius is to be the other Consul along with Falco, if you care about that. The two of them are to address the crowds in the Circus before the sun goes down."

"That ought to persuade the people to go home and go to bed," Eclectus said. He was not a great enthusiast for political rhetoric. He might have had some interest in hearing how the new Consuls tried to explain away recent events, but from what Cilo was saying, it sounded as if they would not even do that. They would probably just pretend that this was like any other New Year's Day, and they were taking their oaths of office like any other pair of Consuls. "I would think the people would be more interested in seeing and hearing the new Emperor."

"The August One will not make an appearance today. He will want to arrange a suitable spectacle, quite unlike what that person we are forgetting had in mind."

"That is wise. Do you know if Pertinax will bring his own staff with him when he comes, or will he retain everyone here at the Palace?"

"Pompeianus expressed a wish that the slaves in the Palace be given their freedom."

"Eclectus is more concerned," Motilenus interjected, "about whether Pertinax has someone new in mind to be head of the household."

"That I could not tell you," Cilo said.

"One thing I would bet is that he will have no use for a mistress. Even if he had such thoughts, Lady Titiana would be sure to put an end to them quickly. Which reminds me. Where is Marcia, anyway? I have not seen her for hours."

"I have no idea," Eclectus said. "I thought maybe you had locked her up somewhere."

Cilo could see that there was something going on here which was none of his business, so he had his men pick up the coffin, without laying a hand on it himself, and departed.

Chapter 16

Senator Tullius was pleased that Cocina was so thoughtful as to arrange a carriage to bring him home after his long day at the Senate, but surprised it was not his own. "Where did you get this rig?"

"That is rather a long story," Cocina said, scrambling to compose an acceptable version of that story. "We took the Portus Way back, thinking it would be faster, but the soldiers were blocking the bridge." It had been an absurdly crowded scene. The bridge led to the Cattle Forum, and the shouting farmers demanding to know why they could not lead their beasts across were nearly drowned out by the bleats and moos of the confused animals. "Alexandrius, the son of Pescennius Niger and a student of Fulminatus Rhetor, was wanting to find out why Fulminatus had not returned from the Palace, but he was not allowed to cross."

"Fulminatus is probably still sleeping it off. He was nearly as bad as the Emperor last night."

"He suggested that we might be able to get across, if we said we were fetching a Senator home from the meeting, but we would need a suitable carriage. So he has our chariot, until we can arrange to get this back to him." She was making it appear that they had met by the bridge, eliding any question about how they came to be talking to each other at all.

But that was not the direction Tullius wished to take his inquiries in any case. "How old is he now, and how are his looks?"

"He is tall, dark, and handsome, and I would say he is not yet twenty."

"I thought he could not be very old. He will not be seeking an office soon, or looking to marry just yet, but he will want to be introduced to women. Sometimes I wish I had not given up the old house. Our house is not really suitable for social affairs. Will we have to invite him to the country, do you think? What exactly did he say when he obliged you?"

"He said to tell you that the son of Pescennius Niger was happy to help."

"Oh! Then he is looking for political support for his father. Pescennius probably wants Syria back. Egypt is a promotion, more or less, but it was an odd business transferring him out of Syria when he had scarcely been there a year. Still, all the same we must have this Alexandrius to the house for dinner, and you must prepare him your best."

"Of course, master."

"What else did you do today?"

"Everything at Ostia was as you wisely foresaw. Everyone was competing with each other to see who could tell the most foolish and fearful story, and prices were bid up to the sky. I sold all that we have, but no more because I did not know if I could get back there tomorrow to make purchases. The soldiers were making it difficult to get into Ostia too."

"Did some obliging gentleman help you with that as well?"

"No, it was our trusty driver. He veered off and cut right past the whole line, almost running down one of the soldiers. I had no choice but to brazen it out and act like some highfaluting Lady, on business that could not be denied."

Tullius laughed. "He shows unexpected skills!"

"On the Portus Way, he got more speed out of the horse than I thought possible. I was afraid he would wreck us, but he did not quite."

When they arrived home, Tullius said to Germanus, "I have a name for you at last. From now on, you are Phaeton. Phaeton! Do you understand?" He did understand, but if he felt any enthusiasm about receiving a new name, he concealed it well. He dealt with putting the horses away in his usual listless manner.

Tullius was surprised to find a litter chair leaning against the wall, and four porters standing around. When Castor unlatched the door to let Tullius and Cocina in, they found Popilia and Tullia Minor also in the vestibule. Popilia was embracing Tullia, saying "Thank you so much for all you have done!" Then she turned to curtsey to Tullius and say, "Greetings, Senator! I was just leaving."

"Are you sure you will not stay for supper?"

"Oh no, I should get back before it is dark. My servants have been so patient."

Popilia went out, Phaeton came in, and Castor latched the door. "So, she came to visit our guest?" Tullius asked.

"Yes, master," Castor replied, "and to return a borrowed robe. I thought there could be no harm in it. She did not ask to bring her men inside, and Master Laetus has been no trouble. He has kept to the back room, but we could move him to the root cellar if you think she came to spy on the layout of the house."

"I do not. You acted rightly."

"What is going to happen to Laetus?" Tullia asked.

"Nothing, I think. The Senate dithered, but seemed in a mind to forget about everything before today, not only the death of Commodus Caesar but his whole life. It is not only a new year, but a new era. It will all be up to Pertinax. Or rather Pertinax Caesar, I shall have to get used to saying. But if I know him, he would rather that Laetus just resume his duties as if nothing at all happened."

"That will spare me some trouble. Popilia asked me to use all my wheedling and pleading on you, to get you to intercede on his behalf. She was afraid he might be put to death."

"Well then, my dear, you must tell her that you did intercede. You should tell her that I was ready to behead Laetus personally, until you wept on my shoulder and made me stop. That way, she will think of you as a person who wields influence."

"I could never tell such a lie to a friend!"

"My dear, you are of age now, and must learn how to play the game."

136

BOOK THREE

The Goddess Looks Both Ways

Chapter 1

A ship was preparing to cast off from the docks of Londinium. Clodius Albinus gripped the gunwale nervously and stared back at the town, deep in thought. At the last possible moment, Servilius came running up the pier and was hauled aboard. "So," he panted, "I catch up to you at last! Were you going to leave without me? Where are we going? And why in such a hurry?"

Clodius turned and pointed an accusing finger at him. "You were the one who advised me to write speedily to the Senate about the supposed death of Commodus, without waiting for official confirmation."

"I thought it vital that you establish yourself at once as one who favors changes. But wait... did you say the 'supposed' death?"

"That is what was in that letter, which the messenger correctly described as most urgent. Commodus, it seems, was not dead at all."

Servilius looked down. "I am so very sorry. You may remove this head from these shoulders."

"No, I think I will need that head where it is. Tigranos sent a warning that Junius Severus has been dispatched to relieve me as Governor and summon me back to Roma."

"Is it really necessary to move so quickly? Few cross the Channel in January, for very excellent reasons. That messenger was lucky to get across."

"The sailors did not want to make this journey. But then they heard that a white-headed eagle, such as is rarely seen in these parts, snatched a big fish out of the river and went swooping off to the south. The soothsayer regarded the white eagle as standing for my name Albinus, the catch of the fish as a sign of success, and the direction of flight as confirming that I should go south. The sailors were readily convinced."

"As well they ought to be, given such a clear omen from the gods!"

"I had to pay the soothsayer very little to make him spin this tale."

"Oh." Servilius was a little crestfallen. He had so wanted to believe in the story about the eagle. "Perhaps we ought not make this journey. The weather can be dangerous this time of year."

"If the gods will that this ship go to the bottom, I will say that they are being merciful to me."

"But why should we rush to answer this summons? Would it not have been better to remain in the far north, and make Junius chase after us?"

"Aha, for once I have thought of something that you have not. His appointment as Governor of Britannia will become effective once he sets foot in the province. If that happens, we are lost. Not even our best friends, I think, would defy an official letter of appointment. We would have to fight most of the forces of Britannia, with only such men as would be crazy enough to be mutineers for us. But if we meet Junius in Gallia, he will have no more men at his disposal than he has brought with him. If he was ordered to proceed rapidly, that will be few."

"We are also moving rapidly, and will have only the men on this ship." The ship was beginning to make its way down the Tamesis as he spoke, rendering any argument about whether they ought to be going rather moot.

"We will ask Governor Placidius to come meet with us. He will bring reinforcements."

"People will ask why we are there. What will we tell them?"

"We need to purchase arms and gifts for our new allies in Caledonia. That story has the merit of being true, even if incomplete. We can say that the barbarians will be more impressed by things not to be found in Britannia, and so we are shopping in Gallia Belgica. I am bringing money, and if worst comes to worst I am sure I can hire some fighters. We will camp by Samarobriva, at the unlucky spot where three roads meet, the roads to Gesoriacum, Durocortorum, and Lutetium. Whichever way Junius is travelling, he cannot get to Britannia in this season without passing through there, and the bad luck will be all his."

"This still sounds very dangerous to me. Suppose Junius has letters giving him authority to commandeer whatever troops he needs to arrest you?"

"In Gallia Belgica, he would have to apply to Placidius, who owes his entire career to me."

"Certainly Placidius will feel a strong duty to protect you, as his patron. But he will also feel a strong duty to the State. Would he dare to defy the Emperor?"

"We may have to put him to that test. I am in deep trouble. You may have tied yourself to a stone that will drag you down and drown you."

"My loyalty is to you, to the death."

Clodius broke with his usual reserve and hugged Servilius tightly. Servilius thought there might even have been a tear in his eye. Clodius said, "All we can do, really, is to buy some time."

"Maybe somebody will kill Commodus after all."

"Or maybe, the horse will sing."

Chapter 2

The throne-room in the Palace, more formally known as the chamber of audience, was left over from Domitian, whose taste ran to excessive size. It was also Domitian who had insisted on making the ceiling in the atrium so high that the architects later had to add unsightly bracings to keep the room from cracking apart. The imposing atrium at least served the purpose of making the visitors feel small and insignificant. The throne, a long shelf running along the wall above an average man's eye-level, with gilded carvings all along the rim and on the wall behind, served rather to make the Emperor look small, like a doll sitting on furniture it was not made to fit. The men who were granted audience had their heads at the level of the Emperor's feet. If this emphasized their subordination, it also meant that the Emperor did not get a clear read of their facial expressions. The oversized door was nearly as grand as the front door to the Palace. Once closed, it was a nuisance to get open again, and so it was typically left ajar. The majordomo of the Palace would have to stand guard in the doorway, and thus would inevitably overhear every audience. This was why no mere Praetorian was entrusted with guarding the entrance. Eclectus had never been known to gossip about who met with Commodus or what was said. That is why Pertinax was inclined to keep him on.

Pertinax began to understand why Marcus Aurelius was said to dislike this room, and to seek excuses to hold audiences elsewhere. Commodus of course had used it all the time, and decorated the walls with murals of the Labors of Hercules, with Hercules of course bearing the face of Commodus. Pertinax was determined to paint over those as soon as he settled on a better theme. His robes, all purple and cloth-of-gold, with padded shoulders, were also made to fit Commodus and needed alteration. Pertinax was developing a paunch and found the robes as uncomfortable as the shelf. He shifted uneasily, trying to find the right posture. Eclectus finally appeared, bowed low, and announced, "O August One, obedient to your command I present Laurentius Motilenus and Diodoros Tigranos."

141

Motilenus and Tigranos followed, and bowed low as Eclectus retreated to the entry. Simultaneously they said, "O August One, how may we serve you?"

"One might almost think," Pertinax said, "that everyone agrees that I am the rightful Emperor. Yet I hear disquieting rumors that this throne is not so steady a seat as it might appear."

"The loyalty of the Praetorians is more solid than oak!" Motilenus rushed to reassure him.

"I hope that six gold in their pouches has helped to solidify that loyalty."

"The men all trust that the other six will be coming shortly."

"Do they now? And if the coins do not come so soon, will that oak turn to corkwood?"

"No, August One! I did not mean to imply that their loyalty depends on the money. Rather, that they have come to trust you completely."

"They have 'come to' trust me? That sounds as if they did not always do so." To this, Motilenus had no ready reply. Pertinax prodded him. "Please speak freely. If the Praetorians have any concerns, I need to hear about them."

"Naturally there was some worry that a new Emperor might not give the Guard the same degree of favor that they have been accustomed to. But any such worries have been relieved."

"Have they now? All of the privileges which have been granted to the Guard must be reviewed. They most certainly should not take it for granted that all will continue as it has been." Pertinax paused, as if waiting for Motilenus to reply. When it was clear that no reply was forthcoming, he added, "One thing will continue. Laetus will remain as Praetorian Prefect. He should be returning to the Guard camp as we speak."

"That is very happy news," Motilenus said in tones that conveyed anything but happiness. "He is loved and respected by all the men."

"Tigranos," Pertinax said without turning his gaze from a spot above both of their heads, "you did not hasten to assure me how strong the City's loyalty is. Do they resent that their six gold has not arrived? Do they trust that it will come soon? Speak freely."

"The men's loyalty should not need stating. Haven't they served you faithfully, when they were called upon to perform so much more than their usual duties? And weren't they serving you faithfully before? There was no call for them to be publicly singled out for disfavor."

"Is that how they see it?"

"I haven't heard them say so. But that is how it appears."

"So you are complaining for them, when they are not complaining themselves?"

"I feel duty-bound to look out for the men."

"And you do not think that I look out for them? If I have not hastened to pay them first, it is a sign of my trust in them. Everyone knows in what wretched indebtedness the State was left, by that man of whom we do not speak. The men must know that my first duty is to redeem the credit of Roma from the dishonor into which it has fallen. The men must also know that I will fulfil my word to them as quickly as I am able. For they have been my unit, and I have been their commander, and that is a very special bond."

"That very bond is the source of some concern. The City is not as strong as any of the legions of the army. Some fear we are put in a false position. The legions may think that we pushed forward our own commander, because we were near to the capital, without regard to anyone else."

"I am no Galba or Otho. I was chosen by the Senate, not imposed by force of arms."

"Yes, but the legions might more readily accept someone in command of more than the City, or a Clodius Albinus or a Claudius Pompeianus with ties to the old imperial family."

"You mean to say that my father was not good enough."

"I beg pardon, August One," Tigranos said as he hastily bowed. "I intended no insult. I'm only conveying what others may think."

"You have been too accustomed to familiarity with me. That level of familiarity is no longer appropriate. You have been acting as the Prefect, but you are unsuited to hold the post. Your father is not good enough.

One whose family acquired citizenship so recently will not be accepted in such a role. I have decided that Sulpicianus is to be the new Prefect."

"Your own father-in-law?"

"I must have someone I trust implicitly. That you would presume to question my choice is another sign of that excessive familiarity which you ought to strive to shed. I shall find some post for you outside of Roma, as supervisor of one of the Latin towns."

"August One, I have been with the Cohorts of the City for nearly thirty years!"

"Then it is time that you served elsewhere. Silius Messala can serve in your place. You are dismissed." Tigranos almost spoke again, but bowed and left. Motilenus stood stiffly. "Both of you! You are dismissed." Motilenus also bowed and left. Pertinax slid off the throne. Dropping his frozen expression, he let his face twist into a grimace.

Eclectus approached him solicitously. "Shall I help you to change into more comfortable clothing? Or perhaps you would like a hot bath first?"

"My back aches dreadfully. Yes, a bath would be excellent. Is this the kind of attention you paid to my predecessor?"

"More often it was Marcia who dressed and bathed him."

"Of course it was. Titiana would kill me if I let her return in such a role. But if you know where Marcia is hiding, do let her know that I am not after her. I would hate for some rumor to start that I had killed her." Pertinax leaned on Eclectus as they walked. "How do you think I handled them? Both of them are more concerned about their own personal advancement than about fulfilling their duties. I simply cannot abide men of that sort. I wanted to dismiss both at once, so neither would spread rumors that the other had conspired against him."

"O August One, it is not my place to have any opinions on such a subject." He had many opinions, but he had long practice in biting his tongue.

"Is Tullius here? He will know how to squeeze out some extra money, if anyone does."

"I sent word that he was wanted. If he is not here already, he should be soon."

"Will he expect me to receive him in the chamber of audience?"

"No, he will expect to work directly with the treasurers and let them report to you. And he has said that he has a dinner engagement, so he will not be expecting to sup with you either."

"Good, I need that bath and would prefer no more formalities today."

Chapter 3

Langoria was no longer bleeding, as she was the first few days after her induced miscarriage. She was however still feeling very weak, and sometimes in physical pain, as well as mental sorrow. She sat up when Junipera came to see her. Junipera was more understanding than any other woman in the Palace. "Castor has come again. You should talk to him."

"Who is Castor?"

"He lives with the wise woman. He has advice from her, about how to regain your strength."

"Oh, him. He seemed rather useless, and like he wanted nothing to do with me or my troubles."

"He is a man. Men can be awkward about these things. I am sure he means well."

"Why should I bother to regain strength, anyway? I'm ruined now. Nobody will want me."

"You must not despise yourself. Despise the monster who did all this to you. You know that he's dead, and yet you feel as if he still has power over you. I know. Believe me, I know."

"Narcissus told me you and he wanted to have a child, but Commodus forbade it."

"Forbade it? Is that what he told you?" Junipera hesitated, then decided to plunge ahead. "He must not have been able to speak of it. I never speak of it. Commodus told everyone my baby was born dead, with the cord wrapped around its neck. I never contradicted." She took a large swallow, and began to cry. "He strangled my baby! And the midwife did not live long after. I don't know if he murdered her too."

"Oh!" Langoria gasped. She rose and hugged Junipera tightly. "Oh. And you have been holding this inside you all this time?"

"Yes." She recovered her composure, and looked Langoria in the eye. "But now, I'm alive, and he's dead, and Narcissus and I will have a dozen children, just to spite his ghost."

"If you can bear what you have to bear, then so can I. I feel ashamed now to have spent so much time moping."

"No, you mustn't feel shame. Let the shame be buried with the monster. It is his shame."

Junipera led Langoria to the kitchen, where Narcissus and Castor were having a bite. Castor addressed Langoria tentatively, "I hope that today finds you well?"

"She is still not very well," Junipera answered for her. "What does Cocina say she should do?"

"Cocina says to boil nails in vinegar until they bleed, and to pour the rusty vinegar over turnip or mustard greens. This should restore the lost blood."

"And what prayers should I utter while I do this?" Langoria asked.

"Pray to Vulcan," Castor improvised.

She laughed for the first time in weeks. "Because of the nails, I suppose? Confess. Cocina said nothing about prayers, but I asked, so you made something up." Castor flushed red. "Well, I will pray to Vulcan for your sake."

Tigranos came in. "I'm sorry," he said, "am I interrupting something?"

"Not really," Narcissus replied. "What's the news? I hear you were called to the August One." Narcissus made an automatic little bow.

"He is dismissing me, and banishing me from Rome to some little town."

"Whatever for?" Narcissus was truly shocked. Tigranos had been his contact in the City Cohorts, and he had been the contact in the Palace for Tigranos, for twenty years.

"He was testy about this and that, but basically, he wants his own people in place. Sulpicianus is to be Prefect, with a protegé of his in my position. Motilenus is out, too. Laetus is coming back."

"If I'd known that a few days off duty was all the consequence for killing Commodus, I would have done it years ago."

Castor said, "Well, I did win all the money Laetus had on him."

"So he was punished a little." Narcissus smiled. "With Motilenus demoted, will there be an end to the restrictions on leaving the Palace grounds? That has been odd, and upsetting."

"The August One said nothing about that. You will have to ask Laetus when he comes back."

"I heard that Claudius Pompeianus said all the slaves were to go free. Is that true?"

"It's true that Pompeianus said that. I've seen no sign that the August One agrees."

"And I may never see you again?"

"I'm to be given some post in one of the Latin towns. It's not yet been decided which, so I will not disappear all that quickly. But I don't know if I will ever be asked back to the Palace."

"Then it's time." Narcissus pulled open the leather pouch on his belt, and took out a key. "Take this to Jovialis Rhetor in Nomentum. He knows what it's for." Tigranos took the key and hugged Narcissus in a formal manner, without saying a word.

But to Langoria he said, "I will convey to your brother that you are well."

Chapter 4

Cocina heard Magnus open the door for a runner asking if he was at the house of Senator Tullius. "Yes, this is his house," Magnus confirmed, "but the master is at the Palace today."

"I have a letter for his daughter, Tullia Minor."

"She is here. I will take it to her."

As soon as Magnus latched the door, Cocina berated him. "This is why it is Castor entrusted with watching the door, when he is here. Even Phaeton would do better. He would talk less."

"What have I done wrong now?"

"What haven't you? You should never tell a stranger that the master is not here. What if he works for burglars looking to break into the house, or for enemies plotting an ambush?"

"He was only delivering this letter."

"Did you know that? And whoever he was, it was none of his business if the master is at the Palace. Were you boasting about the master's influence, to make yourself great?" she asked, punning on the name Magnus. "And who are you to take a letter for our mistress? Perhaps it is from someone who shouldn't be corresponding with her. Who is it from?"

"You know I can't read."

"Precisely. So why are you taking her letter? She should decide for herself whether she wants to receive this."

"I am here," said Tullia, coming into the vestibule with Philoxena behind her. "Give it to me." Taking it from Magnus, she broke the seal and said, "Oh, it is from Senator Sempronius!"

"That is excellent," Philoxena said. "Is he courting you now? Let's go sit down in the atrium and read what he has to say."

Cocina was about to tell Philoxena that she ought to let Tullia read her own letter without looking over her shoulder, but Magnus wanted to continue their argument. "Why must you always humiliate me in front of everyone?" he hissed under his breath. "You are not my wife!"

149

"I am the mother of your child, though who would know it from the little attention you ever bother to give her."

"I have kept that secret."

"Secret?" Cocina was baffled. "Everyone knows you are the father. Who else would be?"

"Whoever master shared you with." His previous owner had some female slaves, and naturally shared them with potential customers, and forbade the gladiators from touching any of them. It would never occur to Magnus that he was insulting either Cocina or Tullius by his assumption that similar things happened here.

"How long have you been in this house now, six years? And you have no understanding? There is only one reason you were brought here at all."

"Because of my skills as a swordsman, and so that I could teach Castor."

"Your skills did not commend you. Master wanted me to have children, so he bought me a man. I wish he could have gotten me more of a man, but it was kindly meant."

"I thought you were seducing me behind his back. When you were with child, the master asked if I was the father, and I denied it."

"You foolish, foolish man. There is only one reason why he would have asked." The sound of a carriage approaching could be heard outside, so she dropped the conversation. "That will be Castor bringing him home. I must begin making supper."

In the atrium, Tullia read her letter out loud to Philoxena. "My dearest Lady Tullia, I wish to hold a pageant for the young men and women of Rome, in honor of the Carmentalia, on the second day before the Ides, in the Lateran fields. I should be honored if you would come, but beyond that I have a further favor to ask. I know many respectable young men whom I wish to invite, but alas, I do not know so many young women. Would you be so kind as to help me assemble my guest list? Any friend of yours I should be pleased to be allowed to consider a friend of mine. Please let me know as soon as you can what friends should be invited."

Philoxena found this very exciting. "He called you his lady! And he shows a great deal of trust in you. I think he has his eye on you."

"Or perhaps he just means what he says and wants some help putting together his pageant. Should we invite Popilia?"

"Certainly not! She is betrothed, so we could not invite her without inviting Laetus, and the Praetorian Prefect would be an intimidating guest. Besides, the whole purpose, unless I misread the Senator utterly, is to invite the unattached."

"What about Julia Aniciana?"

"Yes! She must be at the head of the list. Her mother is a favorite of Lady Titiana!"

"Most of the girls I really like are not that highly connected."

"And that is good too. I am sure that Senator Sempronius is also inviting young men who are quite likable but have not yet made the right connections."

"Should we ask if we can invite Alexandrius? Father did say we still owe him, and he was so pleasant when he came." When Alexandrius drove the chariot over to retrieve his own carriage, he had stayed for some of Cocina's pork pies from her own variation of her great-aunt's famous recipe.

"The Senator has no shortage of young men, he says, but you are right that we should consider him. In the case of young men, though, it is also necessary to consider whether his politics agree with those of Sempronius or not. We may wish to do Alexandrius a favor, but does he? Do you know if Sempronius has ever favored or disfavored the career of Pescennius Niger? And what other senior figures are patrons of Alexandrius?"

"He said that his family owes much to Clodius Albinus."

"I cannot know if Sempronius would view that favorably or disfavorably. The Senate condemned him, but that was before, and I hear that he has many friends. You must ask your father."

"Ask me what?" said Tullius, who was coming in with Castor.

"Dearest of fathers, I am so glad you are home!" She rose to give him a hug, as ever. "The question is, is Senator Sempronius a friend or an enemy of Clodius Albinus?"

151

"Taking an interest in politics? You really are growing up! To answer your question, I only know that Sempronius said on the floor of the Senate that Pertinax Caesar ought not have been made Emperor before the views of Clodius Albinus were consulted."

"Is Sempronius an enemy of the August One, then?" Tullia sounded shocked.

"On the contrary, in fact, Pertinax made Clarus a Consul because he is a friend of Sempronius, having risen as a protegé of his father."

Chapter 5

The river cruise down the Icauna would certainly have been more pleasant during the summer months, but Junius Severus thought the men appreciated the break from marching nonetheless. The mules and carts did not last long past Massilia. They only slowed down the pace, and Junius gave the locals some good bargains in his haste to dispose of them and turn them into coin. Where the road touched the headwaters of the Icauna, between Cabilonnum and Augustobona, it was necessary to board rafts which were poled down the shallows until the river became deep enough for more substantial boats. The boatman said it was lucky that there was no hard freeze this year. Two days of chilly drizzle were the worst they had to endure.

Junius did not ride in the boats himself, for Bucephalus could never have been coaxed aboard. Any pretense that Bucephalus was to be the centurion's horse had long since been abandoned, and Junius enjoyed trotting downstream at a reasonable pace, and taking many side trips. The route was through good wine country, and Junius had plenty of coin left over to stock up. The usually taciturn centurion commented that he had once been so unfortunate as to serve under Pescennius Niger, who hardly ever allowed the men to drink. Junius did not dole out large rations of drink to the men, but what he did give them was appreciated.

He rode into the post station at Lutetia ahead of the men. The postmaster, Faustus Parisius, was from a locally-prominent Gaulish family who had held citizenship since Claudius Caesar, and therefore pretended to be entirely Roman. Junius handed him an introductory letter from Quintus Curtius. It said that the unnamed bearer was a friend, and that Quintus would consider it a favor if Faustus would tell him any intelligence he needed to know, and not divulge to any others that he was travelling through Lutetia. Faustus said, "This is all very interesting, but I still must see your diploma." He noted the hesitancy with which Junius turned it over, and expected to find that the diploma did not authorize nearly the level of co-operation Quintus was requesting for him. He was surprised to find instead that the diploma called for limitless support, and then discovered the coded phrases at the end. "How did you arrive here from Massilia? Isn't Lutetia a little out of your way?"

"We hired boats to take us down the Icauna to the Sequana."

"You are entitled to reimbursement for that."

"That is not necessary. Quintus Curtius made certain that we had the money to pay for it."

"Very interesting, but still, if your boatman will sign a receipt the government will pay. Who did you hire?"

"Badogorus, I think the name was."

"Boudogur? I know him. He can write his name, if nothing more. He deals with enough merchants, and with us too, from time to time. I will write up something simple for him to sign. You can fill in how many men he transported and what he charged you."

"I really do not need the money."

"Then do you mind if I have it? Really, when the government is as eager to give away money as this paper indicates," pointing to the diploma, "it would be a shame if no-one took it. It will be our little secret, since you wish us to share secrets. Do this, and I will tell you two very valuable pieces of news."

The centurion arrived, and Junius asked if the men were finished unloading the boats. They were not, so Junius told him to hurry back with the paper Faustus had scribbled, and get Boudogur, or whatever his name was, to put his name to it before he disappeared elsewhere. Faustus gave the men directions to what he commended as an excellent brothel in town, run by a cousin of his. "The women are clean, and reasonably priced. The cheap food is good enough, and the pricier food is exquisite if you have the coin, although I would not recommend the wine. I think they put lead in it, for extra stupefaction. Mention that I sent you, and he may cut you some deals." And kick back a cut to Faustus, Junius assumed.

When the centurion returned with the receipt, and left Faustus and Junius alone again, Faustus said, "I expect you will be interested to know that Clodius Albinus has crossed over, and is encamped above Samar

Bridge, at the intersection of both the roads toward the Channel, the one from here as well as the one from Durocort."

"What makes you think that I have an especial interest in Clodius Albinus?"

"Just a hunch. Do you know that your diploma tells every postmaster who sees it, in words that others would not catch the meaning of, that you are on a mission for Commodus Caesar personally?"

"I did not know that this was known to others, but yes, the August One chose me."

"Then you should be very interested to know that Commodus Caesar is dead. He has been dead since the first of the year, in fact. Everyone will know of this soon enough, but I always know of these things sooner than others around these parts."

"You did not lie when you said that you had valuable news."

"I never lie about something like that."

Chapter 6

Narcissus informed Eclectus that Clemens wished to speak to him. Eclectus had to ask, "Who?"

"He brings the fodder for the horses, and takes it away again when the horses have converted it to something else."

Of course Eclectus knew who that was, although he would never have thought to converse with him, or bothered to learn his name. Eclectus did recall that he had come on the fateful New Year's Day, but so much else had happened that day. It had not occurred to him to draw any connection to Marcia's disappearance. He was surprised, and rather taken aback, when Clemens whispered to him, "Marcia wishes to know whether you regard her as your wife."

At once Eclectus understood that Clemens must have been the one to smuggle her out of the Palace. But there was much else that he could not understand. Why would she use a man of such low estate as a messenger for such an intimate question, and why was the question so oddly phrased? It seemed that she was not asking whether they should become husband and wife, but whether they already were so. That was an intriguing thought. After all the years they had served together, first in the house of Quadratus and then in the Palace, were they not closer than most married couples he had seen? He wished he could be discussing this with Marcia face to face. To Clemens he managed to respond, "Tell her that she has no need to stay in hiding. The August One himself assured me so."

Clemens bowed slightly, and returned to his work, evidently satisfied to take this reply back. Eclectus had much to ponder, and paced aimlessly around the halls. If Marcia abruptly appeared at the gates of the Palace, would that really be as safe as he had just told Clemens to imply to her? Unless she were married, there was no possible place for her in the Palace. Either Eclectus married her at once, or she would have to make a new life for herself somewhere else, perhaps far away, and Eclectus would seldom or never see her again. That thought was nearly unbearable. But even if they did marry, would the situation be awkward? Pertinax might wish to avoid any association at all with the mistress of Commodus. And what about Titiana? How would she react? Eclectus went back to the stables, thinking to tell Clemens some more words to carry back to Marcia, words of caution. But he was already gone.

Eclectus resolved that he must bring up the matter with both the Emperor and his wife, and soon. Fortunately they were dining alone that night. Marcus Aurelius and Commodus had in common the habit of inviting several guests almost every evening, although the kinds of company the two chose could hardly have been more unlike. Pertinax, it could already be seen, would be different. He had not invited any men to his table so far, and seldom ever would, and when he did, he would not serve the extravagant multi-course meals that had become the custom. Some said it was because he was cheap. Perhaps that was part of it, but Eclectus understood that Pertinax was simply not a man who much enjoyed conversation. Titiana returned to their old house many evenings to dine with her friends, but was at the Palace tonight. Eclectus shooed away all other servitors, to wait upon them himself.

When they were nearly finished, Eclectus found the courage to say, "I beg permission to speak on a matter of some delicacy." He hesitated.

"Well, spit it out then," Titiana prodded him.

"I wish to marry, but would not dream of doing so without the permission of both of you."

"That is wonderful news," Titiana burbled, batting her kohl-painted eyes animatedly. "Who is the lucky woman?"

"I wish to marry Marcia."

"Oh, I see." Titiana's enthusiasm disappeared at once, but she did not veto the idea. "I suppose it is past time that someone made an honest woman out of her. If you can put up with the inevitable unpleasant rumors, that is your own affair."

"I would think," Pertinax put in, "that it would rather tend to settle down the rumors which her disappearance has stirred up."

"How little you know of the gossips in this city! Some have long said, though I would not wish to mention any names, that Marcia was never faithful to Commodus even when she was his kept woman. And now they will be certain that she cheated, and with whom. Can you bear it, Eclectus, that some will be saying you have slept with Marcia already? Of course," she added, "I know that to be slander."

Eclectus knew, of course, that it would not entirely be slander. "My Lady, if I only have your good opinion, and that of the August One, what should I care for the opinions of any other?"

"That is quite the right attitude," Titiana agreed. "Well, if you want her, though I cannot imagine why, it would be best for you to marry her at once." Eclectus bowed, unable to utter the gratitude and relief he felt at how smoothly this went.

"There will be another wedding soon," Pertinax slipped in casually. "Cornificia wishes to marry Didius Marinus." Cornificia was a sister of Commodus, living in dignified widowhood since her brother executed her husband and her children for plotting against him. She accepted the losses with Stoicism, and invited philosophers, poets, and men of learning to her salons. Her house on the Capitoline, nestled among all the great temples, was regarded as the stateliest in Rome, possibly not even excepting the imperial residence itself.

"Why him? She could do so much better." Didius Marinus was from a family of naval officers, once common sailors, who had adopted the family name of their nobler patrons, the *gens Didia*. As a protegé of Didius Julianus, Marinus had served ably in several important posts, but was only of equestrian rank. Naturally Titiana thought first in terms of the difference in social stature, rather than of any other qualities he might have. "The rumormongers will all say that he is only out for her money."

"She is not at all the kind who worries about rumors," Pertinax observed. "And I doubt whether she could, in fact, do better. A Senator might find her a dangerous match."

"Then why should she re-marry at all? It is not as if there were any hope of replacing her children, not at her age." Eclectus wondered whether there was any such thing as "replacing" lost children, but Titiana did not seem to care much about her own. "Well, at least she shan't be running off to Africa with Eclectus." That was a reference to Sabina, another sister whose husband Commodus had executed. Sabina had not taken it as well as Cornificia, perhaps because her husband, unlike Cornificia's, had not even done anything. Commodus kept her locked up in the Palace, with daily screaming matches, until Agaclytus, the previous majordomo, smuggled her out and vanished with her. He was the son of a freedman, also named Agaclytus, whom Lucius Verus promoted to equestrian rank and married to a noblewoman with connections to the imperial family. This was all very much against the wishes of Marcus Aurelius, who refused to attend the wedding and dismissed him from service as soon as Lucius Verus was dead. The junior Agaclytus grew up to befriend Commodus, and never failed to pour poison into his ear about Marcus Aurelius. He was blamed by many as one of the worst of the bad influences who turned Commodus down dark paths.

Agaclytus never lost the knack of playing Commodus. From their hiding place he sent an unctuous letter, saying that he had only acted, at great personal sacrifice, out of distress to see the noble family of the August One torn by dissension, and that he hoped the August One would be happier now. Once Commodus let it be known that he would forgive and forget, Agaclytus and Sabina began living openly in Africa as husband and wife, but continued to find excuses for declining any invitation to return to Roma. Eclectus was not happy to be reminded of the circumstances under which he had obtained his position. Most people in Roma had forgotten about Sabina. But Titiana would nurse every reminder that the recent imperial family had not displayed the same Roman virtues as her own. "That was a scandal and a disgrace!" she added for emphasis.

"Cornificia is quite concerned to avoid any appearance of scandal, even after Pompeianus gave his assent." As the second husband of Lucilla, the senior sister of Commodus and widow of Lucius Verus, Claudius Pompeianus was regarded as an heir to Marcus Aurelius equally with Commodus. But he repeatedly and pointedly refused any suggestions that he try to share power, which is doubtless why in that case it was Lucilla who was executed and Pompeianus who remained alive. He was now treated as the official head of what remained of the family. "She told him that she wanted to make sure of having my assent as well. So I was invited to come and meet with her and Marinus to discuss it."

"Why did you not tell me this before?" Titiana asked indignantly. "I made such a fool of myself with Lady Anicia! She told me that there was a vile rumor going about, that you had been seen going to Cornificia's house on the Capitoline. I assured her that it must be a slander."

"It was true, but nobody could say that there was anything improper about it."

"That wretch Falco could! He is the one who spreads these stories. Lady Anicia told me so. You see, husband, what a grave mistake it was to go to another woman's house, without me."

"You were not here. I did send to ask if you were available, but that impudent servant said you were far too busy preparing for another concert by Citharius." Apollos Citharius was one of the great musicians of the day. He was a frequent performer at Titiana's soirées. "It would help if you taught your staff to have proper respect for me." Eclectus had worried that Pertinax might bring in his own household's majordomo to run the Palace, but his job was quite safe. That household answered only to Titiana, and Pertinax was scarcely on speaking terms with them, even if he was the August One now.

"Or it would help if you let me invite my friends here. Or if you attended yourself when we all get together. Do you know that Falco has even put out a rumor that there is something improper about my relationship with Citharius? Anicia tells me everything that is being said. She is such a good friend!" Eclectus did not think that it sounded as if Lady Anicia were any kind of friend at all, but he held his tongue. "Husband, you absolutely must get rid of that Falco. He does nothing but scheme against us."

"He is a Consul."

"And you are the Emperor!"

"That can be an awkward relationship. You will recall what an unhappy time it was when I served as Consul under the man that we forget." It was no longer appropriate to speak the name of Commodus. "We were always being accused of undermining him."

"If you had done anything like what this vile Falco does, you would not be alive now."

"I do not intend to emulate him in that regard. Quite the contrary, I wish to do undo what he did. He weakened our State, by making officials afraid to carry out responsibilities, lest they be seen to be assuming power. Naturally Falco fears that I will not allow him any power. He thinks that the only way to strengthen his position is to weaken mine. But I intend to show him that I understand how important it is to the health of the Roman constitution for the ancient offices to regain their former dignity." He was slipping into his pontificating mode. "I shall allow him authority within his proper scope. The Consulate must no longer be a mere vain title, and he shall come to understand that I mean this."

Titiana, distinctly unimpressed, asked, "What is the use of being Emperor, if you cannot even execute someone when you need to?"

Chapter 7

Roman camps, whether small or large, temporary or permanent, were always laid out according to the same general plan. The perimeter was a square, aligned to the cardinal points with the main gate facing east, unless the terrain dictated otherwise. Even the small party led by Junius Severus lugged a hand-cart full of sharpened stakes to set up, every night, a picket fence that could at least keep out animals. The principal way would be scratched into the dirt across the middle of the square from the dextrous gate, which might be just a watchman's post and not a functional entry, to the sinistrous gate, leading to the latrines. In the center would be a praetorian tent or building, housing the commanding officers. From there to the main gate, the praetorian way ran at right angles to the principal way. This path did not continue all the way across the square, but there might be a partial path from the rear gate, used for hauling in supplies or at least the day's water. Foodstuffs, arms, and the like were housed in the rear half of the square, along with horses or other animals. In the front quadrants, a large permanent camp would sprout buildings, like a shrine to the gods, a bathhouse, and a gymnasium. In the temporary camps of a unit on the move, each tentful had an assigned place. A soldier who was sent out to reconnoitre when the unit broke camp at dawn, and did not rejoin the unit at its new site until late at night, could find his proper place blindfolded.

The men Clodius brought had had time to improve their bivouac. The wooden walls were solid, and surrounded by a ditch. A trench was dug from the latrine pits to a sufficiently adequate stream. Further uphill, a well was dug. Still, it was not so large a camp that Clodius and Servilius would have any difficulty clearly seeing and hearing the sentry at the main gate challenging a horseman as he galloped up. It was evening, not yet fully dark. They were seated on camp stools by a fire, just across the principal way from the praetorian tent. Servilius was stirring a pot of beans. "That might be the advance man for the Belgic troops," he said hopefully.

"Far too soon for that, I am afraid. He has found us." Clodius shouted at the sentry, "Send him over here at once!"

"The surrounding woods are sacred to the Gaulish Diana. Let us pray to that Lady for her assistance." Servilius dribbled some beans into the fire, a meager offering but the best he had, and set the pot down. He raised his hands and eyes heavenward, and whispered praises to her holy name, and curses against Commodus Caesar.

Clodius did not join in this. He watched the newcomer walk his fine stallion up the praetorian way, and tether him to a tent-stake. Bucephalus could easily have pulled out the stake and brought the whole tent down, but understood that he was to stay. "Are you Governor Decimus Clodius Albinus of Britannia?" Junius asked with a polite bow.

Clodius replied, "I am he. You are Junius Severus. I knew your father. He was an excellent man. And you are a brave man, to come right into the middle of my camp with no guard at all. You must be carrying three sealed letters in your saddlebags, besides the diploma commanding all postmasters to assist you on your travels."

"You must be a soothsayer. But the letters are not so meaningful now, in view of the news."

"What news is that?"

"You have not heard? Commodus is dead."

"I have already heard that rumor, to my sorrow."

"But this time it is true. The postmaster at Lutetia told me. Pertinax is now the Emperor."

Servilius clapped his hands with glee. "You see? And you doubt the efficacy of prayer!"

Clodius pointed out, "Commodus must have died some time ago, so that could hardly be in answer to your prayer just now."

"Lady Diana must have known that I would make this prayer, and answered it in advance?" But even he himself did not sound convinced by this argument.

Clodius rose and embraced Junius. "You bring us such relief! I wish we had more hospitality to offer you than some beans and stale beer."

"I have a wineskin in my saddlebags."

"I knew that I was going to like you, the moment I set eyes on you!"

Junius fetched the wine, and gave it to Clodius, who took a slug and passed it to Servilius, who poured a bit on the ground as a thank-offering before drinking. Junius returned to his saddlebags and fetched out three scrolls, variously adorned with wax seals and ribbons. "And here are the letters. This one, I was ordered to give into the hands of Clodius Albinus and no other." He passed it over. "There, now I have fulfilled my mission."

Clodius did not even bother to open it. "It says that I am to go to Roma and explain myself." He tossed it into the fire.

"And will you go to Roma?"

"Perhaps. Pertinax will want to adopt a successor, and I might want to offer myself. Except that I would have to divorce Plautilla, and marry his daughter. That would be a pity. We get along so much better now that we hardly see each other." Plautilla had recently borne him another son, years after they had pretty much given up on having any more children. The daughters were married off long ago.

Servilius asked, "But doesn't Pertinax have a son also? Wouldn't his son be the successor?"

"His son is a congenital idiot. I know that idiocy has never been a bar to the imperial throne, but if I know Pertinax, he will want a kinder fate for his son than the role of a puppet to conniving men."

"If you are not outright refusing to go to Roma..." Junius tossed another scroll into the fire. "That one I was to open, if you would not take the first one from me, or defied what it said."

"A warrant for my arrest, I presume? And authorization to commandeer troops for the purpose, if I would not come quietly?"

"I would presume so as well. But nobody actually told me anything, besides my orders. And this one..." He held up the last and most ribbon-bedecked scroll, ready to toss it to the flames. Clodius grabbed his wrist to stop him.

"Wait! Are you mad? Do you not know what that is?"

"I know that I was ordered to open it the moment I set foot in Britannia. But I do not want to do that to you anymore." Junius wriggled his hand

164

free, and tossed the scroll into the fire. Servilius rose, bowed very low to Junius, and handed him the wineskin. The three stood and watched the fire blaze up, as the wax and the parchment fed it.

Clodius broke the silence. "My dear boy, governorships do not come along every day. Especially not the governorship of such a prestigious province. And they are not offered so early in a man's career very often. Someone must think very highly of you."

"Or rather, they thought that I would look harmless, so that no-one would stop me from getting to Londinium." Junius took a brush from the saddlebags and began gently grooming Bucephalus. "It is more than I can understand why this appointment was given to me. I do not know, really, how highly anyone thinks of me."

"Well, they cannot think more highly of you than I do. I shall do whatever I can to make this up to you. Governor Valerius Placidius of Gallia Belgica is to rendezvous with us. I did not tell him the purpose, but it was in the hope that he would bring enough men to intimidate you." He laughed. "I shall insist that he make you his deputy, and recommend you to be Governor after him. Now you should know that Gallia Belgica is rather an unusual province. There are the cantonments, where Gaulish chieftains still have autonomy. There are the supply bases, answerable to the generals in Upper and Lower Germania. Indeed, supporting the Rhine legions is the main purpose of holding the province at all. The post calls for diplomacy, not merely command. I think it will suit a man of your talents quite well."

"But perhaps this Governor Placidius will have a different man in mind."

"I have been his patron for many years, and he owes his governorship to me, so he can scarcely refuse me anything."

Chapter 8

Senator Tullius had a fine clock, imported from the same workshop in Alexandria that made the one Pescennius Niger kept in his office. But Tullius did not prize it very much. He kept it in the slaves' quarters, next to the bed, a heap of sacking really, where Magnus slept. Every evening as he went to sleep, Magnus set the chime to ring at midnight. And every midnight, he awoke before the chime went off, and disabled the alarm lest it disturb anyone else in the household. He was proud that the clock had never yet caught him dozing. Castor had the first shift watching the door at night, and Magnus would relieve him until dawn. Magnus always kept the clock refilled with water, and sometimes adjusted its pointer, although no-one but he ever consulted it. He believed that there was a numen in the clock, which might feel neglected, as he so often felt. He made another offering of clean water to his little deity, and asked "Is it time?"

Ordinarily he relieved Castor with no more than a silent nod, but this time Magnus asked, "Can I talk to you?" At Castor's shrug, he said, "I need to know. And I can't ask the master. Why am I here?"

Castor hoped that he did not mean anything deep and philosophical by that. "You're relieving me as watchman."

"I mean, what use am I in this house?"

"You're a second guard if needed. There's been no trouble at the house in years, but you can't be too careful these days."

"Did you know that I am the father of Cocinilla?"

This puzzled Castor. "Of course. I'm not, and the master doesn't do that kind of thing. Who else would be?"

"Some guest that the master lent her to?"

"The master most certainly doesn't do... that kind of thing."

"Cocina was not a virgin when I took her."

Castor shrugged. "She gets out a lot, and she is an attractive woman." He and Cocina had grown up together, and he thought of her like a sister, but he was not blind.

"Is that the reason I was bought? Just to be a mate for her?"

"I wouldn't know the reason. I wasn't asked for advice when master purchased you."

"When Cocina was pregnant, master asked if I was the father, and I denied it."

"You must never lie to master!" Not telling master everything was a different matter.

"Cocina said to me that she could only think of one reason why master would even ask. Do you know what she meant?"

"If you acknowledged the child, he might've freed you and her before the birth. It makes all the difference in the world to a boy's prospects whether he is freeborn or freed later. Do you think Pertinax Caesar would be where he is, if he'd been born before his father was free?"

Magnus sighed. "I've made a real mess of things, haven't I?"

Castor shrugged again. "The child turned out to be a girl, so it made no difference."

"I'm not likely to get her with child again, now that she hates me."

"She just wishes you'd be more attentive."

"She doesn't want my attentions."

"Attentive to the little girl, I mean. Don't you understand anything at all about women?"

"Not much, I'm afraid." When would he have learned, after all? "I have failed the master's purpose for me. Will he sell me away?"

Castor made the sign of the fig against such an unlucky thought. "Of course not! What even put such a thing into your head?"

"When I took Cocina to the market, I saw a man I knew from Lanuvium." Commodus had turned the imperial summer home in the Alban hills into a school for gladiators. His former master had paid five gold to send Magnus there. "He told me all the gladiators are on the auction block. A buyer from Vindabona is likely to snap them all up. Do you know about that place? The fighters call it Vendamala." The pun meant "bad sale." The province of Noricum was not too far northeast of Italy, yet it might as well have been at the end of the world. Even in the capital there was little to do. So fights were staged frequently, to give the soldiers and the locals some meager entertainment. Few gladiators sent to Vindabona ever returned, and even fewer returned with any good memories of the place.

"So thank Lady Fortuna that no such thing is happening to you!" Fortuna was Castor's favored deity. "Look, you are trusted to wear a sword. Do you know how many houses there are where a freedwoman has to come in and cook, because the masters are afraid to let a slave near a sharp knife? Where the slaves are hairy and bearded, because they can't have a razor?" Like most men who actually fought, Castor and Magnus kept their hair close-cropped and chins clean, to leave nothing for an enemy to grab. Toffs now tended to affect beards, precisely to show that they had no need to fight hand-to-hand, much as many ladies grew long fingernails, to show that they did no work. Tullius was only in the army briefly, but still favored the trim look. "You don't appreciate how lucky you are."

"I can't help but worry."

"Forget it. The Tullies haven't sold a slave in living memory. They seem to think that it is bad luck or something."

Magnus knew that the master, like many aging men, or even some who were not so aged, often awoke in the middle of the night. But Magnus did not know that the master had crept into the kitchen for some leftovers from supper, and into the atrium to sit down and eat them, all without a torch since he knew every inch of the house. Castor, as soon as the conversation with Magnus wound down, walked through the atrium on the way to his bed. He saw the Senator sitting there, munching on some of Cocina's excellent pork pie, but rather than greet the master as he usually would, any time that he encountered the Senator after even a brief time apart, he only gave a wordless bow.

Castor didn't want Magnus to know that the Senator had probably overheard most of their conversation.

<u>Chapter 9</u>

It was not quite true, Marcus Tullius Secundus reflected, that the *gens Tullia* had not sold a slave in living memory. He thought back to his childhood. He must have been only six or seven years old when Ceionius Commodus came to visit. That was in the old house, of course, which passed to Tullius Primus. Secundus sold it after Primus died, finding the artwork Primus had put up to be too graphic for his taste, but not wishing to destroy it. Sometimes he did miss the old house, and now he wondered what had ever become of the little toy that Ceionius gave him, a carved horse on wheels. How he used to love playing with it, setting his toy soldiers on its back, as a boy! Ceionius was a jolly man, fond of children, laughter, food, and drink. He had just been named Hadrian's heir, and given a new name "Aelius Caesar" that he hardly ever used. The previously intended heir, it seems, was a little too happy to hear that Hadrian took ill, and not at all happy to hear that Hadrian recovered, and so had to die.

Smaragda cooked the feast. She and her brother were captured in a retaliatory raid after some Hibernians raided a Roman settlement in Britain. No name for her brother was ever settled upon, so he remained just "Hibernius" all the rest of his days. But she was named for the emerald, because of her amazing green eyes. Her skills in the kitchen were also amazing. Ceionius insisted on meeting the cook after he tasted her pies, of honey cake, pheasant, gamy boar-ham, and sweet udder-sausage, a recipe that he would claim credit for, when he served it to the August One. And after only one look into her eyes, he was smitten. He asked to purchase her, and how could the imperial heir be refused?

His wife, Avidia Plautia, did not accept the situation. Most wives of noble Romans had to reconcile themselves to the knowledge that their husbands had other women, but discretion was expected. For him to flaunt his affections the way he did was an intolerably public loss of face for Avidia. She demanded that he get rid of Smaragda. He refused. She began to snipe at him constantly, even at gatherings full of prominent people. Now it was his turn to find the public loss of face intolerable. He forced her into a divorce, but wanted that kept quiet until Hadrian was safely dead. The financial settlement was generous, but did nothing at all to appease her anger.

Since he was giving Avidia their house in Rome, he bought another from a Senator Vectilius who was in financial difficulties. Unusually, Secundus and some other youngsters were invited to the housewarming party. Ceionius was describing it as an informal get-together of the families, perhaps as an excuse for not inviting the August One. His father warned Secundus not to mention Avidia's absence, which he would never have thought of doing anyway. Smaragda circulated among the guests. It was not until much later that Secundus understood how strange that was. She said that she was glad to see him, but seemed worried and distracted. Secundus got a bloody nose from telling one of the Sempronius boys that it was very wrong to call Smaragda a whore. He had to tell his father that he had bumped into a table. He had never lied to his father before. Their host got roaring drunk, and said some unfortunate things, indicating that he knew what some of the guests were saying behind his back.

The August One, who had spies everywhere, must have heard about this surreptitious party. He dispatched Ceionius to a tour of duty on the Danube as Governor of the Pannonias, although Ceionius was one of the least military men in all of Rome. He returned at the end of the year, looking very ill, and promptly died. Given how poorly he had always taken care of his health, it was probably natural. Then again, given his rank and how many people resented his elevation, it might not have been. It was said that he had taken a large dose of strong medicine just before he collapsed, and someone might have put something in it. But nobody inquired too closely, or even indulged in the usual Roman sport of finger-pointing. The question of who would be the successor now was far more interesting. Ceionius had lost his elder son, and had no son-in-law. Negotiations with suitors for the hand of his daughter Fabia had been interrupted by the Pannonian trip. He left a seven-year-old son Lucius, eventually known as Lucius Verus after his name and status changed multiple times. But Hadrian knew that he was not going to live long enough to see the boy grow up.

Some remarked that it would have been easier if Hadrian could just have impregnated his wife. They might not have thought so, if they could have lived to see what a boy raised from birth to be Emperor would turn out like. Hadrian would rather have remained married to Antinoos all his life, but that poor boy died young. He married a grand-niece of Trajan's for form's sake. He did value his wife's learning and advice, and never got rid of her despite her tendency to curl up in bed with a good author. He even seemed genuinely sad at her funeral. But his preference was always for the male gender.

Hadrian cast his own horoscope every morning, and one day it told him to expect to see an omen. He saw Antoninus, a nephew-in-law of his late wife, helping an old man up the stairs. He took it as a sign that Antoninus would help him become deified after his death, something that was not done for every Emperor and which not many felt inclined to do for him. So he nicknamed Antoninus "the pious" and asked him to be the heir. Antoninus did not want the throne at all, which was his best qualification. As Emperor he would let the Governors handle their own provinces and Consuls run the city, without interference, while he devoted himself to reforming the legal system. Antoninus had lost both his sons, but was in the process of betrothing his wife's nephew Marcus Aurelius to his daughter Faustina and adopting him as heir. Hadrian believed that such first-cousin marriages raised the danger of monstrous children, and thought it unfair to cut Lucius out. He insisted that Antoninus make Lucius his son-in-law and heir instead. Marcus Aurelius was to marry Fabia, leaving him in an ambiguous position which he resented Hadrian for creating. Little Lucius was presented to the Senate, and charmed them all by asking that they erect multiple statues of his mother. How could they refuse him?

Hadrian declared that he could now die happy. On the day that his horoscope told him to expect death, he was annoyed to still be breathing at nightfall. So he attempted suicide, but Antoninus Pius stopped him.

No matter, he died soon enough. Antoninus married Faustina to Marcus Aurelius as originally planned, not wishing her to have a husband younger than she was. Lucius was promised the first of their daughters, since it would not at all be unusual for the wife to be younger. Poor Fabia was left out in the cold, and never stopped accusing Faustina of adulteries, hoping that Marcus would divorce, and come back to her. It was taken for granted that Marcus would succeed Antoninus, and that Lucius Verus would have to wait his turn. But when that time came, Marcus insisted that Lucius was his brother, and made the Senate confer the title of Augustus on him too. The army was paid twenty per man, instead of ten as usual, to swear their oath of loyalty to both of them. That was an unfortunate precedent.

For his first act as co-Emperor, Lucius Verus commissioned more statues of Avidia, with inscriptions detailing her matronly virtues. By that time, it was widely understood that this was a backhanded slap against the memory of his late father. But Lucius Verus never treated Smaragda cruelly, even if he never let her near any food that he would personally eat. Avidia had always told him that she thought Smaragda had been imposed upon. And Smaragda's son Achilles was not treated too badly either, though a single glance at his face was enough to confirm his paternity, for anyone who knew the story. Those who did not know sometimes speculated that he was Fabia's son, and that this indiscretion was why Marcus Aurelius wouldn't have her, and why she kept pointing fingers at others. True, the name "Achilles" that was imposed on him was the sort of name only given to a slave, but he was never made to perform any kind of service in particular, and he was given a very generous peculiar account. However, when at thirteen he precociously got one of the maids pregnant, he was ordered never to see her again. After that he followed his father's path of heavy drinking, which cut short his life. Few knew that Narcissus was his son. Narcissus did not continue the Ceionian family resemblance. He was prettier, taking after Smaragda more, Tullius thought. But when Marcus Aurelius, ever conscious of history, gave him that name "Narcissus" he may have been intending more than just an imputation of vanity. Narcissus was the name of a servant of Claudius Caesar who was given his freedom and eventually a great deal of responsibility. Of course, that first Narcissus came to a bad end under Nero, but was not remembered any the worse for that.

Senator Tullius shook his head. That was an unfortunate affair, all around. Loath though he was to criticize his father, he had to consider Smaragda's sale a bad mistake. Slaves should be taught Roman ways and prepared for freedom, perhaps even rank in subsequent generations. But not from slave to empress in one leap, if that was what Ceionius thought he could pull off! No, it should be by gradual degrees. His own ancestor, Servius Tullius, had become King, the builder of Roma's walls and of the Tullian Hole, its oldest prison. Some tale-tellers wanted to give noble or even divine ancestry to Servius Tullius, but that first name of his said otherwise. The family tradition was that his grandfather had been freed by the earlier King Tullus Hostilius, and given responsibilities. Of course that grandfather would not himself have been considered for the kingship, but his freeborn descendants could be. That was the ancient and proper path. It was one thing to send a slave who did not work out in the household away to the estates to work in the fields, but to sell one, that was quite another thing altogether.

No, that was not the sort of business a Tullius should be engaged in.

Chapter 10

"This is an intriguing object indeed," Fulminatus Rhetor said, trying to buy time while he studied it. He had to appear as if he were an expert. It was a statuette about twice the length of his hand, of hammered silver, depicting a female figure with her arms in front of her, the right hand holding a scepter and the left a bowl. The left side was hinged, but on the right side prongs curved out from one set of slots and back into another set of slots, holding it closed. Under these prongs ran a line of multi-colored sealing wax. In the base was a keyhole, but aside from whatever pin-and-tumbler locking system was inside, the image was hollow, to judge by its light weight. Something blocky rattled in the head when he shook it.

"I'm told it's very valuable," said the potential client, who would not give his name.

"It is intended to be presented to the Vestal Virgins," the Rhetor ventured. The scepter and bowl indicated that it was the goddess Vesta who was depicted. "It is to be opened only in their presence." The sealing wax was an odd touch. Evidently it was not permissible to open this lockbox, even with the key, until the proper time. "It contains the seal-stone of a man who left valuables or documents with them." That would be the best guess about the object concealed in the head. The Temple of Vesta was a repository for wills especially, but other things might be left in their charge. The Virgins were of course absolutely trustworthy, and no-one would dare to attack their Temple. The very existence of Roma, it was believed, depended on the sacred hearth of Vesta. "Whose seal is it?"

"That's what we want you to find out." He gave no indication of who "we" might be.

"Then open it, if you are so curious. But if you break the seal, the Vestals may no longer accept it. Do you have the key?"

"I don't," the client confessed.

Of course not, he thought. "How did this come to be in your possession?"

"I'm not at liberty to say."

Fulminatus was beginning to lose patience. "I am not sure what you want me to do for you."

"Maybe you know someone who could pick the lock, and gently remove the wax strip whole, so that it can be stuck back on."

Fulminatus did of course know several people who were talented at picking locks, but he was offended anyway. "If you are looking to hire a criminal, you need not have come to me."

"But I'll need legal assistance to make my claim. Whoever is now holding the property that I'm entitled to, he won't give it up without a fight."

"And which property is it that you think you are entitled to?"

"That's what we have to find out."

"Which of your relatives owned large properties that they might have left to you?"

"I'm not sure."

"You have so many wealthy relatives, who all love you so dearly, that any one of them might have slipped this under your pillow while you were sleeping? And you don't even have a guess as to which one it might be?"

"I... I don't really know for sure who my family is, or might be."

"Oh? Let me guess. You were found floating down the river in a basket, and were raised by kindly cottage folk. They have always been sure that you are really a prince." There was no response to this. "Who are you? What is your name?"

"I'd rather that my name not be known. I have enemies."

Of course, Fulminatus thought to himself. The hidden prince always has a wicked uncle who is looking to kill him. But aloud he said, "My career as a lawyer depends upon my reputation for discretion. Whether I take your case or not, I would never disclose anything that I learn from you, to anyone else, without your consent."

"Some call me Mercurius," he relented.

That did not exactly sound like the name of a great Senator's heir. "That is better. But you must understand that I am most unlikely to take your case, unless I start hearing something from you that makes a little sense."

"I can pay you well." Mercurius slapped down a coin-pouch of fine whitened leather, closed with a large seal of red wax, onto the desk. It made a satisfying jingle. Fulminatus had practiced ears, and could hear that the coins were gold, not silver or copper, and numerous. The seal was easier to understand than the seal on the Vestal lockbox. It was common to clip metal off the edges of coins, so rich men often set aside good coins in mint condition, and when they had a nice round number of them, sealed them into bags like this one. There was a marking "XXV" to indicate that there were twenty-five in this one. "I can bring more, if that's not enough." Whatever Mercurius might be, he did not seem to be any good at haggling.

"It is not a question of the money," Fulminatus began, and then stopped. He was staring at the other marking, the design of the seal-stamp on the red wax closing the coin-pouch. He decided to reverse himself. "Of course, I am very eager to take on what promises to be an important case."

The seal-stamp was a soaring falcon, the mark of Consul Falco.

Chapter 11

A Roman marriage could be a very religious affair. The strictest form of marriage involved very solemn oaths, binding the couple to each other tightly, of course more restrictively for the woman than for the man, administered by a priest with solemn rituals, emphasizing the wrath of the gods which would be called down on anyone breaking such an oath. Pertinax, naturally, had been elected Pontifex Maximus by the college of priests soon after the Senate conferred the title of Augustus on him. So he would have been qualified to perform any level of ritual which Eclectus and Marcia wanted for their marriage. Marcia wanted none at all, not even a little prayer of blessing. Eclectus suspected that she was turning Christian. He did not think any the less of her for that.

A Roman marriage could also be a very legalistic affair. Often there would be a detailed contract drawn up, specifying which properties would be transferred from the bride's family to the groom's, with rarely some property also moving in the other direction. It might also indicate what level of financial support the wife could expect, and which properties she could treat as her own. In this case, Marcia had no surviving family. Marcia owned no lands, either. She had money, and simply gave all of it to Eclectus for her dowry. Eclectus wanted to draw up some papers, but Marcia would have none of that.

Or a Roman marriage could involve neither ritual nor contract. It was sufficient in the eyes of the law for a couple simply to begin living openly together, assuming neither was already married to another, and that was enough to create enforceable obligations. Some among the lower classes did nothing more than this, without any kind of ceremony or celebration. That would be unthinkable in this case. Marcia wanted as close to a traditional wedding as was possible in the circumstances. Normally, the groomsmen would kidnap her from her father's house and take her to the groom's house, where the guests would celebrate after her father formally give her to the groom. In this case, her old room in the Palace, which she was grateful to find had not been disturbed during her absence, would have to substitute for her family's home, and his room for his family's home, and Pertinax for her father.

Everyone was anxious to see what kind of stunning ensemble Marcia would put together for her wedding dress. Surprising everyone as always, she chose to dress all in plain white. A simple veil of loosely-woven mesh, held onto her head by a plain wreath of pressed flowers, topped it off. Junipera and Langoria, her bridesmaids, fussed with the veil to get it set just right. Laetus and Narcissus would be the groomsmen. Ordinarily there would be many more than two of each, but a large procession for such a short distance would look a little silly. It was customary for the bride's family to give gifts to the guests, and especially to the bridesmaids, but Junipera and Langoria were astonished when Marcia began giving them all her jewelry. "The ring Eclectus puts on me will be my only adornment from now on," she said.

"But they would never allow me to wear these!" Langoria exclaimed.

"You are a free woman, and have every right to look as pretty as you can make yourself."

"But I don't have any such right," Junipera observed sadly.

"You will need to sell these, when you make your escape."

"I would never..." Junipera stammered. It could mean anything from a severe flogging to death by torture for a slave to admit any desire to run away.

"You must," Marcia insisted. "For your child's sake." Junipera put her hand to her belly reflexively. She had not even felt sure yet that she was pregnant, but trusted now that Marcia somehow knew.

Eclectus, Laetus, and Narcissus arrived, noisily. They did not want to surprise anyone in a state of undress. Marcia made hurried gestures, and the bridesmaids scooped the jewels into the leather purses tied to their belts. They went out, holding little oil lamps as if they could not see in the brightly torch-lit hall. They shrieked, in reasonably convincing mock-startlement, "The bridegroom has come!" Laetus and Narcissus entered the room and seized Marcia by the arms. Marcia had been afraid that Laetus might be rough, but he was not like Motilenus, and did not take advantage of the opportunity for any unauthorized groping. They marched her along, Eclectus ahead of them, Junipera and Langoria behind. Hyacinthus, released from manacles for the first time since New Year's, began to sing from somewhere unseen. The groomsmen joined in on the male parts, and the bridesmaids on the female parts. It was an old traditional song, about how the Sabine women decided that their rapists might not make such bad husbands after all. They slowed down as they neared the bedroom of Eclectus, who was one of very few in the Palace, free or otherwise, to have a room to himself. They did not want to end the procession before they finished the song.

They had to slow down anyway, because everyone in the Palace, from slaves to Praetorians, seemed to be trying to crowd into the hall. People parted to make way for them, until they stood before the August One. Pertinax asked, "Eclectus, do you take this, my daughter, to be your wife? Do you promise to be faithful to her, and to support her, and any children she might bear you?" The promise of faithfulness was not always taken very seriously, but the duty of support was.

"I do," said Eclectus.

"Then I freely give her to you." Some modern-minded couples included a question to the bride as well, asking whether she was willing, but there was none of that here.

Narcissus produced the ring. The ring had been the subject of their only quarrel. Marcia wanted a traditional iron ring, to symbolize that she was like his slave. Eclectus wanted to give her a gold ring, in the more modern style. Marcia certainly did not want anything that showy, arguing that it would seem as if she were trying to pretend she were still somebody of importance, and asking if Eclectus would ever dare to wear a gold ring himself. Of course, it was quite a different thing for a man to wear gold. That would very much look like a claim to rank. Eclectus argued back that an iron ring would also attract attention these days, and Marcia reluctantly conceded that such a showy humility would in its own way be ostentatious. So they compromised on a silver ring. He put it on her finger, and said, "I give you this ring, and with it I give you all that I have, and all that I am, for as long as I live." This was purely improvised on his part, not at all what he was supposed to say. Astonishingly, a sniffling sound was heard from Lady Titiana.

It was then the job of the groomsmen to hoist her over the threshold. Marcia was grateful that both Laetus and Narcissus were strong men, so that there was no chance of them dropping her. Quite aside from any hurt or embarrassment that this might cause, such a thing would be horribly unlucky. Now she lifted her veil. For many grooms whose marriages had been arranged by a matchmaker, this was the first time they got a good look at the bride, now that it was too late to do anything about it. Eclectus knew every inch of her, but still his heart melted to see her. He stepped into the room and kissed her, accompanied by the traditional hooting from the crowd. At this point, ordinarily the guests would enter the groom's house to begin the festivities. But then, ordinarily the bride would not enter the bedroom until after a late-night charivari. It was necessary to adapt a little to the circumstances. Titiana announced, "There are refreshments laid out in the atrium." It was the first time the atrium had been used that year. Naturally, no-one could help but think about the last time they had been in the atrium. Titiana was aware of this. "It is past time," she said firmly, "that we reclaim that room. We cannot allow a ghost to own it forever. Let us banish everything but merriment from there!"

The crowd parted, and bowed as Pertinax and Titiana led the way, arm in arm. Eclectus and Marcia followed. Narcissus took the arm of Junipera, and Langoria with a little hesitation gave her arm to Laetus. The first cup of wine was, of course, for the August One. Pertinax spilled a little on the tiled floor, but said nothing about which spirits that was intended for. He respected Marcia's wish to have no religious mention, but did not wish to be unlucky. He then proceeded to make a very peculiar toast, which all who were present would remember to the end of their days. "All day long," he said, "people keep wishing me, Long live the Emperor! I could not possibly endure all the long lives that they wish for me. So I offer some of my life to you. Join me in this drink!" He paused. The waiters understood that they were now to pour for the others, for Lady Titiana first of course, then Eclectus and Marcia, and finally Laetus, Narcissus, Junipera, and Langoria. Pertinax raised his goblet. "May you live even longer than I do!"

Eclectus knew the vintage, and was amazed that Pertinax was going to such expense. Narcissus had never had any wine so good in all his days, and even Laetus was impressed. Titiana, like most Roman women of breeding, was no drinker, in fact had not touched a drop in years, but would drink a sip for form's sake. Junipera and Langoria had never tasted wine at all before, and found that they did not like it. Each saw in the other's eyes that she was not alone. They giggled in relief when Titiana, never one to be wasteful, started pouring her wine into her husband's cup, making it seem all right for them, too, to donate their wine to the men.

Eclectus heard Marcia mutter something over her cup before she drank, which might have been, "The blood of Christ."

Chapter 12

The weather in northern Gaul turned foul. Junius Severus was awoken by a pitter-patter noise which disoriented him for a few minutes. He finally recognized that it was the sound of a wind-driven mix of rain and sleet pounding a tin roof, and remembered where he was. The camp had changed considerably since Governor Placidius arrived with his ten centuries of men. The ditch had been filled in and replaced with a deeper ditch surrounding a wider perimeter, and the wooden fencing pulled outward. This made the gaps in the fence too wide for proper gateways, but they had brought more wood and were filling those sections in. More wells had been dug uphill, and the engineers had constructed a sluiceway with remarkable speed. The flow could be switched to fill a tank above the latrine pits, or to continue past the rear gate through a cloth filter into the main cistern. The tank would be dumped to flush the latrines once a day. If a hard freeze came, it would be necessary to heat rocks to set on the ice and make it flow, but this problem had not arisen yet. Besides the cistern, the rear of the camp now housed horses, oxen, wagons, and a considerable store of food. The camp was beginning to take on the appearance of a permanent village, as many such camps had become.

The men had also brought four walls, of uneven height, and a sloping roof of wavy tin, to make a better praetorian headquarters than a leather tent. The praetorian tent which Clodius had used was still there, next door, now housing the camp prefect, military tribune, quartermaster, and a couple other staff officers. The new headquarters contained a little desk and, behind some partitions to give the semblance of a separate room, an actual bedstead. Nobody would call it a luxurious house, but even commanders should not expect luxury out in the field. Placidius had given up the bed to Clodius, and slept in a bedroll on the floor. Junius was also invited to sleep in the house, as the commander of a little independent unit. His centurion was in the praetorian tent, not out among the men like the ten newly arrived centurions. And

Servilius too was in the house, like a body-servant who could not be separated from his master.

Placidius rose, used the chamber pot, and washed his hands and face in a bowl of water. Junius had no need to pee, and did not fancy splashing cold water on his face on a day like this. But he saw that Servilius was eying the pot and the bowl, and apparently wishing to give Junius precedence. So he used both, so that Servilius would feel free to. Then they heard Clodius stirring. Of course, Clodius had his own pot and bowl. They dressed and stood, waiting for Clodius to emerge.

Placidius started the salutations. "Good morning, most honored of patrons!"

"Good morning, he whom I should be honored to call patron," Junius improvised.

"Good morning, most generous of patrons!" Servilius finished.

"It does not sound as if it will be a good morning at all," Clodius said. "It is said that pilots gain their reputations from the tempests they endure," quoting the Stoic Epictetus, "but I doubt that any pilot will wish to gain a reputation for crossing the Channel in this."

Placidius quoted the philosopher back to him, "He is wise who does not mourn what he has not, but rejoices in what he has. I shall rejoice if this weather means that I can enjoy my patron's company for yet a while longer."

"I am at that unhappy place where three roads meet. I can return west to the Channel and Britannia, and my enemies will accuse me of ignoring a summons to Roma. Or I can go south and on to Italia, and my enemies will accuse me of abandoning my post. Or I can go east to shelter with you in Belgica, and be open to both accusations."

"We need not go to Durocortorum. We can remain here, while we await clearer news about the situation back at home." The men would be miserable in their tents until they could build cabins for themselves, but then, they were in the army. "I like to make visitations to different parts of the province. The merchants of Ambiantum will be happy if my men spend some money around here." Ambiantum, from the Gaulish for "river town", was the market that grew up around the best place for boats from up the Samar to put in, above the bridge, whose arches were too low to let large boats through. The river town and the "bridge town" of Samarobriva were both prospering, and beginning to grow into each other to form one city. "This would preserve the option for you to hasten back to Britannia, if the weather breaks and that course seems best."

"If I might make a suggestion?" Junius put in. "You must write at once to Pertinax, congratulating him upon his accession. The Senate could not possibly have chosen a better man, et cetera, et cetera."

"I am not so sure about that," Clodius said. "His term in Britannia was marred by a mutiny, when some of the men felt he was paying no attention to their needs. But, you are right, that is not what I should say in any letter. I have written enough impolitic letters for one lifetime."

"Then you ask the August One's guidance, as to whether your presence in Roma is still desired, and pledge to remain on this side of the Channel until you know his pleasure. That way, no-one can accuse you of anything."

"And what do I say about the fate of one Junius Severus, headed this way to relieve me when last anyone heard from him?"

"Why, you say nothing at all. And then, if you are accused of doing away with me, I can appear in Roma, all indignation that anyone would slander my good friend and honored patron."

"There is a deviousness about you. I like that in a man."

"Naturally Governor Placidius will join in this expression of congratulations, reminding everyone that you are not without allies."

"Quite right." As Clodius nodded, Placidius rummaged in the desk for clean parchment, some quills, a brick of red wax, and a carefully stoppered bottle of ink. He began laying these out on top of the desk, but Clodius fetched a satchel to put them in. "We ought to move to the mess tent. I hope the cooks have got a good fire going. I am as anxious for the heat as for the breakfast."

Servilius took it upon himself to dump the chamber pots outside. Fortunately there was nothing that had to be carried to the latrines. Some engineers were already out spreading gravel on the principal and praetorian ways, trying to prevent them from turning completely to mud. Placidius was shivering before they reached the mess. "And I have a wonderfully warm coat hanging on a peg on the wall back in my office," he said.

"Do you need to get back to Durocortorum?" Junius asked. "Is it dangerous for you to be away from there so long, and for Clodius to be away from Londinium?"

"My boy, when you have a province of your own, you will find that governors are not so indispensable as they like to imagine. Why, governors have been known to die, and then weeks go by before Roma hears of it, and more weeks before a substitute is chosen, and more weeks before he arrives. And then he finds that the men who really run things have scarcely noticed the vacancy."

"Priscus knows who the men are that he can rely on," Clodius added. "And he has Plautilla to advise him. Tossing a boy right into the water may not be the kindliest way to teach him to swim, but it is effective."

In the mess there was vegetable broth, and sausage for the officers, beans for the men. Placidius told the men to be at ease, but when he sat down with Clodius, Junius, and Servilius, the other soldiers at that table quickly finished what they had and vacated the table. The letter was written in one draft by Servilius, who knew what needed to be said. None of the others found any fault with what he had written. Servilius suggested that Placidius add some concurring lines at the bottom in his own hand, to emphasize, as Junius had suggested, that Clodius and Placidius were together. They signed it, and sealed it with their two stamps.

"I will take it to the post," Junius volunteered. "I have the best horse." He had a hidden motive. It occurred to him that his omnipotent diploma would let him order the postmaster at Samarobriva to send by fast horse relay, all day and all night, to the office of Placidius in Durocortorum, to fetch back his coat, at once. That ought to be a pleasant surprise for the Governor.

And the Governor would know whom to thank.

Chapter 13

The weather was fair and pleasant in the Lateran fields. Three dozen girls gathered in front of their host, Senator Sempronius, who was standing between his mother Camilla and the priestess of Carmenta, attended by a younger acolyte. The aged priestess was beaming. Her little shrine was not much visited, and even during her time of the year she seldom got this much attention. Camilla was costumed as the Cumaean Sibyl, with a wide band of red cloth going around the back of her neck to hang down over both sides of her white robe. They stood in front of a large lumpy object hidden under a canvas, behind which were two hastily built huts. On the little lake, just a pond really, was a mock boat with a high forecastle and a convincing sail, but actually it was only a stage, resting on the mud at the bottom of the pond. A real boat could not sail in the pond. The girls giggled as they speculated among themselves as to which of these hiding places might conceal the young men they had been promised. When the last of the late-comers had arrived, the Senator raised his arms for silence and began speaking in his loudest voice.

"Welcome, ladies, one and all! Welcome, first of all, to those of distinguished age!" He bowed to the priestess, and then to his mother. "And welcome to the young! For you are the future of Roma! You are the ones who will bear the Senators and warriors! But how can we build our future, if we do not know our past? Let us honor the face of Carmenta which looks to the past!"

This was the cue for the priestess and her accompanying acolyte to begin singing, not entirely in tune, a long and rather tedious but traditional song about her goddess. The first verses described the pleasant forests of Arcadia, and the bears which haunted them. Several male servants had been drafted to play the bears. They emerged from the larger of the huts behind the canvas-shrouded mystery object, wearing furry suits and capering about. Phaeton made a particularly convincing growl which startled the priestess. Then she began singing

186

about how Carmenta taught the Sibyls to prophecy, and Camilla in her Sibyl costume sat at her feet. The song then told of her son Evander. Jovialis Curtius emerged from the changing-hut, with a wax tablet strapped to his belt and a quill behind his ear, to sit at her feet while she taught him letters and then taught him how to alter the letters to write Italic, for in Italia his destiny lay. She told him to sail across the sea and found a village at a spot that would be revealed to him, where seven hills came together by the riverside. He arose and marched over and onto the boat as she finished her song.

From the forecastle emerged dozens of young men in their finest military tunics. The girls all clapped as they marched smartly off the boat. The priestess took a bow as if they were applauding her song. The canvas was cranked back by machinery hidden in one of the huts behind it, to reveal that it was a scale model of the seven hills of Roma. Hydraulics within it could roll back trap doors and push up models of the major buildings. As the men vanished behind the contraption into the changing hut, Jovialis sat at the foot of the Palatine and a model of the imperial palace rose up. This was a grossly anachronistic representation of his village, but Sempronius wanted to use every one of the buildings. The contraption had been built by his father for a spectacle at their country estate many years ago, and the staff of servants had worked hard to haul it here and get it all in working order. Some of the girls now squealed as Apollos Citharius and his band emerged from the changing hut. He struck up his lute and began singing a new composition, all about the history of Roma. For the little village founded by Evander would be replaced, he sang as Jovialis withdrew, by the great city planned by the mighty king Romulus. Sempronius had ducked into the changing hut and now reappeared in a purple robe with a supposedly golden crown. As he waved his arms over the seven hills, the temple of Jupiter sprang up from the Capitoline hill. Citharius sang that the gods decided to take Romulus. In the trickiest bit of mechanics, a pipe running by the side of the machine let out a burst of steam from a boiler in the control hut. Sempronius vanished into the fog, as the temple of Quirinus rose from the Quirinal hill.

Now Citharius transposed to a minor key, and sang mournfully about the dangers of being ruled by kings, for not all kings were virtuous like Romulus. Roma fell into the wicked hands of Tarquin the Proud. Sempronius came back, now with red splashed on his robes to symbolize his bloodiness, his crown askew to symbolize that he had wrongfully usurped it, a sneer on his face. The song told how Tarquin even lusted after the fair virgin Lucretia. Camilla handed the red cloth that was her costume as Sybil to the priestess, and now posed demurely in white robes as the temple of Vesta emerged. If she did not quite match the song's description of a beautiful young maiden, she displayed convincing shock and horror as her son in the guise of Tarquin lunged at her. She fled, to kill herself according to the song. Now Consul Clarus appeared, having changed in the hut from his tunic to his best Senatorial toga, with a laurel wreath on his head and a mock sword. Citharius returned to a major key and sang how the noble Brutus drove Tarquin from the city and ended the monarchy forever. A few flicks of the sword were enough to chase him away as the Senate House sprang up in the Forum.

Several other young men got to be heroes. Alexandrius held a torch while Fabius Cilo, as Scaevola, impressed the girls by passing his hand through the flames. Planks painted with wavy blue lines to represent the Tiber had been added to the front of the seven hills, so that a little bridge could span it, for Fortunatus Curtius as Horatio to stand on, waving a mock sword back and forth to hold off single-handedly some of the men still in tunics, as Etruscan soldiers. The song's coverage of history grew spottier. There was Cincinnatus refusing to keep power, but no Gauls wrecking the city. There was Scipio wrecking Carthage, but no Marius and Sulla fighting to the death to keep power lifelong. Finally, Sextus Cornelius Repentinus, a freshly-minted Senator just returned from a tour as governor of Lusitania, got the plum role of Julius Caesar. He led the servants, now free of their bear-costumes, in chains, or rather holding a length of chain and pretending to be locked to it. Citharius sang about how Caesar had conquered Spain and Gaul and Britain, and his band joined him in a chorus of "Io! Triumph! Io!" Of course, most of Spain had been conquered before Caesar, and Britain would not be conquered until later, but in the song Caesar was bringing captives from all over the west, to fight and die for the entertainment of the Romans. The Colosseum sprang up, although it was not really built until Vespasian. The slaves all started fighting each other and falling down. Some died more convincingly than others, Phaeton making a particular spectacle of himself.

Citharius stopped playing, and shifted into a sad recitative. Another Brutus, unworthy of the name, was filled with murderous jealousy. Clarus reprised his role as Brutus, but now the later Brutus, the difference marked only by the loss of the laurel wreath, and his scowl as he sneakily came up behind Caesar and stabbed him over and over in the back. In this version, Brutus acted alone. Repentinus as Caesar turned to look at him sadly as he sank to his knees and expired. Some of the girls gasped. But then Citharius struck up the music again, and sang how ever since, the Senate and People of Roma have wisely chosen to be ruled by just and kindly Caesars. This was an excellent place to stop the history. Not all of the subsequent Caesars had been either just or kindly, nor were they all exactly chosen by the Senate or People. And among the good Emperors it was not agreed by everyone which deserved the highest praise. It would have been awkward to try to praise Pertinax Caesar as the greatest Emperor of all time, as would surely be necessary if the story were to continue to the present, given that he had not yet done anything.

The rest of the men now re-emerged dressed in their togas. Sempronius led them, and called out, "Ladies! Didn't the men play their roles splendidly?" The girls applauded enthusiastically. "Now that we have looked back at the past," or as much of it as they wished to remember, "let us also honor the face of Carmenta which looks to the future! Come, ladies, and visit the Sibyls, who will tell you your fortunes!" Since there were dozens of girls, and the priestess only had one disciple, Camilla resumed her costume as the Cumaean Sibyl, and several female servants, including Cocina, were also drafted as fortune-tellers. Each had a bit of crystal to gaze in. The priestess herself had a great crystal ball which she had difficulty hoisting up on to the table. Of course, every girl's fortune was going to be that she was about to meet the man of her dreams, marry and bear many children.

Tullia Minor drew Camilla. She expected to hear some hints that marriage to Senator Sempronius was her destiny. It was not a destiny that she was averse to. But the mother said, "I see a man who has been sent far away. After his long journey he will return here. He is the one for you." Tullia had to wonder if she had given offense somehow, and was seen as not a suitable daughter-in-law. But apparently Camilla had no hostile intent. In response to Tullia's quizzical look, she said, "I can only tell you what I see."

The servants were disassembling the contraption, and the majordomo of the Senator's household began showing all the guests to their assigned seats. There were nine tables seating eight each, numbers which a numerologist had assured the Senator were the most auspicious. The brick ovens which were set about the park for the convenience of the public were superheated by bellows, to bake thick flatbreads slathered in olive oil and covered with shredded cheeses, a paste of mashed chickpeas and herbs, and fresh anchovies, lightly soaked in brine rather than reduced to a garum sauce as usual. This was not the sort of delicacy that would be served at a banquet, but could be prepared in quantity quickly. Camilla was taking the priestess and her disciple, and Citharius and his band, back to the house for a more formal luncheon, and to make a substantial donation to the shrine of Carmenta, and pay a handsome fee to the musicians.

At the highest-ranking table, Senator Sempronius sat with Tullia Minor at his right and Julia Aniciana at his left. Consul Clarus sat between Tullia and Clara Didia, the daughter of Didius Julianus, named Clara for her mother's mother, who was a cousin of Clarus. The Consul was older than any of the other men invited, but had recently become a widower. Alexandrius, honored as a favor to Tullia, sat between Julia Aniciana and Maria Sempronia, a dull and not very good-looking cousin of the host who had to be invited. His younger brother Florentius, a smooth-talker with whom he did not get along well, was at another table, since it would not do for two brothers to be attracted by the same girl. Jovialis Curtius was separated from Fortunatus Curtius for the same reason. Florentius was annoying Jovialis and Fabius Cilo by monopolizing the attention of both the girls seated to either side of him, while across from him the author Dio Cassius was monopolizing the other two girls with tales of the preparations underway for Lady Cornificia's wedding.

The head table was completed by Cornelius Repentinus, seated between Maria Sempronia and Clara Didia. Maria was asking whether he had captured a whole string of barbarians in Lusitania, like Julius Caesar did. Repentinus was having difficulty explaining to her that Lusitania was actually a rather sedate province where not much happened. Clarus was boring Clara with the doings of various mutual relatives whom Clara had little contact with or interest in. Tullia was complimenting Sempronius on how well the spectacle had gone. Sempronius admitted that he had been worried about it, since the men had had so little time to rehearse, and thanked Tullia for lending him the services of Cocina, who had instructed his staff on how best to feed seventy without the use of a real kitchen. Julia was questioning Alexandrius about his ancestry. The career of his father sounded impressive enough, but she wanted to know the parentage of Pescennius Niger and did not at all seem satisfied by his replies. He asked if her father was from the *gens Anicia* and she said sharply, "I do not use the name of my father." That sounded as if there were a juicy story behind it, but if so she was not willing to tell it.

Alexandrius took her silence as the signal to change sides. He soon had Maria laughing at an absurdly exaggerated tale about how his father wrestled crocodiles in Egypt, which at first she had been taking seriously. Repentinus and Clara were both relieved to change conversational partners, and hit it off at once. Tullia tried to ask Clarus how he enjoyed his duties as Consul, but he had to admit that Falco insisted on running nearly everything. Julia was far more satisfied with Sempronius, who could praise his late father's virtues unreservedly, now that it could be openly said that Commodus often killed men for no good reason. Julia expressed the proper condolences, and Sempronius tactfully avoided discussing her father, instead saying some pleasant insincerities about her mother, Lady Anicia.

Everyone agreed that the event had been a smashing success.

Chapter 14

Did Frida and Tausias really have anything in common? Frida was brooding on that question all day. She knew that she ought to be happy after the news she got from Cocina. And the deal with that Senator to sell a large load of anchovies had been more profitable than she expected. She raised her prices, expecting to be paid with newly-minted pennies. She knew that Pertinax Caesar would act quickly to flood the streets with coins bearing his face, and took it for granted that the Pertinax pennies would be even worse than the last batch of Commodus pennies. Senator Sempronius paid her price without question, and all in new pennies, but to her surprise, the Pertinax pennies appeared to be of better metal content than recent mintings. She would save them, and spend the Commodus pennies where she could. She would have told Tausias about this good fortune, but he did not come home that night, and was late tonight. Of course, mid-month was when he got his pay, and he was doubtless out spending it. Perhaps it would be better not to let him know about the money. She kept him around because it was pleasant to have someone she could speak to in her native language. She knew the number-words and curse-words needed to haggle in the markets, but beyond that was not very comfortable in Latin. But was that enough of a reason?

Frida and Tausias were of the Tungri, a German people who settled in Gaul well before Julius Caesar conquered the place. So they considered themselves every bit as Roman as the Gauls, even if the Gauls didn't. Italians of course did not really consider Gauls to be Roman either, and looked down their noses even further at the Tungri. The villages where they had been born were within an afternoon's walk from each other, but they had scarcely known each other by face in childhood, and never spoke of those days. Perhaps that was what they had in common, that neither wanted to be buried where they were born. Especially they did not want to be buried there while still alive. They really met in Lugdunum. Tausias was working for the Tigranos family as a guard on the caravans bringing their Armenian rugs and other Eastern luxuries into Gaul and sometimes even Britain. Frida had advanced from housemaid to mistress of Arpentus, a merchant who dealt in such goods. Arpentus even started a works up north in Atrebat, by Gesoriac, making tapestries in imitation of the Armenian patterns. He could not imitate the firm burlap backing on the Eastern carpets, since jute was not a crop known in Gaul, but only the most pretentious put carpets on the floor. For hanging on the wall, his manufactures were fine, and even sold in Italy.

Some rich men prefer hiding their women away, but Arpentus was more the type to put his woman on display. He made her sing and dance for guests. Frida never sang or danced again in all the years since. She amused Tausias in those days, and he amused her, but of course she would never have been unfaithful to Arpentus. Then Tausias was transferred to the East, and she did not see him again for a long time. There he learned Greek and Armenian to go with the German, Gaulish, and Latin he already knew. Frida could not even master Gaulish without a thick German accent that Arpentus found amusing. When Arpentus tired of her, he did right by her, giving her enough money to set up in business, and sending her to Roma since she expressed desire to see it. His firm's office in Ostia had standing orders to provide her safe passage back, if she found that Roma was not to her liking. All in all, it was. The great buildings around the Forum were as beautiful as she had been told, and if the filth and violence of the back streets were also as horrid as she had been told, she was enough of a woman of the world to accept that the beauty and the ugliness would both be found in any large city. She was pleased when she met Tausias again, and happy to see that he had come up in the world. So had she. She had a large enough house to hold coops full of laying hens. And she no longer rented it, but owned it outright after the last flooding, when the landlord lost a lot of tenants and was looking for some cash infusion. Between her home and the river she had put up a brine-house, where she rendered fish to paste and sauce, and a smoke-house, where she dried other fish. She let a local sausage-maker use the smoke-house, in exchange for the use of his ox-cart. She hoped to buy her own wagon and animals, as soon as she could acquire space to keep them. It saddened her sometimes that she was unlikely to see her children again for years, if ever, but she knew that they would have a better life with their father, and she had no desire to go back to Lugdunum.

Tausias came home at last, obviously very drunk. She did not like it when he was in this state, but had to tell him the news. "I saw the wise woman today. She confirmed that I am with child."

"Oh? I thought you were just getting fat."

Frida had thought of various reactions that he might have, but this was not one of them. But she went on. "She had me lie down while she swung a weight over my belly. She can tell from that whether it is a boy or a girl."

"Can she tell whether it is mine?"

This she had certainly not expected. She almost challenged him on whether he had spent the last night at a brothel. Instead she just asked, "Do you want to know what she found, or not?"

"I hope you didn't pay too much for her conjurors' tricks." Frida had paid ten farthings for the consultation, but that was beside the point. "I'm sure she always says it is a son."

"She could not tell, so she put her ear close against my belly. She says I am carrying twins, one of each."

"And how are we going to raise two brats?"

Now the tears started to flow. "I was hoping you would be happy about it."

"Happy? I should be happy? Do you know what the Cohorts got with their pay? One gold piece! One!"

"One is better than nothing."

"And nothing, nothing, is what the Watch got! And that's all we'll ever get!" It seemed that Frida was not the only one who had been brooding all day.

"We will manage. I have been making good money." She did not say "more money than you make" but immediately worried that he might take it that way.

"And how will you tend to business with two babies?"

"Maybe when your sister is freed, she can help."

"You are going to make Langoria your slave, when Pertinax is done with her?"

"I'll pay her. She will need a place, and some employment."

"She will never be free," Tausias said morosely. "I see the Praetorians, every day, in the Cattle Forum, running market errands like menial servants. You know what that means? It means the August One," he spat, somehow making the title into a curse, "is never going to let anyone out of the Palace."

"The Praetorians can't like that. Maybe they will make him change his ways."

"Like the way that one of them made Commodus change his ways!" he shouted.

"Keep your voice down! One of the neighbors might hear," Frida fretted. Tausias was not speaking Latin, but German was hardly unknown in this part of town.

"Don't you dare tell me what to do!" Tausias backhanded her, hard, across the jaw, and she fell down.

"Do you want me to miscarry?" Frida's tears were flowing rapidly now, mixed with a little blood from a cut on her cheek. Tausias looked remorseful, and tried to offer her a hand to get up, but Frida refused to take it. "No! Don't you touch me again! This is my house, you understand? My house! I will not be treated like this in my house! You get out of here! Get out of here right now!"

Tausias opened his mouth to say something, thought better of it, turned around, and left.

Chapter 15

Pertinax was putting on a spectacle in the Circus Maximus to celebrate his accession. This was long overdue, everyone agreed. "And from what the cryer had to say," Battanitha told Cocina, "it is not going to be much of a show. I scarcely know why I troubled to come here from Ostia."

Cocina would just as soon that she had not bothered. But having run into Battanitha, and knowing that there would be no escaping the flow of words from her, Cocina followed her into the bleachers to find seats. Senator Tullius had given all the household staff leave to attend, except for Phaeton who was to drive him out to the country. He had no need to prove his loyalty, and no interest in fighting other Senators for the most prestigious seats in the Circus. Not since last harvest had he been out to talk to his estate managers, and a time when the Emperor would be busy with something else and unlikely to call on him seemed most appropriate. An armed escort would meet them when they turned onto the Appian Way, since there was no Watch out in the country, and a fine-looking chariot with only an old man and a driver would be too tempting a target. Cocina wondered if Phaeton understood that he was being tested, and might be swapped for a slave from the country if his driving or his conduct was erratic.

Magnus uncharacteristically volunteered to watch Cocinilla, so that Cocina and Philoxena could both go. He said that his time with the gladiators had cured him of any interest in these shows, although it did not appear that there would be any combat this time. Philoxena went to sit with some relatives of her husband's, while Tullia joined Sempronius and Camilla. Castor was outside working the crowd. He challenged some oaf who was bigger than he was, but doubtless less skilled, to a fight, and was likely to make good money on a day like this.

"At least," Cocina said, "they have brought out some of the big cats." Around three sides of a large trap door, four lions, plus a striped tiger and spotted leopard for variety, were pacing in their cages, or lying back and yawning. They had not been fed in a few days, but did not seem to have the energy to protest about it much.

"But I bet they don't even have any captives or atheists to feed them," Battanitha sniffed. By "atheists" she meant Christians, of course. "There was no mention of gladiators fighting the beasts, let alone each other. I wonder if we are going to see a single drop of blood."

"It is not really the season for such sports." The lions were not enjoying the chill, and would rather be sleeping in their pens under the Colosseum. In the summer they would be livelier, until they were cut down. That was assuming, of course, that the Colosseum would open for business as usual that summer, which was not entirely clear. The Colossus out front was still headless, and it did not appear that Pertinax put much priority on getting his own head displayed.

"It will never be the season, under this Emperor. He pinches a coin until the head cries out for mercy, I hear. And it is said that he is squeamish." To hear Battanitha say it, squeamishness was a dark secret which ought to have disqualified Pertinax for the throne.

Flavius Genialis, the impresario, raised his arms for attention, and shouted out, "Who is the greatest man in Roma?" That had been the opening line of the script at such games, since even before the days when the correct answer was "Pompey the Great!" who had first built bleachers here in the Circus Maximus. But in the late Republic, the chants in praise of whichever politician was sponsoring the games often had to compete with claques shouting out the name of a rival. For two centuries now, there had been only one correct answer at any given time, except for that embarrassing occasion when Marcus Aurelius had first been talked into sponsoring games, and some in the crowd answered "Lucius Verus!" out of habit, since his playboy colleague had always been the sponsor. This time there was no uncertainty about what to say. The crowd stood and chanted "Publius! Helvius! Pertinax! Caesar! Augustus!" with emphasis on the "Augustus" and repeating over and over while Pertinax and his entourage entered and made their way to the imperial box.

"Ungrateful wretches," Titiana said to Pertinax. "They cheered louder for Commodus."

"But that was the voice of fear," Laetus pointed out. "This is sincere admiration, and therefore more to be prized." He hoped his flattery was sufficient. It did at least quiet Titiana.

When the imperial retinue took their seats, giving the crowd permission to stop shouting and sit down as well, Battanitha pointed. "Look at her! I wouldn't have thought she would dare to show her face."

"Lady Titiana? Of course she has to be here."

"Not her! I mean Marcia! See her there, right next to Eclectus? I hear he has even married her. He will have to watch out for daggers in the night. It is all Victor's doing, I tell you." Battanitha lowered her voice to a conspirational whisper. "She has killed one Emperor, and she will look to do it again."

"At least she is dressed modestly," Cocina noted. "I would scarcely have recognized her without all the glittering jewelry, if you had not pointed her out."

"Yes," Battanitha conceded, "she looks a little less as if she belongs in a brothel."

The trap door in the middle of the arena was pulled up, and over onto its back, to reveal a pit containing three stags with impressive racks of antlers. They must have been brought from German forests. The cats caught the scent and let out some roars. Their cage doors were lowered to become ramps allowing the cats down into the pit. The stags stood together and lowered their antlers, and got in some blows, but they were outnumbered and the battle did not last long. The tiger got around to one side and sank its claws into the flank of one stag who bellowed with rage. The leopard got under the head of another and sank its teeth into the neck, letting loose a spurt from the arteries. When all the stags were dead, the cats fought each other a little for position, but then settled down to their meal.

Pertinax had not wanted even this much, but Laetus insisted that some in the crowd would not be happy if there were not at least a little bloodshed. Not everyone who wanted blood was satisfied, however. "I can't see a thing!" Battanitha complained. "They should not have done this in a pit. The edges of the pit obstruct the view." The purpose of the display was not very clear. If armed warriors killing lions would have shown Roman prowess in arms, or unarmed prisoners dying haplessly would have shown that Rome could subjugate enemy nations or violators of her laws, this showed only some ability to trap and transport animals. The trap door was raised and lowered again to cover the pit. The business of luring the cats back into their cages would be left until later.

But while the crowd was left wondering if that was all, the trumpeting of elephants was heard. A section of the bleachers had been blocked off, and now it became apparent that this was in order that elephants marched from the Colosseum could be brought under the stands and through a gate into the arena. "Commodus ordered them," Battanitha explained. "They are going to be very expensive to keep, and I hope that Pertinax will not kill them too quickly. The big bull is well known in Leptis Magna." The male elephant who entered first was indeed of impressive size. Unlike the elephants who followed, he was not chained at all. He broke loose from the others, raised his trunk for an especially loud blast, and made as if he would stampede. The crowd was suitably frightened, but this beast was, actually, quite well trained and just putting on an act. He stopped in front of the imperial box, and knelt on his forelegs in homage to the Emperor.

Cheers went up, and the impresario shouted, "Isn't he magnificent? Let him show you how he can dance!" The bull elephant reared up on his hindlegs and made a couple of hops, then down onto his forelegs to kick up his hindlegs almost into a headstand. The other elephants did a few tricks as well, and then they were all led back out. The impresario said, "If the lion is the king of beasts, then surely the elephant is the Emperor of beasts! But what is any beast compared to a man? And what is any man compared to the Emperor? All hail Publius Helvius Pertinax Caesar Augustus!" The crowd understood that this was a signal for them to rise and chant the name again. Pertinax would have to come up with some more chants beside just the repetition of his name. Commodus had several chants that he made the crowd perform, but some had been subverted. "Hail the gladiator who fights without fear!" had to be abandoned when a couple syllables were changed, *sinist' manu* replacing *sine metu*, to make it "Hail the gladiator who fights left-handed!"

Pertinax rose and raised his arms for silence. Then he waved downward, and it took the crowd a little while to understand that he was telling them to sit. Commodus always kept everyone standing for his whole speeches, which could go on for hours. Cocina strained to hear what he was saying. "Most grateful am I to the Senate and People of Roma for" something, something, something. "Always have I endeavored..." It was no use. The Emperor's voice was thin and reedy. It was never going to carry across the Circus Maximus. The cryers trying to echo the imperial words from section to section in the stands were not succeeding. Cocina remembered how much better Sempronius had been at speaking to a crowd. Of course, Sempronius had been raised as a Senator's son, forced even when quite young to shout at public assemblies some words in addition to his father's, supporting whichever candidate the assembly was supposed to vote into some office. Pertinax did not have that upbringing, and even when he advanced from a staff officer to a general, he never got the knack of haranguing the troops in the way that they expected.

Citharius led in some musicians, dancers, jugglers, and acrobats, drawing some cheers. Then Pertinax said something which made the crowd roar. Apparently, at the next doling out of the grain ration, the poor would get some cash along with the food. Many stood to shout their approval. When things grew quiet again, Citharius struck up a chord, only to find to his embarrassment that Pertinax was not, in fact, finished. The Emperor went on and on to some anticlimax about how the loyalty of the soldiers would never be forgotten. Cocina asked Battanitha, who seemed to have a better ear, what he was saying. "The rabble will get some silver, but the troops will have to wait for their gold," Battanitha explained. "Oh, he didn't put it quite that way, but that is what he means."

When Pertinax sat down, Citharius began playing again. With no military triumphs to sing about, he was reduced to singing praises of the Emperor's economic policies. He was re-using the tune which had been "History of Rome" at the Carmentalia the week before, and as some in the stands knew, also "In Memory of Vespasian" at Titiana's the week before that. All the people treasure the pennies of Pertinax, above those of any tyrant, whom Citharius carefully did not name. They cannot bear to be parted with the kindly, generous face of Pertinax, which reminds them of his comforting presence. No more shall money-lenders shake their heads in rude refusal, for all know that Pertinax is an Emperor of his word, and that prosperity shall be coming to all. Neither shall they demand excessive interest any more. This was a legislative proposal to cap interest rates, which was unlikely to pass the Senate without amendments which would render it toothless, but the threat was making lenders try to give out money so that they could lock in high rates of return before it was too late.

The currency revaluation, the move against usury, and especially the promised welfare payments were all popular, but not very thrilling. Citharius seemed relieved to stop singing, and play instrumental interludes while dancers capered about with long ribbons. Then the acrobats performed. The most skillful juggler tossed three balls into the air, did a back-flip from a standing start, and caught them all, then repeated the performance, but on his third try dropped the balls to a chorus of boos. Afterwards this was recalled as an ill omen. Gymnasts shinnied up the outer bars of the lion cages with startling speed, tumbled and flipped on the cage roofs, then vaulted off spinning, to land flawlessly on the trap door, their thumping feet provoking leonine roars from beneath. This was moderately impressive, but all in all, Cocina had to agree with Battanitha.

As Roman spectacles went, this was not much.

Chapter 16

Pescennius Niger called a halt as his men approached a cross-roads by the Palestinian city of Neapolis. He spied a procession coming down the other road. "Let them go first," he ordered.

"Shouldn't they be the ones to give way to us?" a centurion asked in puzzlement.

"We would be in their way for longer than they will be in ours."

The procession was led by a man wearing some kind of priestly robes, and a skullcap. Behind him came an oxcart bearing a large ornamented box from which oversized scrolls protruded. The priest stopped hesitantly, but when Pescennius waved him on, he shouted *"Barakah rabbah aleikun!"* with a flourishing wave of his right arm and a deep bow.

"He wishes a great blessing upon you," the centurion translated. Pescennius had picked up little Aramaic during his time in Syria. Everyone he dealt with spoke Greek.

"You see? Is it not better to receive blessings from the people, rather than curses?"

It was apparently a wedding procession, with a veiled bride, a groom dressed in what was doubtless his best, and singers of both genders, followed by what must have been a substantial fraction of the whole population of the town. "Are these Jews?" Pescennius asked. "They appear to venerate holy books rather than any image, and I thought only Jews did that. Yet I also thought that Jews were forbidden to live in these parts."

"They are, sir," the centurion answered. "These would be Samaritans. They say they are not Jews, although they keep the Jewish law, and the Jews also say they are not Jews. It would be beyond me to tell you what the difference between the two is, but Jews and Samaritans despise each other heartily."

"Why would they keep the Jewish law, if they despise the Jews?"

"They say that it was their law first, and that it is the Jews who stole it from them. The Jews, of course, say the reverse."

"Of course," Pescennius chuckled.

An old man rushed forward, bowed before Pescennius, then sank to his knees, and then to the ground in a full prostration, lifting his head but keeping his eyes lowered, as he began to babble rapidly, his hands clasped above his head. On closer inspection, he was not so old, probably only middle-aged, but worn by years of hard toil.

"He is explaining that this is the day of his son's marriage," the centurion said. "He cannot adequately express his profound gratitude at the favor you have shown him, O most mighty of generals, favor far beyond what such a wretch as he could ever deserve, and so on, and so on."

There was obviously a considerable element of fear behind this effusion. A general named Severus had ravaged this whole area in Hadrian's time, during the second revolt of the Jews. This man could not have been born then, but memories were long in the East. Did he perhaps think that the Romans were trying to trick them, letting them go ahead, in order then to punish them for their insolence in doing so? Pescennius decided to put him at ease.

He turned around and shouted "Quartermaster!" Receiving an answering hail from the rear, he ordered, "Bring up the fattest sheep we have with us." The quartermaster complied, tying a rope around the sheep's neck to lead it with.

Pescennius asked the centurion to translate. "Tell this man that Pescennius Niger wishes the bride and groom all happiness, and desires to make a present to them on this blessed day. Slaughter this animal according to your own rites, and feast on it in good health."

The father of the groom was utterly astonished at these words. Murmurs ran up and down the procession, and the priest turned around to come before Pescennius again. He prostrated fully, which Pescennius knew to be the rarest kind of concession from a holy man devoted to that most jealous God of the Jews, assuming the God of the Samaritans to be the same deity, or at least of the same mind.

"He says that everyone in Neapolis will remember this great kindness, and keep the name of Pescennius Niger in all their prayers, and that if ever these people can do you a service of any kind, it would be an honor to them."

"Tell them to rise, and go in peace." Pescennius thought this would be the most reassuring response. The priest took the sheep from the soldiers and passed on.

Only when he was sure that the entire wedding party had cleared the crossing did Pescennius order his own men to resume marching.

BOOK FOUR

The Badger Calls for Storms

Chapter 1

"I am afraid that I have some bad news," Servilius said.

Clodius was pacing about in an open space toward the rear of the encampment, re-reading the letter from Rome which Junius Severus brought from the post the day before. It brusquely told him to return to his post in Britannia. Clodius hoped to find some hints in between the lines, but if Pertinax had any thoughts of adopting Clodius as a successor, he was showing no sign of it. Clodius was becoming fretful with inactivity, and was starting to worry how Priscus was coping without him. The wind kept trying to pull the letter out of his hands, and he finally let it. The wind pressed the letter against the fencing of a pigpen. Servilius hurried to retrieve it. "Are you afraid the pigs will read it? Even if they eat it, nothing of great value would be lost," Clodius said. Servilius handed him back the letter anyway. Clodius then asked, "So what is your bad news?"

"This is the day, precisely forty-five days after the solstice, and forty-five days before the equinox, when according to the wise men among the Gauls, one should look for the brock, which is the local species of badger, to come out of his den."

"I never knew that badgers were such precise astronomers and mathematicians."

"The brock will determine whether the weather from now until the equinox will be temperate, or whether the winter is to continue harshly until winter's end."

"Neither did I know that they were soothsayers."

Servilius was never deterred by Clodius' inveterate skepticism. "If the brock sees his shadow, he will return to his den, but if he does not, then he will stay out."

"I take it, then, that you have seen one of these badgers, who kindly prognosticated for you?"

"I have not," Servilius admitted. "However, it was sunny all day until just now." The sky was turning very gray as the sun lowered. The harsh wind was blowing out of the west, bringing chill dampness from the sea.

"Any creature who came out today must surely have seen his shadow. And that means that the weather will be bad. We cannot expect to cross the Channel safely until late in March."

"But that makes little sense. Surely sunshine on this very special day, if indeed it is so special, is an omen of good weather to come."

"One might think so. But I am assured that it is the reverse. I have spoken to multiple seers who are of the highest repute hereabouts."

"I have never yet known a seer who could foretell weather with any reliability."

"There is more. When I was out looking this morning, to see if I could find a brock myself, I saw in the west two towering clouds, and knew that they would be over our heads before the day was out."

"That much forecasting, even I might have accomplished. The wind is from the west, and so what was in the west might well blow here."

"But see, what the sign must mean is that the clouds stand for the months of February and March, and both will be gray and grim."

"Perhaps the two clouds stood for tonight and tomorrow, and after that the storm will be gone."

"When I consulted the seers, they told me also that many shearwaters have been seen close to the shore. That bird has always been an omen of storm."

"Cicero once called my ancestor Clodius Pulcher a shearwater, bringing storms wherever he went. So perhaps the birds were simply an omen that something important is soon to happen to Clodius, if indeed they were an omen of anything."

"Clodius Pulcher came to a bad end. Perhaps you ought make an offering to Brigita, the local goddess whose day this is, to ward off such a fate. She favors a cross with four bent arms, woven of rushes, and left beside a running spring. We have very suitable springs up above camp."

"I have never learned weaving of even the simplest sort, and Plautilla is not here."

"Offerings of food are also accepted, if you wish her aid in avoiding the fate of Pulcher, of which perhaps you are being warned."

"His fate? He died, in the end. Every man dies, in the end. If I wish to live longer than he did, then I should avoid repeating his errors. He made an enemy of Tullius Cicero, but the present Senator Tullius has always been my friend. So in that respect at least, I am not following his path."

"But what path shall we follow? We are ordered to return to Britannia." Servilius often said "we" automatically. Only Clodius was ordered back to Britain, but Servilius could not separate himself from Clodius. "But we cannot do so safely."

"Then we shall wait, until the weather improves. We could not have sailed today, not in the teeth of such a contrary wind. But we should be prepared for any break."

"But now it is too late. See? The rain is starting already, and will be hard." The first few drops were falling, and quickly it worsened. They were not far from the tin-roofed praetorian house, but even the short walk left both soaked.

"And are we doomed to repeat this same day over and over?" Clodius asked.

"Yes, for six weeks. So the badger says."

Chapter 2

Tausias was only slightly acquainted with Alexandrius. But it was important to keep up all his contacts with upper society. He knocked on the door with some hesitation, but Alexandrius was all smiles. "Come in, Tausias!" he said with a nod and a sweeping motion with his arm. "Is there something I can do for you?"

Tausias bowed. "I am not come to seek favors. But I was in the neighborhood, and thought it proper to pay my respects to you."

"What brings you this way? You look as if you have walked far. Take your ease here," he said waving at a brocaded bench, "and I will fetch some wine."

"Water would be enough for me," Tausias said. He was embarrassed to sit while his host was standing, especially on such good furniture. He looked ruefully at his dusty and sweaty cloak. And he did not think it right that Alexandrius would fetch for him, as if a servant. He knew Alexandrius only a little, from when they helped Diodoros pack his things and move, and was surprised at the familiarity. "I have more walking to do and may need a clear head. I am looking for a new place to live. I am afraid I may be evicted... again." Bitterness came through in that last word.

"As you wish," Alexandrius said as he poured some water. "Now please, sit, and tell me all about it. You were living with a woman who sold fish? Happily, the last I heard."

"Frida threw me out last month. I am in the barracks, with a couple units of the City and some other watchmen who are at loose ends. That might not last much longer."

"Have you asked this Frida whether she would take you back?"

"No I haven't." Tausias looked down at his feet ruefully.

"You were in the wrong, and have not found the courage to admit it? Well, it is none of my affair. I am sorry that I cannot offer to share this place, but I have already taken in another."

"This would be too rich for my blood anyway." Tausias looked up and out through the window, which showed a fine view toward the city. Most apartments in Roma had no such dangerous openings to the outside, but this building was guarded, which was bound to cost, and every apartment had a door. Tausias did not even want to think what a half-share of the rent would be. He remembered how ashamed he was, when Diodoros let him live with him on the Palatine, to learn how trifling a fraction his contribution was. "I will look in lowlier neighborhoods, but here across the Tiber. I don't like what I'm finding in the Subura." The Subura stretched across a large part of the central city, from east of the Forum toward the northeast hills, filled with some respectable shops, a lot of seedy taverns and brothels, and residences for the humbler classes. "All I'm seeing are places on the ground floor next to the entrances, and too many times I've told tenants in that kind of room that there's no hope of catching the burglar, or up on the tippy-top, and if there's a fire you're done for. I still have nightmares, of pulling out bodies."

Tausias was recalling the Great Fire. A couple years ago, a blaze in a bookshop burned so hot that a large swath of the neighborhood was in flames before it could be put out. Commodus made a speech about how he was going to build a brand new city there, to be called Colonia Commodia of course, which would be so grand that the name of Roma would be forgotten. People were afraid of what he might do, but the worry proved to be for nothing. No government money for reconstruction materialized, and Commodus turned his attention to renaming legions and the months of the year after himself. Private enterprise replenished the housing stock quickly, and shoddily. Some of the new buildings had already collapsed, and more were likely to. Vacancies, as Tausias had discovered, were still in short supply, and mostly in the least desirable locations.

"Is there some reason you cannot remain in the barracks?" Alexandrius was asking delicately whether Tausias was in some trouble with his commanders. Tausias claimed not to be seeking any favors, but perhaps he needed strings pulled.

"There's this weird lawsuit. Vectilian Barracks used to belong to some rich guy, an almost Emperor, you can still see it was a nice place once, even if it's kind of trashed now with all the men practically on top of each other. Some guy says he's the rightful heir, and the State should give him the house back."

"Oh! I know who that is." Narcissus had never told Alexandrius much of his story, but Diodoros Tigranos had.

"So it's true then? Some of the men were saying the courts would never rule against the State, but some said there were papers from the Vestal Virgins, and the Virgins never lose."

"What does your commander say?"

"Messala?" Tausias hawked up some phlegm, then thought better of spitting on his friend's floor. "That useless twit! He never even comes around except on payday, wants to make sure we all get the coins straight from his hand, as if he had anything to do with it. Mostly he just hangs out with the toffs, angling for some better job."

"But if a large number of men might be displaced, he will have to do something about it." It did not look as if Tausias was convinced. "At least, though, I can see a bright side to this. If Narcissus can get out of the Palace to pursue a lawsuit, maybe your sister will be released soon too."

"I haven't heard a thing from her in weeks." Tausias started clenching his fists. Alexandrius regretted having brought up the subject. The awkward silence was broken when a ruddy-faced young man entered, wearing a lawyer's robes and carrying a satchel filled with papers, which he was quick to set down. Alexandrius rose to greet him, and Tausias sprang to his feet.

"Tausias, this is Quintilian Viterbius, my comrade," Alexandrius said, using a word that meant both roommate and close friend. Tausias bowed. "Quintilian, this is my friend Tausias, an officer of the Watch." Quintilian nodded, as it was clear that Tausias was a protegé, not an equal. "He lives in the Vectilian Barracks. Have you heard of some litigation claiming ownership of that building?"

Quintilian brightened. "I have just been assigned to that very matter! Poor Fabiolus, that's the judge who drew the case, nearly sank into the earth when he heard what it was about. He adjourned it, saying he did not want to judge it and also represent the interests of the State. He requested that the State hire counsel. I hurried down to the Palace to apply for the job. I'm awfully junior, but see, the Palace usually hires Fulminatus when they need outside counsel, and he's been hired by the plaintiff. And I thought the senior rhetors might not want it, because it looks controversial, and like a loser."

"What do you mean, it's a loser?"

"The heir has all kinds of documents, and I don't know how I'm going to refute them if the Virgins say they're valid. It will be a pain if the City has to find new housing for all those men."

"So you think Narcissus is going to win?"

"Is that his name? The plaintiff didn't want to identify himself, said he was afraid of enemies. That didn't make sense, when he's appearing in open court, but there's a lot that doesn't quite make sense here."

"You've met Narcissus. Remember when your class graduated? And the Palace invited the whole school, to see you put on rhetor's robes and get pontifical blessings from the August One?" This was not at all usual. A man involved in a lawsuit would be well advised to hire a spokesman who had completed a course in rhetoric and law at a school like the one Fulminatus ran, but that was his own lookout. The government did not require a license to act as a rhetor, and if Commodus had thought of such a scheme he would have charged a heavy fee for it. But Commodus made money from the law the old-fashioned way. When a thorny legal dispute from the provinces was appealed to Rome, Fulminatus was the one to draft the imperial rescript, announcing the legal principle to be applied, after canvassing the parties to see which of them could offer the heftier bribe. Commodus found this a lucrative stream of revenue, and specially favored the students of Fulminatus to keep Fulminatus loyal.

"I mostly remember that we got really drunk, especially Fulminatus."

"And we watched those slaves box, remember? I bet on Castor. You bet on Narcissus, and won money off me if I recall correctly."

"You paid. But no, that's not him. The plaintiff without a name is a really weedy looking guy, no kind of athlete at all."

Alexandrius sat back down on the bench and started stroking his cheek. "Something is very strange about this."

"You must have him confused with someone else. The plaintiff says his father was a secret son of old Ceionius Commodus, falsely enslaved although freeborn. The grandmother was given her freedom before her child was born, and Ceionius married her and everything, even left a will giving the property to her descendants. Or so his story goes."

"You just told me the story of Narcissus. I never heard of Narcissus having a brother."

"If Narcissus is that boxer, no, they're not brothers. They are not alike at all. Maybe he is an impostor? It would be great for my career if I could prove that, save the State some embarrassment."

"We need to talk to Diodoros Tigranos. He's the one who knows all about this."

"I'll go," Tausias offered, eager to prove useful.

"To Nomentum? On foot? It would take you all day and all night. There is a messenger service right by the school. We can hire a fast chariot."

Alexandrius rose, but Quintilian forestalled him. "I really must be the one to go," he said, gathering up his satchel. "How do I find him?"

"He is the town supervisor. Inquire at the forum. Just mention my name and he will see you."

"A hundred thousand thanks, comrade!" With his free arm Quintilian gave Alexandrius a quick embrace, and departed.

"My thanks also," Tausias said. "It was a lucky spirit that put it into my head to see you. But I do not wish to trespass on your time further." Tausias bowed, but then Alexandrius embraced him, embarrassing Tausias with the unexpected familiarity.

Tausias made a desultory effort at looking over apartment buildings by Aurelian Way. But rather than actually make any inquiries about vacancies, he decided to stop in a tavern for a beer or two. He had turned the problem over to his patron, who seemed more eager to help than he had any right to expect. He had to have faith it would be handled. That did not mean that he stopped feeling angry about it. Before, he had not been sure which way to read the situation. Perhaps the place he was living was someone's home, which the State had stolen, just the way the State grabbed anything it wanted, just the way the State had grabbed his sister. Or perhaps the lawsuit was all fakery, some fraudster trying to get away with something. From what Alexandrius and Quintilian said, both were true. It was simply another thief trying to steal what had already been stolen. "I bet there aren't five honest men in this whole city," he muttered into his mug.

Tausias was not the only unhappy drunk in the place. He overheard another customer's mutterings, which were very uncomplimentary about Germans. He was not sure whether this was in reference to himself, but that hardly mattered. "What did you say?" he demanded loudly, swaggering over to confront the offender, who rose to reveal that unfortunately he had an inch or two of height on Tausias. Tausias wondered if he had bought more trouble than he could handle. But so did the other fellow, who could see from the tunic that Tausias was of the Watch, and glanced down at the left hip to see if Tausias was carrying his blade.

It was not entirely forbidden for officers to be armed while off-duty, but it was strongly discouraged. In theory the entire city was a weapons-free zone, except for those authorized to be armed at specific posts. In practice this was becoming more difficult to enforce. The official city limits, the *pomerium* traversed yearly by priests with holy water and chanting, now extended well beyond the walls and the bridges, and there were no checkpoints that anyone entering this Trans-Tiber region of the city would have to pass. As it became more common for unauthorized persons to be armed, officers became less concerned about bearing arms only when they had authorization. Praetorians trained, drilled, and mostly lived in an encampment just outside the city, because within the limits they were only supposed to be armed on the palace grounds or accompanying the Emperor in his movements. Yet they regularly carried their arms in transit between the Palace and the Encampment, and no-one dared to challenge them. When Tausias lived with Frida, he carried his blade to and from home routinely. He had even walked across the Forum armed without giving it a second thought, although in former times the lictors would have struck him dead at once for such an effrontery. Now that he lived in a secure barracks, he left his weapon there when not on shift. But the scabbard still hung from his belt, and his antagonist could not be blamed for peering down to check that it was empty.

But that turn of the eyes cost him, giving Tausias the chance to give a roundhouse sucker-punch to his temple. The blow staggered him, but did not lay him flat. As he fell to his knees, the bartender hurried over, shouting angrily, "Not in my establishment!" The bartender was burly enough that neither of the men felt like continuing the fight. Tausias gave an apologetic bow, fished another farthing out of his pouch to toss at the bartender, and left. He glanced behind, but his opponent was not following, simply returning to his beer.

Tausias crossed the bridge and passed between the Circus Maximus and the Palatine, then turned left toward the Caelian hill and home. The sun was going down, and a vast murmuration of starlings gathered, swirling like a storm cloud come to angry life. Tausias saw out of the corner of his eye a falcon soaring above the shimmering mass of birds. With a shriek, the falcon stooped, but failed to kill any of the starlings. Instead it smacked into the Vectilian House. Tausias could not see whether the falcon was dead or only knocked out. He was astonished to see a falcon be so clumsy. Then the murmuration took on a new shape. Tausias thought it looked like a skull for a moment, and wondered what the omen meant. It would not occur to him to think that he was important enough for such a sign to refer to himself.

He hoped that it meant that one of the thievish bastards running Rome was about to get what was coming to him.

Chapter 3

Octavius Emesianus, the new Governor of Syria, led his predecessor Pescennius Niger to a seat high in a stand of rough wooden bleachers overlooking a large, sandy field. The rise on which the bleachers stood was not quite the horseshoe shape preferred for amphitheaters, and the bleachers were intended only as temporary markers, to indicate how much earth would have to be piled up to create the desired form. Once the ground was filled in, the wooden seats would be replaced with permanent stone benches. Or such was the plan, and had been the plan for years, but two local Greek families were still fighting over the right to pay for the construction and get their honored ancestor's name put on it. So only the bottom row was finished, and the upper structure was becoming a little unsteady. But Octavius said he wanted to take the highest seats to get the widest view of the war games which would take place in the field.

An unspoken motivation was that he wished to be able to speak without any danger of being overheard. Servants followed, carrying jugs of wine and water, cups, trays and bowls with flatbreads, raisins, figs, dates, hard cheeses and pickled eggs. But Octavius told them to set everything down. Some assumed that he wanted to be served first, and picked up a wine jug and a pair of cups, preparing to pour, but Octavius shooed them away. On the field a company of soldiers, with some light cavalry and archery mixed in with the infantry, prepared for the games. Some were dressed as Parthians in distinctive yellow uniforms, and a few officers, acting as referees, wore red plumes, and had small megaphones hung around their necks.

Octavius said, in a somewhat apologetic tone, "I cannot promise that this will be very entertaining. Even with blunted weapons there are bound to be injuries, but I am hoping to avoid deaths." He started pouring a cup of wine.

Pescennius replied, "I know the difference between training and spectacle." He noticed that Octavius was filling the cup near to the brim with wine. "Please, make mine more than half water, not so much wine." Octavius made him a cup which was more than half wine, if not as strong as the cup he poured for himself. Pescennius reflexively spilled a little over the side, as a libation to the local spirits, before drinking any. Octavius had been about to sip himself, but hastily spilled a droplet first, seeing that Pescennius was pious.

Octavius really wanted to talk about such current events as the death of Commodus, but until he had a sense of the other man's sentiments, that seemed a dangerous subject. He would also like to have known why Pescennius had come here in the first place, when he could have sent the detachment of men without any need to accompany them. But he thought it safer to keep to the subject of the war games. "Even as training, this may not look good to your eye. The Roman side is all made of rather raw recruits, though I hope they know one end of their weapons from the other by now. The Parthian side is heavily outnumbered, but they are not told to let the Romans win. The veterans are told instead to use genuine Parthian tactics, from what they have seen of the enemy. I am hoping the recruits do win, to build up their confidence, but if the veterans stomp them, that will be valuable too, teach some lessons."

Pescennius said, "If I were a betting man, I would take the Parthian team." He was not, actually, much of a gambler, any more than he was a drinker.

"No bet. I would also." Octavius took a big slug of his wine, and broached one of the subjects he wanted to talk about. "Look, I am sorry to have been such a nuisance about a small number of men, but every experienced soldier is precious to me right now. I hope you are bearing no grudge about it."

"Not at all. I understand completely. You were in the right. That unit belongs to the province of Syria. And I want to clear up any quarrels or misunderstandings we might have, at this perilous time."

"I am trying to expand the legions here, as rapidly as I can. It is time that we stopped just defending on the Euphrates, and went on the attack against the Parthians."

"I thought the same thing, but I had to give that idea up."

"Really? I heard you were all in favor of an offensive." Octavius drank some more. "Look, if you think there is anything to be afraid of to our east, you are mistaken. Parthia is fragile as an eggshell right now! I hear even the Persians are getting rebellious. The Persians! That is pretty near the core of their Empire. If we march against them now, there is no limit to how far we can go. But if we wait too long, mark my words, they will choose better leadership and we'll miss our chance."

"It was not the East that made me pause. It was the West. As soon as I let Roma know that I was serious about a Parthian campaign, it was decided to transfer me to Egypt, where I am free to contemplate an invasion of Ethiopia if I wish."

"But why? I will do the best I can, but you have a hundred times my experience! Why don't they want the best commander possible on this front?"

"Because no-one except the glorious Commodus Caesar was ever going to be allowed to win a triumph, and he was too much of a coward ever to come to the front."

Octavius was greatly relieved at this confirmation that Pescennius also had a low opinion of Commodus. Now he could speak freely. "Good riddance to bad rubbish!" he said while hoisting his cup. Then he drained it, refilled it, and offered Pescennius the jug. "Do you want some more?"

"I am fine for the moment. Have you heard all the gossip from Rome? I have been on the road, and know only that he is dead, but none of the details. The first time I heard it, I doubted if it was even true. I remember that rumor last year that tricked Clodius Albinus. Are we completely sure now?"

Octavius laughed. "I had the same suspicion! That poor messenger who brought me the news, I clapped him into detention, just in case my face had given something away. I didn't want to give any response until I knew for sure. But don't worry, I gave him a few extra pennies for his trouble when I let him out. Yes, we're sure now. I have just had a long letter from Cassius Dio, do you know him?"

"I do. An excellent fellow!"

"He tells me all the gossip. It was New Year's Eve, that's the only thing everybody agrees on. The juiciest version has it that Commodus, in his Hercules get-up and all swaggering around, tried to rape the girlfriend of the head Praetorian Guard, and got stabbed for his troubles. That's so delicious I want it to be true, but Cassius doesn't buy a word of it. He says this Praetorian, Laetus is the fellow's name, vanished out of sight for a while, and then, what do you suppose? He re-emerged in the company of some leading Senators. What do you think? Does that imply some dark midnight meetings or what? Another version has it that Commodus was indeed being even more loutish than usual, but that was only because his wine was drugged. He suspected a plot, and tried to make Pertinax drink all the dodgy wine that was left, so somebody stabbed him. Or else, he was about to get rid of his mistress and his chamberlain, so they got his wrestler friend to strangle him. Or a more lurid story says, one of the eunuchs mutilated him right proper. But then again, everybody knows Commodus liked opium, so maybe the wine was just drugged because he liked it that way. Then there's also a version, where Commodus started another rumor he was dead, to see who would cheer this time, just like you and I were thinking. But when the word was put out on the street, the mob started celebrating and tearing down all his statues, so everyone decided it was best just to get rid of him quickly, and pretend he had already been dead for a while. We will never really know." Octavius shrugged. Pescennius paid attention to all the stories, but didn't seem terribly interested in contributing any speculation of his own. Octavius moved on to a more vital topic. "So, what do you know about this Pertinax? He doesn't sound the type to plot that kind of thing, but *cui bono,* eh?" The conversation was in Greek, but sometimes Emesianus threw in some Latin. "Of course I don't really know much about him. I've heard of him, who hasn't? But we've never exactly moved in the same circles."

Pescennius replied cautiously. "He was patron to some who have been patrons to my career, so I have sometimes been counted as a member of his faction. But I have seldom met him face to face, and cannot say that

I have ever known him really. I think that he would be a difficult man to get to know well. He is very reserved in his manner."

"I asked some people who've been around since his term as governor here, and it was funny. It was almost as if they'd forgotten he'd ever been here, until they were reminded. Of course, he brought his own team of people with him, and took them away with him when he left. Hardly anybody else got to speak to him. He hated appearing in public, and made little impression when he did."

"That will not serve him well as Emperor, I fear. The people of Rome are used to seeing their ruler perform. But in the more substantive duties, we may hope he will do well. He has been everywhere and done everything. Everyone says he is very capable. He will need to be."

"Well, all I know is that he wrote at once, wanting his revenues, now now now. I bet you have a similar letter waiting at home. Isn't that how it always is? We send boatloads of coin to Rome, and what do they send back? Boys, raw as hatchling chicks. Half of them unarmed, and those who have any, look like they saw their weapons for the first time the day before yesterday. And scarce a word of Greek! What am I to do with this latest batch from the back-end of Gaul," he said, sweeping his arm over some of the soldiers on the Roman team, now walking around the field aimlessly, "who think they can speak some Latin, but it's all a barbarous drawl, half the letters never make it out of their mouths? Equipping them properly, training them, supplying them... That all costs money, how can Rome not understand that?" He was getting agitated now. "I've had to resort to all sorts of scurvy tricks, to raise the funds for this buildup."

The Parthian team had ridden back behind a hill. The Roman team was supposed to mill around, as if they were unaware that the Parthians were near. Then the scouts announced that the enemy had been sighted, and their officers called them to formation. They were not very quick about it, and looked scarcely more organized than before. Octavius was making some noises of disgust. Pescennius chose his words carefully. "It is those fund-raising tricks, as you called them, that I need to discuss with you. Some of my Greeks, from Alexandria, complain that at the end of the shipping season, they put into your harbors and were hit with all sorts of new fees, a fee to drop anchor, a fee to unload, a fee to load, a fee if they could not move on soon enough. Their profit margins are small and they need to know about such things in advance, to decide whether the venture is worth it."

Octavius noted that, while Pescennius had not governed Egypt long, he already thought of the Alexandrian Greeks as "his" Greeks. But was he expecting to get their money back for them? That was not going to happen. He said nonchalantly, "Well, now they know in advance for next year, don't they? I would remit the fees, to please you my friend, but the plain fact of the matter is, I need the money."

Pescennius pressed on. "And my Jews complain to me that there was a desecration in Antioch, that was clearly the work of the Christians, but you imposed a fine on the Jews. The Jews had been collecting a fund for much-needed repairs to the main synagogue of Antioch, but then they had to give it to you."

"And what business is that of anybody in Egypt?"

"You know the Jews all stick together. The Jews of Antioch write to the Jews of Alexandria, and they complain to me, and will keep after me about it. So what happened?"

"Most of the gates have some kind of icon at the top of the arch, but there is one gate to Antioch that is left blank, so that those who have some scruple about images, whether Jews, or Christians, or whoever, we try not to inquire, can use it."

"I know that gate."

"Well some stupid fellow hung a wooden eagle over it. The prefect should have taken it down at once, at the very least as an ugly excuse for a piece of art, and disciplined whoever was responsible. But he didn't want a fight with the town guards. It really has to be some of the soldiers guarding that gate who did it, or helped whoever did it, but I have to pretend not to know that. Anyway, in the middle of the night when the portcullis was down, someone set up a ladder on the outside and got up there to soak the eagle with oil and set it on fire. They got away before the guards inside heard the noise and could raise the portcullis, or at least, so the guards all say. I have half a mind to crucify the lot of them on general principle. But everybody said I had to avenge the insult to Rome." He sighed. "Well how would I dare look disloyal to Rome? But then there was the problem of who to blame. There was a sign of the fish painted at the scene. Perhaps the Christians boasting that they did it?" He shrugged. "Or perhaps somebody else trying to point the finger at the Christians. But who can ever find out who the Christians really are? My advisers told me that even if I did catch some Christians, they probably wouldn't have any money anyway. There's Serapion, of course, but I didn't want to arrest him."

Serapion was the leader of the Christians of Antioch, and did not make the slightest attempt to hide that fact from the authorities. He often spoke publicly, and even people with no sympathy whatsoever for Christianity would go to hear him, out of curiosity to know what his positions were. There were other philosophers and religious leaders who gave talks, and attending such talks was a popular form of entertainment. Attendance need not imply agreement with whatever radical ideas were uttered. The crowd did, though, have some limits to its tolerance. Alexander the Oracle, with his supposedly living, talking dragon named Glycon, which was really a hand puppet, had died twenty years earlier of an apoplectic seizure while trying to argue with his many hecklers. But people who tried to shout down Serapion were generally shushed by the crowd, for many non-Christians had a grudging admiration for Serapion.

Pescennius was one such. "I found Serapion quite helpful during my term as governor."

"Really? Do tell."

"There was this seditious book causing an uproar. I obtained a copy, to read it for myself. Supposedly it was a story about Paul, that renegade whom the Christians revere second-most after the criminal Jesus, and his friend Thecla. She was a wonder-working beauty, who gained her powers by the simple expedient of remaining a virgin, despite all the men wanting to marry her, or to rape her, which in the eyes of the Christians seems to amount to much the same thing. And we evil governors were always trying to burn her alive, but she magically snuffed out the flames, or feed her to the wild beasts, but she magically tamed them."

"Sounds like an entertaining book."

"It was, better than that book of Sobek that is all the rage in Egypt these days. But it was pernicious, because its moral was that Christian women were permitted to preach. Usually the Christians keep their women quiet, preferably in veils, and we have not been sufficiently grateful to them for that. Suddenly there were babbling women on every street corner, spouting their crazed versions of the Christian message and defying us to execute them. I am not sure whether they expected to be miraculously preserved, or whether they really hoped to die. You know that the Christians think it a good thing if they are hurried along to their Elysium, though for some reason they have scruples against dying by their own hand."

"Perhaps you should have helped them meet their god, then."

"I had no taste for it. Anyway, Serapion proclaimed that the whole book was full of lies, and exposed the rogue who had forged it, and said that anyone who read that book was not a true Christian. You know that Christians fear being expelled from the ranks of their community more than anything else. My agents tell me that this whole affair helped him to win some kind of leadership struggle among the Christians, despite his most unfortunate background, from a family inclined to worship the Egyptian gods." He said this last with an ironic gleam in his eye, since he himself was inclined toward Egyptian gods. "I was glad to learn that they have a somewhat sensible leader, someone that we know and can keep an eye on. It would be worse if he were to be replaced by someone more deranged, especially if it were someone underground whom we could not track."

"My advisers said much the same. So I was not about to seize Serapion and try to force him to tell me who burned the eagle, or who pays the bills for him to live in his ostentatious poverty. Instead, I just fined the Jews. I had to blame someone, and they had a pot of money all collected in one spot."

224

Pescennius was going to reply, but the action had started. The Parthian team was charging over the hill, and the Roman team was ordered into shield-wall formation. They did form up, out of their previous disorder, with commendable speed. Could they have done so if they really had not known that this was coming? Well, that was another question for another day. Little space was left between the shield of one soldier and the shield of his neighbor, and through that little space each soldier stuck out his spear. They were not using real spears, but rather sticks whose tips were wrapped in rags, to pad the blow if the shield-wall held but some horse neither had the sense to shy away from charging the spears, nor was properly controlled by the rider. There was only so much that could be done to minimize the danger, however. If the shield-wall broke and the horses got in amongst the men, many would be trampled and there was no help for it.

At first, the formation held solidly, and the Parthians had to pull back from the front of the square. Then some tested the flanks. The right side of the square stayed solid, but one man from the left charged out at a horseman, trying to stick the horse with his fake spear. He got a kick in the shield for his trouble, which sent him sprawling in the sand. He tried to get up and continue, but the referees shouted at him to lie there, because he was dead. In a real fight, of course, the Parthians would have picked off this exposed man readily. The "dead" man started weeping, realizing that he was in for some severe humiliations at the hands of his fellow soldiers. The other men on the left flank of the formation were hooting and jeering at him as they did their best to close up the gap he left.

Octavius muttered, "Always one, isn't there?"

Chapter 4

Junius Severus was on a mission to the coast, and having a desultory time of it. The White Eagle, as the ship which brought Clodius and his men across the channel had been renamed, should be adequate to take them all back again, but Clodius asked Junius to inquire about the possibility of hiring a second ship as well, to take across the men whom Junius had brought north. Clodius insisted that he could not go back to Britannia without taking these men with him also. When the face of Junius had shown his puzzlement as to why this was, Clodius laughed and said, "Clearly your education has not taught you much about the ways of the army."

To this, Junius pressed his palms together in front of his chest, bowed slightly, and said, "Teach me." This was a gesture which a youngster used to his tutor. To those raised in well-born families, the tutor was an important authority figure. Here the gesture was a self-deprecating admission of ignorance.

"The army has despatched these men to be a personal guard to the governor of Britannia. The general staff will not care overmuch which governor of Britannia they guard, but to Britannia they must go. Then, after a decent interval, I can write and say that they have served me faithfully, but are no longer required. That is their only hope of obtaining a new posting in some more decent climate. If I leave them here, they may be stuck here for the rest of their lives."

So he rode to Gesoriacum on the first fair day once the foul weather let up, hoping to secure a second ship, but found that even one ship was not secure. The storms had knocked the White Eagle off her anchor and run her aground, leaving her tilting awkwardly on the sand. The rains had turned to snow and sleet, leaving the ship encrusted with ice. The long mast from the center of the ship was pointing somewhat away from Junius, in what would have been the vertical direction if the ship were upright. The furled cloth and dangling ropes from the mast were flapping languidly in the sea breeze. The harbor master had a team of men looking over the damage. Junius had some slight interactions with this man before, and recalled that he had been introduced as the cousin of Boudogur, the boatman who had taken his men down to Lutetia. But he had not caught this man's name exactly. "Arbagas" perhaps? Actually, it was Ardogent. Junius still found the weakening of final consonants and slurring of many vowels in the Gaulish pronunciation of Latin very hard to puzzle out. He did manage to decipher what was meant when Ardogent hailed him with, "Ye'r one o' Clod's men, ain'tchee?"

"I am honored to call Clodius Albinus my patron," he replied.

"Will 'e pay well?" Ardogent wanted to get straight to the point.

"My patron is well known as a... just man." He had been about to call Clodius a "generous" man, but did not want to say something that might lead to his patron being overcharged. "Your men can rest assured that they will be properly compensated for... whatever it is that needs doing." Junius was wary of exposing exactly how ignorant he was about ships. "How long will it take?"

"The keel's no' busted, gods ha' mercy, nor the mainmast." Junius did not recognize the word he used for "keel" but understood it was something vital. He did understand "mast" and caught that the reference to a "main" mast implied that there ought to be more than one mast, though only one was now visible. Presumably the not-main masts were broken. "A plank or two an' a spar or three needs replaced, an' a mite o' tar an' caulk. But 'auling 'er down to the water, now that'll need a fair day we can trust to stay fair. Only gods know when that'll be, an' they're no' telling." He smiled at his own wit.

"Do what needs to be done, as quickly as you can do it, and be assured that your men will be paid." Clodius had, after all, given Junius a mission to obtain two ships if he could, so Junius was hardly over-reaching his authority by making sure that at least the one ship would be available.

"All new sails and rigging would no' be amiss," Ardogent ventured.

"Very well," Junius replied, hoping that he was not being cheated. Did "rigging" mean the rope-things that attached the sails? How expensive could that be?

An elegant carriage rolled up, and a man dressed in stylishly trimmed furs stepped out. "Have you heard aught of the Golden Fleece?" he called out as he strode rapidly across the sand, eying the state of the White Eagle. He spoke Latin, with an accent that was noticeable but not as lower-class as that of the harbor master, who answered him in Gaulish. Junius gathered that Ardogent was saying that he had not heard any news of the Golden Fleece.

The newcomer looked Junius over, and evidently decided he might be somebody important. "I don't believe we've met, sir. I am Arpentus, at your service," he said, while giving a fairly deep bow. The harbor master, whose social rank was decidedly inferior, had not bothered with any such deference.

"I am Caius Junius Severus Lepcius," Junius replied with a half-bow, certainly more than a nod. He did not know how important this man might be, and did not want to offend by being insufficiently deferential. At the same time, he felt compelled to add his praenomen and agnomen, which he hardly ever used, to emphasize what kind of family he came from.

"Is that your ship, so sadly grounded?"

"The White Eagle belongs to my patron, Decimus Clodius Albinus, Governor of Britannia." Again he used a fuller form of the name than was strictly necessary, since Arpentus doubtless knew who Clodius was, and added the title, to emphasize the importance of his patron, and therefore of himself.

"I fear that my own vessel, the Golden Fleece, may be in a similar pass, on this coast or t'other, if she's not at the bottom." Arpentus raised his eyes heavenward in a prayer that his words not be true. "The fault is all mine, all mine. I should ne'er have dared another crossing in this season. I know how hard it is to tack westward in the teeth of a wind from that quarter." Junius had no idea what he was talking about, but nodded his head gravely. "But my cap'n assured me he could make it, he was a good man, they were all good men, I should'a ne'er let them risk themsel's." Now he cast his eyes downward, as if already assured that these good men were all dead.

Junius let a moment of silence pass before saying, "My patron was hoping to hire the use of a second ship."

"Well, in summer he would'a had his pick. But these months most'll be parked up the Sequana or up the Tamesis, away from Lear's ragings." Lear was the Gaulish Neptune, Junius gathered. "That's what I ought'a done, but I got greedy."

"Messire Arpong!" the harbor master interrupted, touching his hand to his forehead in a "pardon me" gesture. Junius noted that Arpentus was deemed worthy of such little gestures of respect, even if he himself was not. Ardogent continued with a burst of Gaulish while pointing out to sea. Junius could pick out the word "cursa" which was obviously borrowed from the Latin word for the postal service. He could see a few men in a boat rowing toward shore.

Recently the Cursus in Samarobriva had given Junius a dispatch from Britannia for Clodius. So despite all this talk about how it is nearly impossible to cross, Junius mused, boats must be crossing all the time. Evidently large ships were more dangerous than smaller watercraft, the reverse of what he would have naively guessed. Of course, ships with sails were at the mercy of rough winds: how had he not understood this before? He remembered red-facedly a conversation from back when he first set out on his mission. He had been advised to take a ship from Ostia to Massilia, and requested a ship to Londinium instead. Oh no, came the reply, with barely concealed sniggering, ships could not go past the Pillars of Hercules into the open Ocean. Junius took that for a bald-faced lie, knowing that Lusitania faced the Ocean and was famed for its fishermen, so he petulantly refused to deal with those people any more, and made his men go to Massilia on foot. That, he now realized, had been a senseless prolongation of the journey. The thought suddenly struck him that, if he had finished the journey by crossing the Channel, it would have been the first time he was ever on a boat of any kind. He had stepped on Boudugur's raft, but not while it was moving, so that hardly counted.

Was he secretly afraid of boats, a secret kept even from himself until this moment? Would an island people like the Britons have mocked him, if they learned of his ignorance and fear? Clodius recently chided him for his lack of education about the army, as well. Was he utterly unqualified for the governorship Commodus tried to give him? Really, there had been no reason for the appointment except that he was counted as a loyal friend, when Commodus had so few left that he trusted. He could match Commodus drink for drink, could gamble and lose without making it too obvious that he was allowing the August One to win, and could improvise some witty remarks. Was that all that he was good for? He had not even been a loyal friend, not really, harboring very low opinions of Commodus which his smooth mask had never hinted at. And if he had been a better friend, would friendship with such a person really have been anything to be proud of?

Junius tried to shake off these gnawing doubts as he followed the other two men down to the beach. Ardogent was gesturing to some of his men to stop tinkering with the White Eagle and help the postmen haul their boat inshore. Arpentus was shouting questions about the Golden Fleece. His ship was, they assured him, safely tethered to the docks in Londinium and unloading its cargo. "Cargo not even jettisoned? It all arrived whole?" he asked. That was more detail than they could tell him. But he was so relieved at the news that he started fumbling through his pouch for some coins to give them. Then he just decided to hand the whole pouch to them.

One of the postmen startled Junius out of his reverie, handing him a scroll and saying, "For the governor, but it is not important."

Chapter 5

The few horsemen assigned to the Roman team charged in, symbolically standing for a larger cavalry which would be available in reality. The Parthian team fell back, as if faced with many horse. Octavius said, "Oh look! The Parthians are making their fake retreat. I bet the rookies are all going to chase after them. You have seen this game before, I think?"

Pescennius replied, "Indeed I have. But won't their officers tell them not to fall for it?"

"The pretended officers are simply the most promising of the decurions. They're given no instructions. I want to see what they do with a larger command than a squad." Some of the "Parthians" were peeling off to the right, and others to the left, but the "Romans" were paying no mind. Their horsemen were trotting forward, with the square of soldiers at double-time behind them. "Well, at least the cavalry know not to leave the infantry in the dust. But it will just make it easier to surround them all."

It was exactly as Octavius said. Once the Roman team was deep enough into the cul-de-sac, the Parthian team let loose with volleys of arrows from three sides. The arrows, like the spears, had wads of rags in place of tips, and did not fly as they ought to have, but still, they came in at great speed. The infantry could make a roof of shields. The cavalry were more exposed. Some of the horses that were hit threw their riders. Other riders managed to control their horses, but the referees, following at a safe distance, shouted that anyone whose horse was struck must dismount. Some of the soldiers lowered their shields, looking to the sky to see if the arrows were done. "Don't look up, you fools!" Octavius shouted. They probably could not hear him. It was too late, anyway. One last arrow came down straight into a soldier's eye. Padded arrow or not, that had to hurt. "Oooh! I bet he loses that eye!" Octavius was becoming enthused by the action, and poured some more wine for himself. "Oh! Oh! Do you hear what he's shouting?" The poor man's screams were piercing the distance quite effectively.

"Is that a local boy?" Pescennius asked. "It sounds like Aramaic, but I confess I have never mastered that tongue."

"He is saying he can still fight! What bravery!" The referees, however, were declaring the game over, a Roman defeat. Some of the Romans wanted to argue that they were still not whipped. One threw his spear at the Parthians. It was a good toss, but he was angrily reprimanded for it.

Pescennius shook his head sadly. "That was not bravery. That was fear. He worries that he will be discharged from the army and unable to make a living. Make sure to find him employment, in the supply train or somewhere. Nothing helps morale more than assurances that the soldiers will be taken care of, if wounded."

"Can't we leave him in the line? Bravery or fear, he shows spirit!"

"That would be unfair to the comrade on his blind side. In desperate times, of course, we have used soldiers much worse off than he is, but shortage of men is not your problem."

"No, it isn't." Octavius looked down at the field with disgust. "Well, fun's over for today. I could go down and shout abuse at the men, but I suppose the officers, the real officers I mean, already have that covered."

"Better that they learn the lesson here, rather than deep in the East."

"Deep in the East... Do you think our army can get deep into the East?" Octavius grew thoughtful, his voice dropping to a whisper. "Once, when I was little, my father and I, with a load of purple dye, got further east than I think the Parthians meant to let us go. Across a valley, up on top of the next rise... I saw them!"

"Saw the Parthians?"

"No, we saw the silk people! They wore funny-looking cone-shaped hats, and had strange scrunched-up faces. Too alien to be from anywhere but the end of the world. I got a good look at their faces because they were staring back, I think they knew we were from the purple country, must be as much of a mystery to them as the silk country is to us. Parthia keeps us apart, and robs both blind. If we can punch our way through those thieves in the middle, don't you know what that would mean? I wish those people whining all the time, about how I take money for the army, could just understand, there'll be so much profit if we win this. More money for the Jews! More money for the Greeks! More money for the Syrians! Money for everyone!"

Pescennius smiled. "Now there is a rallying cry! I think more people would be roused by 'Money for everyone!' than by 'Glory for Roma!' Mind you, I love Roma with all my heart, but I have cousins who hate it. Money, though, is beloved by all."

"I have cousins who hate Rome too."

"Really? I heard you were related to the imperial family."

"My mother's father's mother was of that *gens Ulpia* family, whoop whoop whoop," Octavius said, waving his hand in little circles. He was beginning to get sloppy-drunk. "Her honored brother did something or other for his cousin Hadrian Caesar, but she was in disgrace, pregnant by a common soldier. The brother could have had his balls for that, he was paterfamilias over her at the time. But he was content just to ignore them and disown them. So my grandfather grew up rather incognito. He did reasonably well for himself, ended up here in Syria, married off his daughter, my mother that is, into an up-and-coming mercantile family, the Qutb-a-din." He spat out the Syriac name.

"That is easy for you to say!"

"So you see why in Rome they just called my father Emesianus, because we are from Emesa. He sold finery to all the best families, never hurt that he could say, did you know that my wife is related to...?" He hit the wine some more. "Do you know why I am called Octavius?"

"After the first Augustus Caesar?"

"No. When my birth was announced, Marcus Aurelius quipped, well at least one-eighth of him is worth something, and the nickname stuck. Commodus never really acknowledged me as kin, until... you remember that year when Pertinax and Julianus and all them others were banished?"

Pescennius grimaced. "I had to leave Roma rather suddenly myself."

"There was some kind of big conspiracy."

"Nothing was ever proven."

Octavius waved the thought away. "Of course not. Anyway, Commodus had to fill the offices with somebody, so he gave me this job and that, and I did better than he expected, better than I expected too. Still, it was a surprise to be given a Governorship. But now you tell me he only sent me here to fail, trusting that someone like me would never win any triumphs." He finished his wine, and was disappointed to find the jug empty. "So, what is your story?"

"Much the same as yours, in many ways. Some of my ancestors were Roman equestrian, not imperial by any stretch, but solidly respectable. Others were servile, and others in between. The army, of course, posted me to the other end of the world from where I grew up, out to the Rhine frontier, where hardly anyone believed that someone who looked like me was a citizen. But my commanders judged only by ability. They gave me administrative jobs, which like any foolish young man I resented, but I worked hard. So they sent me to Rome, to law school. Soon I was a magistrate, and now, if I go to Rome to visit my sons, who are attending a very good school, I can walk into the Senate House, and have a vote. So can you, now that you have been a Governor. How could I not love the Empire?"

"You know, I thought you were coming here to take Syria back from me. My shaky family tie to Commodus isn't much protection any more, is it?"

"I assure you I wished only to make peace between Syria and Egypt. The East must be unified."

"You are not worried that someone is grabbing power in Egypt, while you are away?"

"I never wanted Egypt in the first place. Mantennius was in line to be the next governor, and Commodus only gave it to me out of a kind of spite. Mantennius has been prefect long enough, and really he is governor in all but title and salary. I let him know that I trusted him to run things in my absence, and if he embezzles a little money for himself, he is welcome to it."

"Governor Asellius of Asia is in Tarsus, to attend some relative's wedding. He wrote to assure me that he had no intention of trespassing in my province. He must have known that I was feeling insecure about my position. I sent an urgent messenger to intercept him, to tell him you were visiting, and to ask him to come and meet us."

"He is an excellent man. He will have ideas about the Parthian campaign."

"If there ever is a campaign. Instead I suppose the West will just bleed us dry, of all the money we need for this glorious campaign." He waved his hand at the scene down on the field, where officers were haranguing the men. "Not that it looks very glorious right now, but you know what I mean."

"I do know what you mean. The revenues from the East are needed in the East."

"I am half tempted to tell that Pertinax to... no, forget I said that. I don't dare be a rebel. If Pertinax came out here himself to take command, I would be glad to obey him. But I don't suppose there is much chance of that."

Pescennius thought about this. "No, the situation in Rome is probably too uncertain for him to leave. But, for a while there were separate Emperors on the western and eastern fronts. Unfortunately Lucius Verus died too soon. We should write to Pertinax and the Senate and ask that a co-Augustus be named, to be in charge of the East."

Octavius asked slyly, "Do you have anyone in mind for that position?"

Pescennius laughed. "I do not think that I would be their first choice. Assuming that Rome agreed, we would probably get someone like Septimius Severus. He has managed the Danube front for years, and is well connected on the Euphrates front as well. His wife is sister to the high priest of Elah Gabal, from your own hometown of Emesa."

"Oh, spare us! Do you know what the Elah Gabal cult is like? They're worse than the Christians! I hear they still make eunuch priests, despite the law. And their women circle-dance around the sacred phallus going ulu-lulu-lulu. That's who I would really like to feed to the beasts!"

"It might not be him. Rome might not agree to the idea at all. But if we are slow in sending the revenues, that will pressure them to reply. Egypt, Syria, and Asia will have to act together. We will have to be delicate about what we say, avoiding any implication that we would be disloyal to Pertinax."

"You write the letter, I'm sure you're better at this than I am, and I will sign it also."

Chapter 6

The pathways in the base camp were now strewn with cinders, but still a little slick. Junius knocked the snow and grit off the bottoms of his boots before entering the command house. This had lately been improved, with a more solid roof, and a slanting chimney hole, so that smoke from a fireplace could go out without letting rain and snow come straight down in. As was his way, Clodius had not allowed any of this work to be done on his own dwelling until wooden huts had been constructed for all the soldiers. The men had not gotten out of the tents any too soon. Every morning, some would start to cough, and the contagious sound would set the whole camp to hawking up phlegm raucously. At least, no-one was yet sick to a life-threatening degree.

As Junius entered, Servilius rose, bowed to him, and poured him a cup of hot herbal infusion. Placidius nodded but did not rise, and Clodius asked, "How did you prosper, my son?"

"Not well. The White Eagle was driven up onto the sands. I have had to hire some locals to repair the damage."

"Is the keel broken?"

"No, nor the mainmast."

"That should not cost too much money or time."

"There was another ship, the Golden Fleece, but it was sent across the water before the storm. It belongs to a local merchant called Arpentus."

"I know that name. The British legions have bought many greatcoats from him."

"So have the Belgian troops," Placidius added. "His reputation in these parts is high."

"He was angry at himself for venturing another crossing in this season. He feared that all of his good men were at the bottom of the sea."

"He worried about losing the men?" Clodius asked. "Rather than worrying about the goods?" Junius nodded. "Well then, his friendship is worth cultivating. I did put it about, when we first came here, that I was here to purchase trade goods for the Caledonians. Does this Arpentus make woolens that are ornamental as well as functional?"

"He does indeed," Placidius said. "Some of his wall hangings would make this place more beautiful, as well as warmer."

"And some of our men need new coats, if I can judge by the morning chorus that always greets us. Very well, we shall spend some money on his wares."

"He will not easily be persuaded to risk his ship again until later in the season. The post did bring word that the Golden Fleece was safe in Britannia," Junius said. "That reminds me. The postmen gave me this dispatch for you, but said it was not important." He pulled out the scroll.

Clodius did not reach to take it. "Open and read it. See if it is from my son Pescennius Priscus." Junius nodded. He had the art of reading a text silently, without speaking the words aloud, something that few could do. "See if it is a list of all the men he intends to promote to this post or that, come spring."

That was exactly what it was, Junius saw. "You are a soothsayer."

"Not at all. I see that for all your dealings with them, you are also not well educated in the ways of the Cursus."

Rather than beg instruction, Junius decided to try a guess. "When dispatches must cross the Channel, they send them in duplicate, in case one boat goes down? They said it was not important because this is the same dispatch I brought you yesterday?"

"Well answered," Clodius said, as a tutor would say to a clever pupil. He took the scroll from Junius and tossed it into the fire, which was needing a little more fuel. "So I have been told twice that I am a useless old man who need not bother coming back."

Junius was shocked. "Your son addressed you with the highest respect!"

"He is a disrespectful son of a whore and a dog!" Clodius was too agitated to consider what this insult said about Plautilla and himself. "How dare he tell me what he is going to do, and not even ask whether I approve? Better yet, he ought to have sent me alternatives and asked me to choose." He stared into the fire. "I have sat here too long, waiting for a summons to Roma that will never come."

Placidius intervened. "I know something that will cheer you. I asked one of my men to look for something in the archives, and among the records from your time governing Belgica, he found a most interesting letter from Commodus. Yes, it is still preserved. Why did you never tell anyone that he granted you the title of Caesar and named you the rightful heir?"

Clodius shrugged. "Because I wrote back promptly to refuse that offer. I thought that he was trying to trap me into expressing eagerness for the throne, so that he could condemn me. It turned out to be something different. It was right after he beat poor Crispina into a miscarriage, and sent her off to an island, never to return. Some Senators were worried because he was never going to beget an heir, and managed to tell him so. I think it was that silver-tongued Tullius, who said something to the effect that it was grossly unfair for poor Caesar to bear all the burdens of the Empire alone, and did he not deserve to have a helper?"

"All the better then! If there are respected Senators who know the truth of it, nobody can accuse us of forging this document."

"But how self-serving would it look, for me to dig that buried corpse up now? I should be like the cat who refused to go out when the door was open, but begs to go out after the door is shut."

"It would not be you yourself bringing this to the Senate's attention. I would write to friends in Rome, and tell them, I was not looking for this, I was looking through the archives for something else, which is true, but isn't this document interesting, and so on, and so forth."

"And you can say," Junius added, warming to the theme, "that Clodius is so modest, not only did he decline the honor, but he has never told any of his friends about it."

"Very well," Clodius said. "Junius, you write the letter. You always know how best to put things." Junius was gratified by the praise, forgetting all his self-doubts of earlier. But he saw that his patron still was not happy. "I doubt that it will make any difference, anyway," Clodius sighed as he turned his gaze back to the flames.

Junius knew he was still upset about the high-handed conduct of Priscus. "If you need me to, I could cross over to Britannia as your agent."

"As my spy, you mean? I am not yet reduced to fearing plots against me by my own son."

Servilius was rummaging among his things, and came up with some scraps of parchment, charred around the edges, stuck together by some molten sealing wax. He handed this to Junius, who needed a moment to recognize, with some astonishment, what it must be. "If ever you do go to Britannia, you must take this with you. It is the last remnant of the scroll you swore to break the wax on, the moment you set foot in Britannia, and it would be terrible luck to fail to keep your oath."

Junius and Clodius looked at each other in amusement. "There is not much wax left here. I am not sure I would know how to go about breaking the wax, anymore."

"You could scrape some off with your fingernail... no, not now! If and when you get to Britannia! That would convey to the spirits your oathkeeping."

"But what would have been the meaning if I had simply stirred the fire that evening and made sure that every last bit of this was burnt?"

Servilius shuddered a little. "That would mean that you were telling all the gods you never wanted a governorship or any other such honor, ever again!"

At this, Clodius laughed out loud.

Chapter 7

Fabiolus Prolectus was an inexperienced elderly judge. This was an unusual combination. There were young judges of high birth, serving a lowly magistracy for a short term, as a first step in what they hoped would be a glittering career. And there were elderly judges, for whom this was the entirety of their career. Those would be from respectable families whose patrons had political power even if they themselves did not, and their service would lead to their sons or nephews being considered for such appointments, and perhaps further advancement. Fabiolus had dubious family, but the highest level of patronage. He had served the *gens Anicia* in various capacities all his life, and Lady Anicia was a personal friend of the Empress. So Pertinax was persuaded to name Fabiolus to the "white list" from which judges were chosen to hear legal cases, to provide some dignity and steady income in his later years.

He had only the rank of *iudex*, meaning that he was empowered to investigate the factual issues, but would have to submit the case to a judge with the rank of *praetor* if there were unresolved legal issues. Of course, in most cases, findings of fact on such questions as which witness was lying or whether a document was forged completely disposed of the case. He was afraid that this would be so in the case before him, and that he, rather than any praetor, would take the blame for the outcome. He rued the day that he had wished for some case less boring than the ones he had been assigned in his first month on the job. He gingerly climbed the steps to the raised podium. The podium was in the middle of a basilica, which was an open space covered with a domed wooden roof in case of rain, on most days used as a marketplace. Romans were proud that their legal proceedings were conducted in full public view. At least, in theory the public watched the legal proceedings, but most Romans avoided the tedium on those days when judges sat. The first hearing of this case had the usual small audience, but word must have gotten around. This time there were some notables in attendance, and several curious lawyers, and

240

a disquieting number of soldiers in the uniform of the City. They were doubtless from the Vectilian Barracks.

Fabiolus was glad that the servant climbing beside him with a satchel of documents was a tall, stout Mauretanian. He had never had a servant before in his life. The cryer standing to one side of the podium with a ceremonial mace also had a formidable aspect, since threats of violence to the judges were not at all unknown. Fabiolus waited until the servant laid out the documents and anchored them with lead paperweights, and set beside them the curious lockbox in the form of Vesta, before climbing the last step. The cryer thumped the ground with his mace thrice. "All rise for the Honorable Fabiolus Prolectus Iudex! If any have disputes, come forward and let truth be found!" If Fabiolus had been a praetor, "let justice be done!" would have been the phrase. He paused briefly, in case anyone wished to exercise the customary right to come forward at this point to plead a cause. In practice, anyone wishing to initiate a case would hire a lawyer, who would have had the courtesy to inform the court in advance.

Once satisfied that there would be no surprises today, Fabiolus sat on his high bench behind the podium. He was not entitled to the curule seat of a more ranking magistrate. Spectators could sit once he did. "In the matter of Anonymous Plaintiff versus the Senate and People of Rome, I recognize Fulminatus Rhetor for the plaintiff." Fulminatus rose and bowed, and tugged the shoulder of his client to make him do likewise, and when he resumed his seat, he had to pull his client back down as well. "And you must be Quintilian Viterbius Rhetor for the State. Have you had a chance to review copies of the documents received into evidence, purportedly executed by the late Lucius Aelius Caesar, also known as Ceionius Commodus?" Fabiolus reflexively stood and bowed at the mention of a Caesar, although he was not supposed to make any gestures of obeisance while on the bench. A judge was supposed to be practically a god within the court, and not to take any notice of any man's rank, but habits were difficult to break.

Quintilian rose and bowed. "I have, Your Honor."

"We have, firstly, an emancipation of his slave Smaragda, and secondly, a divorce agreement with his wife Avidia Plautia, settling most of his property on her and her issue, but retaining the house called Vectilian. Then thirdly, we have a marriage contract with the aforesaid Smaragda, and fourthly, a will leaving the Vectilian house to the issue of Smaragda. Will you stipulate to any or all of these documents, and if not, what would you dispute?"

"Your Honor, the State is not prepared to yield anything at this juncture. We require authentication of the documents' provenance from the alleged testator." Here Quintilian showed off his expensively-acquired legal vocabulary. "And we require proof that this nameless person is of the issue of Smaragda, if such parentage is of any worth." Here he displayed a talent for sarcasm. "Moreover, we note that under the Julian statutes, a Senator may not marry a freedwoman, nor can a child from a legitimate marriage be disinherited in favor of irregular offspring."

"His firstborn, the late and much lamented Lucius Verus Augustus Caesar..." Fulminatus paused to bow with a flourish, at the mention of an Emperor. This forced Quintilian and even Fabiolus to make bowing motions, if they were not to look boorish. Then he resumed, "...was not at all disinherited, as the bulk of his father's property had already been conveyed to his mother. All that my poor client seeks is the one piece of property which was reserved for his branch of the family, of which he has been unjustly deprived for so long."

"If this purported divorce is to be believed, then the Vectilian house was the entirety of the estate which he retained at the time of executing this purported will. Therefore, he could not bequeath his entire estate to the fruit of an illegal marriage."

"It was not illegal for him to marry if he wished, only for him to marry as a Senator. My learned, though young, colleague misapprehends how the Julian statutes have been applied," Fulminatus said condescendingly. "A man of any rank may freely renounce his rank at any time, as the mighty Cincinnatus did repeatedly."

"Are we to believe that the very man whom the divine Hadrian Augustus Caesar..." Quintilian paused for some bowing. Two could play at that game. He continued, "…entrusted as his own heir, would abandon his rank and his duties as a Senator?"

Fulminatus was not flustered. "Are you implying that a Caesar," with a slight bow, "could not experience true love, or that he should not be free to act in accordance with his heart's promptings? You demanded proof of some facts. Let me then demand proof that the testator ever voted in the Senate after his remarriage."

Quintilian of course had no records with him as to when Ceionius Commodus had last gone to the Senate. To his best recollection of the history, Ceionius seemed to have been in some disgrace in his last months, for reasons that nobody knew. He was not sure what to say, but the judge rescued him. "All of these questions," Fabiolus pointed out in a tone of relief, "as to the legality of the remarriage, or of the bequest of property to the second wife's children, are exclusively within the jurisdiction of the praetors." Perhaps, Fabiolus thought, he could duck this case after all.

Quintilian looked around nervously. The parties he was waiting for had not appeared. Did he want the case kicked over to a praetor, on the purely legal issues? No: then the factual questions might be assumed against him. "Your Honor, we don't know the facts. We don't even know who this guy is." His formal classical diction was slipping away from him as he started to feel rattled.

"My client will reveal his true name and relations once he is assured that his property rights and his station in society will be appropriately protected by the law," Fulminatus answered smoothly.

"There is an outstanding demand for proof that your client has any right to claim under these documents," the judge observed.

"If the documents are even genuine," Quintilian added. He was fairly certain that they were, but could not waive the issue. Besides, he needed to stall for time. "Consider the factual implausibility of this scenario, an imperial heir voluntarily degrading himself…"

The judge shook his head. "The Maximal Lady, Eldest of the Vestal Virgins, gave me these documents herself." She was in the court, but not up front as one might expect. Rather, she sat demurely in the back, as if not wishing to be noticed. "I know that you were not present at the earlier hearing, but you ought to know that."

"I call the Maximal Lady!" Fulminatus declaimed loudly.

The cryer pounded his mace on the ground and called out in his most booming voice, "Is the Maximal Lady present? Come forward and be heard!" There were few in Rome who knew her personal name, even fewer who were entitled to use it, and he was certainly not one of them. He thumped with the mace again. "Is the Maximal Lady present? Come forward and be heard!" Third time was the charm. "Is the Maximal Lady present? Come forward and be heard!"

"I am here," she replied. She still needed a little more time to complete her mincing progress to the front. Her long dress covered her feet, and her steps must not let even a toe peek out. She also preferred to keep her arms within her sleeves, and she wore a mantilla completely covering her hair. The drab grey color of all her clothing gave no hint of the power she wielded. Ordinarily the cryer would at this point make the witness clutch his testicles and swear an oath to be truthful, and since women and eunuchs could not do this, any statements a court allowed them to make would not bear the same evidentiary weight. But the Vestal Virgins guarded the very sacredness of Roma, as well as records and treasures, and to question their honesty in any way would be an impudent sacrilege.

"Maximal Lady," Fulminatus opened in his most unctuous tones, "I pray, explain to us, concerning those documents which you gave to this court, how you know from whom they issued, and how you can know who is their beneficiary?"

"They have been in our treasury since the days of my predecessor's predecessor. The record clearly states that the depositor was Lucius Aelius Caesar." She made no gestures of obeisance at the mention of a Caesar. "The claimant was to give us a token, in the form of a silver figure of Our Lady of the Hearth, Vesta..." At this point she closed her eyes, bowed her head, and muttered under her breath the more sacred names of her goddess, which those not in her service ought not use and need not hear. "The figure was hollow, and locked. Within was concealed the seal-stone of Ceionius Commodus,

244

that is, the name which Lucius Aelius Caesar used before his elevation in rank, and the hinges were sealed with multi-colored wax. We had a paper with a rubbing of the wax seal, and the stamp of the stone seal, for verification."

The judge held up the figurine. "Is this the token which the plaintiff presented you?"

"It is."

"And are you satisfied that my client was the proper claimant?" Fulminatus asked.

"Not entirely." This took Fulminatus aback, and he could not entirely conceal the look in his eyes, as if to ask why she had not mentioned any objections before. "The claimant ought to have had a key. We had a duplicate key, but ought not to have needed it. The wax seal appeared slightly askew. But I thought that perhaps my eyes have grown too suspicious after squinting at so many forgeries in my time. A challenge question was left with us, in case of doubt. Who first prescribed *tetrapharmaka*? That is Greek for the four remedies."

The plaintiff sprang to his feet. "And I answered! It was Epicurus the philosopher, and the Four Remedies are: never to fear the gods, never to fear death, always to remember that evil is easy to avoid, always to remember that good is easy to find!" He looked smugly proud of his erudition.

"Fulminatus Rhetor!" the judge admonished. "You will control your client." Fulminatus put both hands on the plaintiff's shoulders and pushed him back down onto his seat.

"That was not the correct answer," the Vestal said sadly.

"There is also a medicine by that name," the judge observed.

"That also was not the answer sought."

"I suppose the answer was: My great-uncle!" came a voice from the back. Four men were hurrying into the basilica. Quintilian turned around, and smiled to see them.

"That was correct," the Vestal confirmed.

"How dare you interrupt these proceedings?" the judge erupted. He must regain control of his court. "Wait, I know you! Are you not Diodoros Tigranos, commander of the City?"

245

"I am, Your Honor, although my post is now elsewhere."

Many of the soldiers in the audience cheered him and shouted Ave. Fabiolus was thoroughly annoyed, and slammed lead paperweights down to make some noise while shouting, "We will have order!" He wished that he had some kind of little hammer, or something, to pound more effectively. When quiet was restored, he asked, "But what does your uncle have to do with this? I thought that your family was from Armenia?"

"Not my great-uncle, the heir's. Smaragda's brother created the dish tetrapharmacum, for which the household was renowned."

"I object!" Fulminatus was looking stricken. He had been to imperial banquets, knew the dish, and ought to have made the connection. Somehow he had to stop this case from unravelling. "A bystander cannot just stroll in, and start spinning stories for the court."

Quintilian was quick to rectify. "I call Diodoros Tigranos!"

The cryer, of course, had to go through the entire ritual of asking whether Diodoros was present, and commanding him to come forward, three times, even though he was right there. "Lower your right hand and repeat after me!" Diodoros put his hand on his scrotum and repeated promises to let Jupiter Optimus Maximus do terrible things to him if he either spoke untruth or withheld any truth. The phrases were from such an archaic version of Latin that Diodoros could not be quite sure exactly what things Jupiter would do to him, but it sounded as if castration would be the very least of them.

"So is it your testimony that the true heir, from the issue of Smaragda, should be expected to know the story of the origin of tetrapharmacum?"

"It is how Smaragda first caught his eye, by making that wonderful dish. He would know that, if he were from that family, instead of a runaway slave from the Curtius household!" He pointed his finger very rudely at the plaintiff, who belatedly looked around to see that three other men had come in with Diodoros. It was Senator Sempronius and the Curtius brothers. The plaintiff gasped, jumped up, and made a run for it. The cryer dropped his mace and gave chase, and the Mauretanian joined him. The two soon had the struggling man pinioned in their arms.

Fabiolus swore. "Pluto, Hecate, and the infernals! What is going on here?"

"This slave's name is Mercurius. He may not know me, but you see that he knows his masters. He stole the figure of Vesta..."

"I object! I object! I object!" Fulminatus was waving his arms. He would not go down without a fight. "This is simply inadmissible! He admits that he has no personal knowledge."

"Then I call Jovialis Curtius Rhetor!" Quintilian's call forced the cryer to let Mercurius go, but the Mauretanian could easily hold him alone. The cryer retrieved his mace and his dignity, and formally called and swore in the next witness.

"Let me get this straight," the judge said, and held up the figure of Vesta. "Are you the rightful owner of this?"

"No, Your Honor," Jovialis replied. "It belongs to a client of mine, who entrusted it to me for safekeeping. I was quite embarrassed when it disappeared."

"And what proof have you," Fulminatus sneered, "that it belonged to your client?"

"I have the key. Your Honor, may I approach?" As Jovialis pulled out a key and passed it to the judge, Fulminatus sat down in weary surrender. Never ask a question if you do not know the answer.

The judge slapped the Vesta figure shut until it locked, then opened it with the key. "Now we are getting somewhere. Does this client of yours have a name, or does he also prefer anonymity?"

"My client is not pressing any claim for possession of the property at this time," Jovialis carefully answered. The soldiers in the audience let out some audible sighs of relief.

"And are you the owner of the slave Mercurius?"

"I was, until I sold him to my brother Fortunatus for a farthing, to show him how worthless he was. He was one of a pair of twin brothers, Hermes and Mercurius. I trained them in law, history, philosophy..." He looked at Mercurius sadly. "They could have earned their freedom, become men of substance. But they were always low schemers. Hermes ran away and the Vesta was missing. I have since heard that he died at the hands of that one of damned memory himself." He avoided the name of Commodus Caesar. He added, "It is said that he was trying to blackmail the Palace about the existence of a secret heir, but," he added carefully, "I have no personal knowledge of that. I do know that I put Mercurius to the questions," a euphemism for torture by professionals, "about where his brother or the Vesta might be, but he denied knowing. Clearly he lied."

"You are the liar!" Mercurius shouted. "I am a man of high birth! I told the court that enemies would plot against me. You see now, I was right."

"Strip him, and you will see how many times I had to flog him."

Mercurius was wearing an undistinguished tunic. Fulminatus had pressed him to wear a toga for court, and only now understood why he had refused. Mercurius started to squirm again, protesting "You have no right to make me expose myself!"

"Shy, are you?" the Mauretanian laughed. "Never go to the baths? That might account for the smell!" Without waiting to be prompted, he tore the tunic off effortlessly, and spun Mercurius around to show everyone a back that was one solid mass of stripes from shoulders to buttocks.

"I see. The court finds that this claim was fraudulent," Fabiolus concluded. "The slave Mercurius should be put to the questions, as to who put him up to this." His eyes were squarely on Fulminatus. He might not be allowed to torture the rhetor as he could the slave, but he was obviously wishing to.

"It was Consul Falco!" Mercurius blurted out. He had withstood torture before when there was a potentially profitable secret to protect, but he had no wish to undergo it again if he could avoid it. "I tried to sell the statue, and somebody told me Falco would be interested!"

"It is true, Your Honor. The Consul paid for this case to be brought. Naturally I assumed it was a valid claim. How could I have imagined that a man in such an honored position could use me so dishonorably?" Fulminatus was trying to make himself the victim.

It was the turn of Fabiolus to regret asking a question he had not known the answer to. The Consul was bigger game than he wanted to hunt. "If there is nothing further, is this your brother, the present owner of the slave? You may take him home. We can find manacles if you need them."

"Yes, Your Honor, I am Fortunatus Curtius, but I would never trust this wretch under my roof again. I would prefer that he be punished in some exemplary fashion."

Punishing a perjurer was well within his jurisdiction. "Very well. I order that his lying tongue be torn out by the roots, and that he be hung by his hands from a bar and flogged until death." The crowd's cheers drowned the incoherent protests of Mercurius.

Executions were a popular entertainment, and there had been so few since Pertinax took over.

Chapter 8

A festival of Fervor in late winter, when all the rules were relaxed, was a good idea, as everyone agreed in both empires. But there was no agreement about when exactly to hold it, or what to call it. Rome had its Februalia in the middle of the month named "February" for the festival. Then the young men ran around naked and tried to whip the women with leather thongs, and any women they tapped was sure to become pregnant. Parthia had its Frawar about a month later, in the last days before the Nawruz at spring equinox. But where Nawruz was a normal holiday with exchanges of food and gifts between friends and neighbors, Frawar was a time for slaves to go free and even order their masters about, although they would not go too far if they knew what was good for them. Syria held its Pherurin somewhere in between, although not always at the same time from one place to another, or from one year to another. This year Antioch was holding it on the last new moon of winter, to avoid clashing with the Jews' Purim on the full moon. Either was an occasion for masquerades and drunkenness. If someone did something he shouldn't have, perhaps he wouldn't be recognized in his mask, or if he were, the drink would be an excuse.

Demetrios was a wealthy merchant of famously abstemious habits. He never indulged in any of the pleasures of the flesh. But his youth had been quite different. In his more dissolute days, he had gotten a young girl pregnant, and had denied all responsibility. He had even hired men to beat up her brother, to stop his persistent pursuit of the matter. Then she and the child both died during the birth. An unexpected remorse overwhelmed him. He confessed all his sins and dedicated himself to God. He credited his piety for his prosperity, and made sure to donate generously to the poor. And yet, the Demetrios of the past was not dead, but only sleeping, and lately, not sleeping very deeply.

On this night, the urge to cut loose for once was too strong to ignore. He changed into worn and dirty clothing which he had been on the point of giving away. He did not wish to be obviously rich and a target for thieves. He put on a mask of a sheep's head which somehow he had never gotten rid of. Only someone who had known him thirty years ago would recognize it, and those people were mostly dead or moved away, or would hardly expect that Demetrios would still have kept it. He slipped out without any of the servants noticing, evading them as if they were the masters and he were the one guilty of some petty mischief. Soon he was mingling with the crowds.

He fell in with a group of three soldiers, one of whom had a patch over one eye. He bought them wine, saying that he always wanted to be good to veterans, especially the wounded. He lied to himself that his motive for being out here was to be charitable to the poor and to forgive them their day of indulgence. The one-eyed soldier said that he was not so badly off, really. The governor himself had promoted him to quartermaster after the valiant way he had kept on fighting after losing his eye, and this gave him opportunities to sell goods on the sly. This was so obviously a lie that Demetrios felt challenged to come up with tall tales of his own. He drew upon and exaggerated some of his youthful escapades, and soon had them all roaring with laughter.

They got drunker and started swapping their assessments of the women they passed in the streets, in various states of revealing dress but all with faces veiled. Most of them were whores, of course, expecting a profitable night. Many of them however were respectable ladies, out for a fling if they could find one. Some of their husbands would not even mind. It was said that a woman who had not been able to have children might become pregnant if she gave in to the ways of Astarte on this night. The notion that fertility problems might ever reflect male sterility rather than female barrenness was inconceivable, or if anyone thought it, the barriers against speaking such a thing were impregnable.

Demetrios was not drinking as much as his companions, but he had not drunk at all in years and it was going to his head. The warmth and stuffiness inside his mask were not helping either. The others were starting to mock his unsteadiness on his feet, but it was all in good fun. The trouble started when they got hungry, and stopped at a stall selling some bread and meat.

Naturally, the one-eyed soldier had to haggle down the price by disparaging the goods. "What is this, the remnants of some sickly horse who died in the road?"

"No, no!" the vendor insisted. "This is beef from the priests of Elah Gabal! You know they accept only the finest cattle as offerings! It is especially blessed."

The vendor might have been lying about where he acquired the meat, but Demetrios could not take that chance. When a price had been negotiated and the transaction completed, his companions offered him his share but he would not take it. "I ate earlier," he said weakly.

"Well whenever you ate," one of the others said, "it was too long ago. The wine is not sitting well in your empty stomach. Just look at you!"

"I will take some bread," Demetrios conceded. Part of the piece of bread he was given was contaminated with juices from the meat. He tried to eat carefully around that part.

The one-eyed soldier had a shrewd guess about what the problem might be. "You're a Jew, aren't you?" Demetrios shook his head, but it was unconvincing. "You're a Jew!"

The more friendly-seeming one of his two friends shrugged it off. "So what if he's a Jew? He's not a tight-fisted one, at least!"

"I'm not a filthy Jew!" Demetrios insisted.

"Let's have a look," the least friendly-seeming of the soldiers said. With only an exchange of glances, the one-eyed soldier grabbed Demetrios to prevent him from resisting while the other lifted his robes. "Huh! His cock's not cut. We must have been wrong."

"I told you I'm no Jewish swine!"

"Then you must be a Christian!"

Demetrios closed his eyes in a silent prayer for strength. This was a just punishment for his sins. The snares of the world were everywhere, and he had walked right into them open-eyed. Words that might have been from Scripture came to him, "A fool acts wickedly, while thinking, no-one sees me, but the Lord sees all." Would these men let him get away with silence? He doubted it, and that would be so cowardly in any case. And the temptation to lie must be stoutly resisted. "Whosoever denies Me before men, him will I deny before My Father in Heaven." He had heard those words from the preachers many times, but now he heard them in the voice of the Lord. "And whosoever acknowledges Me before men, him will I acknowledge before My Father in Heaven."

The prefect of Antioch did not have as many watchmen as he would have liked, but all of them were out on the streets tonight. Unlike the off-duty soldiers, they were armed. This scuffle was attracting attention, and a few watchmen trotted over to maintain order. They arrived just in time to hear Demetrios proclaim, "Jesus Christ is my only Lord and Savior!"

This was a breach of the unspoken rules. Serapion was left alone, but he confined his preaching to the usual Speaker's Corner, where more tolerance was allowed for the outspoken of all stripes. Otherwise, it was understood that no-one said aloud that they were Christian, and no-one asked another about it. There had been that rash of preaching women a few years ago, but everyone was thankful that that had soon been suppressed. The watchmen looked to the most senior officer for some guidance. "Now, now, my good sir," the officer said calmly, "why don't you just go home and sleep it off? You should not say such things in public. No-one will know tomorrow who said that, so let's just pretend that I never even heard it."

Demetrios took the silly sheep's head off, threw it down and kicked it. "My name is Demetrios, and Jesus Christ is my only Lord and Savior!" He shouted more loudly this time. He hoped that it was the Holy Spirit speaking through him, but it might have been the wine. Several men who heard his outburst started running away from the scene.

Obviously the officers had no choice but to arrest him.

Chapter 9

Pertinax sat on his uncomfortable throne in his uncomfortable robes. This conversation was bound to be awkward, he knew, so he might as well make it a formal audience and hope that the Senator was made as uncomfortable as he was. He glanced over at the new decoration on the wall. The Labors of Commodus-as-Hercules had all been white-washed over, and one of the panels had been replaced, with mosaic tiling that should last much longer than a mere painting. It now showed the god Vulcan, with the face of his father, forging weapons for the goddess Roma, with the face of his wife the Lady Titiana, while Vulcan's wife Venus, with the face of his mother, looked on adoringly. The artist had gotten a little above himself, asking why Pertinax did not want his own likeness in the picture somewhere, but he had done a good job, Pertinax decided with satisfaction. The artist wanted to do more work in this room, of course, but Pertinax could not justify the expense at this time.

Finally, Eclectus came in. "O August One, pursuant to your command I present to you Senator Caius Titius Sempronius!" It was the Senator who had sought the meeting, but the fiction that the Emperor had summoned him had to be preserved.

"How may I serve you, O August One?" Sempronius exaggerated his flourish, and went down on one knee during his bow.

Oh, so he was going to play it that way. Pertinax sighed. "Should I not rather ask how I should serve you?" Sempronius looked perplexed. "Oh come now, let us not pretend that you are here to ask me what you should do. You are here to ask me to do what I am most loath to do."

"I seek only what is needful for the weal of the State, and the honor for which the August One is renowned throughout the world entire."

"And what is that, pray tell? Less honey and more meat, if you please. Be blunt like a soldier, not coy like a maiden."

"Falco must die."

Pertinax laughed. "Well, that was blunt enough. But is not one source of my world-renowned honor the fact that I have not put a single Senator to death? I am not certain which Emperor was the last to manage that, but there have been few."

"The August One must be aware that the Consul has done nothing but connive against you from the start, whispering in dark corners to Senators and Praetorians and who knows whom else. But this last scheme was so public that it must not be ignored. He sought to portray a runaway slave as a secret imperial heir. He was hoping to unseat you!"

"I heard all about it. Supposedly this fellow was descended from a Caesar and a kitchen maid?" Pertinax waved dismissively. "Even had the story been true, how would that have qualified him to wield the imperial powers?"

"Of course he would not have power! Falco wanted him for a puppet, to dress up gaily and sit on this throne like a child's doll, while Falco controlled everything!"

"Calm yourself!" Perhaps he should not have asked Sempronius to drop the highfaluting formality. That remark about sitting on the throne like a doll was a bit too rude. "The story was quickly exposed, so no harm came of it."

"No harm? It has brought the State into disrepute. A mocking poem about it is already circulating on the streets, and more will follow." He began to recite the words in his head: *Quam stultum Falconi consilium...* Then he shuddered. Had he spoken the words aloud? No, thank all the gods. Only now did he suddenly realize that the verse, while overtly directed at Falco, was really a sly dig at Pertinax: How stupid of Falco's conclave / To forget that the son of a slave / Could only be viewed with disgust / As purported heir to the August.

"I can agree with you that it is unfortunate if the rabble lose respect for authority."

"It is a step toward utter lawlessness!"

"I doubt that the number of thieves on the streets will be greatly affected by a few jests at the Consul's expense. His embarrassment might cause him to be more restrained in his behavior."

"He will launch some new scheme to retrieve his position, if he is not removed from power."

"Suppose for the moment that the Consul must be replaced, though I have not yet agreed to that. Who would take his place?" Here Pertinax expected Sempronius to press for the promotion of some friend or connection of his. The other Consul, Erucius Clarus, was too close to Sempronius as it was. Wasn't there a rumor that Clarus was about to marry that unattractive cousin, Maria Sempronia? It would not do for both Consuls to be allied to the same faction in the Senate. Whomever Sempronius wanted, Pertinax would have to find some objection, without being overly rude.

"The August One has reposed great confidence in Silius Messala."

"He is a good man," Pertinax temporized. The truth of the matter was that Messala had proven to be a useless nonentity. But he was entirely the creature of Pertinax. It seemed that Sempronius was not, after all, seeking personal advantage out of this situation. He was willing to let the Emperor fill the vacancy with his own man. Perhaps Sempronius was even acting out of genuine civic concern, as he portrayed himself. "Yes, Messala might do, if you are so determined that Falco must go."

"I am. Falco is a man of abilities, which makes him all the more dangerous. When Commodus chose him, I was relieved, thinking that he would be a steadying influence. Now I feel foolish for ever having thought well of him. But it is not me he has betrayed, it is you, O August One." This time his bow was not overdone. "And for that I cannot forgive him."

"Very well. The Senate may vote to censure Falco and remove him, so long as Messala is named in his place. But let us not speak any more of executions."

"We must condemn him to death."

Pertinax began to lose his patience. "Do not presume to tell me what I must or must not do."

"I should never presume so, August One. I meant that we in the Senate must show that we do not shrink from condemning our own. The gravest offenses call for the gravest punishment."

"Not everyone will share that opinion. He has many allies in the Senate."

"I have been counting. I have the votes to pass my motion."

"And I have the tribunician power of veto." It would require a difficult search of the records to find the last time that an Emperor had needed to veto anything in the Senate. The Senate for a very long time had known better than to enact something which the Emperor opposed.

"Then let each do his duty, as the gods give us light to see our duty. I see my duty to call for justice, but you may extend mercy. It is a singular man who can love even those who have wronged him." That last was a quote from Marcus Aurelius, as Pertinax would be sure to recognize.

Pertinax considered the political appearances. Yes, it might be best if the Senate voted to condemn Falco to death, showing that even Senators were not above the law, and then the Emperor reprieved him, showing his reluctance to execute anyone. His record of killing no Senators would remained unspoiled, and he would also demonstrate that he allowed the Senate to speak even when their views disagreed with his own. "I have underestimated you, for which I am sorry." This left Sempronius speechless. The notion of an Emperor apologizing for anything was alien to him. "We should become better friends. You must stay, and dine with Titiana and me."

Sempronius bowed low, knowing how rare this invitation was.

Chapter 10

It was unusual for three governors to be walking together through an unfashionable district of Antioch, outside the walls. It was scarcely unusual that they would be guarded by a sizable number of soldiers, who chased everyone unfortunate enough to be in one of the narrow alleyways when this party shoved its way through. This area could not even be called a suburb. It was under the direct authority of the prefect of Antioch, like much of the outskirts of the city proper, and had never been granted the dignity of its own town council, or even a formal name. Informally it was called Persian Town for the large number of residents of eastern origin. Aramaic often gave way to Iranian tongues here. The main open plaza, to which they finally emerged, faced a fire-temple of the Zoroastrian Magi. Octavius Emesianus raised his hand to tell the soldiers to stop here and wait.

"So where is this fellow that you were so anxious for us to meet?" Asellius Aemilianus, Governor of Asia, asked.

"My spies tell me that he is coming here today." It required very little time for his spies to be proven correct. A tall middle-aged man in fine robes with purple stripes down the sleeves and across his chest emerged, wearing also a silver filigreed headband, in a leafy design like an Olympic victor's wreath, to keep his long hair out of his face. He was surrounded by scruffier men in shabbier clothes, almost every one of them carrying a dagger. "Ho, Prince Narsai! We would speak to you."

"Prince, you call me?" Narsai replied. He looked at the governors and their armed entourage with mild curiosity, while his own men nervously fingered their dagger hilts. They knew they were no match for the soldiers with their short swords, even if they had not been outnumbered. Narsai turned to face his men and said in Aramaic, "Go home, all of you. I will be fine." Then he strode unafraid to the other side of the plaza. Octavius led them into a busy tavern, shooing out all of the customers. He told the proprietor to let the soldiers have whatever they wanted, but the soldiers understood that this did not mean that they could get as drunk as they pleased. Octavius commandeered the thermopole room in the back for a private talk. A thermopole was a long marble table, with circular holes cut out for pots to sit in, of both hot and cold food. The proprietor and his staff quickly removed the partially filled dishes left by the hastily ejected patrons, laid out more jugs of wine and water, and hustled out with much bowing and scraping. It was evident to the others that Octavius knew this tavern well, from times before he held such an exalted position.

Pescennius Niger said to Narsai, "It looks as if you have prospered since last we saw each other."

Asellius said, "So you know him also?"

Octavius took charge of the introductions. "Narsai, this is Asellius Aemilianus, the Governor of Asia." He introduced Asellius first, as the higher-ranking personage, but Narsai made the slightest of nods, as if Asellius were his inferior. "Asellius, this is Narsai of Adiabene, that is Assyria. He is heir to the former royal house of that country."

Asellius did not even nod. "I thought Trajan made certain that there were no such heirs."

"It is said," Octavius explained, "that his father was smuggled out of the palace as a baby. The nursemaid left her own baby instead to be killed by Trajan."

"That is a familiar trope in folklore," Asellius sniffed. "I could cite many similar stories." Pescennius could barely repress a smile. Asellius was famous for pedantically reciting ancient lore at length. However, he refrained from listing all the tales of smuggled baby princes this time. "But ordinarily, a usurper begins circulating the story of his secret descent from the old line only after he has successfully seized power." Asellius sank down on a bench, and put his feet up on the bench as well to stretch out and relax, and the others did likewise. He was not about to let Narsai act like the ranking person in the room by taking a seat first. He had chosen a spot in front of a pot of mutton stew, and ladled some of it into a bowl, again as if the others could not begin eating before he did.

"I care not," Narsai responded in a lofty tone, "whether you believe it. My father, may he rest in the Elysian Fields, never sought to take advantage of it, even though many knew his identity. For a long time he remained in the east, and traded with India. He stayed well away from Adiabene, until the Parthians let it be known that they saw no threat in him."

"But you keep to the Roman side of the border in recent years," Pescennius observed, "as if the Parthians no longer see you as harmless. Do you expect to take Assyria from them?"

"That is in the lap of the gods."

"And the gods have not kept you informed? I thought that they granted you all manner of special revelations."

"And why should they not? Everyone knows that the gods look after the disinherited. But that is only as long as they are obedient to divine will. You will have heard of Jesus, heir to the old Jewish royal family which lost power so long ago. The astrologers said at his birth that he would be king of the Jews. So the gods granted him wisdom, and powers of healing. But he foolishly said that he wanted no kingdom in this world, demanding rather to be king of the heavens. So the gods struck him down and he came to a miserable end."

"I believe that the Christians tell the story somewhat differently."

"And in India they revere a man called the Buddha, have you ever heard of him?"

"There were Buddhist preachers in the market of Alexandria one day. They told me not to be attached to material things, and to be compassionate to all living beings. The wisdom of India sounds little different from the wisdom of any other place."

"He was heir to a little principality in the eastern mountains that had lost its former grandeur. The astrologers said at his birth that he could be either a world-conquering king, or a world-renowned teacher of wisdom. His father naturally preferred the first destiny, and kept him confined within the palace, learning only martial arts. But he had no taste for bloodshed and ran away. So he became head of a monastic order, but lost his kingdom. Now, at my birth the astrologers said that I might be high priest, or king, or both."

"So you hope to outshine those failures, Jesus and Buddha?"

"If I do what is right in the eyes of the gods. I have sworn that if ever I come into my rightful inheritance, I will honor them all properly, and build twenty-four temples, for the divinities of each of the twelve planets and twelve signs."

"The twelve planets?" Asellius asked. "Everyone knows of seven. And Pythagoras taught that there are really ten. This Earth on which we stand, he said, is but another planet, and there is an anti-Earth which we can never see. All revolve around the secret central Hearth, which is the source of all light and power in the other nine."

"But you do not know the wisdom of India. There they teach that there are nine planets, the seven that everyone knows, plus the Sun-Eater and the Moon-Eater. Combine that with the Pythagorean lore, and we see that there are twelve, and that," Narsai said while gesturing with his hands animatedly, "is why there are twelve Olympians."

Asellius shook his head. "The mathematicians tell us that eclipses are but the result of occasional direct alignments. The Sun-Eater, as you call it, is only the Moon's shadow falling on the Earth, and the Moon-Eater is nothing but the Earth's shadow falling on the Moon."

"But those shadows are themselves planets!"

"My shadow is a close friend of mine, though only a fair-weather friend. But I have never been deluded into thinking that the shadow is another person, like poor Bucephalus who thought that his shadow was another horse."

"They are divinities nonetheless. There are not seven thrones on Olympus, nor ten, but twelve. The Moon is Artemis, Mercury is Hermes, Venus is Aphrodite, the Sun is Apollo, Mars is Ares, Jupiter is Zeus, Saturn is Kronos, but then also the Earth is Demeter, and the anti-Earth is Poseidon called the Earthshaker, and the Hearth is Hestia, and the Moon-Eater is Dionysius, for does not the Moon turn the color of wine, and what sort of mere shadow does that? It is also said that the eclipsed Moon has the color of blood, which is why the legends speak of Dionysius as Zagreus torn to pieces, shedding his blood for our sins. And finally the Sun-Eater is Hera, who sent snakes to kill baby Hercules, who is the Sun."

"I thought the Sun was Apollo?"

"He is! But he is also Hercules, whose twelve labors are obviously an allegory for the Sun's journey through the twelve signs. And the Sun is also Horus, who is also called Ra, the great god of Egypt. All the divinities are known through many names and many aspects, but the lore has become confused. It is up to me to straighten it all out, and learn the proper place of each."

"But you have included Hestia, who is said to have given up her throne so that Dionysius could have it."

"Hestia's modest retirement is allegory for our inability to perceive the central Hearth."

"Yes, but if you include her as well as her replacement, that makes thirteen Olympians. You must have left one out. And you included Kronos, who was the father of the Olympians but dethroned by them, so you must be missing two." Asellius squinted and began counting on his fingers, ticking off names of the Olympians. "Ah, what has become of Hephaestus?"

"Hephaestus, that is also called Vulcan, is the same as Kronos and Saturn! Do not the legends say of both, that Zeus hurled him down into the pit? He is also Ptah, the Egyptian god of potters and smiths, who created all things in this world in the beginning. For he is the original Father, whom the Jews call Iao."

"The secret name is pronounced a little differently I hear, but I will not try to speak it, for the Jews say that it offends their god to utter the name unworthily. And the Jews would be most offended to hear their god, whom they think the only true God of the entire universe, spoken of as one amongst twelve."

"Yet they themselves say that they are descended from twelve fathers. And if their god is not Saturn, then why is their holy day Saturday?"

Asellius sighed. "And what of Athena? That is the other one whom you have omitted. Those who slight the Grey Goddess have often come to bad ends. Arachne turned into a spider, and Odysseus was made to wander for years after the impious theft of her image."

"Athena is the Virgin, one of the twelve signs."

"How did she get demoted to the lesser set of deities?"

"The Zodiacals are by no means inferior to the Planetaries. Is not the Bull, who is called Serapis in Egypt and Mithras in Persia, the most popular divinity in both countries? Do not sailors of all nations pray that the Twins preserve them? And the Ram, or Lamb, is the divinity of all sacrifices. The Christians say that their Jesus has become one with him."

"The Christians use, rather, the sign of the fish."

"The Fish is Oannes, ancient Babylonian god of wisdom, called Dagon by the Palestinians. And in India..."

"But what about the Balance, say? You cannot pretend that all the signs are worshipped."

"I told you I would restore the proper worship of all neglected divinities. The Balance is Themis, goddess of justice. Indeed she is not honored in this sorry world as she ought to be, else a prince would not have to beg for his rightful inheritance."

Pescennius could think of other injustices in the world which he would sooner see rectified. And he did not wish to sit through a discussion of what the Fish meant in India, or what deities the Crab and Scorpion might represent. "Theology is too complex for a simple man like me. I pray to Mother Isis, and she sees to all my needs. There must be many like myself who have little interest in all these intricacies."

"In my realm, every man will be free to worship the divinity who best suits him, and need not honor any others if he does not wish. You wish only to worship the Virgin, in the form of Isis, and that is fine. The Jews also wish only to worship one god. But Asia here," gesturing toward Asellius in a somewhat rude manner, "thinks the Jews will not be grateful if I give them a temple, if there are other temples in the country. Adiabene has been a friend to the Jews for a long time." Adiabene was the only country to send troops in support of Judea during the revolt against Rome, and neither the Jews nor the Romans had ever forgotten that. "They know we have other religions in our country, and do not mind, so long as they are not asked to participate. From Rome, they have learned what it is to have their freedom to worship taken away. Perhaps the Magi need to learn that lesson. They lack the wisdom of the Jews in this regard."

"So your negotiations with the fire-temple did not go well?" Octavius asked. This was the subject he had expected to discuss in the first place.

"I revealed to them that Hormuzd is the central Hearth, the same as Vesta. Surely the power which gives life to all beings has both male and female aspects. Surely the power which guards the empire of the east is the same as the power which guards the empire of the west. How could it be otherwise?"

"But the Magi didn't see it that way?"

"Sasan's men are so arrogant that they told me Hormuzd will be the only divinity to be worshipped anywhere, in the days to come. And they demanded that I swear fealty to Artaxerxes, their wonder boy." He said this last with a sneer.

Asellius was not one to be shy about asking when he did not know something. That is how he had become learned. "Pardon my ignorance of eastern potentates, but who is Sasan, and who is Artaxerxes? I do know that the name Artaxerxes was a recurrent one among the Achaemenid house of Cyrus the Great."

"Sasan is the Grand Magus," Octavius put in. He was always one to show off, when he knew something. "He claims to be descended from their prophet Zoroaster."

"And he married the daughter of Papak, who is called the king of Persia," Narsai added. "Maybe half the princelings of Persia actually obey Papak. He will be the last of the house of Bazarangus, since he has no sons or brothers. When I was young, Bazarangus was said to be a divine monkey. But Sasan teaches that he was the rightful heir to the Achaemenid emperors, exposed as an infant by a wicked uncle, only to be rescued and raised by monkeys."

"Like Romulus and Remus, suckled by wolves? Another familiar trope in folklore."

"So Sasan gave his son an antique name, and made the astrologers say that he was destined to restore the Zoroastrian religion and Persian Empire to their former glories."

"And this time you do not believe the astrologers? Do I sense some jealousy? Do you fear that he could outshine you as a priest-king? Well indeed you might. As an ancestor, Cyrus the Great is more of a name to conjure with than, pardon my saying so, any king of Adiabene."

Narsai sat straight up, and glared down at Asellius. "I trace my genealogy to Tiglas Ninurtus, whom the Greeks call Ninus and the Jews call Nimrod. Ask any historian from either nation. He was a mighty emperor long before Persepolis was even a village."

"But his capital city of Nineveh was burned to the ground many hundreds of years ago, and was not much lamented at that time, so I hear."

"I shall refound it, and make it a site of pilgrimage for many peoples. You will see. But Sasan will never accomplish any of his mad imaginings."

"He will not manage to establish his son as the priest-king of Persia, or half of Persia at least? That sounds as if it will be easy for him to do."

"You know nothing of his ambitions. He dreams that Artaxerxes will retake every patch of soil where a Persian foot has ever stepped. Asia, Syria, and Egypt, he claims all your provinces, and Ethiopia and Greece besides!"

"That does sound a little mad. Does he propose to capture Roma while he is at it?"

"No, he would concede that Rome is master of Italy, and that you took Carthage fair and square. But everything east of that he thinks is Persia's by right."

"How do you know so much about the intentions of the Persian court?"

"There are men there who are loyal to me."

"Could these men perhaps see to it that the wonderful Artaxerxes has a misadventure?"

"The boy has been sent to Lesser Armenia as a hostage." Roma and Parthia had grown weary of wrangling, every generation, to find a mutually acceptable king for Armenia, and had agreed to partition the country. Rome chose the king for Greater Armenia and Parthia for the lesser subkingdom.

"Who rules there now? Vologases can hardly contend for the throne of the whole empire, while still giving personal attention to that far corner of it." Vologases, son of the late emperor also called Vologases, had been king of Lesser Armenia until his father died.

"He turned it over to his son, who is immature and rude, or so Artaxerxes recently wrote to complain. But Papak wrote back that Artaxerxes should keep his head down and ignore any disrespect." Narsai seemed especially smug about knowing the contents of this high-level correspondence. "Sasan does not wish Persia to be seen as grasping for power at this time, not until Artaxerxes inherits."

"Who rules in Media Atropatene?" Octavius asked. "I heard that Vologases the father, as one of his last acts, overthrew king Osroes."

"Chosroes," Narsai corrected. Again he seemed smug, to be able to correct Octavius about the name. "Vologases the son wants him ousted even more, but Chosroes is not going anywhere. He stakes his own claim to be the rightful heir to the empire."

"He is a younger son, but from a nobler mother?"

"You have it backwards. Vologases is the son of the queen. Chosroes is the eldest son, but from a dubious mistress. Vologases casts doubt on his paternity, and accuses him of conniving at the poisoning of their father. There can be no reconciliation. Vologases is amassing his shaky allies to invade Media Atropatene from the south, while Lesser Armenia attacks from the west. Sasan sent his precious hostage, as reassurance that he would not go over to the side of Chosroes. He wants to be seen as loyal, despite all his meddling in Hyrcania."

"What is happening in Hyrcania?"

"How can you not have heard? You must know that they are building a magnificent wall of red brick, all along the frontier." Blank stares told Narsai that none of the governors had heard of this. "Sasan sends builders and soldiers to help with the project, and compelled the late emperor to divert some of the taxes on the silk and purple trade to pay for it. The son of course now wants that money back, for the war with his half-brother. But Sasan argues that the revenues of the empire ought to go to the defense of the empire."

"We try to tell Roma that, all the time."

"It is not a new idea in Rome. But in Parthia, each kingdom is accustomed to fend for itself, and the money that the emperor takes, he feels free to waste as he pleases."

"This is excellent intelligence that you bring us," Asellius said, in a much friendlier tone than he had been directing at Narsai hitherto. "We hear much less from east of the border than we should like to know."

"My knowledge and my wisdom are the only coins I have to barter for your friendship. I am not so vain as to think that I can reconquer my homeland without a powerful ally."

"But you would have allied with the Persians, if they would have you."

"I would ally with anyone who would help me to regain my proper place."

"That is answered honestly enough."

"Or are you leading us into a trap?" Octavius asked, disregarding a glance from Asellius that suggested he keep silent. "You say Parthia and Lesser Armenia are moving on Media? So if we move our army to Assyria, might we find all the armies of the east, ready to set aside their differences to smash us?"

"I know Vologases. He is a coward and a weakling. If Roman armies approach, he will scurry south, to defend Seleucia and Ctesiphon, and his money and his women, and leave his son to face both you and Chosroes all alone."

Asellius rose, to force the others to do so. "If you will excuse us, we must discuss this amongst ourselves." Narsai bowed, finally. In the outer room, Octavius attracted the attention of the ranking officer with a curt finger-snap.

"Detach a squad, to escort the Prince home safely."

Chapter 11

The large anteroom adjoining the throne room was known as the counting room. It was equipped with two sets of counting tables which could stack, each table fitting over a slightly smaller one. When stacked together, the tables could be shoved unobtrusively into two corners of the room. But today they were all spread out, for the monthly reconciliation of accounts. Treasury officials paced from table to table with wax tablets hanging around their necks, to make notes of various figures, while clerks performed their calculations. Each table had rows from one to nine, and columns for ones, tens, hundreds, thousands, myriads, and on the larger tables also columns for hundred-thousands, millions, and beyond, or perhaps an irregular column, left of the ones, to mark simple fractions. Tokens in the form of round disks, like mock coins, in bright iron, dark lead, and ruddy bronze were used to mark the numbers. Usually two of the colors marked numbers to be added or subtracted, with the third color used to create the sum or difference.

Those operations were easy enough. Sometimes two numbers needed to be multiplied or divided, which were trickier procedures. To multiply, the smaller number was halved and re-halved until it vanished, while the larger number was doubled and re-doubled. Each time that the halving left an odd remainder, the corresponding power-of-two multiple of the larger number was added into the total. Senator Tullius was supervising as two tables independently performed the same multiplication, to see if the results checked. A desired appropriation for each legion was being multiplied by the number of legions, and it was vital to know whether this was less than the grand remainder on the largest table. That remainder was the difference of cash on hand minus all of the other bills Tullius wished to pay. He sighed in satisfaction when the result was as he hoped, and began stamping a large stack of warrants, authorizing the disbursements of funds, with the imperial seal.

Pertinax came in as the tokens and the tables were being put away. He led Tullius into the throne room. He did not clamber up onto the throne, or expect any ritual obeisances from Tullius. He simply wanted a little privacy. "So, what does the kalends of March announce to us?"

"We have cleared all arrearages, except for one. Most soldiers have still not received the full donative they were promised at your accession."

"How much money is left over?"

"About a million farthings."

"Is that all?" For an ordinary citizen, that would be a lot of money. For the entire Empire, it was a pathetically small sum, but better than enormous debt. "Well, use it to pay off some of the soldiers."

"We could only buy a thousand gold with that, and at six gold per man, that would only cover two centuries of men, if the centuries were a little short-handed." Tullius had a greater facility for mental arithmetic than Pertinax, but Pertinax saw that he was right. "And those two centuries would then be the targets of envy from the others in their unit."

"At least revenues are now outpacing expenses. So we should be able to pay all the men soon?"

"No, O August One," Tullius said with a bow. He did not ordinarily bother with such formalities in the course of working together with the Emperor, but felt that he must when broaching an unpleasant topic. "The results of this past month depended upon sources of income which will not be repeated. We enforced taxes which were still legally in force, but which Commodus had allowed to lapse through negligence. We required settlements for the amounts which should have been paid in the past. These taxes will produce revenues in the coming months, but not the retroactive lump-sums again. We pressed importers to pay in advance for license to continue operating, so we will not even get the regular payments from them in coming months. Also, we raised much money from sales of surplus property, such as the gladiator school and the gladiators themselves, and estates which Commodus seized from those he put to death, but for which the State had no particular use."

"But will revenues exceed expenses in the coming month?"

"I expect that we will fall a little short."

"And there is no way to pay off the donatives to the soldiers?"

"We will fall very far short of that. That is, unless we again start witholding payments for our other expenses, or start borrowing money, or both as Commodus was doing."

"We must not go back into debt. And we must not be dishonest with those who give us service. That road we shall never go down again. Instead let us raise money by selling more surplus property. There are plenty of useless things all over this house."

"But there is little market for them. We have already sold everything that anyone would want. Chariots with gold-plated spokes? Those are an invitation to robbers, or something to show off like a peacock's tail without ever being used. Even trying to scrape off the gold would require so much labor that it would scarcely even be profitable. There were no bidders for those. And who wants mugs with lids made to look like phallus heads? Or any of the other obscene artworks Commodus has left us?" Tullius had faced the same sort of problem when trying to liquidate the estate of his brother, whose taste was also execrable.

"What if we sell this house? I could move into the house of Tiberius." That older imperial residence, further up the Palatine hill, was not in a good state of repair. But it was still used to house members of the imperial family from time to time. Commodus had sometimes let his sisters stay there. At present it was sitting vacant except for a skeleton staff.

"Oh no, August One! That would be quite impossible."

"What? You do not think that there are any Senators who could raise or borrow enough money to give us a proper price?"

"But consider how that would look to the public. Whoever took over the Palace would appear to be one of the leading citizens of Roma, perhaps even the highest ranking, a rival to yourself, if you pardon my saying so. Imagine Falco, for example, living here and holding court."

Mentioning the name of Falco gave Pertinax a shudder. Of course, ever since Falco was condemned and pardoned he had been trying to wheedle his way back into favor and prominence. A spider cannot stop spinning webs. Tullius was right about how unacceptable the idea of selling the Palace was. "Then... there is really only one other possible sale." Tullius remained silent, hoping that he was wrong about what the Emperor must be meaning. Pertinax became more explicit. "I know that Claudius Pompeianus spoke of emancipating them all, and I would hate to go against what that very honorable man proposed."

"It was rather more than a proposal. As I recall what he said in the Senate, it was a condition of his renunciation of the inheritance."

"So there might be a legal issue as to whether these slaves are even our property? Well, there might also be legal issues as to whether they were property of Commodus personally, or of the State. Commodus seldom made any such distinction. Even if they were personal property, there might be issues as to whether Pompeianus indeed was the proper heir, and had any right to attach conditions on their disposition."

"I much doubt that Pompeianus or anyone else would dispute the matter in court. That is not the question. It will appear very dishonorable."

"I agree. Yet it seems that I must break faith somewhere. Above all, I think it necessary that the financial credit of the State be restored. We must pay those we owe, without delay. We must pay the soldiers what they were promised, even if we must borrow. We will be charged lower interest if it is known that we no longer allow accounts to fall into arrears, and if we show that we make every effort to raise as much of the money as possible ourselves."

"I thought we were resolved not to go back down that path?"

Pertinax had indeed said just moments ago that he never wanted to go back into debt. But of course Tullius could not stop him from changing his mind. "On the one side is Scylla, the unpaid soldiers who might bite our heads off. On the other side is Charybdis, the moneylenders who might suck us down into a whirlpool. I might have to choose Charybdis.

Did you not tell me that, even aside from the donatives, we are likely to run out of money to stay current with expenses?"

"Sometime this coming month, yes."

"And there is worse, that you do not know about yet. A letter arrived today that will be read in the Senate soon enough. Three governors in the East want me to commit to a war. How will I finance that? With the loot that my glorious conquests will bring us? We have heard that Sirens' song before. And they demand that I share my power and my revenues with another Emperor to command on the eastern front, and I suppose that all the glory will go to him."

"Demand?" Tullius was shocked to hear the Emperor use such a word.

"Oh, they are very polite about it, pledging undying loyalty and all. There is no hint that I will be faced with open rebellion. But Egypt, Syria, and Asia between them can make things quite uncomfortable for us all, if they choose to be just a little tardy, not so much as to be obvious, in remitting taxes or making grain shipments." Tullius began stroking his chin, contemplating some dire arithmetic in the months to come. And the arithmetic today had gone so well! He had expected the conference with the Emperor to be a happy one. "So now, if I must approach the moneylenders, I need to rely on you to obtain for us the best deal, even if I cannot rely on you to manage that sale which is so distasteful to you."

"O August One, whatever you call upon me to do, you may rely on me."

"But for traffic in slaves, you are not experienced. I will find another to manage that, if it must be done. I am sorry that you disapprove of the business." Like Sempronius, Tullius was shocked to hear the Emperor apologize. "But I have never liked having so many people in the Palace. I enjoy my solitude, and never feel that I am truly left alone." Tullius wondered if this was a hint that he should find some excuse to leave now and leave the August One to brood in his preferred solitude. "But I shall put off the decision as long as I can. Are you truly certain that we will run short of money this coming month?"

"Who can be truly certain of anything in this world? We must do what we can, whatever comes." Stoicism brought Tullius comfort in troubled times. "But I do expect us to face a shortfall that forces us either to borrow a little or to go back into arrears."

"We shall not go back into arrears. But we shall put off borrowing as late as we can. And when it comes time, I shall make the sale, in order to give you every argument with the lenders that we have been doing everything possible to raise money. Can I avoid taking such actions past the Ides, at least?" Everyone knew that the days around the Ides of March were the unluckiest for any Caesar to do anything.

"You can survive through the Ides, but not much longer."

Chapter 12

Asellius finished his stew. Pescennius contented himself with mopping up some chickpea and sesame paste with pieces of flat bread. Octavius poured himself more wine, and asked, "What did you gather from that interview?"

Pescennius said, "He reminded me of a soldier I knew on the Danube, whose skull was split open by a German mace. The surgeons barely saved him. After that he had to be given his own tent, because he would babble incessantly, and drive his comrades mad. Worse, his favorite topic was himself, and his own greatness."

Asellius said, "But can he be a leader of men? That is the question."

Octavius shrugged. "He has built up his following quite rapidly these past couple years."

"What kind of a following?"

"You know, a young man whose beloved does not return his affections, an old woman with vague complaints of illness, a merchant who wants a business venture to prosper or a rival to be ruined. He, or one of his acolytes, decides which god they need to placate, devises a spell for them to recite, and an amulet for them to wear, all for a quite reasonable fee, of course."

"Oh, he is one of those." Asellius wrinkled his nose. "I should have gathered as much. Something like Alexander the Oracle, then? Are you old enough to remember him?"

"I grew up around here in his heyday. All the women he had! And their rich husbands would pay him to be cuckolded! I couldn't understand how he did it. And I never understood why that wasn't enough for him, but he wanted to be adored by the crowds. Too bad the public saw him as a fool."

"Does the public see Narsai as a fool?"

"Not really. He offers them gods they can understand, with a touch of secret lore from Persia or India if they want something exotic. Too many teachers of sacred gnosis talk about layer upon layer of heavens

274

above the planets and signs, all filled with divine emanations whose names are impossible to pronounce or remember, names you can only learn, of course, by paying the master money. Lots of money. Much more money than the modest sums that Narsai charges."

"Will Assyria be eager to have him for a king?"

"The Assyrians will be eager to have anybody for a king. Since the Parthians took Adiabene back, they have appointed eunuch governors. Assyrians find that disrespectful to their ancient realm. The current governor has the quavering voice and permanently mournful look of one who was castrated after puberty, and knows what he lost. He commands neither respect nor fear. Narsai should not lack for support among the people."

Pescennius said, "His glittering project of two dozen temples should excite. It would attract a lot of pilgrims with money, I expect, assuming that he can ever raise the money to build them in the first place. Perhaps he would start with a little temple for the Jews. It would not be Jerusalem, but maybe he is right that the Jews would be glad to have anything."

"It would be odd to have either the Jews or the Assyrians on our side," Asellius said. "But any sincere support would be important. If easterners can ever be sincere, that is."

"But what do you think?" Octavius asked. "Is this a good idea or not? I am less experienced than either of you. I don't know how to weigh my hopes against my misgivings."

"Let us review the past history," Asellius said in the tone of a tutor addressing a child, "of the campaigns against Parthia by Crassus, Trajan, and Verus, to learn their lessons. Crassus made an ally of the king of Osroene, but then treated him with the same disdain and haughtiness which had lost Crassus every friend in Italia. So Osroene led him into an ambush. He and most of his men perished, and it was many years before Augustus could ransom the survivors and the legionary eagles."

"The lesson is not to trust Osroene. I have disturbing news from that quarter... but it can wait." Octavius felt unaccountably guilty about interrupting the recitation, as if he had spoken out of turn. He folded his hands in front of his chest, and nodded. "Tell us of Trajan's campaign."

"A royal of Osroene named Yalur wanted to kill all his kinsmen, for some good reason. Trajan installed Yalur in Edessa, with a co-king to keep an eye on him, but rival candidates for the throne held out in Nisibis through a long and bloody siege. He took thorough revenge on the Assyrians for fighting against him at Nisibis, though today I learned that his extirpation was not so thorough as I had been led to believe. Finally he marched south into Babylonia, and sacked Seleucia and Ctesiphon. But we could not hold it all, and Hadrian wisely withdrew."

"But why was that?" Octavius unconsciously pressed his palms together again. He really did want to hear Asellius explain. "I have never understood. Didn't Trajan conquer all, smash everyone who stood in his way?"

"It is not always enough to smash. A Briton once said of us Romans, 'You leave a wasteland, and call it peace.' We can do that in Britannia because they are few and barbarous. The easterners are numerous, and have been civilized longer than we have. If they will not have us rule over them, they have subtle ways of making trouble. Hadrian simply found that it cost more than it was worth to keep all of Trajan's conquests, and settled for Osroene, knowing it was the key to any resumed campaigns in the east. Hadrian kept the garrison in Nisibis, since it cost so dearly to take it, but lowered the tribute from Osroene, to much less than the Parthians had taken. He wanted Osroene to be happy, more or less, to be a Roman ally. And Osroene did help to guide and supply the armies of Lucius Verus. Marcus Aurelius advised Verus, 'You must woo them like a bride, not rape them like a captive woman.' So Verus gave Seleucia and Ctesiphon very generous and attractive terms. They opened their gates to him, trusting his word that they would not be looted. But then he found feeble excuses to break his word. So the gods smote him with plague, as an oathbreaker. And then his soldiers brought back the plague to our whole Empire. Further, Marcus Aurelius was left with no heir but his worthless son

Commodus. One might say that the plague Verus brought upon us never fully abated until this year."

"Seleucia and Ctesiphon are cursed," Pescennius said. "Babylonia is fool's gold. We do not even want it. We want to move northeast and punch through to the silk road. So if I take your meaning, we begin by promising the Assyrians whatever their hearts desire, and then keep our word."

"We must also make certain that Osroene is on our side."

"They will never rebel while we have a military base deep in their territory."

"But they could spy against us for the enemy, or sabotage our supply lines. The present Abgar of Osroene has favored the Christians, has proclaimed his land a haven for those who feel unsafe under direct Roman rule, has even undergone their rite of baptism to make himself fully one of them. Or at least, so I hear. Have I heard wrongly? Octavius?" Asellius pressed his palms together.

Octavius drained his cup and smacked it down on the marble table. "This is what I know. Nine days ago, during that festival that we all enjoyed so, a man named Demetrios was arrested for public Christianity."

"Oh no," Pescennius said. "What fool decided to start a Christian hunt? If you know that scorpions are hiding down in the holes, better to leave them there than force them out."

"It was not the officers' fault. This Demetrios was loud and rude. They had to bring him in. Some fellow called him a Jew, because he would not eat meat butchered by priests, and he started shouting that Jews were filthy swine and Jesus was his only god."

"But did he insult the gods of others?" Asellius asked. "That is the only real offense of Christianity."

"He did insult the Jews."

"I thought that the Christians also worship the god of the Jews?"

Octavius threw up his hands. "Some say yes, some say no, what do I care? I am besieged by letters from local toffs, oh what a good man Demetrios is, he is totally loyal to the Roman Empire. Are they just friends, or business partners? He is wealthy and well-connected, to be sure. But I have to suspect that I am suddenly discovering just how many Christians there are in high places, more than I would have ever imagined. Surely they know that they are bringing suspicion on themselves, to write for him? But they don't seem to care."

"That is the frightening thing about Christians," Pescennius said. "Sometimes they truly do not care, even if you threaten them with death, and mean it."

"The letters all seem coordinated, as if they all met in secret, like Christians do. And how can I be getting a letter from Abgar of Osroene? For a rider to go from here to Edessa and back, surely that takes many days. Perhaps Abgar is nearer than Edessa, waiting on the border with Syria, for some reason best known to him? Or did they kill horses to deliver that message? Who set it in motion so quickly? Do I have spies loyal to Abgar in my own household?"

"Men loyal to Serapion, more likely."

"That is much the same thing, isn't it? It would be a great favor to him, Abgar says, if I were gracious to his friend Demetrios. Since when does a king seek a favor from a governor, on behalf of a merchant? He has never corresponded with me before. Did he ever write to you?"

"Never," Pescennius agreed. "He may pay tribute and endure the presence of our troops, but he insists that he is master in his own house, and ranks above the likes of us."

"I begin to think that this whole Demetrios affair must have been set up in advance, to trap me."

"But see now, this could be a great opportunity."

"To do what? I can demand that Demetrios burn incense to the divine Caesars, and watch him refuse, and have to kill him in some ugly way, and interrogate all his friends and kill some of them, and poison relations with Osroene just at the wrong time. Or I can let him go unpunished, announce that Christians are now tolerated in Syria, flouting the laws of Rome when I have no authority to do so, and give any enemies that I might have the perfect chance to denounce me as a traitor." Octavius poured himself some more wine.

"This is what you should do. Punish Demetrios by ordering him to pay to the synagogue of Antioch the exact sum that you fined the Jews for that affair with the eagle. Everybody knows, you say, that it was really the Christians at fault for that. But say that Demetrios is being punished for insulting the Jews. If he does not have the money, all these well-to-do Christian friends of his will raise it for him. This will be good for me, because the Jews of Alexandria will hear that I successfully intervened for their brothers in Antioch, as they asked me to. And it will be good for the Christians, to have it established that they will only be prosecuted if they breach the peace. You do not announce any changes in the law. You simply let your actions speak for themselves."

"You are a genius. But how do I describe it when I write to Osroene?"

"You do not write anything to Abgar, which might be used against you. Let Serapion notify him. But we ask Narsai to write, and say that he would like to visit Abgar on his way back to his home. The implication will be clear. If Abgar responds favorably, then we march. We send the rawer troops from here to relieve the garrison of Nisibis, who then proceed, along with the better troops from here, into Assyria. We do write to Nisibis now, telling the commander to start making logistical plans."

"And if we are attacked from multiple directions in Assyria?"

"Then we pull back quickly. But if we take it, then we offer this Chosroes to recognize him as king of Media Atropatene, and to protect him from Vologases. We do not undertake to conquer the whole Parthian Empire for him, or even to invade Media Parthica. It would help if we could induce Armenia to break the truce and invade Lesser Armenia. That would be one less direction from which we would face threat, and we may need their experience in mountain fighting. But the king of Armenia is even less likely than the king of Osroene to take direction from us."

"We can approach him indirectly," Asellius said. "My good friend Cheironios of Byzantium has done many favors for some Armenian merchants who are cousins of the royal family."

"Excellent. Send word through your friend that we mean to cut off Lesser Armenia from Parthia and make it easy for them. We cannot wait for their reply, when the message goes in such a roundabout way, but must trust that they will see how this serves their own interests." Asellius nodded deeply, as if a servant acknowledging orders. Asellius was given deference on scholarly matters, but Pescennius was the one the others looked to on matters of military planning. "If we tear Assyria Adiabene, Lesser Armenia, and Media Atropatene away from Parthian allegiance, then we have a clear road to the Hyrcanian Sea. I hear that the silk people used to build boats sometimes, on a sandy bay on the eastern shore of that sea, and come to us that way. If they can reach us without paying the Parthians, then Vologases will starve for money, and Seleucia and Ctesiphon will eventually fall into our laps, like overripe fruit that nobody bothered to pick."

"That will not work," Octavius said. "The silk does not come that way anymore because a new nation of savages has settled on the eastern shore. A traveller told me all about them. They call themselves the Chshiungu," spitting out the barbarous syllables, "but we call them the Hunnoi. They are hereditary enemies of the silk people. They are splendid horsemen, and the women give birth in the saddle, so the babe rides before he crawls. Then they mash the babe's skull with boards, so that their heads are pointed and their faces hideous, the better to terrify their neighbors. They make the finest bows, shoot further and harder than anyone in the world, but that is the only art they know. So they live only on mare's milk and what they can steal by raiding."

"Could we make allies of these Huns?" Asellius asked. "Might they be trouble to the Parthians?"

"Armenia sent an expedition around the north end of Parthian territory and across the sea. The ambassador and some of his party came back in pieces. The one who told me all this only survived because they wanted the mutilated corpses to return home, as their answer to the embassy. He said they brought gold and other gifts, but there were many squabbling petty kings, who were greedy for more, and they gave presents first to a king whom others thought was lower ranking, so the other kings decided that they were insulted. The man who told me the story considered himself lucky to come home with all his parts attached. I would bet a large sum that they're already trouble to the Parthians. That must be why Hyrcania is building a wall. We may thank all twenty-four of Narsai's gods that they have not found their way further west, or they might be trouble to us."

"What do you know of Hyrcania? I confess I know it only as a distant name."

"I was there once, but that was when I was young. And I was only in the western portion, on the southern shore of the sea. There they fish for giant sturgeon and sell the eggs, they're supposed to be a great delicacy, but I didn't like the taste. From there it stretches off east, I don't know how far, but the land is mostly waste. They used to make money back then from the silk and purple traders who came through that way, but nowadays the route goes more southerly, through the very heart of Parthia, out of fear of the savages I suppose, and I suppose too that the wall is meant to bring the trade back."

"Perhaps then we can convince Hyrcania that the Roman Emperor is better able than the Grand Magus to man and maintain their wall?"

"But if we stretch so far east," Pescennius objected, "then we will have a very long southern flank exposed, with no ready defenses. Can we build another wall and make the Parthians pay for it?"

"And is the east end of Hyrcania even far enough?" Octavius asked. "Or would the silk still have to come through lands where the Parthians can extort money? Does anyone know if Parthia still controls Margiana these days?"

"I know that Margiana is where the legions of Crassus were banished," Asellius said, "before they were ransomed. But any intelligence they might have brought back would be two hundred years out of date. How much do you know about Margiana?"

"I know that it is the name of the kingdom northeast of the very end of Hyrcania. And that is the very end of my knowledge. Maybe Narsai would know a thing or two."

Pescennius gave in, and poured some wine into his water. "Are we doomed to march ever eastward, like Alexander, until the army can bear it no more?"

Asellius said, "We are worrying about whom our grandchildren will marry, while our children are still sucklings. Let us proceed one step at a time."

"Tomorrow we'll just get a letter from Rome telling us we're forbidden to do anything anyway," Octavius said. He was beginning to enter the morose phase of his drunkenness. "We should never have sent that letter."

"No, it was absolutely necessary to write to Roma," Asellius replied. "And we only sent it three weeks ago. We will be lucky if it has even arrived. Perhaps in April we will be sent a commander. Then we can lay our plans before him, and it will all be his problem."

"If I know Pertinax at all," Pescennius said, "we will get a very ambiguous response committing to nothing. We shall have to decide what to do for ourselves."

When this war council broke up, Octavius made sure to pay the proprietor handsomely.

Chapter 13

That same day, Tullia Minor received three letters, all of the same kind. This was not a coincidence. If one was planning a large wedding, it was vital to consult a priest about the appropriate day to hold it. Not that the priest would be invited, unless it was to be a confarreation, but that old-fashioned style of religious wedding was completely out of fashion. But a large assembly must not be held on an unlucky day, lest the gods be angered. Then any misfortune which befell Roma might be blamed on whoever had the temerity to celebrate, without consulting a priest. And if one has gone to the expense of providing a sacrificial animal, to pay the priest for his oracular advice, one might as well also ask which day would be the luckiest to send out the invitations. The kalends of March, unsurprisingly, seemed to have been named by multiple priests as an excellent day for announcements.

The first one was received with unalloyed joy. Clara Didia opened, "My dearest sister, if I may still call you sister..." It was slightly indelicate to allude to the death which had prevented them from becoming sisters-in-law, but it stirred only the tenderest feelings in Tullia.

"Of course you shall always be my sister, O dearest Clara!" Tullia gushed. She read the rest of the letter in a rush. Philoxena was pleased to see that Tullia really could read perfectly well, when she was interested in what was written. The letter confirmed that Clara was engaged to Senator Repentinus, lately governor of Lusitania, and thanked Tullia again for helping to arrange the Carmentalia pageant where they had met. Clara asked Tullia to lead the bridesmaids at the wedding. "Oh! We must make the most beautiful dress that anyone has ever seen! What colors can we use? Do I dare to use a splash of purple? Or make use of a silk scarf?" A woman wearing purple or silk was announcing social status, though a man less than the Emperor would scarcely dare to dress so arrogantly. But on the occasion of another woman's wedding, it might not be appropriate for a bridesmaid to appear to outshine the bride.

Philoxena was happy to see Tullia express any enthusiasm for making clothes, another art that she was often sullen about practicing. Philoxena expected that she would end up doing most of the work on this bridesmaid's dress. But there was the matter of etiquette here to teach. "Before you consider what color or design to use for your dress, you must ask her. Perhaps she has her own preferences, depending on what she herself will be wearing. You may make suggestions, but in the end, it is her day. Now, we must not be tardy in replying. We must use a fresh sheet of parchment, not one that has been scraped, the whitest we can find. The entire reply must be in your own hand." Writing was yet another art that Tullia did not practice nearly as much as she ought. If gossiping with friends in the bathhouse could be considered as one of the arts which a young lady needed to master, that was the one for which Tullia had shown most aptitude, Philoxena thought to herself ruefully. "Think carefully before setting each word down. We do not want a single scrape-mark."

Composing and writing out the reply to Clara was an enjoyable chore. As they were finishing, Philoxena began to worry about whether Phaeton could be trusted to deliver it. Castor of course had taken the master to the Palace, and Magnus was watching the door. Phaeton's Latin was improving, but the house of the Didian family was on the Viminal hill, very nearly to the opposite corner of the city, and if Phaeton got lost he might not be up to the task of asking directions. Perhaps it would be safer to ask Cocina, or even Cocinilla, if they knew a likely boy in the neighborhood who could be hired as a runner. But then, Magnus rescued her by announcing that another letter had come to the door. The runner who brought it was happy to get another job, doubly so when he heard that the delivery was to the house of Senator Didius Julianus. Rich people always paid better for deliveries, and getting the houses of two Senators in the same day was unbelievable luck.

The second letter was more problematic. Popilia opened, "Most gracious lady, I can never express, let alone repay, your great kindnesses to me. If you cannot attend, I shall understand perfectly, but I should be greatly honored…" She was, as she had announced two months earlier, going to marry Laetus, the Praetorian Prefect.

"But of course I must attend!" Tullia exclaimed. "Dear, sweet Popilia…"

"I do not think that is at all a wise idea. The Praetorians are a rough crowd, very rough indeed. The guests at this affair will not be at all like those you meet at the house of Didius Julianus. I hesitate to broach such an indelicate subject, but some might even try to force themselves upon you."

"Castor will take me. No-one will want to start anything with him."

"Well certainly your father will not take you. It would be beneath his place. But you know that you cannot be alone in the company of Castor. Your virtue must be protected."

Tullia laughed. "I am not worried about Castor. He would never do anything wrong."

"But your reputation, my dear… Surely you must know how vicious the rumor-mongers can be." Philoxena's voice trailed off. It began to occur to her that she was talking herself into a corner, where she herself might have to be the chaperone, witnessing that Tullia was never alone with a male slave. She had no desire whatsoever to attend the wedding of a Praetorian. Was there any way of making Cocina go instead? But it was Philoxena's job, not Cocina's, to look after Tullia.

Again Magnus rescued her. There was yet another letter at the door. The matter of Popilia's wedding could be set aside while Philoxena prodded Tullia to read what Julia Aniciana had to say. "My dearest friend, I do so hope that this is not too much to ask…" the letter began. Tullia was again being invited to lead the bridesmaids, at Julia's wedding to Senator…

Tullia stopped reading. Philoxena thought that perhaps she was having trouble making out the name. She leaned over Tullia's shoulder to see what it said, and gasped. "Sempronius!" It said "Caius Titius Sempronius" in fact, to leave no room to wonder if there might be another Senator Sempronius.

"How could she?! How could she?!" Tullia shrieked, and then began to sob. "And how could he? I shall never speak to either of them, ever again!"

Philoxena tried to comfort her, but was somewhat at a loss for words. She also felt that Senator Sempronius had led Tullia on, rather rudely. There had never been the slightest hint that he was courting another, not even from the gossips. Philoxena ransacked her memories for anything anyone might have said this past month hinting that Julia and Lady Camilla had ever been seen together, or that Julia seemed like less than a friend to Tullia, or that Camilla did not want Tullia as a daughter-in-law. She came up empty. All Philoxena could really do was let Tullia cry on her shoulder and say "There, there!" Eventually the emotion was spent, if not the lingering sense of betrayal.

Magnus opened the door again, this time for Castor and Senator Tullius returning home. As the Senator came into the atrium, his daughter weakly rose to hug him. Her upset state still showed plainly. "I gather," he said, "that you have heard about the engagement of Sempronius and Aniciana."

"So you knew about this? And you didn't tell me?" Tullia was seldom angry with her father, but if he was part of this betrayal too, that would be too much to endure.

"I only just heard. Lady Titiana stopped me when I was finished with the day's work. She told me, and said that Lady Anicia wanted to know if I would be willing to give the bride away, if Anicia's brother cannot come from Graecia in time."

"You would do that? Act as the father? To her? Would I have to start calling her sister?"

"It will never happen. If the uncle does not get the invitation in time or is otherwise delayed, then the wedding will be postponed until he is here."

"Then why did Lady Anicia even ask you?"

"My dear, you must learn to understand how the game is played. Anicia meant that she still wishes our families to be friends, and that no disrespect was intended."

"But why didn't he want me?" Now the tears began to flow again.

"My dear, it had nothing to do with you. Sempronius needed to improve his fraught relationship with Pertinax Caesar. He opposed conferring the imperial titles until the legions were heard from, and more recently he wanted ex-Consul Falco put to death, which the Emperor vetoed."

"He is an enemy of the August One?" Tullia was horrified at the thought that she might have given her heart to a traitor.

"Not at all. They are good friends now, and sealed it with a marriage alliance to the daughter of Lady Anicia, who is the best friend of the Empress. You see, he is practically in their family now. And if you are wise, you will continue your friendship with him, and with Julia."

"But what do I do now?"

"You attend the wedding with a happy smile on your face, and charm all the potential suitors who will be there. Come now, show your father what a beautiful smile you have!"

"I will make the most magnificent dress for Clara's wedding, where I can really smile."

"Good!"

"And then I will wear the same dress to Julia's wedding, unaltered."

Chapter 14

Tigher Inissean was king of the Horse People of the western isles, who were called Eqendi or Epidi depending on whether you were of the Q or the P persuasion. He looked up at the great hall of Struyvaethin. The hall was in the center of a compound atop a craggy outcrop, overlooking a strategic ford on the best path into the northern highlands. The compound was only fenced along the easiest slope, depending on the difficulty of the climb for its defense from other directions, and the houses were built merely of blocks of turf, with straw-thatched roofs. But the hall was solidly built of stone, rising to three times a man's height. There were no hinged doors as one would find on a Roman structure, but only two narrow entryways on opposite ends, permitting one man through at a time, and easily barricaded in case the hall needed to become a refuge. There were small window openings, which a man could not crawl through but an archer could shoot through, adding little light to what came through the central hole in the roof, but drawing in air when, as now, a central fire was sending up smoke. Over the front entryway hung a large semicircular varnished wooden panel, carved to show a smiling head with a full beard, and a right hand hoisting a horn of frothy ale, surrounded by intricate knotwork in which the forms of several animals could be discerned. A Roman would have scorned this hall as rude, but it was the greatest in Caledonia. Tigher might call himself a "king" while Qenmaethin was only a "chief" but Qenmaethin was the more powerful, and both of them knew it.

Inside, Qenmaethin was growing impatient. He had told his guests to present themselves around sunset, and there they were waiting, and the torches were lit and the food prepared, but where was Kuglas? The Horse People had brought a fine gray as a gift. The horses of the islands were small, and Qenmaethin was a little too stout to ride one well, but Kuglas was lithe and wiry, and could not resist taking the gray down to the fields. Was that the sound of hooves outside? Was Kuglas belatedly returning? There was no way to know without going out, so

Qenmaethin stepped through the door and boomed out, "Welcome, my good friends! My hall is your home!" He gave each man in turn a hearty hug, and as the guests entered the hall, the servants within greeted them with offerings of bread and salt. As Qenmaethin followed the last of them in, he saw that Kuglas was going around to the back and entering through the postern doorway and the kitchen area. Kuglas rushed to take his proper place, and Qenmaethin muttered to him, "You smell of horse sweat and man sweat. Could you not have taken a moment to splash water on yourself?"

"No time, I was late!" Kuglas said, drawing a glare which silently said, Yes, you were indeed.

Tigher Inissean smoothed things over. "You enjoyed the ride, then? It is so gratifying to see a gift received with genuine pleasure!"

"As I hope that my gifts shall be!" Qenmaethin returned to the rituals of hospitality, distributing necklaces, armlets, and rings among the guests. And he gave a silver penny to Tigher's young page-boy.

"For me? Wow!" The boy had never seen any coins but the three worn copper quarters which his grandfather had given him. Those might have been minted under Hadrian, although it would be hard to tell anymore. In Rome they would not have been of any interest even to an antiquarian, but to the boy they were his treasure, something Qenmaethin had apparently heard. "Thank you, thank you, thank you!" the boy shouted, bowing up and down in a bobbing motion that amused all the men.

Qenmaethin gave Tigher Inissean the seat that was usually his own, one of only two chairs with a back in the hall. He took the other chair, ordinarily his wife's, and sat Kuglas besides him on a folding stool. The other men were directed to stools or benches depending on rank. The women from both peoples were out in the eastern hills, doing whatever ritual the full moon of this season called for, in whichever of their sacred lodges they used for that occasion. The men did not inquire too closely about such matters. The visitors would stay through the equinox, when the women would perform other rites by the great cairns. The first rites in which the men would partake were the pole dances halfway between equinox and solstice. The Horse People could not stay nearly that long. For tonight, the men were quite content to be left to themselves, to get as drunk and talk as ribaldly as they pleased.

The tables were heavily laden with food. There were puddings of organ meats and oats baked in the stomachs of sheep, and a variety of gamebirds, and kippered herrings, and a soup of nettle broth with chunks of salmon. All of this was washed down with plenty of ale. When the honey cakes were brought out, and the ale was replaced by a fine mead, it was time for some serious talk.

"Has Guvnor made you any gifts of late?" Tigher Inissean asked. Caledonian leaders were always referred to by their titles, forgetting any personal name they might have had, so naturally they referred to Clodius by an eroded form of the Latin *gubernator*.

Qenmaethin shifted uncomfortably. "He sent much iron. My smiths have been busy all winter."

"But there was talk of gold."

"When Southrons speak of gold, they often mean the equivalent quantity of silver pennies, and not actual pieces of gold." He was evading the question.

"And has Guvnor even been so generous to you, as you have been to my page? Have you seen even one penny?"

"MaqGuvnor assures us that Guvnor will honor all pledges in the spring." He had no way to refer to Priscus Pescennius except as the son of the Guvnor, not knowing of any title he held in his own right.

"Does he now? A bird whispered in my ear that after speaking words of honey to you, Guvnor received some bad news, and vanished, never to be seen again."

"He looked as if he wanted to sink into the earth," Kuglas interjected, chuckling at the memory. Qenmaethin kicked him under the table.

"MaqGuvnor assures us that Guvnor will return in the spring," Qenmaethin repeated.

"And since when is it the Southron custom for Guvnor to turn his power over to his son?" Tigher asked. "My understanding was that Guvnor serves at the pleasure of their faraway king Qaysar, who can raise up or cast down whomever he pleases."

"That is my understanding as well." Qenmaithin himself wondered how it was that Priscus was now in charge of Roman Britannia, but felt that he had little choice but to take him at his word.

"Perhaps Guvnor is in bad odor with Qaysar, and none of his pledges are worth anything anymore."

"If that were so, then surely Qaysar would not replace him with his son. Little birds sometimes whisper in my ear as well, and say that the old Qaysar is dead, and that Guvnor is among those who might become the new Qaysar. Then his friendship will be valuable indeed."

"Perhaps. Or perhaps that is a tale which it suits MaqGuvnor to spread about. Perhaps Guvnor went to fight his enemies and has lost. What do we know of Southron affairs?"

"Not so much as we would like," Qenmaethin conceded. "We can only wait and see what happens in the spring."

"That is rather too long to wait. All winter you were full of grand talk. We were going to crush all the wildlings of the north. We were going to gather every chieftain from my isles to the eastern sea. If we were going to do so, we should be buying their loyalties already. You may be content to be bought with words of honey, but few others will be. This cake is very good," he said, pausing to appreciate one of the desserts, "but alone it would not have made a meal."

"Have I ever failed to set a good table?"

"Nay, you never have." He made a dedicatory gesture with his horn of mead toward his host. "But you have never before relied on the Southrons to set it for you."

"They did feed us well when we met with them," Kuglas put in. Qenmaethin, who did not like the direction Tigher was going but was running out of things to say, was not displeased this time.

"We are of a mind to hunt some game for ourselves," Tigher said. "Mon's island is becoming rich and careless." Mon's island, separated from the northwest tip of Cambria by a narrow strait, was at the outermost fringe of Roman control, a center for trade with both Hibernia and Caledonia. Once it had been a holy place for priests of the area, a place to burn malefactors as an offering to the gods, until the Romans made sure to wipe them out, having taken some distaste to the practice, regardless of their own swiftness to deal death. "A raid there might yield much profit at little cost." Some of his men made huzzah noises to signal their support. Evidently, the islanders had been discussing this before coming to Struyvaethin. "The garrison by the sacred pool has been empty since the summer. It would take time for them to bring up reinforcements. Long enough for us to be in and out."

Qenmaethin distinctly wanted to head off any raid by Caledonians on Roman territory, which could poison any possibility of the alliance he sought. "You know, better than I, the traders on the islands. But I know, better than you, the soldiers on the wall, how they wish for friends in the north."

"Better than I, surely, but you don't know enough. You have admitted so yourself."

"Could I persuade you to hold off on your raid a while, if I get a spy among the Southrons to inform us better?"

"Can you capture a red-capped dwarf?" Little sprites who make hats out of clotted blood were said to haunt old battlefields and to pester men at arms. "Or is there a woman who has winked her way into an officer's lodgings?"

"Neither. Burranus!" A man seated on a stool, so near to Qenmaethin as to indicate that he was held in high esteem, rose and bowed. The mannerism was more Roman than Caledonian, and Qenmaethin waved him back down. "How long have you been with us?"

"Six years now, my lord." Burranus spoke with little remaining trace of a foreign accent, though most people found Caledonian a difficult tongue to learn. He was Italian by birth, and his complexion was rather swarthier than most of the men around the tables, but some men with Hibernian blood in them had that look. Tigher would not have guessed that he was not Caledonian.

"Would you like to go home?"

"My home is now here, with you, my lord."

"With Malduve, rather." Some of the men laughed, and Burranus flushed.

Malduve healed his wounds when the Caledonians captured him, half dead, the only survivor of a Roman punitive raid. She sometimes sang as she worked, a popular tune about the thistle and the heather, how the thistle loved the heather and said she was too beautiful to bear, how the heather scorned the thistle and said he was too rough to endure, though in the last verses the heather seemed to be relenting. One day Burranus began singing along. He had an ear for language and a fine voice. Now the couple had a son and a daughter.

"If I send you back," Qenmaethin asked, "Malduve and her children will be well looked after." They would be hostages for his continued loyalty, in other words. Of course, no Caledonian would refer to Malduve's children as "his" children, since paternity was never certain and was no-one else's business, but it was certainly known that he loved them. "But can we be certain that the Southrons will keep you on the wall? If they transfer you elsewhere, I should lose you, and I should hate that."

"The army will reckon that I still owe years of service to the unit on the wall, and will not credit me with these years of, shall we say, unauthorized leave. And besides, the commanders will want to keep me there for questions, about every scrap they can learn."

"But would you hear in turn any scrap about where Guvnor has gone, and when he might return, and what is planned?"

"Soldiers cannot stop gossiping about their superiors. Some of the things they say are even true. And they must be told what the plans are, sooner or later."

"So, one fine day a trader will seek permission to cross the wall, and will whistle that tune of the thistle and the heather, as a signal that you must find some way to take him aside and tell him everything that you have learned. And I will tell it to our friends in the isles."

"We shall wait, then," Tigher agreed. "You shall doubtless be too busy yourself, but you must send some lads and lassies to dance around the poles with us." This indicated the limits of how much time he was prepared to grant. "Let us hope that we learn more of them than they learn of us."

Qenmaethin asked Burranus pointedly, "How have you been treated here?"

"With more respect than my meager deserts, my lord."

"Nay. You have endured the most miserable thralldom, filled with labor and torment. You hate the Caledonians with the passion of a she-bear whose cubs have been hunted down. Every day you have looked to escape, until at last you succeeded." Burranus nodded. "Hmmm, I should not have let you feast tonight. You look too well-fed. I shall have to starve you a dozen days. And I shall have to beat you, and reopen your old wounds."

"I will not flinch, my lord."

Chapter 15

The ides and the equinox had passed, when Castor drove Senator Tullius to the Palace again, expecting another dull day of waiting for his master to finish whatever business he was attending to. He knew his way around the Palace better now. All during the reign of Commodus, he was usually confined to the same few rooms on the lower level. Under Pertinax, things were both laxer and stricter. Castor could wander about more freely, but always a Praetorian would trail after him. Conversations between servants of the Palace and anyone from the outside had to be monitored, in case there was some plot of escape. But Castor had become accustomed to this.

He sought out his friend Narcissus, hoping to pass the time with dice. But Narcissus said, "This is the day when I must shovel horse-shit. Let me take you to the kitchens. There should be some fine leftovers there this morning." And indeed there proved to be sumptuous foods spread out all over the tables, with only two people picking at them. "You will remember my wife Junipera?" Castor knew that they were a couple, but did not know that Narcissus had taken to calling her his wife. "And Langoria, of course?"

"Castor! How wonderful to see you again!" Castor blushed a little at the warmth of Langoria's greeting, and bowed awkwardly to each of the women. Narcissus went out, but the Praetorian who had been trailing Castor remained, standing stiffly where the hall entered the room. "Sit," Langoria said with a smile, "and try some of the tetrapharmacum, it's delicious. There was another banquet without guests last night, so there's plenty."

"A banquet without guests?" Castor wrinkled his brow in puzzlement.

"The August One," Junipera said while rising briefly to make an awkward curtsey, "seldom feels that anyone is worthy to dine with him. But some days he still makes the kitchen cook for a hundred." Castor noted the beginnings of a belly bulge when Junipera stood up.

"He sends food around to the houses of any toffs who happen to be in the city," Langoria added. "Just so they don't feel slighted. Not as good as being invited, but what can we say?"

"So the cooks are allowed to go outside now?" Castor hoped that this might mean that the Palace was starting to ease up its confinement of all the servants.

"No, of course not," Langoria said sadly. "The Praetorians have to make the deliveries. I'm sure they hate that." She dared to turn and look at the Praetorian standing silently watching them. "Don't you?" He did not respond, of course, but his expression spoke of resentment.

"Well, a banquet without guests is better than guests without a banquet." Castor laughed weakly at his own attempt at humor. He was so nervous around Langoria. He nibbled on the dainties which she passed to him, grunting his satisfaction.

Another Praetorian entered. "You two! There is someone who wants a look at you." This did not sound good. The leer on his face made it a little worse. But Junipera and Langoria had little choice but to rise and follow him out. Castor also stood up, then thought better of it and sat back down. The Praetorian who was monitoring him shot him a glare, for even having a passing thought about interfering. Castor tried to finish the tetrapharmacum he had been working on, but suddenly had no more appetite. He sat in silent worry.

After a few minutes, the awkwardness was broken by the entrance of another Praetorian. This one was leading a man who was wearing a Senatorial toga, and yet managed to look disheveled. Castor thought he recognized the face, but could not quite recall. "Are you the slave of Senator Marcus Tullius Secundus?" the Praetorian asked.

"I am." Castor wondered if he was in some kind of trouble.

"This gentleman wishes to speak to you."

The gentleman in question said, "If you please, we require privacy." The Praetorians exchanged glances and withdrew. Not until they were out of earshot did he continue, "You may or may not remember me..."

296

"You are Geta." Now Castor placed him. Geta Severus was the brother of the renowned general Septimius Severus, but had never had much of a political or military career. He had not aged well since Castor had seen him last. "You were a friend of my late master." Castor keep the disdain he felt for the friends of Marcus Tullius Primus out of his voice, but he neither rose nor bowed.

"I was at his deathbed," Geta said. "Do you know what the last words Primus spoke to me were?" Castor was in no mood for a guessing game, and would not even ask. "He made me swear by Venus and Bacchus that if ever there were anything that I could do to help Secundus, I would do it without question, even if it meant my life."

"What could you possibly do for my master?" The disdain was beginning to leak out.

"I can warn him. A terrible thing is about to happen. He must leave the Palace at once."

"What terrible thing?"

"I cannot say without betraying those who told me. But if you love your master, find any excuse to take him home, now."

"Of course I love my master!" Castor was offended that this should even be in question.

"Then do as I say. Find some excuse, any excuse, and get him out of here." Castor made no reply, so he insisted, "Swear to me!"

"By Fortuna and Hecate, I will do it." Castor was not about to swear by Venus or Bacchus.

Geta made a hasty exit. Now what? Castor wandered toward the atrium. His master was not in the atrium, and Castor had to break down and address his Praetorian tail. "Where would my master be? I must find him." The Praetorian said not a word in reply, but led him to the counting room.

There, aside from several Praetorians, he found Tullius, Pertinax, Eclectus, and a man he did not know, who was examining Junipera and Langoria. The strange man turned an icy glare in Castor's direction, and Castor was paralyzed, like a bird facing a viper. The ugly sneer on his face gave Castor a very good idea of what kind of person this must be, some leading figure in the slave-traders' guild, whose eyes were rapidly calculating Castor's price, down to the farthing. One of the counting tables was out in the middle of the room, and Castor felt sure what the tokens on it stood for. But he could not even move his eyes until the slaver turned his head back, to resume appraising Junipera's belly and the bonus that might be within. Then Castor turned to look at Tullius, whose face was grim and ashen. "Master..." he blurted out, without knowing how he was going to continue the sentence.

Then he realized that he was nearly face to face with the August One. He had been in the same room with the Emperor before, but always with head bowed down, and silent. Now he had spoken, and had committed the horrible error of not addressing the Emperor first! His legs were wobbly, so as he bowed he fell to his knees, then sprawled on the floor in a full prostration. He clasped his quivering hands above his head as he pleaded, "O August One, forgive me!"

"Forgive you for what, my child?" Pertinax did not sound angry at all, merely curious, and perhaps even kindly.

"My master is not at all well. Might I have leave to take him home?" If that cursed Geta had not made him swear an oath, Castor would never have found the boldness to speak.

"Your concern for your master does you credit." Pertinax turned to Tullius. "Your devoted servant is right, you know. You look wretched. I did promise not to force you to deal with this dreadful matter. We can manage without you. I dismiss you. Go home, or to the baths, and rest yourself."

Tullius bowed, and walked over to Castor. Almost unbelievably, the Senator offered his slave a hand, to help him pull himself up off the floor. Castor's head was spinning. He was trying to compose some explanation for why he had dared to intrude in such a manner. Surely the master would have many questions.

But Tullius spoke not a single word, the entire way home.

Chapter 16

Pertinax and Eclectus were alone in the counting room now, if one disregarded the Praetorians in the corners, as Pertinax and Eclectus certainly did. The slaver was off surveying the personnel in some other part of the Palace. Pertinax stared glumly at the total entered thus far on the largest of the counting tables, while Eclectus stared at a blank space on the floor. A distant sound of shouting, and blaring trumpets, caused them to look up curiously. Laetus came running into the room with some more Praetorians following. "Into the throne room, quickly!" Laetus shouted, without the slightest effort to appear deferential.

Pertinax was not about to hop to his commands. "What is the meaning of this?"

"Mutineers from the City have broken into the atrium. They say they have some grievance."

"What do I pay you for?" The Praetorians felt that they were not paid nearly enough, if their duties were to include unsoldierly menial chores. But this was scarcely the time for Laetus to complain about that. He said nothing. Pertinax persisted, "How could you not repel them?"

"We were not expecting such an attack. And there were too many of them." These were both very feeble excuses. The guards ought to have been ready for an attack at any time. And the entryway through the vestibule was specifically designed so that the guards would only have to face a handful of invaders at a time, no matter how many were in the twisting passage behind. The truth was that the Praetorians simply had no stomach to fight the City. And Pertinax knew it, to judge by the look he was giving Laetus. The Praetorian Prefect could only say, "Never mind that now. Go into the safer room and close that door. The door is stout and we can guard it against however many, or if need be go out through the tunnel." Opposite the great door to the throne room was what appeared to be just another panel in the wall, but it could be pushed aside to reveal stairs that went down to an underground passage, which emerged near the stables.

"I will go into the throne room, but we will not shut the door. If they have a grievance, then I will hear them." Laetus did not think this was at all a good idea, but followed him. The efficient Eclectus was already in there and had brought out the silk and purple robes. He helped Pertinax into his costume, and boosted him up onto the long shelf that was the throne. He could sense that the Emperor was in a state of anxiety that he was unaccustomed to. But he hoped, as doubtless Pertinax was also hoping, that reflexive habits of obedience would reassert themselves.

When Eclectus came back out into the counting room, soldiers of the City were already pressing in. There were many more Praetorians now, forming a wall to block the mutinous soldiers from the throne room. Blades were out on both sides, but neither seemed eager to engage. The counting table in the middle of the room was now tipped on its side, the tokens scattered. "Back!" Eclectus shouted. The Praetorians parted to let him through. He raised his hands over his head and made a hurling motion, as if tossing a gigantic boulder at the mutineers, as he repeated, "Back! Back!" in louder tones. The soldiers actually fell back into the corridor in the face of this fury. Then Eclectus was startled to recognize their leader. "Diodoros Tigranos? What are you doing here?"

"Vindicating the rights of my friend!" Diodoros put his left hand on the shoulder of the man next to him, his right hand still holding his short sword. "This is Tausias, granted citizenship for valor in the service of the Emperor. He has a grievance which must be heard."

"Must?" Eclectus snorted. "The August One, out of the abundance of his grace, sees fit to hear your grievance, little though your conduct merits any such consideration." Diodoros bowed in response to these words, and his hand pressed Tausias into bowing as well. "But only the two of you may enter the presence. The rest of you are to stay back." Diodoros and Tausias stepped forward, but then halted, nervous about running the gauntlet of angry Praetorians. "Sheathe your weapons," Eclectus said calmly, and they sheepishly complied. Then he turned to Motilenus, the highest-ranking of the Praetorians, since Laetus remained in the throne room. "Motilenus, you will have your men sheathe their weapons and stand aside!" He turned back to face the men of the City. "Sheathe your weapons, all of you!"

Eclectus seemed to be the only one who was sure of what he wanted. So naturally the City obeyed, without even a nod from Diodoros. And Motilenus also did not need to relay orders to the Praetorians, who sheathed arms and got out of the way. Eclectus gathered his dignity, and strode into the throne room, with Diodoros and Tausias at his heels, as if it were any other day. "O August One," he said with his usual bow, "I present to you Diodoros Tigranos, the former commander of the City." He emphasized the word "former" with a sneer.

"And town supervisor of Nomentum," Pertinax added, "until today."

Diodoros of course understood that his career was over, and possibly his life as well. "I am your slave," he said as he bowed deeply.

"And this is Tausias," Eclectus added, "who purports to be a citizen."

"I recall the case," Pertinax said. When he was Prefect of the City, he made it a point to familiarize himself with the records of anyone in that service who had received commendations. "You were honored for fighting off robbers, when the Praetorians were rather useless." He was not feeling warm towards the Praetorians at the moment. Laetus felt stung. Eclectus hoped that his voice was not carrying into the next room. He wished that he had been able to clear that room entirely.

Tausias bowed and said, "I am not a slave, and neither is my sister."

Pertinax was shocked at his insolence. "Tigranos," he said, pointedly ignoring Tausias, and addressing Diodoros by his less familiar name, as if to erase any surviving trace of friendship, "you wound my heart. How is it that I find you in the company of rebels?"

"O August One," Diodoros said, eagerly taking the chance to abase himself again with a deep bow, "this man is no rebel, but a loyal servant of the State, who has been wronged beyond endurance. His sister Langoria was kidnapped by your predecessor of cursed memory. She was enslaved contrary to law, and is now in peril of being sold."

Pertinax would rather have completed the sale of the Palace slaves before any word of it got out, but was not surprised that the news had leaked. "I seem to recall the name Langoria." He was not as well acquainted with the identities of all the people in the Palace as he was with other matters that attracted his interest more. "Eclectus, do we have someone here by that name?"

"We do indeed. She was among the last that we examined, not the pregnant one but the other. I know not her whole story, but I do know that Commodus Caesar, cursed be his name, often used her very ill." Marcia would know all about it, he thought to himself. He would have to ask her.

Pertinax addressed Tausias in a stern but not hostile tone. "The previous Caesar acquired much property in dubious manners. If we have been eager to liquidate surplus property, for which the State has no use, it is out of our love and concern for the soldiers, whom we wish to pay, as promptly as possible, the generous donative which we have promised. We deeply regret if your sister has been treated as State property in error."

"She may not be a citizen, but she was as freeborn as I am!"

"Are you attempting to insult my father?" Pertinax was always sensitive on this point.

Tausias blanched in horror, and bowed deeply. "I would never dream of it! I honor your father, may he rest in the Elysian Fields!"

Pertinax saw that he was sincere, and felt sorry to have accused the man wrongly. He waved his hand dismissively, anxious to end this uncomfortable audience. "Go now, and describe your complaint to Eclectus in detail. We will investigate this matter."

"I am not leaving here without her."

Pertinax was stunned into speechlessness by this backtalk.

Laetus had heard enough. "That is not how one addresses the Emperor!"

"I am a citizen, exercising my legal right to appeal to Caesar." Tausias had never liked the Praetorians, and was not going to be bullied by one.

"Your appeal has been heard, now trust to his justice. Or are you one of those who won't be loyal if you don't get your coins fast enough?"

"You lot were certainly paid speedily! I suppose he could trust your loyalty no other way?"

"You mind your tongue, boy! Or I will see that it is torn out!"

"For speaking truth? I saw that wretch have his torn out for lies, but that Falco, who was behind it all, was pardoned!" He turned his gaze to Pertinax, who flinched at the anger in his eyes. "Is that how it is? One law for the toffs, and another for the rest of us? I am a citizen! I know my rights!"

"You have no right," Laetus said in the tone of a debater who has thought of an irrefutable point, "to force your way in here like this. You are armed, in the presence of Caesar."

"And what of you? They say that you have even used your arms, to kill a Caesar!"

Laetus was stunned. He had thought that hardly anyone outside the Palace knew about his role in the death of Commodus. He moved his hand toward his sword-hilt. But Tausias was moving quicker, and already had his blade half out of its sheath. Abruptly, Laetus turned and ran. He pressed the panel on the back wall and slid it on its secret track, then bounded down the hidden stairs.

Tausias said, "So it is true, then? And yet, you let him continue in your service?"

Pertinax was desperate to calm the situation. "You were not there, or else you would understand. Laetus was provoked. Commodus behaved abominably."

"You are saying, then, that sometimes it is right to kill the Caesar?"

Pertinax turned pale. Tausias ran up to the throne, placed his hands on the shelf, to the right of where Pertinax was seated, and hoisted himself up in one motion. Pertinax was so astonished at this effrontery that he had no reaction at all, not even when Tausias drew the blade and plunged it into his chest. Tausias let go of the hilt and sat staring, horrified by what he had just done. Diodoros was also frozen, repeating helplessly, "No, no, no, no."

Eclectus, however, sprang into action. With a running leap, summoning strength he did not know he had, he jumped up onto the throne behind

Tausias. He reached around the unmoving Tausias to pull the blade out of the Emperor's chest. Tausias did not even resist when Eclectus slit his throat and shoved him down to the floor. Eclectus tried to put pressure on the chest wound, but it was too late. Pertinax was gurgling out his last breaths. Diodoros was screaming loudly now, "NO! NO! NO!"

The tallest and burliest soldier of the City was one of those who loved Diodoros Tigranos, and hated that Silius Messala had replaced him. He rushed forward and picked up the overturned counting table, using it as a battering ram to push through the Praetorians. Several men of the City followed him into the throne room. Eclectus jumped down, with the blade that had belonged to Tausias. He stood behind Diodoros and pressed the blade to his throat, shouting, "Get back! All of you! Or I'll kill him!"

But there were too many of them. One of them got behind Eclectus and cut him down. Eclectus at least took Diodoros out with him. Praetorians also were flooding the room now. "They've killed Caesar!" Motilenus cried out.

The melee which followed was bloody and confused.

www.ingramcontent.com/pod-product-compliance
Lightning Source LLC
Jackson TN
JSHW021353171224
75420JS00006B/30